Telford's
Odyssey

DAVID EBSWORTH

SilverWood

Published in 2025 by SilverWood Books

SilverWood Books Ltd
14 Small Street, Bristol, BS1 1DE, United Kingdom
www.silverwoodbooks.co.uk

ISBN 978-1-80042-312-1 (paperback)
Also available as an ebook

British Library Cataloguing in Publication Data
A CIP catalogue record for this book is available from the British Library

Page design and typesetting by SilverWood Books

DAVID EBSWORTH is the pen name of writer Dave McCall, a former negotiator and workers' representative for Britain's Transport & General Workers' Union. He was born in Liverpool but has lived in Wrexham, North Wales, with his wife, Ann, since 1981.

Following his retirement, Dave began to write historical fiction in 2009 and has now subsequently published fourteen novels: political thrillers set against the history of the 1745 Jacobite rebellion, the 1879 Anglo-Zulu War, the Battle of Waterloo, warlord rivalry in Sixth Century Britain, and the Spanish Civil War. His sixth book, *Until the Curtain Falls* returned to that same Spanish conflict, following the story of journalist Jack Telford, and is published in Spanish under the title *Hasta Que Caiga el Telón*. The third of his Jack Telford novels, *A Betrayal of Heroes*, takes Jack into the turmoil of the Second World War but through a series of real-life episodes, which are truly stranger than fiction. *Telford's Odyssey* continues to follow Jack's career and misadventures from 1945 onwards, including the story, *The Lisbon Labyrinth*, previously published as a novella.

Dave's *Yale Trilogy* tells the story of intrigue and mayhem around nabob, philanthropist (and slave-trader) Elihu Yale – who gave his name to Yale University – but told through the eyes of his much-maligned and largely forgotten wife, Catherine.

The eleventh novel, *The House on Hunter Street*, is a mystery set during the political turmoil of Liverpool in 1911 and, more recently, Dave has published a non-fiction guidebook of Wrexham history, *Wrexham Revealed*. It was his research for the guidebook which inspired him to write his twelfth novel, *Blood Among the Threads*, and its sequel, *Death Along the Dee*.

Each of Dave's novels has been critically acclaimed by the Historical Novel Society and been awarded the coveted B.R.A.G. Medallion for independent authors. He is also a member of the Crime Cymru Welsh writers' collective.

For more information on the author and his work, visit his website at www.davidebsworth.com.

Also by David Ebsworth

The Jacobites' Apprentice
A story of the 1745 Rebellion.

The Jack Telford Series
Political thrillers set towards the end of the Spanish Civil War and beyond.
The Assassin's Mark
Until the Curtain Falls
(published in Spanish as *Hasta Que Caiga el Telón*)
A Betrayal of Heroes

The Kraals of Ulundi: A Novel of the Zulu War

The Last Campaign of Marianne Tambour: A Novel of Waterloo
The Song-Sayer's Lament
Another political thriller but this time set in the time we know as the Dark
Ages, 6th Century post-Roman Britain

The Yale Trilogy
Set in old Madras, London and northern England between 1672 and 1721
The Doubtful Diaries of Wicked Mistress Yale
Mistress Yale's Diaries, The Glorious Return
Wicked Mistress Yale, The Parting Glass

The House on Hunter Street
A mystery set during the political turmoil of Liverpool in 1911.

Blood Among the Threads
Death Along The Dee
Victorian crime novels set during 1876 and 1884.

Wrexham Revealed
Non-fiction. A walking tour with tales of the city's history.

Dedicated to Mila-Rose and Lyla-Rein

One

The Nuremberg Effect

Thursday 17ᵗʰ October 1946

'You guys saw them swing?'

Telford decided to ignore the man, and stared out through the train's window to the stabbing blackness of Nuremberg's bomb-shattered central station. On the platform, a press of German women and children, a very few men, all laden like donkeys. They pushed and jostled each other among their suitcases and belongings. Everything but the proverbial kitchen sink. The whole heaving queue harried into order by shouting train guards in immaculate uniforms. All so horribly reminiscent of other images; other trains; other destinations; other uniforms.

'I said, did you fellas see them Nazi bastards swing?'

Nobody seemed inclined to answer the fellow, an American major, smoking a corncob pipe. Combat jacket, forage cap. Alongside him, the officious lieutenant from the platform, who had waved his clipboard in Jack's face, insisting he had no right to a space in this carriage reserved for the military.

Telford still felt out of place in his civvies whenever he was in military company. He'd been out of uniform for almost two years, but he had taken delight in waving his own authorisation papers in front of the lieutenant and, now, his portable typewriter was stowed up on the luggage rack, while his satchel and Rolleiflex camera sat on the empty seat opposite.

'We had that privilege, Major,' said Antonvic, who had been there, covering the trials and their aftermath on behalf of *Krasnaya*

Zvezda – the newspaper of the Soviet military. He leaned across, translated for another Russian captain.

'Not me, I'm afraid,' Telford's companion decided to tell them, absently wiping a finger along the beads of moisture clinging to his pencil-thin David Niven moustache. 'Just the Lucky Eight. Like Telford here. And I'm Fox, by the way. Good afternoon, gentlemen. Military attaché. Liaison with the French Sector.'

Fox and Telford had been together through much of the war, though they'd often been at odds, one with the other. Jack scowled at him, and used his handkerchief to mop away the sweat gathering beneath his eye-patch.

A one-armed Frenchman peered over the top of the seats and offered Fox a greeting.

'*Commandant* Falco,' said Fox. '*Bonjour.* We meet again.'

Telford didn't know the Frenchman. But the Lucky Eight? Jack wondered. He supposed that lucky was one way to put it. From those crowds of journalists covering the trials of the Nazi leadership, just eight of them selected to witness the hangings, along with a handful of other observers. Eight. Yes, he'd seen them swing.

'Did those bastards suffer?' said the American major.

Telford saw them again now. Not a single clean execution. The blood which had poured from Frick's eyes, nose and ears. The twisted, bloated features of von Ribbentrop after the fourteen minutes during which he'd choked to death. And Keitel – it had taken him almost twice as long to die. Telford saw them and felt not a shred of sympathy.

'Suffer?' Antonvic laughed, 'I think your Master Sergeant Woods made quite certain of that, Major.' He shared the jest with his companion.

'They should have used Pierrepoint,' said a British naval officer, the sixth of the carriage's other passengers. 'They say he made a tidy job at Belsen.'

Jack remembered Belsen. Eleven of them. The three women. Evil personified. Then there'd been Dachau – not Pierrepoint, of course. How many? Two dozen? He'd been unmoved by every single one. The crimes they'd committed. And something else, naturally: Danielle, taken from him. Maybe not by *those* Nazis, but by others like them. He wished them all dead. Every last filthy fascist one of them. It was

8

the reason he knew he might be wasting his time when he finally reached Strasbourg, his unfinished business. The Frenchman waiting for him, imprisoned there in the Maison d'Arrêt.

'Our friend, Mister Telford here,' said Fox, 'has seen them all. Haven't you, Jack? He's become quite the *voyeur*, so far as executions go. Disappointed with Mauthausen though, I think. Am I right, old boy?'

The train whistle screeched twice, and Jack glanced at his watch. Nine o'clock. The last of the German women and men, their whimpering children, hurrying for a place on the balconies between the carriages, the interiors already full to bursting. They looked pinched; cold, regardless of the unseasonal warmth. But despite the lack of food and fuel, the trains still ran on time. German efficiency making a defiant last stand here on the railways. The locomotive eased them along the tracks, trundled them past the final station nameboard. *Nürnberg Hauptbahnhof.*

'Mauthausen?' Jack replied. 'They'll get their turn.'

Fifty-eight of them, quaking in the condemned cells at Landsberg prison – death row, as the Yanks called it.

'You wrote about it,' said the American major, chewing on the lip of his pipe. 'That was you, wasn't it, Telford – in the *New York Times*?'

That bloody corncob pipe. Who did he think he was – MacArthur? Pretentious fool. Looked too wet behind the ears to have seen action; though, something about his demeanour chimed with the equally pompous, soft-seated décor of their carriage – a stark contrast to the third-class coaches he'd peered into while boarding, most of them without glass in the windows, the dark green livery, flaked and fading.

'Yes,' said Jack. 'The *New York Times.*'

It had been Telford's last assignment for Barea and the Beeb's Spanish service. And Bunnelle at the Associated Press picked it up, as well. The trial not held at Mauthausen itself, but at Dachau. Yet some of the Spaniards who gave evidence had invited him to visit the Mauthausen and Gusen camps, and he'd travelled with them, that long road east from Munich.

'*Monsieur* Telford is a celebrity, I think,' said the one-armed Frenchman. 'Covered the war with General Leclerc's Division – all the way to Berchtesgaden.'

It had only been as far as Strasbourg and the Rhine in truth, but Jack let it pass.

'It was your boys who liberated Mauthausen, wasn't it, Major?' he snapped at the Yank. 'Maybe you should tell the story.'

'You must forgive him, Major,' said Fox. 'He used to be such an affable fellow.'

'It's this damned war,' said the naval officer. 'Time we all went home.'

'It's not the war,' Jack murmured. 'It's the bloody lies and betrayals that go with it.'

'Telford is correct,' said Antonvic. 'Our reports tell us those who truly liberated the Mauthausen camps were the prisoners themselves. Not the Americans, my friends.'

'Soviet propaganda?' The major sneered. 'How could that be? And anybody want a beer?' He reached down into the nearest cooler, produced a dripping brown bottle. 'Or a Fanta?' A bottle of Nazi Germany's favourite soda appeared in his other hand. 'Liberate themselves? I never heard such shit.'

'Ignorance is bliss,' said Telford. 'Isn't that what they say? Have you any idea how many poor sods passed through Mauthausen? Have any of us?'

'A quarter million maybe,' said the major. 'That's what we reckoned.'

'But among them, Major, around ten thousand Spaniards.'

'Spanish Reds,' said the major, passing around more of the beers.

'Just Republicans, sir,' Jack snapped back at him. 'Like you Yanks. Republicans. Refugees from Franco's fascists. And handed over by Vichy to the Nazis. Ten thousand. And probably half of them killed there. Gas chambers. Or the Stairs of Death. Heard of those, Major?'

Jack saw again the granite quarries. Labour camp prisoners simply worked to death. Almost two hundred steps up from the depths, carrying hewn stones so heavy Telford had barely been able to lift them, let alone carry one up the rock face.

'They organised themselves, those Spanish comrades,' said the Russian. 'And not just the Spaniards. Frenchmen, Czechs, our own Russian prisoners of war. Many of them died, resisting. But when the SS abandoned the camp, it was those same groups who held everything together.'

'Still,' Jack muttered, 'the SS didn't abandon the camps without managing to gas a final three thousand.'

Those memories of the gas chambers, the ovens, had kindled in Telford's brain a fire of his own. Fox was right, it *had* changed him. He fished in his jacket pocket, pulled out his pack of Lucky Strikes and the gold lighter. It had once belonged to the German commander of Paris, von Choltitz. A souvenir of Jack's time with Leclerc.

'Mind if I take one of those?' said the Frenchman, making his way towards Jack's seat, steadying himself as the train began to sway, gathering speed as it left Nuremberg's suburbs behind.

'Of course.' Jack switched into easy French, offered the packet, tapped its side until three of the Luckies protruded from the opening. The Frenchman's empty left sleeve was pinned neatly to the shoulder of his tunic. Next to the sleeve, an impressive row of medals and ribbons.

'This is Major Falco,' said Fox. 'We met a while back at de Gaulle's headquarters.'

'Henri Falco,' the Frenchman smiled, stuck the cigarette in the corner of his mouth, and shook Jack's hand.

Jack looked at the four gold bars on the fellow's epaulettes. Yes, a major. A *commandant*. Four more strips of braiding around the upper part of his *képi*.

'Falco...' Jack puzzled over the name, and Falco smiled.

'My uncle,' he said. 'One of our judges.'

Of course. Jack remembered him.

'He argued that Göring, Keitel and Jodl should be shot by a firing squad, no?' said Jack.

Falco shrugged his shoulders.

'If it had been a military court-martial,' he said, 'I suppose he might have been correct. But the crimes they committed wiped out any entitlement to an honourable end, don't you agree *Monsieur* Telford?'

The crimes, yes. Jack was still struggling with the parameters of that new word. Genocide. And the new phrase which sat alongside. Crimes against humanity.

'Just a pity,' he said, 'Göring managed to avoid the noose.'

Göring was dead. Suicide, two days earlier. And the circumstances had sowed seeds in Telford's mind. A plan. Thoughts of justice. Or, perhaps, just simple revenge.

'Cyanide,' said Falco. 'Do they know how he got hold of it yet?'

'Just theories,' Fox told him. 'Don't suppose we'll ever know.'

But Telford knew. He'd managed to track down the Yank from the honour guards who'd obliged the former *Reichsmarschall*, retrieved the "medicine" hidden among Göring's personal possessions. It had cost Jack a fortune to get the story out of him, naturally. And he couldn't actually *use* the story, of course. Otherwise...

'And you, *Monsieur* Telford.' Falco leaned across, touched Jack's knee, brought him back from his memories. 'Where now for you? England?'

'Me? No. Berlin. For the BBC's German service. I'm keen to follow up some of the stories about all these refugees still here. The camps, you know?'

'Really, *monsieur*? Then we must speak some more. I'm at Baden-Baden. Still serving General Koenig, I'm pleased to say, but now find myself with responsibility for public health in the Zone.'

'You were with him at Bir Hakeim, sir,' said Fox, and pointed at one of the medals.

'I had that honour, Captain, yes. But we have our fair share of problems to resolve. And among those problems, of course, our Displaced Persons. Baltics, Ukrainians, Poles – we have them all.'

It had been complicated, Telford recalled. He thought about the Poles. At the end of the war, they'd been just one group among the millions upon millions of displaced persons crowded into Germany, Austria and Italy. Refugees from the bombing and conflict of mainland Europe. Or the Nazis' army of forced labourers. And both sides' prisoners of war. Survivors of the death camps, as well.

Jack had witnessed the astonishing logistics of the repatriation programme. Until, now, only a million remained.

Only a million, Telford smiled to himself. The last million. Yes, take the Poles. Those who were left, refusing repatriation to a land now controlled by the Soviets. Many because they couldn't stand the prospect of living under Russian tyranny any more than under the Germans. So still having to be housed in the DP camps.

Among them, of course, were others, those Poles who'd collaborated, to one extent or another, with the Nazi invaders. Returning those to Soviet-controlled Poland would have been a death sentence – and thus they also had to be housed in the camps. And the same for each of the other nationalities. The Latvians, Lithuanians, Estonians and the rest.

'And the Jews?' said Jack. 'You forgot to mention the Jews.'

The Polish Jews, for example, who'd somehow miraculously survived the Nazi extermination programme. And they, quite rightly, now refused to be held in the same camps as non-Jewish Poles – either Polish *collabos* who'd helped transport their families to the gas chambers and stolen their homes, or those who'd simply stood aside and let it happen. Non-repatriable as well, naturally, these Jews, since what was left for them in Warsaw or Krakow? Or the cities of any other European country, for that matter? Hence, separate camps for the Jews, as well.

'Yes,' Falco admitted. 'Jewish camps too, naturally. But you have a particular interest in the issue, *Monsieur* Telford?'

Jack was almost tempted to tell him the story. About how Danielle had been lost to him. After the fighting at Châtel-sur-Moselle. How he'd found the ambulance she'd been driving. Run off the road. Dani disappeared without trace. But her dog tags left behind, thrown under the vehicle. His search for her at every German prison camp. Every internment camp between.

He knew in his heart that she couldn't still be alive, but there was always that glimmer of hope he couldn't quite extinguish. And, in his search, he'd stumbled across all those other stories. Among them, the story of a young man, now in the Maison d'Arrêt in Strasbourg. Jack's unfinished business there.

'Maybe we should keep in touch,' said Jack, stubbed out his cigarette in the ashtray below the window.

'Of course, *monsieur*. Perhaps you might give me your address. Berlin?'

'I have no settled address in Berlin yet. But you can reach me through Paris. They'll forward mail for me.'

He was still at the apartment in Montparnasse – the apartment Josie Baker had so graciously allowed him to use.

Telford lifted a notepad from his satchel, reached into his inside jacket pocket and took out the pen – the pen gifted to him, eight years earlier by Spanish Republican President Juan Negrín. Then, he remembered. His little secret, fear that Fox might somehow have seen it in his eye.

'I'm an idiot,' he stammered. 'Completely forgot. Out of ink.' He put the pen hastily back into the pocket. 'Would you mind?' Fox obliged, seemed to have noticed nothing untoward. He offered Jack his own pen, and Telford scribbled down the Montparnasse address.

'And presumably,' Jack turned to Falco, 'if anything comes up from my end, I can reach you at the French headquarters in Baden-Baden?'

Indeed, he could.

They spent most of the remaining couple of hours before the halfway point at Würzburg arguing about the war, an occasional amusing anecdote to lighten the mood, smoking cigarettes and cooling themselves with the bottles of Henninger-Bräu. The Fanta remained untouched.

Jack glanced back through the window in the door connecting their own coach to the carriages behind. Folk had come and gone at the various stations along the route, but the open railed porch of the following carriage remained as crowded now as when they'd left Nuremberg.

'Would anybody mind,' he shouted, 'if we shared some of those drinks with the kids out there?'

He didn't wait for an answer, moved to the back of the carriage, threw open the door. Across the gap, women in headscarves and pinafores stared back at him, hollow-eyed children huddled among the baggage.

'We have Fanta,' he yelled in his best German. 'Might the kids like a drink?'

A few of the youngsters stirred, tugged at mothers' sleeves, and Telford soon found himself lifting one after another over the couplings, passing them through to Fox and Falco, much against the protests of that American lieutenant.

'I told you, mister,' the lieutenant mouthed against the wind. 'Reserved.' The lieutenant grabbed at Jack's arm. 'Against regulations.'

He pulled so hard that Telford's grip loosened from the child, an urchin – a girl of perhaps three or four – he was trying to swing across the gap.

The child screamed. Jack stumbled forward, the child dangling from his arm, her feet pedalling in thin air, terrified eyes wide with panic.

'Christ,' he yelled. 'Somebody…'

And Fox was there; Falco, too, the American pushed aside, the girl finally heaved to safety. By the time they pulled into Würzburg, the military carriage was full. Men and women, as well as the children. But the train would be there for a while, so a chance for Telford to stretch his legs, see if there were any decent photo opportunities.

Twenty minutes went by. The same twenty minutes it had taken the RAF to entirely obliterate this old, historic town. Nothing to photograph except yet more ruins, before the locomotive's whistle screeched once more and they hurried for the military carriage. They climbed aboard just in time to see the last of the civilians being bullied back to their own section of the train, uniformed guards wielding wooden clubs to persuade them.

'Your doing?' Jack snapped at the American lieutenant.

'Reserved,' the Yank repeated. 'I told you. Anyway, they're just krauts.'

Telford was the first to leave the military carriage. There were always those bloody moments – the ones that pressed down so hard upon him; a man alone in a world entirely shattered. Nothing to do but bite down on the thing, to press on. To Strasbourg. To that impossible dream that, at last, he might discover the truth, painful as it might be. Danielle. The damned flicker of hope.

Frankfurt am Main Hauptbahnhof, principal station for Frankfurt on the Main, that longest tributary of the Rhine. More signage here in English – well, American, Jack supposed, in reality – than in German. The reservations office for trains to Paris. Local route schedules and timetables. Notices for the Roundup trams. Menus in the smoke-filled Mitropa station canteen.

'That kid was lucky,' said Fox. 'And you, too, Jack.'

'I hate to admit this,' said Jack, trying to wipe out the memory, 'but I seem to be developing a taste for Spam.'

He cut a slice, dipped it into the yellow of his egg. The incident had, in truth, terrified him as much as it had terrified the girl.

'Good job,' Fox laughed. 'If you're coming to Berlin, there won't be much else.'

'I dread to think what would have happened, if you and Falco hadn't...'

The captain had declined the offer of food. Eat later, he'd said. At the Park Hotel, his room booked there until tomorrow. Stuck in Frankfurt overnight until the early train, while Jack now had a ticket for the seven o'clock to Strasbourg. He'd be there by midnight with luck.

'My god, so many Yanks,' Jack muttered.

Fox lit a cigarette, turned to survey the canteen's other customers, his features illuminated by a flash of lightning flooding the room from the window above, dispelling the twilight's gloom.

'Made themselves at home here, haven't they?' he replied.

Telford had never been in the United States, but he could imagine himself at Grand Central in Midtown Manhattan. The clamour. The khaki crowds. The cacophony of accents: Brooklyn and Bronx New Yorker; Deep Southern drawl; the maritime echoes of Massachusetts; others he couldn't identify.

With remarkable prescience, the Yanks had calculated, much earlier in the war, that the terminal building would one day be important for them and thus they had avoided direct aerial bombing. Destruction of the surrounding city had, of course, damaged roof glass in the dome of the station's great platform hall – though even those shattered panes had now been replaced.

The weather had remained hot and humid all the way from Würzburg, but now the inevitable thunderstorm. Outbound civilian passengers, with nowhere to wait but on the concrete floors of the concourse, huddled among their baggage. The smell of damp dogs clung to their clothes and GIs stepped over them as though they might have been invisible.

'And this business in Strasbourg,' said Fox, 'it'll keep you there very long?'

'Not long. Just a few more questions.'

'You think he really knows anything?'

He'd searched everywhere. Two years since Danielle disappeared. Taken, and Telford had hunted for clues about her fate. In the midst of his search, a rumour had reached him. More than a rumour. There'd been the massacre of a Waffen-SS unit, just before the war came to its conclusion. No ordinary SS unit, however. No, these had been members of the krauts' Charlemagne Division – French fascists who'd continued fighting for Hitler until the very end. Leclerc's troops had shot them all. Summary justice.

But not quite *all* of them. One had claimed to be the son of a general – a general loyal to de Gaulle. But what the hell to do with him? Jack hadn't cared much, not until the rumour. That this wretch had previously been with the *Milice*, a unit of the *Milice* which had spent time in Lorraine. Possibly, at Châtel-sur-Moselle.

They'd thrown him into the prison at Strasbourg while they checked out his story – it had turned out to be true – and then while they arranged a military tribunal to hear his case. But the wheels of military justice turned slowly.

'When I spoke to him,' said Jack, 'he made no bones of his involvement with the *Milice*. Proud of it. Still claiming the Communists are the enemies of us all. That the *Milice* were the only true French patriots. You've heard it all before. But Châtel? Wouldn't say a word. Not until after the tribunal. Well, the tribunal's all over now. So, we'll see.'

He tapped at the breast pocket of his jacket, an unconscious communion with the photograph hidden there. Danielle in her fatigues.

'And then?' said Fox.

Telford's fork paused halfway to his mouth. Then? He toyed with the word. Then, he thought, I close the chapter. One way or the other. But he couldn't explain this to Fox. Part of him was hesitant to explain it even to himself. Why? Because he was far from certain that he was even capable of carrying out his plan.

'Then,' he smiled, 'I get on with the writing. Bunnelle's asked me for a piece about post-war hardship.'

'Don't you get fed up with it?' Fox groaned, stubbed out the cigarette. 'We lost people. Of course, we did. Too many people. But now? Back in Blighty? A bit of rationing. Bomb damage that looks like a picnic when we see what's happened in northern France. Or Belgium. Holland.'

It was harsh. Jack knew that.

'I'm not the only one who's misplaced his affability, then?' he said.

'It's being here, Telford, I suppose. And every letter from home seems to whinge about some new bit of nonsense. Some petty...'

'Bunnelle's only thinking about the American market. The Yanks who'll read the Associated Press pieces in the *New York Times* or the *Washington Post* seem to have a real thirst for knowledge – about what's happening here on the ground in Europe. Mainland Europe. Shocked by some of the pictures, according to Bunnelle. More than half of Berlin simply gone. Hard to comprehend, isn't it? Unless you've been here.'

Jack knew the war, its aftermath, would shape the character of European nations like France, Germany, Belgium and Italy forever. About Britain he was less certain.

'But you think they'll learn, Telford? Your readers. Personally, I doubt it. The majority of Yanks still see war as a game played on somebody else's pitch. I'm sorry to say that's pretty much the attitude at home.'

'And here?' said Jack. 'What will it be for Germany? Bitterness until they spark another powder keg?'

Jack glanced at the black-cased wall clock. Six-thirty. Only half an hour until his train.

'Christ, no.' Genuine surprise in Fox's voice. 'Rebirth, I think. There'll be those who cling to the Nazi ideal – of course, there will. The self-pitying fanatics. But the majority? Unless I miss my guess, they'll turn their backs against it. Like the Japs have done.'

'You think that settles the debt? To the Jews, in particular?'

'If your Socialist friends would listen to reason, that debt could at least be reduced. If the Jews here were all given permits for Palestine. Get them out of the camps. New beginnings – for everybody.'

Jack pushed his plate away, accepted one of Fox's cigarettes while a waitress filled his coffee cup.

'As it happens, I'm quite proud of my *Socialist friends*, as you call them.'

The new Labour Government had been elected with the considerable help of Jack's old friend and former editor, Sydney Elliott. He'd left *Reynold's News* a while back and now, with the *Mirror*, he'd been one of the masterminds behind Attlee's winning campaign.

'Just how long, d'you think,' said Fox, 'the Yanks can afford to keep the camps open here? The obvious answer – sending them to Palestine. It's costing them billions. Billions.'

'The obvious answer? Only if Attlee and Bevin are wrong – about the inevitability of civil war between the Arabs and the Jews, Britain caught in the middle. My god, haven't we let them down enough? The Arabs *and* the Jews.'

The waitress had also left the bill – the check, as she'd called it – and Telford rummaged in his wallet, threw down the requisite amount of the new Military Payment Certificates, MPCs, plus a generous tip.

'More reason,' said Fox, 'to give them what they want. Jewish homeland. And how the hell were we supposed to know, Telford? The full extent of it. Not in our wildest dreams.'

'Ignorance was bliss – that what you're saying? No, it was more than that. All the time after the war ended. We wrote about the camps. We talked about the mounds of bodies, about the ovens, about the gas chambers. We talked about the typhus. But you know the one word none of us ever used in our reports?'

'I've no idea, old fellow,' Fox replied.

'Let me tell you, Captain. None of us ever used the word "Jews". When we wrote our articles. Not once.'

He stood from the table, picked up his hat.

'That can't be right,' said Fox. 'Ed Murrow – all the others. Here, might as well walk you to the train.'

'Sure. Go and check, though.' They wandered out onto the concourse. 'Now, we just take it for granted. After the trials. But back then? I understand why that might have been. There were so few Jews left in the camps. Outnumbered by others. How could we know how many had already been exterminated? But that doesn't stop me feeling guilty.'

The sense of personal guilt had never left him. Yes, of course, in many of the camps, there weren't many Jews left. But how could six million Jews simply have disappeared? Where had all the children gone? The older people. But the survivors had, at least, expected help; though, no help came. And while the world prevaricated about the fate of those survivors, typhus raged through the camps. At Bergen-Belsen alone, it claimed another fourteen thousand lives. In the absence of anything else, the Jews began to organise themselves in each of their Jewish-only camps and in each of the occupied zones.

'Guilt,' said Fox. 'And betrayals. In war, aren't those the price we pay for victory? And will your guilt be any the less after Strasbourg?'

There it was, again – the doubt. But, he filled that space with all the old images. The abandoned ambulance. The dog tags. All those godforsaken prison and internment camps. Danielle's face.

They checked the departures board. Platform Eight. Strasbourg. Telford had an image of Chrétien de la Marielle's face. Then, recollections of some of the atrocities in which the *Milice* had been involved. Their collaboration with the Gestapo.

'Yes, Captain,' he said, 'I'm certain of it.'

Friday 18th October 1946

The Detention Centre, the Maison d'Arrêt, on Strasbourg's Rue du Fil, was ancient. It leaned against the back of the Palais de Justice, its exterior paintwork flaking away, untouched for a hundred years or more. The lattice shutters hung all askew, most of them offering little protection to the barred windows.

'Did they reach a verdict?' Telford asked the superintendent.

'Yesterday afternoon. He's back before the tribunal tomorrow morning. Sentencing.'

'Can you tell me?' Jack slipped him a pack of cigarettes. 'And don't worry. Mum's the word. But I have to be on the early train for Berlin.'

Telford stored away the information, followed the superintendent through the cockroach-infested corridors leading to de la Marielle's cell.

'Remember, *monsieur*,' said the superintendent as he unlocked the door, 'I have your parole.'

'What was that about?' said the young prisoner. The door slammed shut at Telford's back. Chrétien had been sitting on the edge of his striped mattress, but now pushed himself to his feet.

'Nothing much,' Jack told him. 'Promised not to stay too long. That's all.'

As before, Jack was struck by just *how* young this fellow looked. He must be twenty-five but something distinctly adolescent about him. The inflamed acne, perhaps.

'I'd invite you to sit down, *monsieur*, but...'

He waved his arm around the space. Six feet by six feet. Black metal bed. A bucket with a lid and, above the bucket, a single dripping tap. Barely enough space for each of them to stand. A single light, which flickered constantly, despite this being almost noon. And an angry bluebottle, buzzing and buffeting at the bulb.

'I was sitting all day. Yesterday, that is. Train from Nuremburg. Then to here. Delayed, of course. Still, I promised to come back, didn't I? The tribunal's over, I understand.'

'I tried to tell them.' De la Marielle's features twisted in childlike tantrum. Haughty. Aristocratic. Educated. 'War crimes, I said. Let me tell you about war crimes.' He'd become almost hysterical. 'The twelve men captured with me. Twelve loyal Frenchmen. True Frenchmen. And shot like dogs. That traitor Leclerc and his Commie Red rabble. Shot them. All good Catholics.'

'At least, you lived to tell the tale, Chrétien.'

'I did.' The fellow's face relaxed, the youth again, his smile disarming. 'And you know what he said to me – Leclerc? Asked me whether I was ashamed to serve in the uniform of the Waffen-SS.' He scratched at his spots. 'Do you have a cigarette, *monsieur*?'

Jack unfastened his trench coat, threw his trilby onto the bed, set his back against the green iron door.

'Here,' he said, holding out his remaining pack of Luckies. 'Help yourself. And I bet you had a clever answer for him, no?'

De la Marielle took the cigarette, waited while Jack lit the thing for him.

'Answer?' said the Frenchman – though, Telford had difficulty thinking of him as such. *Salopard*, he thought. Worse than a *collabo*. 'I told him *he* certainly looked good,' Chrétien went on, 'wearing the uniform of America. What sort of Frenchman wears the uniform of America?'

'Clever,' said Jack, and lit up his own smoke. 'Leclerc was never a man to appreciate being contradicted. But he sent you here.'

'Told me I was going to meet my father. Had me pulled out of the line. Then called for one of his so-called officers to get rid of the others. Awful people – that's what he called them. Those "awful people". My comrades, *monsieur*. They took them away. Four at a time. Shot them.'

Jack knew the details. Maybe, knew them better than de la Marielle. A wood near Kugelbach. Karlstein. He'd once tried to speak with Leclerc about it.

'But they died like true Frenchmen, *monsieur*. Each of them refused a blindfold. Each died shouting "*Vive la France!*" That is patriotism, is it not?'

Passion in his voice. And bitter regret. He thumped the wall, grazed and bloodied his knuckles.

'You would have preferred to die with them,' said Telford.

'I begged Leclerc to let me die. But he looked down his nose at me. Something about Vichy corrupting the young. Young. He said I would live because I was young. Because of my father.' The hysteria again. 'The bastard. I am a man, *monsieur*. A son of France. The son of a traitor. Not some damned child.'

'You told them all this at the tribunal, Chrétien?'

'They didn't want to know. Objection this. Objection that. Irrelevant, they said. All they wanted to hear about was the Jews.'

'And, like you told me last time I was here, you're no Jew hater. Isn't that what you said?'

'Of course not. Who cares about the Jews, one way or the other? Not me, that's for sure. I knew about the camps. The transports. Sure, I did. Everybody knew. But not the gas chambers. Not those.'

'The tribunal swallowed that nonsense? After all, the Waffen-SS and the death camps - two sides of the same monstrosity, no?'

'To the ignorant, perhaps. To the stupid.' De la Marielle waved his arms in the air like a madman. 'Those fools. Their so-called tribunal.'

He spat on the floor.

'Well,' said Jack, 'we all sing the anthem, don't we? The dear *Marseillaise*. That line about watering our furrows with the impure blood of France's enemies. That's the Jews, isn't it?'

'No, not Jews. Worse than the Jews. Communists. Freemasons. Republicans. All those who took up arms against Vichy. De Gaulle, Leclerc and their lackeys.'

'And when the Jews were also Communists, Chrétien? Or took up arms against Vichy?'

'Then, of course. Then they deserved...' He paused, lifted the lid of his toilet bucket, dropped the stump of his cigarette inside. A hiss, and he looked back at Telford. 'Are you trying to trick me, *monsieur*?'

'Why would I do that? The tribunal's over, after all.'

'They've not said when I'll hear the sentence,' said Chrétien.

'At some of the camp trials,' said Telford, as casually as he was able, 'they didn't find out the verdict until they came to take them to the hangman.'

Jack lifted his arm behind his head, jerked his hand upwards, a mummery of the hangman's noose.

'Don't be a fool,' the young man sneered. 'I was promised leniency. A couple of years in prison. You've got this wrong, *monsieur*.'

Jack shrugged his shoulders.

'Chrétien, listen. It might be you that's wrong, I'm afraid. What if they've decided to make an example. Sentencing...'

'What?' he laughed. 'Firing squad? You must be mad. Prison's the worst that I'll get. You'll see.'

'I've just come from Nuremberg,' said Jack. 'The hangings...'

He watched the colour drain from the young man's face, de la Marielle slumping down onto the grey-striped ticking of the meagre mattress.

'They can't,' he said. 'My father…'

'I expect it's all something of an embarrassment for them. Has he been to see you?'

'No. But…'

'It wasn't pretty, Chrétien. I remember Streicher. They put the noose around his neck. Then the black hood. He managed to yell one last '*Heil Hitler!*' as he dropped out of sight behind the curtain. The rope should have snapped his neck. But we could hear him choking. It just went on and on. God knows how long. Until, eventually, that American Master Sergeant – the executioner – he ducked behind the curtain, too. Then it all went quiet at last.'

De la Marielle was silent for a long while.

'But Streicher,' he said, finally. 'It was Streicher who stirred up the worst of the hatred against the Jews. I'm no Jew hater, *monsieur*. You know that.'

'It's true Streicher wasn't in the military. And he played no part in planning the extermination programme. But the pen *is* mightier than the sword, Chrétien. They decided his articles in *Der Stürmer* were so inflammatory, so vile, they made him an accessory to murder. As guilty as those who'd ordered the extermination itself. Like the stuff you wrote for *Le Pays Libre*. You might not have mentioned the Jews specifically, but preaching about pure blood, all that collaborationist nonsense – it all amounts to the same thing, I suppose.'

'Nonsense?' Chrétien jumped to his feet again. 'I was proud to *collaborate*, as you call it. Serving France – that's what it was.'

Yes, thought Jack, I bet you believed the lie. His heart began to hammer in his chest. But he needed to know.

'In a way,' he said, 'I understand.'

Telford paused for effect, prodded his finger aimlessly into some paintwork peeling from the wall, as though he were thinking of something – something else.

'You know,' he went on, 'maybe you can tell me about it. Châtel-sur-Moselle. Remember? Last time we spoke you said perhaps after the tribunal…'

'Proud,' Chrétien insisted. 'To have served France. Served the Führer. If I have to die for him, too – well…'

But Jack knew it for bravado, saw the tremble in the fellow's lip, heard it in his voice.

'It was cruel,' said Telford, 'if they hinted at leniency. Cruel. But, I suppose, they were looking for some sign of contrition. Yet, here you are, still insisting that the maniac was right.'

'He *was* right, wasn't he? And if he wasn't right, why did your so-called Allies sit back and watch happily when the Vatican signed its Concordat with him? When he marched his troops and flew his bombers into Spain? When he annexed the Sudetenland and then the whole of Czechoslovakia? And when Hitler invaded Poland, why did France and Britain simply go through the motions? Did Churchill himself not say that if Britain were defeated in war he hoped you should find a Hitler to lead you back to your rightful position among the nations?'

'I've heard the speech before. And spent many nights wondering about the same things. But I need to know about Châtel, Chrétien.'

Yes, he thought, I've wondered about those things. But in a different way, of course. By the time of Munich, we might not have been strong enough to fight Germany militarily. Yet, if the bloody European powers had stood firm economically, choked off Germany's trade routes, called Hitler's bluff, stopped him gaining all those millions in gold when they allowed him to take Czechoslovakia…

'If Hitler had been left,' said de la Marielle, 'to lead Germany back to *its* rightful position, there'd have been no need for war. Britain, France and Germany in glorious alliance against the Bolsheviks.'

Jack laughed.

'We were talking about Châtel,' he said. 'The mayor. He was the town's doctor too, did you know?'

'Communist scum. A traitor to France.'

'You were there with the *Milice* – when they shot him?'

'Perhaps. I don't remember. Not everything. A long time ago.'

'Two years. Not *so* long.' Yet, to Jack, in truth, it felt like a life sentence. Time might heal, but never fast enough. And this… 'But I understand,' he lied. 'So many deaths. Too many men shot. On both sides, yes?'

'They can't hang me for that. They can't. We all killed our enemies, didn't we?'

'Perhaps the tribunal was more concerned about those you sent to their deaths elsewhere. That's what they asked about, wasn't it? All they wanted to hear about was the Jews, you said. The Jews, condemned by your writing, Chrétien. Or prisoners. You took prisoners, didn't you?'

De la Marielle's features changed again, reptilian, calculating; the penny beginning to drop. He wagged a suspicious finger in Telford's face.

'You're looking for somebody. Is that it, *monsieur*?'

'The last of the prisoners taken in Lorraine and Alsace,' said Jack, 'did they end up at Rebstock or somewhere, when the *Boches* retreated?'

'If I help – you'll tell them? Tell them I cooperated with you?'

'I thought you were happy to die for the Führer. For your vision of France?'

'Happy? Yes, if I must. But I prefer to live. Wouldn't we all? Well, we heard rumours. When the SS abandoned Strasbourg they took their prisoners. But not far.'

'The SS? Your own bunch, you mean?'

'I joined the Charlemagne Division later. After Strasbourg. Training in Franconia. Then fighting the Reds.'

'Splitting hairs, Chrétien. They must have talked about it. Your new comrades. Boasted about it, I suppose.'

'It was war, *monsieur*. Prisoners shot? Scum like those traitors in Châtel – of course. And yes, I heard stories. But none I remember now.'

'There's one I thought you *might* remember, though. Also at Châtel. Your group of *Milice* friends. You were driving around in a black Citroën sedan, weren't you?'

De la Marielle laughed.

'Black Citroën? Are you serious? You know how many black Citroëns there are?'

'This one is a bit special, I think. I saw it in the courtyard of the Hôtel de Ville in Strasbourg. Left behind, they said, by a section of the *Milice* that had been operating in Lorraine. Damage on the wheel arch. The side of the bonnet. Running board, as well. Missing paint. Scratches. And traces of olive green. From an ambulance, which the *Milices* had driven off the road.'

The colour drained from Chrétien's face.

'The girl,' he said.

Telford felt something like an electric shock to his whole system, and had to hold his breath, while he regained control.

'Yes,' he said. 'The girl.'

'Hostage. We thought she might be useful. But the Gestapo took her. The other one was dead. But the one we took – she meant something to you? Why take all this time to look for her? She does, doesn't she – mean something?'

Telford swallowed. He swallowed, hard.

'We were going to be married. And the Gestapo – you know where they sent her?'

A spark of hope. Stupid hope. It almost made him weep.

'They thought she might be useful, as well. And one of the boys – André, who was murdered at Karlstein – well, André had taken quite a shine to your girl, *monsieur*. He went a few times. To Gestapo headquarters. They let him see her. She had no identification tags, wouldn't even give them her name. They thought she was American. Like we did. But then everything changed. Seems they'd seen a report from Toulouse. Her photo matched with a girl who'd been one of those terrorists from the *Maquis*. What was her name? Can't recall now.'

Jack fumbled in his pocket, took out the dog-eared photo, Dani in her fatigues, face smudged with oil.

'Zidane,' said Jack. 'Danielle Zidane.'

'If you say so.' Yet de la Marielle refused to look at the image.

'And then?'

'Then? André found out they'd sent her to Haslach. You know Haslach, *monsieur*?"

'I've been there. Christ...'

Yes, he'd been. The closest of the camps to Strasbourg. Only thirty-five miles away, across the Rhine in the Black Forest. Just one of the secondary camps – in truth, Haslach was three camps – to which prisoners from Alsace and Lorraine had been relocated.

'I'm sorry, *monsieur*. Perhaps, if we'd known. If André had known…'

'Known?'

'By then, they weren't keeping anybody at Haslach anymore. It was just a convenient place… Look, it was the Gestapo.'

'Convenient place to get rid of the bodies? But, there's no crematorium at Haslach.'

Telford tried hard to remember; though, he was certain. That's what they'd done elsewhere. Burned as many as possible of those they'd butchered in those final months.

'No,' said de la Marielle, 'but there are burial pits. In the forest.'

How close Jack must have been. To Dani's lonely grave. Yet, lonely? He wondered how many others lay alongside her. It was the thing she'd feared, falling into their hands. And he'd promised her, hadn't he? Promised he'd never let that happen. He looked at the photograph, choked back the sob threatening to suffocate him and, somehow, an echo of the terror she must have felt – it brushed down his spine. Yet, he knew, now. The truth of it. And, as the truth flooded his brain, the doubts entirely ebbed away.

'You know, Chrétien,' he said, taking a last glance at the snapshot before he tucked it back into his pocket, 'I hope when they come for you, tell you your fate, you'll get to taste the fear Streicher must have felt – that the girl felt. Ambulance driver. Nurse. She saved lives. Our own soldiers. Germans, too. But hanging really *is* too good for you, boy.'

'I'm no boy,' de la Marielle raged, jumped to his feet. 'Not a boy. And you promised. I told you what you wanted to know. It wasn't us, anyway. The Gestapo…'

'You took her,' said Jack. 'You. And your Nazi friends. But you're the only one of them left. Just you. Killed her as surely as writing your filth for *Le Pays Libre* sent Jews to the gas chambers. You useless little bastard.'

Telford pushed him back onto the bed.

'You promised,' Chrétien sobbed.

'I promised nothing. But I can help you, Chrétien. I don't owe you a thing. Not a damned thing. All the same, Nuremberg – it left its mark on me, I suppose.'

There was a hammering at the door, the superintendent's voice.

'Time, *monsieur*,' yelled the superintendent. 'Getting late. And we've preparations to make.'

'Yes, yes,' Jack replied. 'Five minutes.' They heard the fellow's footsteps retreating back up the corridor. 'You see, Chrétien? They want this done and dusted.'

'Help me, how?'

Jack reached inside his jacket pocket, pulled out Negrín's pen. He unscrewed the black Bakelite barrel. No rubber ink sac attached to the nib and feed section. Instead, he shook from the barrel's interior a small glass capsule. He held it between his thumb and finger. Caution. Some disdain. Feigned reluctance.

'I've got this,' he said. 'Just not sure – it came from the *Reichsmarschall* himself. Or, rather...'

It had cost him a pretty penny. For the cyanide as well as the story. That Yank from the honour guard who'd inadvertently or otherwise helped Göring avoid the noose. And he'd been glad to help get rid of the evidence – for a handsome price, naturally. Telford hadn't formulated a specific plan at that stage. No, it was rather that the idea of possessing the capsule had insinuated the plan into his brain. And, of course, the plan made it even more certain he couldn't use the story itself.

'You just happened to have it with you?' said Chrétien, his eyes fixed on the ampoule.

'Honestly? I just wanted it for a souvenir. Help me sell my story about Nuremberg. Had to smuggle it out this way. And I'd be happier to keep hold of the thing. So, if you don't want it...'

'What if you're wrong – about the sentence? They've already kept me here eighteen months. If they'd wanted me dead...'

'Fair enough,' said Jack, and slid the capsule back inside the pen's barrel, picked up his trilby from the bed. 'Well, I'd wish you good luck, Chrétien, but you know I'd be lying through my teeth. In truth, I wish you a slow and painful death.'

De la Marielle jumped to his feet yet again, gripped Jack's arm.

'Wait. If I take it, I could keep it hidden until after they tell me, and then...'

'Are you stupid? You think after Göring, they won't search you as soon as they come for you?'

'But you can't know, *monsieur.*'

'Of course, I know. Why do you think the superintendent gave me that warning when I got here. Made me swear not to tip you off.'

Jack unscrewed the barrel again, tipped out the cyanide capsule.

'Then, I will die for France,' said Chrétien.

'Your decision,' Jack told him.

'Is it…?'

Jack passed him the poison.

'Painful? Apparently not. All over in a heartbeat.'

'If I wait until I hear them in the corridor, and then…'

Jack screwed Negrín's pen back together. He wasn't entirely certain what Negrín would have thought about this. Mightier than the sword had certainly been part of Negrín's philosophy.

'I'm sure God will have mercy on your soul,' he said. A final piece of satisfying hypocrisy. But Telford the agnostic decided it might provide one last encouragement. 'To a better place, Chrétien, no?'

Jack thumped on the door again, as de la Marielle palmed the tiny glass vial.

'For France,' Chrétien shouted when the door opened and Jack slipped out of the cell. 'For the glory of France.'

The door slammed shut once more.

As Telford signed himself out in the Maison d'Arrêt's visitor book, the superintendent came bustling after him.

'You didn't tell him anything, I hope, *monsieur?*'

'Of course not.'

'That *salopard* will gloat, I suppose,' said the superintendent. 'When he finds out. Only another eighteen months. Is that what they call justice?'

It gave Telford satisfaction that he hadn't directly lied to Chrétien de la Marielle – simply allowed him to hear what the Nazi swine wanted to hear.

'Justice?' he said, 'Sometimes in the night I hear the screams of people I've known, crying out for justice. And sometimes, Superintendent, it's only we, ourselves, who can deliver it for them.'

Two

The Berlin Protocol

Saturday 26th June 1948

The war in Europe might officially be over but Telford knew, these three years later, that liberation from Hitler's grasp was a far cry from true freedom.

Jack lit a Capstan, began to type.

In Berlin, one does not experience any sense that the war is truly finished...

And not just Berlin, he thought. There'd been Paris, the previous December. Leclerc's funeral. Everybody had expected such great things of Leclerc, only to have him die so uselessly in a plane crash. The funeral had been enormous, naturally, but Jack had avoided meeting up with too many old comrades – all those reminders of Danielle and everything he had lost.

He gazed again at the words; though, they weren't his own. Not anymore. Plagiarism was alive and well, living in a boarding house, just off the Kreuzberg's *Oranienplatz*. He wasn't proud of himself, naturally, and often thought of the way his old gran had scolded him as a boy – and even as a young man – whenever she considered him to be guilty of even minor deceptions.

'If you cannot be true to yourself, John,' she would say, 'then you will never receive truth from others.'

His pay from the BBC was hardly generous; yet, as one of the Corporation's foreign correspondents, he earned a fortune compared to the many Berliners formerly of his own profession, now without work.

So, Jack merely commissioned a piece, claimed credit and payment for its completion, converted the finished copy to script format. Even the typewriter wasn't his own. It belonged to the offices of the *Konsumergenossenschaft* offices, along with a miscellany of other equipment, including a Peirce 55-B dictation recorder acquired, they said, from the *Tiergarten*'s black market. Ah, the joys of international capitalism, thought Jack.

A modest payment to the Queen Bee, *Fräulein* Erika Vogel, ensured access to the machines whenever they were not otherwise in use.

'*Bitte, Fräulein,*' he said. 'Today? The recorder?'

'Today?' she replied. 'Make the most of it, *Herr* Telford. For us there may be no tomorrow.'

He knew little about her. Except that she walked here every morning from her home in Friedrichshain, one more of the sixty thousand who crossed each day from the Soviet Sector to work in West Berlin.

'The blockade?' said Jack, hoping he'd chosen the correct German word. 'It is touching you?'

'They violate the city for revenge, *Mein Herr*, the same way that their filthy soldiers...' She paused. '*Reichsminister* Goebbels warned us about them. The Communists.'

It had begun yesterday. Road and rail traffic closed. Berlin no longer simply adrift in the sea of Soviet eastern Germany but supplies to the stricken city suddenly severed.

Funny, Jack thought, that even now, despite everything, they still speak about the Nazis as though they'd been the voice of reason.

'They fear the black market,' he said. 'And the new *Deutsche Mark*. The Soviets. They think Germany will rise from the ashes. Threaten them all over again.'

'With what? They dismantled all the factories, took them to Russia. American cigarettes worth more than money. How could we be a threat to anybody now, *Mein Herr*? We are trapped here. Animals in a cage.'

Ah, thought Jack, now there's an irony!

It was precisely how he spent much of the time he had freed for himself by having others do his work. Visiting the few remaining inmates of the Berlin Zoo. A sad place. Confusing. Less than a hundred beasts had survived from the original almost four thousand before the war. And most of the hundred subsequently eaten by starving Soviet soldiers. The place was slowly being rebuilt, of course, partially restocked, but he still went there to weep for those other cages he'd seen. Empty now. At Dachau. And Sachsenhausen.

He took the scripts and entered a small office that housed the dictation recorder. The window was open. All the windows of Berlin seemed open today. Futile hope of relief from the June heat wave that permeated the building. That and the stink of excrement and stale food – the predominant smells of both war and its aftermath, he'd found. Telford closed the window, arranged his papers, switched the machine to *On*, turned the central dial to *Record*, and began to read his introduction.

'In Berlin,' he said, with his best BBC accent, 'one does not experience any sense that the war is truly finished.' Two fluent paragraphs about the crisis. The British, French and American sectors now cut off. Only enough food left in West Berlin for the next few weeks.

He halted the recording, opened the window again. The noise would give his next piece the authentic feel of an outside broadcast.

Jack selected *Record* once more, introduced *Herr* Spiegel.

'The Nazis put me in prison,' said Jack, in a weary and ancient German accent, 'because I was active in my union. I am socialist but I do not like what is happening to my city.'

Jack was entirely carried away with the *Herr* Spiegel performance, almost jumped out of his skin when he heard the applause behind him.

'Bravo, *Herr* Telford,' said *Fräulein* Vogel, closing the door behind her. 'A performance worthy of the Opera House.'

'Perhaps, I could take you there one evening?'

'To see the Bolshoi trying to demonstrate that the Russians have more culture than their defeated enemy? I think not.'

'I was just practising,' said Jack. 'To make sure...'

'Please, *Herr* Telford.' She held up her hand. 'I am no fool. I have seen the spools dispatched. Remember? I have listened to the broadcasts. Your Radio Newsreels. The rest of the world may not recognise your accent. But you cannot deceive me, *Mein Herr*. Your employer would not appreciate the joke, I imagine?'

'What exactly would you want, *Fräulein*? For the joke to remain strictly private?'

'It is my father, *Herr* Telford. He is not well. But at least until now I have been able to take him food and medicine.'

'He is too ill to leave the house?'

Fräulein Vogel hesitated.

'Yes,' she said. 'Too ill. And… Well, he is not in favour with the Reds. They say he is a Trotskyist. An enemy of the state.'

'I'm afraid I still don't see…'

'Yesterday, today also, they began to search us. To confiscate things at the checkpoint. And there are rumours, *Herr* Telford. That the Soviets may build a fence around the whole of West Berlin. After that, we may not be able to cross at all.'

'Just a stupid story, surely?' said Jack.

'Maybe. Meanwhile, I have only one solution. To bring my father out of the Soviet Sector.'

'If they won't let him leave, how can he obtain an exit permit?'

'The local police chief runs a small business. He is happy to accept ransom payments. To allow my father's release.'

'You have this all thought out,' said Jack. 'And exactly how much will this cost me? I assume that you *are* holding me to ransom also?'

'An ugly way to put it, *Mein Herr*. But a modest price. At least, for a non-Berliner. One thousand *Ami-Zigaretten*.'

Fifty packs, he thought. Have I got that many stashed away? If not, he knew how to acquire them. And at sensible prices. A fiver, perhaps, but no more. Yet, the mark-up? A quick calculation. A single pack of twenty was selling at the *Tiergarten* for about ten pounds. Fifty dollars. Two hundred times their original value. So, fifty packs would turn a pretty profit. All to ransom a Trotskyist? Jack had his doubts.

'I understand, *Fräulein*. But we need to be honest with each other. About your father. He's a Nazi, isn't he?'

'You say the word as though it poisons you,' she said. 'The Party only brought order from the chaos that the *Juden* had inflicted upon us.'

'He was a party member?'

'Yes, a member. But not active, *Herr* Telford. A member only.'

'Alright. That's good enough for me. And how are we supposed to pay this ransom?'

They arranged to meet later, near the shattered Schesisches Tor station. She could meet *Hauptmann* Hofert at the *Grenzpolizei* barracks on the north side of the river, any evening up to seven o'clock. Jack would bring the cigarettes since he was more likely to get the ransom past the *Hauptmann's* subordinates at the checkpoint. He would show his press pass, confirm that he was crossing to interview Captain Hofert and, naturally, had brought him a small token of his appreciation. He opened a khaki rucksack, allowed her to peek at the contents. Lucky Strikes.

'I brought something for your father, too.'

'A book?' she said, taking the carefully wrapped brown paper package from his hand. 'It's heavy.'

'Of course,' he replied. 'It's Kafka.'

She was too polite to reject the thing.

'Won't they confiscate it?'

'They're looking for food, aren't they? I may see Kafka as the bread of life but I doubt the border guards will be so philosophical.'

He thought about Kafka. *'All too often men are betrayed by the word freedom.'*

They walked together towards the Oberbaum Bridge. It was a fine evening.

'I hate this,' she said. 'Crossing each day. Like returning to an evil dream. Grey. No colour. Full of ogres that can do with you whatever they please.'

I imagine the Jews in their ghettoes must have felt somewhat the same, he thought. But he kept his lips sealed.

'You think the Americans will help?' she continued.

'They'll certainly bring more cigarettes,' said Jack. 'According to the *New York Times*, the Marshall Plan is set to deliver over two hundred million of the things.'

'They will bring food too. Chocolate, don't you think?'

'So, you didn't believe Goebbels when he told you the Americans would use chocolate to poison German children?'

'No,' she laughed. 'That would be absurd.'

But not the bits about the Jews and the Communists, he thought. How could monsters like Goebbels still have such a hold here? He'd lost count of the times he had seen people involuntarily begin to give the Nazi salute.

The upper deck of the Oberbaum Bridge, with its brick-red turrets, no longer carried the U-Bahn across the Spree, and the lower level was empty of road traffic, too, since yesterday – now simply a wide pedestrian thoroughfare, with the wire, oil drums and tables of its checkpoint at the nearer end. And, given the hour, there was a queue, whispered gossip about whether the Americans and British would, as they had done in April, attempt once more to bring in food by plane. More importantly, if this miracle should come to pass, how would they manage to benefit from the thing, to get supplies past these green-clad border police when commuting back to their homes.

It was the turn of Telford and *Fräulein* Vogel to step forward, to show their papers, open their bags. Erika wanted them to go together but Jack smiled.

'Quicker if we take one each,' he said.

He approached the right-hand table, documents in hand and the rucksack partly open. The guard saw the Luckies.

'For you, comrade…' Jack winked at him, took out a few packs, nothing but a bag full of journals beneath.

At the other table, a different guard examined Erika's gift.

'It's a book,' she was explaining.

The policeman ripped apart the brown paper wrapping, seemed puzzled, stepped back in alarm, shouting to his companions, pulling apart the leather cover from its carefully padded contents - a dainty Czech automatic, .25 calibre.

You can buy anything at the Tiergarten, thought Jack.

'Hands up!' bellowed a guard.

Fräulein Vogel turned towards Telford.

'Why?' she screamed. 'For God's sake, why?'

For a foolish moment, Jack thought she would run.

'*Stehenbleiben, oder ich schieße!*' Stand still, or I will shoot.

So, she stood still, tears running down her cheeks.

'Why?'

They dragged her away and, while the remaining guards began to restore order, there was a low rumbling in the western sky. For Berliners it was a sound that still haunted them, even now. The earth quaked, and they responded as they'd always done, seeking shelter, showing fear, instincts of self-preservation even though, in this instance, it was wholly illogical. The airlift had begun.

Yet, it provided a useful distraction and Jack took advantage to move casually away from the table, pausing only long enough to pick up the Lucky Strikes.

Waste not, want not, he thought, and strolled back towards Skalitzerstraße.

Doesn't really matter whether it's Hitler or Stalin, he decided. Fanatics spring from the seeds sown by ordinary people. And when the fanatics die, they leave more seeds behind them. To start the whole process all over again. What can you do, Jack mused, to keep the garden free of weeds except hoe the soil whenever we get the chance? He considered seeds like Fräulein Vogel and her father. Well, he said to himself, every little helps.

Three

The Vienna Premiere

Friday 10th March 1950

Telford enjoyed the notoriety of having once thumped Hemingway. And now, it seemed, he might be tempted to repeat the performance.

'Say, haven't we met...?' Hemingway waved a finger vaguely towards Jack's eye-patch. It was generally the way people remembered him. In this case, however, Telford knew the fellow was using this pretence at familiarity merely as a decoy.

The foyer of Vienna's Apollo Kino was pure Art Deco; though the whole building had once been a gilded palace. Literally, a palace. The Apollo had survived the Anschluss, the Nazis, the entire war, remarkably intact – unlike much of the rest of the city.

'I don't believe so,' Telford replied, deciding that leaving Papa Hemingway to the mercy of the other journalists and press photographers was more fitting, and less perilous, than a physical response. It was their questions, in fact, and Hemingway's ungentlemanly behaviour which had sparked Jack's outrage.

'*Herr* Hemingway,' Schmidt from the *Salzburger Nachrichten* insisted, 'where *is* Adriana this evening?'

They'd been hounding him since he first made his entrance along the Apollo's red carpet, almost dragging his fourth wife, Mary, behind him. She was pretty. About Jack's own age, he decided. Blonde. Tiny alongside Hemingway. A good journalist, as well. She'd covered the war, mainly from London. And they'd met – just once, before she'd married the brute.

'Jack,' she said now, with a small gasp of surprise and apparent delight. 'Jack Telford?'

Jack touched the brim of his trilby in salute before Hemingway hauled her unceremoniously up the stairs.

It was one of the stories which had followed Hemingway around for the past year or more. His apparent infatuation with the young Italian girl. Or was she Croatian? Anyway, Hemingway fifty, the girl just eighteen. Adriana Ivancich. And flaunting her in front of his wife. Why did she stand for it? Wherever the Hemingways went, there too went Adriana. Though not here, it seemed. Not tonight. Not in Vienna for the Viennese premiere of this most consummately Viennese film.

Well, that wasn't strictly true, either, since Hemingway was actually in town, on a flying visit, to promote both a new German edition of *For Whom The Bell Tolls*, as well as his forthcoming new novel, due for publication later in the year. But what was wrong with a bit of extra publicity? Another glittering occasion, the first showing here of *Der dritte Mann*. The very thing which had brought Telford to town, as well. Yes, *The Third Man*.

Jack's train journey to Vienna, of course, had not been an easy one. But it had been made somewhat more bearable by his sometime acquaintance, *Hauptmann* Hofert, formerly of the *Grenzpolizei*, now the *Ministerium für Staatssicherheit*, the East German secret police. It was a bit of a mouthful and Telford had sent his report about the change, back in February, to London, using the term *Stasi*, for short – just as the *Grenzpolizei* had been more commonly known as the *Grepo*. It might have been coincidence but, suddenly, it seemed the whole world was using the same term. *Stasi*. Still, Jack liked to take credit for it.

His relationship with Hofert was a strange one, but they had "scratched each other's backs" from time to time and Fox had encouraged him, in the hope that British Intelligence might turn the fellow at some point. So, now, knowing that Jack had this daunting ordeal ahead of him, Hofert had provided papers and travel documents enabling him to make the trip by the most direct route, almost a straight line entirely through Soviet-controlled territory. It was easier now, of course, that the Soviets' blockade of Berlin had finally ended the previous year, the Airlift no longer needed. And thank heavens – for no less than two dozen American and British planes had crashed during that one year in the process of flying in food and supplies.

So, a modest improvement in détente and, while it lasted, Jack was happy to take advantage. First, through the checkpoint to East Berlin's Ostbahnhof station, then by train though the sometimes stunningly beautiful and sometimes deeply depressing landscapes of East Germany to Dresden. The place was slowly being rebuilt but still more ruin than reconstruction. The bombing, the firestorm, had killed tens of thousands, even by the most conservative estimates.

Jack had seen plenty of bombed-out towns and cities in the past ten years and more. All Europe in ruins. But the sight of such destruction always took him back to those first places in Spain he'd visited in '38 – the places where German and Italian pilots, flying for Franco, had honed their skills at bombing and strafing civilian targets. At Guernica. And, four weeks before Guernica, at Durango. Yes, somehow it all began at Durango, then ended here, at Dresden. But, after Dresden, there'd been Hiroshima. My god, he thought, where the hell are we heading?

Telford had declined the option of a stopover and opted, instead, for the overnight sleeper from Dresden to Prague. Poor Prague. Poor Czechoslovakia – the sacrificial lamb offered up by Britain and France to appease Hitler at Munich. It had almost been as if a nation only created as an independent state in 1918 hadn't been worth the effort. And sacrificed for what? First, the Reich, now the USSR. Yet, the Czechs themselves were a proud people, whose Bohemian and Moravian territories had simply been subsumed into the Austro-Hungarian Empire, but whose art, philosophy, culture and architecture still shone.

From Prague, across the border into Lower Austria, that farthest third of the Allied-occupied country under the control of the Soviets – while Britain, France and the Americans had their own zones in the western *Bundesländer*. At the heart of the Soviet zone, Vienna: like Berlin, isolated, itself partitioned between the same four Allied powers. And, since he was travelling on Hofert's papers, Telford arrived by circuitous route at the once grand but now badly damaged

Nordbahnhof station in the Soviet zone – Leopoldstadt, to be precise. Russian soldiers in the streets and cafés, huge posters of Lenin and Stalin hanging from its more stately buildings, and trams flying both the Austrian and Soviet flags.

Another checkpoint, and a short walk into the city's heart, the Inner Stadt district, under the joint control of the Americans, British, Soviets and French. This was the famous "four in a jeep" district, patrolled by policemen, one from each of the occupying powers, but the driver always an American – it was their vehicle, when all was said and done. So, this wasn't Berlin. Not by a long chalk. And, at the centre of the city's heart, on Philharmonikerstraße, Telford found the impressive Hotel Sacher.

'No trouble, then?' Fox had said, when they met later in the bar. Still debonair. Still the David Niven moustache.

'Not until I got here.' Telford lit a cigarette and nodded across to the mirror-varnished elegance of the woodwork and the polished brass of the reception area with its silk-draped sofas. Fox followed the direction of Telford's glance.

'What – the lifts?'

'Paternosters,' Jack had grimaced. 'They bring back bad memories.'

Of the Hotel María Cristina in San Sebastián. Blood. Lots of blood. And that style of elevator, designed a hundred years earlier by some fellow from Liverpool and named because its constant motion reminded him of a set of rosary beads in action.

'Our Father...' A smile from Fox while he sipped at his cognac. 'But, here you are – and not one assignment, but two!'

Telford had nodded. Yes; though, not really a coincidence. First, the most simple, since Thompson at the Beeb had simply asked him to write, and then record, a piece about the premiere itself. It would sit well with the broadcasts from Bush House as part of their new East German Service, aimed at listeners behind the Iron Curtain and building on the clever wartime propaganda the Corporation had fed into Nazi Germany. The broadcasts had a strong focus on culture and entertainment, like the new comedy show, *Die zwei Genossen – Two Comrades*. A feature about this first German-language version of *The*

Third Man – Der dritte Mann – would be perfect. Besides, there was a neat link between the film and the Corporation itself. For wasn't Hugh Carleton Greene, recently head of the German Service, not Graham Greene's brother? Perfect.

'The first should be straightforward enough...' Jack had been distracted by the flamboyant and noisy arrival of Hemingway and his wife. 'Oh, my god,' he went on. 'I was just thinking how much better it would have been if Greene himself had been in town, but look who we've got instead. Did you know?'

'I did not,' Fox replied. 'And didn't you tell me you once...?'

'I'd rather not be reminded.' Telford had slumped down on the shared sofa, lest he be spotted.

'You could have a bonus story, dear fellow. Think he might be here for the premiere?'

'With all that luggage? Looks like they're here for a year. Though, with Hemingway...'

Jack had recalled the stories of Hemingway arriving in Spain during the siege of Madrid, in '37. And Martha Gellhorn following him there. Another brilliant journalist. Another of Hemingway's conquests. They married, eventually, of course. His third, wasn't she? The wife before Mary.

'Never mind him,' said Fox. 'Tell me about this story that AP are after.'

Telford was still earning extra income on the side with additional pieces for the Associated Press.

'That's the point. I'm not sure. Their man in Berlin – Thompson, you know him?' Yes, Fox knew him. There wasn't anybody in Berlin he *didn't* know. 'Anyway,' Jack had continued, 'New York have latched on to this legend that there's *really* a "Third Man" operating in Vienna.'

'Borrisov?'

'Borrisov. Benno Blum.'

One and the same person. The man was indeed a legend – for all the wrong reasons.

'What did Greene say about Harry Lime?' Fox had mused. 'Something like, "*The worst racketeer who ever made a dirty living in*

Vienna." Wasn't that it? He could have been talking about Borrisov. And, knowing Greene, maybe he was.'

It was an open secret that the writer had been a spook with MI6 during the war – and, perhaps, later.

'I wouldn't know,' Jack had told him. 'Never seen the film, nor read the book. Remiss of me, but...'

Another distraction. More celebrity arrivals. Two of the film's German-speaking stars, the Austrians Paul Hörbiger and Hedwig Bleibtreu. Telford might not have seen it yet, but he'd taken the trouble to study the cast. It was already established that neither Welles, Cotten nor Howard would be at the premiere, but there was a strong rumour that Valli would be there. Telford hoped so. She was beautiful.

'And your man in Berlin,' Fox had said, 'he seriously thinks Borrisov can be tempted to give an interview?'

Telford had read enough to know the Harry Lime character in the film was involved in the black market, a penicillin smuggler – after the war, penicillin literally worth far more than its weight in gold or diamonds. But the Benno Blum Gang had excelled in smuggling people. Kidnapped people. High-ranking Red Army deserters, or political opponents of the Eastern Bloc, any prominent defectors now in self-exile within the Allied zones. It was said that Bulgarian Nikolai Borrisov was contracted to deliver alive, each and every month, at least one person being hunted by the Soviets.

'I didn't exactly get my travel arranged here for nothing,' Telford had replied. 'Thompson asked me if I could pull strings, and I mentioned it to Hofert. If the show's on, he'll leave a message for me at the AP's Vienna bureau. We'll see.'

'Sounds damnably dangerous, old fellow.'

'It can be a deadly business. And, for you? Vienna?'

Fox had shrugged his shoulders.

'This feels like a vacation, as the Yanks might say. And, speaking of our friends across the Pond, you're sure this is just AP? Not the CIC?'

The US Army's Counterintelligence Corps.

'Why should you think so?' Telford had tried his best to sound offended. The very thought...! 'But your vacation?'

Fox studied him for more than was comfortable before answering. Trying to work out what, exactly?

'You know the score, I think. Always rumours at the Broadway about Reds under each of our beds. And I asked about the CIC because one of our own old boys is now in Washington. First Secretary to the Embassy – though, you'll know what that means, too, yes?'

Indeed. Telford had clear memories of the First Secretary he'd met in Madrid at the end of '38. A spook. And on the wrong side. The devil had tried to have Jack killed.

'Anyway,' Fox had continued, 'this fellow was Greene's supervisor for the Firm during the war. Convinced that Greene wrote *The Third Man* as a warning to us. That we've got a mole. Clues, that sort of stuff. A riddle. If we watch the film closely enough, maybe we can solve it. Flush out the mole. Hoping the German-language version will show us something we couldn't see in the original.'

'But why wouldn't Greene simply have told you?'

'Fear? If this mole has been clever enough to fool us all this time, he would have a long reach, don't you think? A deadly reach.'

'Greene's supervisor, now in Washington, but still keen to expose the mole. That's very diligent of him.'

'Well, old man, that's Philby for you!'

'You think Trevor Howard speaks German?' Mary Hemingway whispered to him behind her hand. Telford had already established that both she, and Hemingway himself, spoke the language reasonably well. Skiing holidays, apparently, and Mary's coverage of the war.

They sat in the best seats – plush red velvet – in the Reserved Section at the front of the upper stalls. Almost a private box, but not quite. Jack had been surprised to find himself on the list, and even more surprised to find himself seated next to the Hemingways.

'I know,' said Jack, 'that Welles and Joseph Cotten are dubbed. Brilliant, too. But Howard? Hard to tell. It certainly sounds like Howard.'

Further along the row were the other celebrities announced with so much pride by the absurdly tall theatre manager before the show began: some of the actors, including the delectable Alida Valli; members of the directorial and cinematographic teams; and "other honoured guests" – who must have included a certain Jack Telford, since he wasn't specifically named. He wasn't offended.

Papa Hemingway leaned across his wife.

'Where'd you say you both met again, my dear?'

'I don't believe I did say.' Mary smiled up at him. A pretence of a smile. Almost a sneer. They hadn't stopped sniping at each other, and Telford wasn't especially keen to be caught in the crossfire.

'It was May '44,' said Jack. 'London. The Instituto Español. Mary was there for the *Express*, I think. Interview with Negrín?'

'May?' said Hemingway. 'Wasn't that…?'

'Coincidence. I met Jack precisely twenty-four hours before I met you, Papa.'

'I'm not sure we did actually meet,' said Telford, somewhat ungraciously, and noticed Fox, waving down at him from up on the balcony tier. 'We were introduced, shook hands and moved on, as I recall. That was it. Amazed Mary remembers me.'

'But made enough of an impression,' Hemingway muttered, 'to have remembered each other just fine.'

Jack offered him a simpleton's smile and turned back to the film. A scene in which Trevor Howard's Major Calloway tells Joseph Cotten's Holly Martins that his friend, Harry Lime, is a murderer and a racketeer. Martins so offended he tries to punch the major in the face and swears he'll prove Calloway wrong.

Telford was due to meet Hegel at the AP bureau in the morning, and then he'd see whether the secret interview with Benno Blum was likely to take place. And for what hidden purpose. In the meantime, all he needed was a few notes about the premiere. If his piece was going to shape one of the East German Service broadcasts, he needed to find the right angle.

'Doesn't look much like the Vienna we've seen,' said Hemingway, as Cotten's character made his way past a vast pile of rubble.

'Apparently,' Jack whispered, 'by the time they came to film it, most of the real damage had already been cleared. They had to bring back heaps of the bomb damage debris. It's why the Austrians are likely to hate it. Too many nasty reminders.'

Yes, that would be his hook. A gentle nudge about the film's messages: look what happens when you follow dictators of any stamp,

Hitler or Stalin, regardless of how much they might pretend to have the interests of the people, of the motherland, at heart; look at the creatures who crawl out of the rubble in the aftermath.

But he'd also carefully craft something more subtle, more subliminal, the film's other lesson: look at the way this Cold War, propagated equally by East and West alike, continues to breed that insane fear and mistrust, the tension, between the nations of Europe at precisely the time the whole continent should be working collectively for the creation of fairer societies, free from the terrors of yet more warfare. He'd have to be careful about that part, but he could see an angle forming in his brain.

He watched the story unfold for the next thirty minutes or so. There was something surreal about seeing parts of the action played out at the Hotel Sacher, where Jack himself was staying. But he was still thinking about his own piece, when Hemingway snorted.

'At last,' he said. 'Thought he'd never put in an appearance.'

It was fair enough. Almost an hour into the show and here was the first sign of Orson Welles, hidden in the shadows of an ornate doorway, a cat nibbling at the laces of his shoes. The haunting zither soundtrack tune. The silky voice of Welles echoing across the darkness.

"*What kind of a spy d'you think you are, satchel-foot?*"

'Clever pussy!' Mary murmured, and Jack felt her rub her leg against his own.

He pulled his knee away fast, turning his head quickly to check whether her husband had seen. But it seemed he had not.

'Not clever at all.' Hemingway lit a cigarette. 'Probably smeared the laces with pilchards.'

Jack looked back at the screen in time to see Joseph Cotten's astonished reaction as a light from above illuminates Welles's face, and the Holly Martins character realises his old friend isn't dead, after all; the chase scene, Harry Lime vanishing into the night; and, then, the Intermission announcement, the theatre lights brightening.

'Buy you a drink, Telford?' Hemingway demanded, as they stood from their seats. Jack tried to demur, desperately seeking an excuse he might invent, but Mary linked his arm.

'Don't you dare!' she laughed, dragging him towards the exit, and the staircase leading to the first-floor winter garden, an extensive glass pavilion full of exotic plants among the tables and reflected in the gilt-framed bar mirrors.

Telford looked around in desperation, praying that somebody would rescue him.

'Fate worse than death?' said Fox, and took a flute of champagne for each of them from the tray of a passing waiter.

Well, not champagne, of course. No, a proud Austrian Sekt, a good vintage Vöslauer, the waiter boasted. 1911. Something else, Telford was surprised, which had survived not only the Anschluss; the Nazis and the war; but, also, the entire break-up of the Austro-Hungarian Empire. Mind, that was their own fault, wasn't it? They had, after all, been mostly responsible for triggering the first of the century's world wars, their impossible ultimatum to Serbia. If he thought about it, he probably blamed the Austrians most for his father's death. And then, of course, Hitler was Austrian, too. Yes, they had a lot to answer for, did the Austrians.

'You saved me,' he replied, swigging his wine so quickly that the bubbles flooded the inside of his nostrils.

'As it happens, it was mutual, old man. The only thing anybody wants to talk about is the damned election.'

Jack grimaced. He'd rather not remember. How had it happened? Only a couple of weeks earlier, and Labour's '45 majority of one hundred and forty-six seats had been slashed to just five. Five! And it was likely that it wouldn't be enough for Attlee to continue to govern. Within a year, they said, Churchill would be back in power.

'It's all Elliott's fault,' said Jack. It was part jest, and partly the truth. Telford's old editor had masterminded the *Mirror*'s remarkable publicity campaign in '45 on Attlee's behalf. But Elliott was now in Australia, supervising the *Mirror*'s newspaper and radio operations there while, at home, it seemed as if its new editor had somehow abandoned the Party. Lacklustre, that was how Jack had seen their coverage. 'Maybe, that's the reason we did so badly,' he groaned.

But the real reason? More to do with a fickle British public, he knew. The Tories had no choice except to swallow the welfare state,

NHS, and nationalisation, all through gritted teeth. But where was the acknowledgement from voters that Attlee, Bevan and the rest had done more for them in five years than all the governments of the previous fifty put together.

'I rather think,' said Fox, 'it was more to do with rationing.'

He was right. While the spirit of Dunkirk and the Blitz had remained strong, their countrymen had happily snatched up every benefit Attlee had brought them. But keep them deprived of sugar? Goodness, a bridge too far. And then there'd been the devaluation of the pound.

'And perhaps, just perhaps,' Fox went on, 'this feeling we're being led by the nose a bit?'

'The Yanks,' said Jack. Strangely, it was the point of what he wanted to write. This Cold War – who needed it? Well, the American arms industry, for one. And there was Churchill, talking about a more European union.

'Not that we're ungrateful to the American cousins, of course,' Fox smiled. 'But our future's here, isn't it?'

No doubt, thought Telford. But it came with a twinge of guilt. Hypocrisy, since he'd not been above stoking up the Cold War himself, had he? Last year's story of the *Amethyst* and the Yangtse Incident: newly communist China flexing its muscles against the Royal Navy. Jack's recorded broadcast into East Germany had turned the ship into an obvious allegory for escaping to freedom. Well, he decided, we all have to earn our bread.

'Yes,' he said. 'Welcome to our future. And the film? Found any clues about this mole of yours?'

But Fox was still none the wiser; though, he regarded Jack with some suspicion.

'Me?' he said. 'No. But what about you, old boy? You're sure the Yanks aren't ahead of the game, here?'

'I've no idea what you mean,' Jack told him, as innocently as he was able, and thankful as the bell rang for the intermission's imminent end. He slapped Fox amiably on the back and turned towards the stairs, heading back down to the seats, with the Hemingways hot on his heels.

'Papa,' he heard Mary's voice. 'Remember in the foyer? You thought you might have met Jack before?'

Telford looked back over his shoulder. He was astonished to see her poke out the tip of her tongue, a gesture of pure spite, accompanied by that form of childish pout he still thought of as a *moue*. Hemingway was busy lighting a cigar, so seemed not to notice.

'Just occurred to me, honey,' she went on. 'You told me that tale – Paris, Liberation Day. The funny little man who threw a punch. The guy with the eye-patch?'

Jack managed a couple of canny manoeuvres to get ahead of them, then side-stepped when he reached the doorway until they'd gone past and resumed their seats, Mary looking all around for him. But, by then, Telford had found another empty place, as the lights went down once more.

The second half, in which Holly Martins finally meets Harry Lime, on the Ferris wheel. The shots of the ground far below managed to unbalance Jack – his vertigo, of course – as much as they unnerved Martins. A clever scene. Menacing.

Then, an interesting piece of the dubbed dialogue. About cuckoo clocks! In Jack's mind, it didn't quite fit the context, but there it was, in the mouth of Orson Welles, yet the voice of some German whom Telford didn't know:

"In der Schweiz herrschte brüderliche Liebe…"

Jack followed it perfectly.

"In Switzerland, they had brotherly love, they had five hundred years of democracy and peace, and what did that produce? The cuckoo clock."

Strange, he thought. The cuckoo clock was actually a product of Bavaria, not Switzerland at all. Besides, the Swiss? Before this past hundred years they'd been one of the most feared military forces in Europe. Landsknecht mercenaries? Bonaparte's Swiss regiments?

But he enjoyed the train station scene with Valli. And the finale, in the sewers – wonderful. The closing scene saw Martins back at the Vienna Central Cemetery for Harry Lime's real funeral. And that superb but strange, sad cliffhanger ending. The last notes of the zither's theme music. Momentary silence. Then, a sparse smattering of unenthusiastic applause.

*

49

In the Café Papageno, they'd hired a resident zither player whose job, it seemed, was to massacre the same theme from the movie endlessly throughout the afternoon.

'You like, mister?' said the big Bulgarian, sitting across the table from Telford and sipping at his glass of colourless liquor, then puffing on a cigar even larger than Hemingway's had been. At his back, a gorilla bodyguard.

'The music or the *rakiya*?' Jack smiled, lifting his own glass in salute.

'Play game with words. You clever man, eh?'

My god, thought Jack. How do men like this manage to fill every word with so much menace?

Nikolai Borrisov – Benno Blum – must have weighed in at sixteen or seventeen stone, and the thick black moustache hung like whale baleen, masking the movement of his lips with each sneering sentence. Yet, despite the malignant pose, there was something strangely effeminate about the man.

'I've been a journalist so long,' said Telford, 'it seems to come naturally, *drugar*.'

He used the Bulgarian word for *comrade*, and was rewarded with a smile flashing across the fellow's face, like a beam of sunshine when the storm clouds briefly part.

'Yes, you clever man. But maybe journalist...' Borrisov had to take his time with the word. 'Journalist,' he said again, 'ask too many question. Look too close at other man's business. Look too close and lose...'

He flapped a hand towards Jack's eye-patch. 'Only one left, mister. Careful, yes?'

Well, it was true. Jack *had* lost his eye through an excess of curiosity. And maybe it was the cigar smoke but, suddenly, he felt the burning pain yet again in the scarred and empty socket.

'These days,' he said, 'it pays for all of us to be careful. Is that why you're here, in the French zone?'

AP's Vienna bureau had made the arrangements. Borrisov, it seemed, was keen to do the interview. And, maybe, something more, he'd apparently hinted to them, though without further explanation. Telford had been advised to tread carefully.

'Safe enough in Soviet Sector.' Then he fell to a whisper. 'So long as I was useful to them.' He laughed, and slammed the flat of his hand on the table. Telford smiled. Hadn't Harry Lime said something similar?

But, once the fellow had started, it was almost impossible to stop him again. Jack took notes. As many as he could; though, he had no idea whether any of it was true. The story came out in a jumble of confused statements.

Yes, the rogue had been a smuggler, mainly of medicines, both in Germany and the Balkans during the war – and been paid for his efforts in even more lucrative cigarettes. Later? Yes again, after the war, he had begun to smuggle people – traitors and defectors from the East – and taken them back to his Soviet paymasters. Until things had started to go wrong.

Acting on his own initiative, he had kidnapped one of those defectors, only to incur the wrath of the MGB when he discovered the man was a double agent, his defection carefully planned and now blown. And, then, earlier in the year, many of his Benno Blum Gang had been arrested, Borrisov's links to the MGB hitting the headlines in the West.

The Soviets had put on a show of indignation, responded by arresting him. Kidnapping? How dare the West suggest they would sanction such a thing. A trial. Imprisonment. And Borrisov's miraculous escape. So, here he was, hiding from Allies and Soviets alike in the French Sector.

'Hiding?' said Jack, and looked around the busy café. 'There were three black Chevrolets parked outside when I came in.' Hardly inconspicuous. The very ones, Jack knew, which had been the gang's signature kidnap vehicles, almost their trademark. 'And my friends at the bureau seemed to have no trouble working out where I could find you.'

'Sometimes,' Borrisov smiled, 'can hide in plain sight if castle has strong walls.' He jerked a thumb back towards the gorilla. 'Josef,' he said. 'And my boys. Those are my walls.'

He nodded his head towards the other obvious thugs lurking around the establishment. A dozen of them. Maybe, more. It would be a bloodbath, trying to prise Borrisov out of his hideaway.

'Anyway,' he went on, 'Boris has trump card. Secret. Your friends in West will pay good price, mister.'

'And this secret, I'm guessing, will repay the Soviets for their perfidy?'

'Perfidy? What this perfidy?'

'It doesn't matter, *drugar*. But you want me to pass on this message? Your secret?'

For the first time, Borrisov seemed unsure of himself, and lowered his voice. He slipped a pencil from his trouser pocket and snatched Jack's notebook, scribbling an address.

'Not here, mister. But tonight. Nine. This place. Ask for Grete.'

'Nice pen,' said Hemingway, making his way past Jack's table.

Telford flinched, as he palmed the signed tab back to the waitress. For such a big man, Hemingway was light on his feet.

'It has something about it, does it not?' he said, and glanced at Mary, who was plainly doing her best to ignore him. 'A gift from Negrín, as it happens.'

She stared down at the pen, now. Plain black bakelite, gold trim and nib. But it did seem to attract attention.

'The event in London?' she said.

'No,' Jack told her. 'Long before. Spain.'

'You were there, too?' said Hemingway.

Telford screwed the top home, and slipped it back inside his jacket, somewhat offended that the fellow should sound so surprised.

'At the end, yes,' he snapped.

'Pretty lighter, too,' said Mary. She lifted it from the table, where it sat next to the pack of Capstans. 'Real gold – my goodness. Another present, Jack?'

He would have told them the story – how it had once belonged to the Nazi commander of Paris, von Choltitz. Yet, it would have just been too much. And he had no intention of reminding Papa Hemingway about Paris again.

'How was dinner?' he asked them, instead.

'Wiener Schnitzel,' Hemingway sneered. 'Why is it always Wiener Schnitzel?'

'But the strudel was just dandy.' Mary's sarcasm sounded as spicy as cinnamon.

'Buy you a whisky at the bar, Telford?'

'Need to go out again, I'm afraid.' He offered Hemingway his friendliest false smile. 'But if you're still there when I get back…'

The street was unnaturally quiet, despite the horse-drawn tourist carriage trotting past, even this late in the evening. The clatter of its wheels, and the *clop, clop, clop* of the hooves echoed eerily between the four-storey apartment blocks on either side. He could almost have been back in the Apollo Kino admiring yet another haunting example of Reed's cinematography.

Telford's destination filled a considerable portion of Thalheimergatse: three lengthy, bow-ended balconies protruding along each floor; the green wrought ironwork illuminated, here and there, by the lights ghosting through curtained windows.

In the flickering shadows of the entrance hall, where a single ceiling bulb stuttered, the head-scarfed old concierge demanded to know his business. The German was broken, her accent eastern European, almost certainly Russian. Indeed, she was a typical *babushka*, wrinkled and formidable.

'Grete?' he said.

'*Vier*,' she said, and held up four fingers, just in case. '*Rechts*.' She waved her right arm sideways. Was she part of Borrisov's gang? He could easily believe it.

There was no lift, of course, and he had to stop halfway up the stairs to get his breath back. Bloody cigarettes, he thought. Here he was, forty-two, and puffing for tugs.

Predictably, on the top landing, Josef stood guard outside that apartment to the right.

'Wait!' said the bodyguard, and leaned over the metal balustrade. He whistled down into the stairwell. Far below, Telford heard the ancient *babushka* muttering some Slavic curse, and the entrance door clanging shut behind her, as she went out into the street. Two long minutes later, she was back inside, and shouting up at the gorilla.

It sounded like, *suchista*. All clear?

'You could have just asked me,' said Jack, while Josef knocked at the apartment. 'But I wasn't followed.'

It was true, as it happened. He knew it for a fact.

In the doorway stood a peroxide blonde, attractive enough in a hard-faced sort of way. Mid-twenties, he thought, and wearing a pink, see-through negligée, which might have been alluring had it not been for the winceyette nightdress beneath.

Telford tipped his hat.

'You must be Grete,' he said.

'Margarethe,' she replied, as had been arranged. Jack saw a fleeting image of comedian Max Weston's wife, a long time past. Marguerite Weston – what the hell had become of her? He shook his head to dispel the memory and followed Grete along the passageway, through a small but lavishly furnished living room – courtesy, certainly, of the black market – and into a small kitchen area, where Borrisov sat at a table, working the spigot of a brass samovar to pour tea into gold-rimmed glasses. Jack could smell the mint.

But the thing which amazed him was the elegance of the fellow's attire. Some form of traditional dress: a green, fez-style hat with a matching drape hanging down his back; a sleeved, velvet waistcoat, also green, with rows of yellow buttons around the edgings; baggy, coffee-coloured pantaloons over white stockings; and ankle boots.

'Mister, you like tea?' He smiled, and handed Jack one of the amber-filled glasses. He reached behind him into a narrow alcove with shelves, a pantry of sorts. 'Here, sugar.' He set a porcelain bowl and a spoon on the table.

Jack shook his head, to Borrisov's astonishment. He knew it was the custom, but his time in North Africa had left Telford with an aversion to the sickly sweetness of mint tea.

'Fine like this,' he said, and nursed the glass, warming his fingers. But before the tea had even reached his lips, there was a commotion out on the staircase. The apartment door burst open.

Josef ricocheted into the passage, set a hallstand flying on one side, and knocked a mirror from the wall on the other. An explosion of glass. Boots on the stair treads. Shouting.

'*La police! Arrêtez-vous!*'

It sounded strange, but they *were* in the French zone; American-accented English, too, but the same message.

'Stay where you are!'

The voice inside Jack's head yelled. Too soon! Too bloody soon!

Josef was deaf to the instruction, charged across the kitchen, yelling as though all the hounds of hell were at his heels, and hit the French windows onto the balcony. He flung them open – admitting a blast of cold wind, which sent the thin curtains flapping – and disappeared out into the blackness, seemingly leaping to the adjacent ironwork railings.

Borrisov had stood, knocking over the samovar.

'You!' he said to Jack. 'Judas.'

'No,' Telford mouthed, as the policemen jostled each other in the passageway, tangling themselves somehow in Margarethe and her negligée, while the Bulgarian pressed himself into the alcove, dragging a revolver from beneath a rag on the shelves and flicking off the light switch above his head.

'Do not shoot!' cried Borrisov. 'I have secret. Big secret.'

Jack knew it. The very reason he was here. What the hell had gone wrong? But he was forced to stand as well, back to the wall, the apartment now plunged into darkness. He caught a blurred glimpse of the policemen, rain capes, two French *képis*, an American helmet, a heavy tweed civilian overcoat. And their own guns. One of them fired, shattering the window, despite Josef having disappeared moments before.

'Wait!' Jack shouted. 'Stop shooting, for Christ's sake.'

Borrisov fired back, blind – his hand and the revolver poking around the corner of the alcove and so close to Telford's stomach that the heat and blast from two return shots seared the wool of Jack's own coat. He was in the line of fire. Right in it.

He could think of nothing else to do, so reached up and grabbed Borrisov's gun – at the precise moment when the fellow pulled the trigger a third time. It was fortunate for the policemen, though unfortunate for Jack, that his grip on the pistol resulted in the hammer closing, not on one of the cartridges in the cylinder but, rather, on the little finger of Telford's left hand.

Agony. Jack screamed.

The civilian overcoat was in front of him. Two more shots, and Borrisov groaned. His arm dropped, though he still held the revolver, yanking Jack's hand down also, his finger trapped tight by the hammer and blood oozing from the wound. He turned to see Borrisov slumped in the alcove, mumbling something through the walrus moustache, trying to push himself up from the floor – until another of the policemen, one of the French gendarmes, delivered the final *coup de grâce*.

'Why?' Telford murmured. 'Why?'

He slid down the wall, looked up into the face of the American – the agent Bob Crowell, to whom Hegel at Vienna's AP bureau had introduced him. Crowell was smiling at him. The lights came on again.

'That was neatly done, Mr Telford. Neat indeed. But let's have a look see...'

He reached down and, less than gently, pulled back the blood-soaked hammer of Borrisov's gun, releasing what was left of that damaged finger and causing Jack to swoon into nauseous, echoing oblivion.

'You lied to me, old fellow,' said Fox. 'You bloody lied to my face.'

If he was honest, Telford hadn't expected him to show. Yet, here they were, sharing *schnapps* and smokes in this grubby bar. He wiped steam from the window and peered out across the square to the checkpoint at the canal bridge. He wouldn't be sorry to see the back of Vienna. All that had happened this past week. And how many prominent Nazis had the place spawned? How many of the scum who'd served in Austria's death camps – at Mauthausen and the rest? The Soviets had taken Vienna in a battle almost as brutal as Berlin, but later determined that Austria should be classed as a victim of Nazism, rather than one of its breeding grounds. The country would therefore likely regain its independence and unity much faster than Germany – but Telford wasn't certain that Austria deserved the privilege.

'I may have been economical...' Jack turned his head and coughed into his handkerchief. He seemed to have picked up a chest infection. And the cigarettes didn't help. 'Economical with the truth. For what it's worth, I feel sorry for it.'

'And now? Heading back to your paymasters?'

'You know it's not like that. Hofert and I scratch each other's backs sometimes. It's damned well suited *you* often enough.'

Well, that was true.

'But not *this* time,' Fox snapped, and knocked back his *schnapps*. 'It's not going to look good, dear boy. Not for you. Not for me.'

'It all sounded plausible enough at the time. Borrisov become an embarrassment to the Soviets. They arrest him but he escapes to the French Zone. Then, what? Risk a bloodbath with his gang at the Papageno just when they're trying to thaw relationships with the West?'

'I understand all that,' said Fox. 'And the plan to lure him away from his thugs? I understand that, too. Give him his five minutes of fame. A modern Jesse James – wasn't that it?'

'More or less.' Telford glanced at his watch. Half an hour until the train to Prague. 'Let the West have him. But, of course, they didn't know about his little secret.'

'You're sure about that, are you, Jack?'

Telford winced. The painful doubt which still plagued him. And the pain from his injured left hand, bandaged two days earlier at the American Hospital. The least they could do, agent Bob Crowell had told him. The tip of his little finger. From the top joint upwards, had been neatly amputated.

'A bit paranoid, don't you think?' Jack sounded convincing, even to himself. 'A thaw in relationships is one thing. But some deal between the Soviets and the Yanks to dispose of a mutual problem?'

'You think the Yanks would have killed him for no better reason than he was hiding in the Allied zone?'

'What else?' Telford finished his own *schnapps*, the liquor spreading a fiery glow across his troubled chest.

'Borrisov's secret,' Fox suggested. 'I asked you – remember? Whether the Yanks were ahead of the game.'

'But if there was a Soviet mole among our spooks, wouldn't the Yanks want to know who that was?'

Fox smiled at him.

'Would they, old fellow? Would they, really? Doesn't that rather depend...?'

Yes, thought Jack. He'd already got there during his time at the hospital. It would depend on whether agent Bob Crowell and his team had been given their orders by some rogue who'd want the secret to die with Borrisov. The mole himself? Well, it was certain they'd never find out the truth of *that* one.

'Complicated world, isn't it?' Jack smiled. He picked up his hat and case. 'But what will they do now? The Soviets. How will they get their defectors back, without the Benno Blum Gang?'

'My God, you can be annoyingly naïve at times.' Fox set his own trilby on his head, left a handful of notes to pay for their drinks and opened the door for Jack.

'Naïve?'

'Well, dear fellow, Borrisov may be gone, but the gang is still alive and kicking.'

'Josef?'

'Still bodyguard to the boss – but a new boss, certainly. And speak of the devil...'

He nodded to the other side of the square. Walking towards them, towards the checkpoint, in a pale raincoat and cloche hat, a slender briefcase under her arm, was Margarethe.

'You see, my friend?' said Fox. 'Going off to meet *her* new paymasters, too.'

'I've told you...'

But Jack was thinking that, maybe, Margarethe was also heading for the Prague train. No, she wasn't Alida Valli, though she was bloody attractive. Maybe, another story. And maybe...

'Listen,' he said, ' no hard feelings, I hope.'

He set down the case and held out his hand. Fox took his time before shaking it, and Jack knew by the hesitation that something was now irrevocably lost between them.

'If you say so, old boy. If you say so.'

Fox walked away in the same instant that Margarethe drew level with them. Jack smiled at her and tipped his hat.

She ignored him and marched resolutely past, onwards towards the Soviet checkpoint, and Telford found himself trapped in that closing scene from the movie: Joseph Cotton's Holly Martins unexpectedly given the cold shoulder by Valli's character. *The Third Man. Der dritte Mann.*

Jack lit a cigarette – just as Joseph Cotton had done – and watched her walk on without a backward glance. He felt like a fool. But then he shouted after Fox.

'By the way, what will you tell him – our man in Washington? What was his name again?'

Fox stopped.

'Philby?' he said. 'No, he'll not be best pleased, I expect. And I forgot to ask you – the black eye. Looks like a recent addition.'

Telford laughed. One eye blinded and covered by the patch. The other swollen and still sore. He touched it with his fingers cautiously, cautiously.

'This?' he said. 'No, this was bloody Hemingway. Hell hath no fury – isn't that what they say? Seems like, with Mary's help, he'd finally managed to remember what happened in Paris.'

Well, he decided, I probably deserved it.

Four

The Suez Triangle

Monday, 22nd October 1956

Twin sparks of light, flashing out a warning of danger – that was how Telford first perceived the low, incoming fighters. He rubbed at the aircraft's window and realised he was seeing the Mediterranean's setting sun gleaming upon the plexiglass of their canopies and casting long cruciform shadows behind them on the blood-dark sea.

It was an hour after take-off from Palma de Mallorca, on this cunningly conceived route from Rabat to Tunis – circuitous to avoid French territory over Algeria.

'Nobody considered this?' Telford asked his fellow travellers in a French now somewhat rusty. 'That their air space extends to wherever their navy might be sailing?'

He pointed down towards the waves, and Ahmed Ben Bella moved across the aisle, shaking his head, a look of weary exasperation on his handsome face, a face younger than his forty years. A cap of tightly-curled, dark hair. He reminded Jack of an actor who'd become something of a star recently. Quayle? Anthony Quayle?

'Truly, *Monsieur* Telford,' Ben Bella replied, 'you have the ability to turn a blue sky permanently grey.'

'They don't worry you?' said Telford.

'What can they do? Shoot us down?'

'You think being on a Moroccan plane will help us?'

'That – and having a renowned BBC correspondent on board.'

'I still have no idea why I'm here.'

'Because His Highness, Sidi Mohammed, asked you to be here.'

It was true. Jack and the Sultan of Morocco had become close during the war. Friends? Perhaps not that close. But close enough. *'Whenever your soul is weary,'* Sidi Mohammed had once told him, *'you may return. Always a place for you here.'* And Telford's soul had certainly been weary these past ten years. Put simply, he didn't like himself anymore. He found he could not remember whether he'd *ever* liked himself.

'He asked me to be here,' he said, 'to help celebrate Morocco's independence.'

'That was seven months ago. What took you so long?'

But Ben Bella didn't wait for an answer. Instead, he called to his four companions in Arabic so that now they all stared through the windows of Jack's side of the plane. The two fighters were climbing towards them now. Climbing fast, their profiles clear.

'Christ!' Telford shouted in English, switched hurriedly back to French. 'Are you sure they will not attack?'

'The French have already tried to kill me twice, my friend.'

Jack tried hard to dismiss the thought, *third time lucky*. He didn't enjoy flying at the best of times and his memories of being shot down over the Libyan desert all those years before still brought him night terrors. But here – over the sea?

'Ungrateful, don't you think?' Ben Bella went on. 'After I fought so hard for them at Monte Cassino.'

One of his comrades – Telford thought it was Mohammed Boudiaf – fingered a string of prayer beads, *mas'baha* – and muttered the beginnings of a *du'a*, seeking the intercession of Allah in their plight.

'But after Monte Cassino,' said Jack, 'there was Sétif.'

And Jack – as well as Ahmed Ben Bella – had both been directly affected by Sétif. The very end of the war and nationalist protestors clamouring for Algerian independence. French soldiers had opened fire. And after Sétif, a whole catalogue of other atrocities. Even official sources put the death toll at a thousand. But Radio Cairo claimed it might be as high as forty-five thousand over the intervening weeks. Telford, still attached to the Free French, had confronted de Gaulle, virtually accused the general of having issued the orders – and been seriously rebuffed for his efforts.

'Sétif changed all our lives,' Ben Bella replied, as the two French planes – Grumman Avengers, dark metallic blue-grey with *Aéronavale* insignia, Jack could now see – fell into formation, one on each side of the Moroccan plane organised by Sidi Mohammed to carry its Algerian passengers to Tunis. 'It changed them forever,' said Ben Bella.

Telford knew his story well enough. Decorated more than once for his outstanding bravery in the Italian Campaign and turned to politics in the wake of Sétif. Seeking independence through the ballot box – but a ballot box the French would never allow to produce fair results. So, Ben Bella had turned to paramilitary revolution. A spell in prison and escape to Cairo. It all played out like the musical score to a movie while Jack's gaze was fixed on the Grummans.

'If they're not going to attack...' he began, as one of their own crew – the pilot, or maybe the co-pilot – threw open the door from the cockpit, shouting in Arabic.

'He says they're insisting we divert to Algiers,' Ben Bella translated. 'Looks like we have no choice.'

'We'll be arrested,' said Jack. He didn't relish the prospect. There were plenty of stories already about the French use of torture. He felt the ruin of his left eye begin to throb and itch like the very devil beneath its piratical patch.

'It's what happens when you travel with terrorists, do you not think?' Ben Bella laughed; though, it seemed to Jack as though the laughter was tinged with trepidation.

Terrorist or freedom fighter? Wasn't this always the question? Was it not entirely in the eye of the beholder? French Resistance. The Haganah in Palestine. Mau Mau. EOKA in Cyprus. And the independence from colonial rule won by Morocco and Tunisia had only made Algeria's demands more strident.

Of course, Algeria wasn't either of those two neighbouring countries. Unlike all France's other overseas possessions, Algeria had the unique status of being part of France herself. Besides, there were the *Pied-noirs* to complicate matters – roughly a million of them, European non-Muslim settlers born in Algeria. France was never going to willingly subject them to independent rule. To Muslim rule. And Ahmed Ben Bella was never going to allow this small matter of the *Pied-noirs* to stand in the way of the National Liberation Front's deadly campaign for independence, assisted by both Morocco and Tunisia.

'You see?' Ben Bella went on. 'If you'd taken up Sidi Mohammed's invitation earlier – but, of course, then your BBC had still not instructed you to follow a story. And now we, *Monsieur* Telford, myself and my friends...' he gestured towards his four companions, '...whether or not they send us to the guillotine, we *are* your story.'

Guns. So many guns. Searchlights, as well; though, it was barely twilight. A cordon of gendarmes, of khaki-clad soldiers, and an army truck mounted with a heavy machine gun. All this weaponry and beams of blinding illumination trained on the plane as it sat on the runway. And there was a loudhailer.

'You shall disembark one at a time. One at a time only. We will tell each of you when to come down. Keep your hands raised at all times – and clearly visible.'

The French officer summoned Ben Bella first.

There was a brief discussion between the Algerians – about their luggage, Jack gathered – but Ben Bella shrugged his shoulders, took a last glance at his own valise, abandoned now by his seat, and shook hands with his comrades.

'Bonne chance,' Jack called to him. The man nodded his head towards Telford – a grim-faced farewell to acknowledge Jack's best wishes – and made his way out onto the passenger stairs.

Jack watched as they handcuffed him, then stripped him of his tie. Ben Bella's four associates had been similarly instructed by name to leave the plane: Hocine Aït Ahmed, another of the FLN's founding members; paramilitary commander, Mohammed Boudiaf; writer and historian, Mostefa Lacheraf; and former member of the French National Assembly, Mohammed Khider. Each arrested, the five detainees lined up for photographs before being bundled roughly into a black police van.

Telford waited for his own name to be called. But nothing.

What to do about his own attaché case? What if they took it for a bomb? The French here had become famous for their "shoot first and ask questions later" approach to their suspects, but it contained too much of his work to simply abandon the thing.

He was left to gingerly make his own way to the plane's open doorway, where he followed the crew down onto the concrete, each of them with their hands tentatively raised – Jack holding the case high in one hand, his white Panama in the other – even though the searchlights had all been dimmed, the tension eased, the gun truck and most of the soldiers driven away.

'*Monsieur* Telford?' said a serious young police lieutenant, waiting at the bottom of the stairs. To Jack's surprise, the fellow saluted him when Jack confirmed his identity, showed his papers. 'Welcome back to Algiers, *monsieur*,' the lieutenant told him. 'This way, if you please.'

Telford was directed to a waiting black Citroën, ushered onto the back seat, but the lieutenant didn't join him. Just Jack and the driver, who remained entirely uncommunicative as they drove north from the airport into the city.

He'd been in Algiers twice before. The war, of course. But how in god's name would the lieutenant have known that?

The first time just an overnight stop, only long enough for him to visit the sights, to wander the famous Casbah, that enormous warren of rebelliously stacked dwellings, a maze of steep and secretive alleyways climbing up towards the old citadel and surrounding palace ruins. The Casbah, he knew, now a sanctuary for the insurgents of the National Liberation Front, the FLN, and turned into a virtual ghetto by the French army.

His second visit? In company with Josephine Baker – and Steinbeck. Algiers which, until Normandy and the eventual Liberation of Paris, had briefly served as de Gaulle's capital of Free France.

It held grim memories as well – for Jack had almost been murdered on his return journey from the city to Casablanca. Was it this which haunted him now? This fear? This confusion? None of it was improved when they stopped on Carnot beneath the austere bulk of the *préfecture*. It stood alongside the equally obdurate town hall, the boulevard sitting high above the ramped roadways and rail lines leading to the dockyards and Maritime Station. Beyond the quaysides below, lights flashed green and red along the outer harbour wall, or were reflected from the wide waters of the port and outer basin by the many vessels already berthed at the piers, or underway. The ebb and flow of Algiers and its place in the world.

Jack's reception was less congenial than his greeting at the airport. A sergeant escorted him inside the police headquarters, up two Gauloises-scented flights of stairs and along a gloomy corridor, its flaking walls painted drab olive green. Deep within the building, somebody screamed.

'Here,' said the sergeant. 'Wait here, if you please.'

The fellow almost pushed him into an office as Jack recoiled from the noise, directed him to a straight-backed chair. There was a desk with typewriter, telephone, large blotter, brass ashtray, scattered papers. In the corner, two roller-slatted filing cabinets. Overhead, a ceiling fan, flies buzzing about its stilled and silent blades.

Left alone, Jack set down his Panama on the desk, and waited. Fifteen minutes went by; though, it seemed like hours. There were no further screams, but somehow the silence was worse. And he filled the silence by living again the waking nightmare of the torture he had himself suffered. The eye. Why did the torment worsen with each year that passed, rather than lessen? He reached nervously for his case, ruffled through the pages, took out his copy of Tolkien's *Return of the King*. But he couldn't settle to the story – these chapters too dark for his mood. A Mordor mood, he decided.

Instead, he lit a Capstan and stared at the maps filling almost every inch of the tobacco-stained walls. Algiers, of course – several, including a nautical chart of the harbour and a large-scale plan of the Casbah. But most prominent? The entire world with France and its former colonies or protectorates, each of those lost since the war marked in ink by a small Cross of Lorraine: French Indochina; Morocco; Tunisia; and their concessions in India, Egypt and Lebanon.

'How long before we lose the rest?'

Telford spun around on his chair, caught unawares by the voice. The terror returning, until he realised that the voice was familiar. Almost forgotten, but familiar.

'Shit!' he said.

'It is – *d'accord*. Shit, indeed! The whole bloody mess.'

Jacques Massu had aged these past ten years and more. But he remained easily recognisable: the swarthy, aquiline features; the distinctive moustache; and a surprisingly silent approach, given Massu's stature. Telford – as a correspondent attached to Leclerc's Free French Division – had covered his exploits on more than one occasion. North Africa, Normandy, and the Liberation of Paris. Yet his bearing, always military, seemed more rigid than Telford remembered.

'Why am I not surprised to see you here?' he said, even though he was – surprised, shocked almost. Still, he got to his feet to shake this old friend's hand, equally surprised by Massu's own momentary hesitation.

'But I'm not – here,' Massu replied, finally taking Telford's own hand in a firm grip. 'Still, it's been a long time, *mon ami*. Too long.'

Telford nodded his head, while Massu regarded him quizzically, released his hand.

'And you have changed, I think,' he said.

'Haven't we all?' Telford replied. 'The world's gone mad again. It tends to age us.' He knew, however, that this wasn't what Massu meant. No, he decided, I'm not the same man I was in Paris. Before… He shut out the thought.

'But you, Jacques,' he said, 'I heard they made you a general. Under cover? Or can they simply not afford a uniform for you?'

'A general's uniform for a man who's not even here?'

'And me?'

'*Eh bien*, you are most definitely here.' Massu sighed, and some of the tension visibly eased from his shoulders. He waved his hand into Jack's cigarette smoke. 'You have one of those for me?'

Jack handed him the pack, stubbed out his own stump in the ashtray.

'You still in contact?' said Massu, lighting the Capstan from Telford's proffered lighter. 'With any of the Spanish comrades – from the regiment?'

'A letter now and again from Granell. Still in Paris. Runs a restaurant on the rue du Bouloi. Calls it *Los Amigos*. It's where they all meet. Republican exiles.'

'Plotting Franco's downfall?'

'Dreamers. All dreamers.'

'See what I mean? You've changed.'

Jack shrugged, the hack's habitual cynicism.

'For how long?' he said. 'How long am I here?'

'As long as it takes.'

Massu gestured for Jack to resume his seat while he, himself, edged around the desk, sat in the swivel chair behind.

'To stop me writing about this piece of aerial piracy?' said Telford.

'Seriously? You know what's been happening here? Since the summer, one atrocity after another. Our citizens' throats cut. Policemen murdered on the streets.'

He jerked his thumb towards the map of the Casbah while, beyond the door, there was a further commotion, a young prisoner yelling in Arabic, being dragged along the corridor by three gendarmes. Although 'dragged' was an inadequate description. Telford watched as, just outside the doorway itself, there was something like a failed rugby scrum, the police officers and the bloodied detainee struggling in a heap on the green-tiled floor.

'And the reprisals, General?' said Jack, nodding his head towards the noise. 'Innocents slaughtered. French parcel bombs.'

'There are fanatics among the *Pied-noirs*, too.' Massu rose from his chair and went to close the door as though this were an everyday inconvenience.

'Children and women killed,' said Jack. A shiver ran down his spine as he recalled his own experience of interrogations by the forces of law and order. He found himself touching the eye-patch. 'And don't you need to sort that out?'

Massu shook his head, returned to his place behind the desk.

'Women? Their women are the worst. Dress themselves like our own. Bombs in their shopping bags. Cafés. The Air France office. Kids enjoying a dance in the Milk Bar.'

'Is that why you're here?'

'Some things need a personal touch.'

'Like sending Ben Bella to the guillotine?'

'They'll decide all that after they get him to Paris. But that part of this affair's not my concern.'

'Then...?'

'What's that you're reading?'

'This? You wouldn't know him. English professor. Wrote this weird little story, *The Hobbit*. Children's story, I suppose. But I was reading it when I first went to Spain in '38. And now – well, this…'

'Worth the trouble?'

'I'm still not sure. Good versus evil? Small people challenging impossible powers? Sounds familiar?'

The cream-coloured dust cover was looking somewhat the worse for wear. All this travelling. But Jack picked up the book anyway, turned it so that Massu could see the front images – the Eye of Sauron and the Ring. He pointed at the runic writing.

'It could almost be Arabic,' he said. 'Couldn't it?'

'Half a million Arabs in Algiers alone,' Massu replied. 'Only a handful who want independence.'

The uproar in the corridor receded into the distance, but the yells of the young Arab now in French.

'*Nous sommes l'avenir!*' We are the future.

'*Nous sommes…*'

'Isn't that what we always say?' said Jack. 'Ireland. India. Indochina.'

Massu made a show of crossing himself.

'Don't mention Indochina, *mon ami*. Please, I beg you.'

'I'm sorry. And are you still – in touch – with Toto?'

Telford did his best to make the question sound innocent, diplomatic, and he lit himself another cigarette. Massu and Toto – Suzanne Torrès – had enjoyed an illicit relationship together in Normandy and beyond, she being second-in-command of an ambulance unit attached to Leclerc's Division. Danielle's officer. And Jack was certain Toto had been in Indochina as well.

'You're sorry?' said Massu. 'About Indochina? Painful memories – for Suzanne. And the rest of us who were there.'

Perhaps, it was Massu's civilian clothes which prompted Jack, some sixth sense, a moment of intuition, but he suddenly felt compelled to ask the question.

'Wait – she's here? Toto?'

'Nobody calls her Toto anymore. But yes. I'm based here now. Since August. She knows you're here. Happy to meet up with you – while you're waiting.'

Jack saw the tension return, some slight trace in Massu's voice that was less than convincing.

Massu picked up the telephone, snapped an order at somebody on the other end to bring coffee.

'Waiting?' Jack groaned, as Massu slammed down the receiver.

'We've arranged a room for you at the Angleterre. I understand Suzanne plans to be dropped off there in the morning. And you go nowhere else. You stay in the Angleterre. Safe there. Understand? There'll be trouble tomorrow; maybe, tonight as well.'

Telford wasn't sure about meeting Toto again. Was Massu lying about her being happy to meet him? And Telford himself? Half of him longed for the comfort of a nostalgic reunion. The other half...

'You'll be in the thick of it, I suppose,' he murmured.

'I have other cats to flog – what do you say in English? *Bigger fish to fry?* But I'll see you at the Angleterre tomorrow night.'

'Meanwhile, I'm under arrest?'

'We don't usually jail our prisoners at the Hotel Angleterre.'

'Though, you still didn't tell me how long I'll be kept here.'

'For as long as it takes to tell you a story, *mon brave*. Or, perhaps, I should say, to *give* you a story.'

Tuesday 23rd October 1956

Two worlds clashed. Waves of protest, rioting, as news of Ben Bella's arrest had spread. Outside, only half a mile distant, the haunting ululations of the Casbah's women, the screech of police sirens, and the slightest whiff of burning onions – tear gas, Jack was certain – hanging over the sedate scents of jasmine and mint tea here in the luxury of the hotel. It had been the same through most of the night, the darkness punctured by occasional eruptions of startling illumination, or the flashing blue lights of *gendarmerie* vehicles.

There had been a brief respite earlier when Jack took some breakfast, but it had all begun again by the time he went back to his room. And there he had stayed until, at ten, a bellboy knocked on his door to announce that a lady was waiting below.

Now, Telford observed her from behind one of the columns in the foyer of the Hotel Angleterre. She was sipping at a coffee in the terrace bar.

Suzanne 'Toto' Torrès had hardly changed. As petite as Piaf. Another sparrow. But spirit? My god, he thought, just look at the fire in those eyes. This was the woman he'd seen, diminutive in stature, gargantuan in valour, facing down the commander of an entire Panzer column during the thickest of the fighting in Normandy to prevent them molesting her nurses, arresting her wounded patients, and impounding her ambulances.

Telford had seen the whole bizarre episode, himself hidden inside one of those same vehicles – hidden with…

Never mind. He wouldn't go there. Just a pity she'd not taken the same care of her units later, after Paris. And yes, he knew it was stupid to blame her. But how was he going to avoid them, the memories? As soon as he stepped out from behind the pillar, there'd be no turning back.

Too late. She had looked up, spotted him and waved; though, without any great enthusiasm, he decided.

'You were hiding?' she said, and eased herself out of the armchair, came to meet him as he crossed the expanse of ornate blue carpet between them. Telford recalled that her English was good – her time spent in New York after the fall of Paris – though some unspoken agreement caused them to continue in French.

'No, I…' He kissed her formally on both cheeks, but then she threw her arms around his waist, and he felt her choke back a sob.

'I thought you would not come, Jack.'

For some inexplicable reason, it sounded to him as though she had *hoped* he would not come. His stupid imagination, surely?

She pronounced his name just as she must address her husband. *Jacques*. But it brought back all the memories he'd tried so hard to bury, and a great racking sadness shook his whole body. He held her tight, trying to make the pain subside, hardly aware of the looks they attracted from the neighbouring tables.

'You never found her,' murmured Toto.

'No. Never.'

He'd visited Haslach enough times. There was talk of a memorial there, to mark the burial sites in the forest where the Gestapo had seemingly buried those they'd killed in the final months. Yet, he had found nothing to comfort him, no sign of Dani's own final resting place. He had no idea whether he'd even been told the truth about her fate. Not really.

'And you,' he said. 'Wasn't it risky – coming here, like this? With all that…'

Another siren outside.

'Not alone.' She slowly pulled away from him, nodded towards the door from the glass-fronted terrace out onto the street. An army sergeant stood guard, in red beret and camouflage fatigues, and a submachine gun.

'Does he belong to Jacques?'

They sat at her table and a white-coated waiter came to take Telford's order. Mint tea.

'Today, it seems,' Toto smiled for the first time, 'he belongs to me. I have a meeting with the Governor-General.'

The siren faded into the distance.

'It certainly seems like they're going to need more ambulances – is that what brings you here?'

'Not since Saigon and Hanoi. Two tours of duty out there. After that, with Jacques in Dakar and Tunis. Brittany, of course. And now…'

'Slow down,' he said. 'With Jacques? All this time? You're…'

'Married. Eight years ago. Henry and I were divorced, and…'

'I mustn't have received the invitation.'

'We never sent you one, *mon cher*.'

'Just as well. I couldn't have faced it.'

'There were too many,' she said, and dabbed away a tear from the corner of her eye. 'Absent friends.'

They fell into silence, a painful interlude for them both.

'Still,' said Jack to break the barrier, 'I don't see you just being the general's wife, Toto. Why all the mystery?'

She raised her eyebrows, looked at him quizzically, as though searching for some hidden implication in his words.

'No mystery, so far as I'm concerned. There's been a suggestion – about organising a women's solidarity movement here. You'll get the idea. Emancipate the Muslim women. Help them develop.'

'Discover the benefits of modern French society? How very colonial.'

The smiles had vanished again, Toto's face set like stone once more.

'Don't patronise me, Jack. We tested the idea in Saigon…'

'Just look how that turned out.'

The waiter was back. The white jacket was immaculate, its collar and cuffs trimmed in crimson, a matching crimson bow tie and fez. He set down the silver tray, then picked up the silver pot by its long wooden handle and poured tea into the gold-mounted glasses, gleaming green with mint leaves. The smell was delicious.

Toto thanked the lad in Arabic.

'There were lessons to be learned, perhaps,' she said, and offered Jack one of the two tiny bowls of *baklawa* from the tray. 'But here? Winning hearts and minds, that will be the trick. If only we could persuade more of the women, the children…'

'The orphans?'

'Yes, if you like,' she said, curtly. 'For the orphans, an Association of Youth Training. Persuade them to think of themselves, first and foremost, as French.'

'Charitable work, then.' He helped himself to a fork, cut through the tissue-thin pastry, the crushed almonds, the syrup, and popped the dripping morsel into his mouth.

'Of course.'

'And the general – here on some mission of charity, as well?'

'None of us are the same, Jack. We all thought the defeat of Germany, surrender of Japan – that it would be the end.'

Telford licked away some of the orange-scented stickiness from his lips.

'Start of something better,' he said.

'Wasn't life simple back then? Knowing who the enemy was – more or less. But now?'

He felt her eyes upon him, looked up from the *baklawa* to find that he was being scrutinised. Was there some implication…? There had been many times in his life when he had known himself to be falling down the rabbit hole.

'A whole new level of complexity,' Jack admitted, unsure whether he was expected to offer her some assurance of his status as either friend or foe.

'And tonight, *Monsieur* Telford, my husband will introduce you to an entirely fresh understanding of that word.'

'Here?' He washed the *baklawa* down with a sip of the sweet mint tea.

'No. A change of plan. Jacques will send a driver. So, make sure you pack your bags – you'll be staying with us.' She hesitated, then, 'For tonight, at least.'

An offer Jack supposed he could not refuse. But why the hesitation. Did she mean *only* tonight and then somewhere else? Or did she mean, perhaps, longer than tonight? Yes, complex.

'Complexity?' he said.

Toto slipped into American-accented English.

'Wasn't it Jolson? "*I tell yer, you ain't heard nothin' yet.*"'

It was a passable impersonation.

'A little excessive, don't you think, Sergeant?' Telford smiled from the back seat of the limousine, as the motorcycle escort ahead of them kicked up a cloud of dust while, behind, the commander of the armoured car stood in his turret and scrutinised every inch of the surrounding orange groves with his binoculars.

The modest convoy had taken an hour to climb westwards, fifteen miles or so, over the rugged hills of the headland separating Algiers itself from the neighbouring town of Zéralda. But now they dropped back down onto the *rue Nationale*, a forested peak up to their left, the turquoise Mediterranean a mile away across the rectangular ochre patches of homesteads on the other side.

The town itself seemed peaceful enough; date palms, tidy, colonial, thought Jack as they passed through the third checkpoint and swung through a gateway in the high barracks wall topped with barbed wire. Within the gate, another town within the town. A garrison town. Busy military traffic. A square with soldiers at their drill. A practice field with a tower from which trainees tested their paratrooper landing skills.

On higher ground, surrounded by a grove of trees, a complex of elegant white villas, outside the most prominent of which Jack's convoy finally came to a halt as the light began to fade.

Massu came down the path to meet him, now in his camouflage fatigues. The Brigadier-General's two stars shone upon the black epaulette flash at his shoulder; the raised eagle-winged Parachute Division insignia on his rolled-up sleeve; and the impressive medal ribbon patch upon his chest. He acknowledged the sergeant's salute with a nod of his head, while Telford climbed from the car with his attaché case. Then, Massu shook Jack's hand, a formal greeting in front of his men.

Inside, there were drinks. It seemed that each of them – Massu, Toto and Telford – needed the *pastis* to help them through the apparent discomfort of this three-way reunion.

'And you're sure?' said Jack. 'About me staying the night?'

The couple exchanged glances. Guilty glances, Jack decided. But what was going on? His case had been taken from him by a young servant boy, and there'd been a promise to show him to his room later.

'Safer,' said Toto, 'than trying to get you back to the Angleterre tonight.'

'And I suppose it's not too late to offer my congratulations. On the wedding?'

There were polite murmurs of thanks, somewhat embarrassed to Jack's mind.

'But tomorrow?' he asked Massu.

'I'm arranging for you to be flown back to Morocco. To Rabat. It seems Sidi Mohammed now fears for his life after our arrest of Ben Bella. You must reassure him. For France, *non?*'

Massu's attempt at good humour seemed, to Jack, just a bit forced.

'I should like to reassure him,' said Telford, 'that Ben Bella isn't going to the guillotine.'

'Nothing so barbaric, old friend.'

74

Jack recalled that it was only a few months since two members of the FLN had suffered precisely that fate here in Algiers. But he bit his tongue.

'Ben Bella and his friends are, as we speak,' Massu went on, 'safely back in Paris and likely to spend many years in La Santé. But at least we've scuppered their plans for a federation to unite the whole of North Africa against us. Without Ben Bella in Tunis, it won't happen.'

'This is the story you want to give me, General?' Jack saw Massu wince and at once regretted the official form of address. 'I meant – Jacques. I'm sorry. The uniform…'

Massu's lips twitched, a forced smiled, and Toto, beside him, touched her husband's arm in a gesture of solidarity, perhaps.

'The story,' said Massu, raising his glass by way of a toast, 'will keep until after we eat.'

They led Jack out onto the verandah. Crickets drowned out any other sound from the barracks and the lights were lit – mosquito repellent candles in green glass balls. A maid or housekeeper busied herself, arranging appetisers of green olives and crispy fried *bourek*, while Toto fussed about the seating, nervously changed her mind several times about where, precisely, Jack should be placed. He'd never seen her nervous before. It was a shock. But, finally, it was all settled and she gripped the maid's hand.

'Thank you, Mimi,' she said, and the girl beamed a smile at her before disappearing back to the kitchen.

'Mimi?' said Jack. 'Isn't she Berber?'

'Her real name is Latifa,' said Toto. 'But she prefers Mimi now. I introduced her to *Bohème*. Would you like some music, by the way?'

She started to rise from her seat, but Jack begged her not to bother on his account.

'You've succeeded, then,' he said. 'Sees herself as French now? You must be pleased.'

Toto scrutinised him, seeking any hint of sarcasm, he decided – and hoped that he'd displayed none. He speared an olive with a cocktail stick and popped it into his mouth.

'Suzanne is a great admirer of the Soroptimists, *mon ami*,' said Massu, opening a bottle of wine. He showed Jack the label – Royal Kebir – and Telford murmured his appreciation.

'Of the Soroptimists,' Massu continued. 'And of Madame Noël.'

Jack knew the name. One of France's first female surgeons. Famous for her reconstruction surgery during the Great War.

'I didn't know she was anything to do with the Soroptimists. But yes, I see the connection. Transform the lives of women and girls. Help them develop. Isn't that the idea?'

'Noël,' said Toto, 'was the first president of the Soroptimist Federation of Europe. And you see? A women's solidarity movement here – to help emancipate young Muslim women like Mimi?'

He didn't want to argue. Massu had poured the wine and waited for Jack to taste.

'It's good,' said Telford. 'And funny you should mention the Soroptimists,' he said, to change the subject. 'When I arrived in Madrid. '38, you know. At the consulate there, they had a copy of *The Times*. Report of a talk by some schoolteacher in Coventry – to her local branch of the Soroptimists. She'd been on one of the same propaganda tours that took me to Spain in the first place, back in the September. By all accounts, from this article, she must have thought Franco was a god.'

'Still the dictator,' said Massu.

Mimi was back, with dishes of charcoal-roasted lamb, a white bean stew, and couscous with vegetables. The smells were divine.

'We should have done something, Jacques,' said Telford. 'De Gaulle should have done something. All those Spaniards who fought for us. You should have given them back their Republic.'

'De Gaulle had other things to think about,' the general replied. 'And there was no appetite among the Allies to have Franco as anything but a friend.'

'And now? De Gaulle? Retired from politics. Doesn't sound like the man we all knew.'

'He had his own family to think about,' said Toto. 'And you, Jack – never thought of settling down? It must have been hard, after Danielle. But nobody?'

It struck Jack as being somewhat formal, the sort of enquiry you might put through politeness. With – well, with a stranger.

'Nobody.' There'd been a couple of women, more recently, in Berlin, but nothing serious. Dinners. The inevitable and clumsy sex.

Mutual partings of the way. 'But de Gaulle,' he said, deliberately dodging further personal questions, 'ten years in the wilderness?'

'The wilderness of retirement,' said Massu, sipping at his wine. 'Precisely that. But maybe soon... And republics? Here we are on our fourth. The Fourth Republic. Just look what a bloody mess they're making of everything. Chaos. Weakness. I sometimes think...'

The remainder of the meal continued in much the same way. Angry politics softened by Toto's excessive concern for Jack's future. But after coffee, she made her exit. She seemed relieved to do so, apparently having promised to continue her nightly knitting lessons for Mimi-Latifa.

'Before I give you the story,' said Massu, as they leaned on the verandah's white-painted balustrade, smoking Jack's Capstans, sharing an ashtray, 'I want you to tell me what's happening with your BBC.'

'Strange question. Mind if I ask why?'

'First, tell me why you're here.'

'Put simply?' said Jack. 'We appear to be in serious competition with Radio Cairo and Voice of the Arabs. There we are, trying to convince them about the benign nature of British colonial rule, and there they are, throwing up nightly tales of atrocities against the Kikuyu, our concentration camps and use of Trioxone in Malaya...'

He turned his one good eye to the heavens, the final hint of orange and purple in the afterglow. Telford had read some harrowing accounts, the curse of his job.

'And all those countless deaths,' said Massu, 'you caused by that absurd bloody partition of India?'

'That too. My connection to Sidi Mohammed's no secret. With North Africa on the boil, some bright spark thought I might be able to get a story out of him. And I'd no sooner arrived...'

'He insisted on you taking the plane with Ben Bella.' Massu stubbed out his cigarette.

'Reckoned he was doing me a favour – the story, a possible scoop.'

'He was right, wasn't he? Though, maybe not the story you were expecting.'

'We'll see – maybe, after your turn, Jacques. Why all this interest in the BBC?'

Telford almost jumped out of his skin with the sudden harsh cry out in the trees. *Kroo-kroo-kroo.*

'Only a nightjar, *mon ami*. And why the interest? Our mutual friend, de Gaulle – he may be in the wilderness but he still hears things. Has this strange view that we could never have won the war without the Corporation. D-Day. But all those other messages, to resistance groups everywhere, year after painful year.'

Jack recalled his last discussion with de Gaulle. About Sétif, of course. The general hadn't been best pleased. Mutual friend? Not anymore.

'This has something to do with Algeria?'

'It does not – or, at least, only in part. More to do with Suez. And the Russians.'

Suez. It was the other big issue of the year, of course. After so many years of French and British control of the Suez Canal Zone, Egypt's President Nasser had finally forced the last of Britain's forces to pull out, and then nationalised the Suez Canal Company back in July.

'You think they're right?' said Jack. 'That it's all part of Nasser's plan? A united Arabia led by Egypt and under Russian control.'

It was Massu's turn to share his smokes. Gauloises, naturally. He flashed the familiar blue pack in Jack's direction.

'They'd have us all by the throat, wouldn't they?' Massu replied. 'Destroy the last vestiges of our influence in the region? Extension of Russian influence instead. Blackmail us by threatening to block our access to the Canal whenever they choose. Endanger oil supplies to the whole of Europe. Unthinkable.'

'Wait! This whole business with Russia – the link to the BBC?'

'It seems to de Gaulle, the Corporation's now defending Western democracy in the Cold War just as it did against the Nazis.'

Telford laughed. You couldn't help admiring de Gaulle, warts and all.

'The problem,' he said, 'and I'm guessing de Gaulle knows this as well, is that our precious government sees this is a good reason to control the Beeb's output. Eden's a fool, thinks that's what happened during the war. He's wrong, of course. Churchill gave the European Service a lot of leeway. And Eden's no Churchill. Not by a long chalk.'

Massu slapped Telford on the back. A first hint of the old companionable *bonhomie* they'd once shared so freely.

'We'd trust the Corporation,' said the general, 'to work out what they should broadcast – to behind the Iron Curtain, or into the Middle East – more than Eden and his cronies.'

'But the Corporation's not likely to have any say in the matter. If they don't toe the line, Eden's made it clear they'll lose their Grant-in-Aid funding. That's going to cripple them.'

Brigadier-General Jacques Massu sighed deeply and turned to face Telford, stared at him with analytical scrutiny. Telford found himself forced to return Massu's gaze, to look him squarely in the face.

'What?' said Jack.

The nightjar shrieked once more.

'Isn't it time we stopped playing games with each other, *mon ami*? Isn't that the real reason you're here? To find a story which will, at the same time, both demonstrate your Corporation's absolute importance and cause their political masters to back off.'

'How did you know? I always had my ability to dissemble down as one of my finest honed skills.'

Actually, Telford felt quite pleased with himself.

'It doesn't matter.' Massu looked at his watch. 'Later we need to listen to the radio. But, for now, here's what you should know.'

'I'm all ears.' Jack heard the nightjar again. 'But, maybe, we could sit?'

He was tired; yesterday's excitement – and its terrors; the disturbed night; and this Machiavellian labyrinth. The white wicker verandah chairs were suddenly very enticing. And, as he flopped onto the Berber cushions, as if on cue, Mimi appeared in the doorway with a tray, two glasses and an attractively curvaceous bottle of Courvoisier, three-star.

'Yesterday,' said Massu, after she'd disappeared again, 'while you were flying to Mallorca, some of Eden's people were flying to Sèvres. For a secret meeting with the Israelis. And with my own superiors. They've all been working on this for weeks, but yesterday...'

'The Israelis - and the British? Seriously?'

Massu poured the cognac, handed a glass to Telford and settled the bottle on the elaborately hand-painted oriental table between them. Red and gold, with the scent of cedar.

'They don't trust Britain, of course. And the British don't trust us. But then, we don't trust the Israelis.'

'Despite all that,' said Jack, 'they've managed to come up with a plan?'

'Six days. The Israelis will launch an attack against Egypt – across Sinai.'

Telford held up his glass to the light, peered through the amber glow. Out in the trees, the crickets had turned up the volume – a racket like machine guns.

'Another war. Christ! But what about Eisenhower? All the work he's put into finding a peaceful solution to Suez.'

'Peaceful? You mean a solution that favours the Americans. But the Americans weren't there – at Sèvres.'

Jack mulled this all over. Dammit, the rabbit hole again.

'And the attack,' he said. 'Only the Israelis?'

'Britain and France shall, naturally, be dismayed…' Massu raised both hands, a mummer's show of feigned amazement. 'Concerned that the conflict might threaten our access to the Canal.'

Telford could almost see the gathering, as though he'd been present.

'An ultimatum, I imagine,' he said, wiping away a bead of sweat running from beneath his eye-patch. 'Ceasefire?'

'Both sides to withdraw.'

'France and Britain to send a peacekeeping force, to reoccupy the Zone?'

Massu pursed his lips, nodded his head slowly, as though appraising Telford entirely afresh, perhaps even a hint of admiration.

'Nasser will, of course,' he said, 'refuse to accept those terms.'

'And then?' Jack blew a smoke ring up towards the wooden ceiling.

'Then, I am to have the honour of leading my parachute division into action. We shall be at war with Egypt.'

There was more than a mere hint of reluctance in his voice.

'Nasser's friends – the Russians – you expect them to sit on their hands? Christ, this could trigger...'

Jack's mind filled with all those images of mushroom clouds, of Hiroshima-scaled devastation, while Massu checked his watch again.

'Almost time,' said the general, and led Telford back inside the house. 'Fetch your glass.'

A comfortable sitting room, with a divan running around two sides, carved occasional tables and cedar-scented stools. In the corner, the general switched on his wireless set, twiddled with the tuner, and settled the Courvoisier bottle on one of the tables.

The language was Slavic. Not Polish. Not Russian, either. But one of the BBC's Eastern European Services, Jack was certain. Something about the delivery. Once you were familiar with the style, there was no mistaking it.

'Hungary?' he guessed, lowering himself onto the divan. Things had been brewing in Hungary for a while.

'Two hours ago,' said Massu, 'just before you arrived, that bastard Gerö made a radio announcement. Unscheduled, of course.'

Telford laughed and tipped back his head, savouring the last heavenly drops of his cognac, as they delighted the back of his palate.

'But you knew it was going to happen.'

Massu dropped into a chair of his own, the broadcast now changed. Piano music. Franz Liszt. *Liebesträume*.

'The Soviets,' he said. 'Nothing if not predictable, *non*? Given a fixed set of circumstances, they will always respond accordingly.'

'Circumstances?'

'Today. Tens of thousands taken to the streets in Budapest. Demanding an end to Soviet rule.'

'I'm guessing Gerö was on air denying there's a problem – saying how much the Hungarian people love their Russian comrades. That kind of stuff.'

'A revolution, *mon ami*. Only the beginning. And your Hungarian Section already working their magic.'

Massu stood again, brought the bottle and reverentially poured more of the amber warmth into Jack's glass.

'Of course,' he said, 'we could have listened on any of a dozen different channels, in a dozen different languages. All courtesy of the BBC.'

'As they spread the word.'

Yes, that's what we do so well, Jack decided, and gazed around the walls. Framed photos. De Gaulle. Massu himself with his officers in Indochina, each of them in battle gear. Toto and her ambulance teams in Normandy. He searched for an image of Danielle but couldn't find one. Time for another cigarette.

'So, the world now knows,' said Massu, 'that Gerö's Communist government has lost control.'

'The Russians will send tanks.'

'That, also, is predictable.'

'Their attention turned away from Egypt.'

'Egypt. And Algeria. You think it's any coincidence – that we picked up Ben Bella yesterday?'

Jack leaned across with his lighter, the flame leaping up before his eyes.

'Without Ben Bella,' he mused, 'North Africa could still have united against you. But without Russian support…'

'D'accord.'

'I think I'd be pleased if I thought Eden – or any of those close to him – had the intelligence to put this one together.'

Jack leaned back against the divan's cushions.

'They didn't,' said Massu. 'None of us did.'

'The Yanks?'

In the distance, a bugle call. *L'Extinction des Feux*, Jack remembered. The French army's equivalent of the Yanks' *Taps*.

'Who else *but* the Yanks?' said Massu. 'Eisenhower wanted a cosy Suez deal for himself. But when he found out about Eden's plan, he spotted the flaw.'

'We go to war with Egypt,' said Jack, 'Russia goes to war with us. If Russia goes to war with us…'

'Then the USA goes to war with Russia, and…'

'Bang!'

They had dominated the news for the past six years. A-bomb and H-bomb tests. Americans, British, then the Russians. How long, he wondered, before we all blow ourselves to hell?

'CIA, then?' Jack went on. 'In Hungary.'

'Looks that way. They've been watching this build up for months. All they needed to do was light the fuse.'

'But the Hungarians…'

'No, they can't beat the Russians. Of course not.'

'Will you think about them, Jacques – when you're parachuting into Egypt? About the Hungarians who'll be dying so Eden and your Fourth Republic can have their glorious little war. Ben-Gurion, too.'

'Oh, I will think about them. And when we lose, as well.'

'Lose?'

'I've seen the plans. Drawn on the back of a cigarette packet. We shall do our duty – naturally. But…'

'Nasser will turn it into a people's war. Indochina all over again.'

'Militarily, we'll do well enough. But the way your fool of a Prime Minister has handled this, the secrecy, the delays…'

'There'll be protests, of course.'

'By then, you're right – the Hungarians will be dying in droves, calling on the international community for help that's never going to come.'

'Eisenhower won't help?' Jack knew very well it was a rhetorical question.

'The Hungarians,' said Massu, 'will simply be collateral damage – so the USA won't have to go to war with Russia over Egypt. Can you imagine how angry he will be? How compromised they're going to feel?'

On the wireless, the final familiar notes of the *Liebesträume* faded away and Massu jumped up to twiddle with the dial again until he picked up a crisp English voice, a piece about that earlier Hungarian Revolution in 1848 and one of its heroes, Lajos Kossuth.

'This is what we're good at,' Jack smiled. 'Turning up the heat.'

'The question is,' said Massu, slumping back into his chair, 'will your BBC turn up the heat on Eden – when Suez goes wrong?'

'Eden? You don't know him very well. Good war record. Resigned in '38 for all the right reasons.'

'Opposition to Chamberlain.'

'Of course. Dashing devil, too; popular with the ladies. But for me? He's a man who's adept – as we say in England – at polishing a turd.'

Massu smiled at him. Yes, thought Jack, Massu knows the type.

'You can bet your life,' Telford went on, 'whatever happens, he'll be bragging about how successful it's all been.'

'There'll be a ceasefire,' said Massu. 'Hard, even for Eden, to claim this one as a victory.'

'Especially if there's a hint he's conspired to create a war.'

'Difficult for a man who's made his name as a peace-maker.'

'But how,' said Jack, 'do I prove any of this?'

'About the Yanks and the CIA? You don't.'

'But the Sèvres agreement...'

'That's a different matter entirely. Eden wanted everything destroyed. All record. But our man, Pineau, he kept his copy of the protocol. The Israelis did the same.'

To Telford it sounded almost too good to be true. And there was something...

'Wait,' he said. 'This doesn't make sense. You're going to give me all this – and let me walk away?'

Jack decided it would have helped if Massu had at least made some show of being shamefaced. But no, this was just business, and it made his blood boil. The dismissive shrug of Massu's shoulders.

'Am I being detained here, Jacques?'

'Only until we have boots safely on the ground, *mon ami*.'

Telford fought to constrain his fury. It burned inside him.

'Was that it?' he growled. 'Toto – Suzanne – she wasn't exactly delighted to see me. What was it, Jacques – embarrassment? The hospitality just a sham?'

'Not the ideal way to renew an old acquaintance, *non*? But better than the alternative, my friend.'

'A cell at the *préfecture*?' Telford raged, and jumped to his feet, waved his glass in Massu's direction. 'Seriously?'

The general stood, too, straightened his fatigue shirt, as if declaring the discussion now on a more formal footing.

'That would never...' he began.

84

'How long?'

'A week or so. Not much more.'

'You said you were going to fly me back to Morocco.'

'I didn't say when.'

'You can't have known I'd be here.'

'*Un heureux hazard*,' said Massu.

'Serendipity?' Jack yelled. 'You're serious?'

'We were trying to find some way to break the story to the BBC – and there you were, getting on the plane with Ben Bella. Our intelligence services have eyes and ears, even in Rabat. Extraordinary, no?'

'Too extraordinary for words,' said Jack. But he decided he didn't need to pursue this path any further, and he knew he must not now overplay his hand.

'But why the hell should I want…?'

'Because it's your job?'

Yes, thought Telford, I suppose he's right. And it was as good a time as any to turn down the temperature a little. He allowed his expression to marginally soften. He sat again, and Massu followed suit.

'I can always claim to have seen it, I suppose,' said Jack, begrudgingly. 'Evidence of collusion – between Eden, France and the Israelis. How we'd known about Ben-Gurion's plan to invade Egypt well in advance – helped them plan it, then played at being surprised.'

'They'll never allow it to see the light of day, of course.'

'They'll slap a D-notice on the Corporation, naturally,' Jack agreed. 'National security.'

'It will give the Corporation,' said Massu, 'plenty of – what do you call it? Leverage? But you'll lose your job, will you not?'

'Certainly. The Director-General will be eternally grateful, desperately sorry.'

'And your carefully crafted article will never see the light of day.'

'The story of my life.'

'Yet, it may just make Eden pull back on their threats to cut the BBC's funding.'

'Eden will have to leave them with more independence than he'd like. But this little deception,' he raised his glass once more – it was now empty again – and gazed around the room, 'was it truly necessary, Jacques?'

Massu took the gesture with the glass as an invitation for peace to be restored. He fetched the Courvoisier yet again and replenished Jack's glass.

'It's been a long time since we were together,' he said. 'People change. But you've missed this other possibility, *mon ami*. A question of timing, is it not? You report your story to the BBC. A D-notice, as you say. Yet, your BBC has the leverage it needs. But then...'

'But then, de Gaulle helps to have the story published in France anyhow.'

'Very good. Eden shown to be up to his neck in triggering a war. British troops will die. And the British public will have been duped, fed lies about why their boys are dying.'

'And, meanwhile, de Gaulle uses the same story to bring down *your* government.'

'If only it was so simple. But no, we would need a military coup of our own to get rid of the fools we have now. To bring him back. It should have been Leclerc, of course, but...'

'But Leclerc is dead. And you see yourself as Franco now, Jacques?'

'Why not? Dictatorship seems to be working well enough for Spain. For Portugal.'

Jack felt sick to his stomach. Had they truly fought all those years against the Nazis to now have fascists like Franco and Salazar lauded as role-models for government? Thank god he had a plan of his own.

Wednesday 7ᵗʰ November 1956

Today, through the plane's windows, not a single French fighter in sight. He had somehow expected them, but they'd not materialised. And the landing at Rabat as smooth as any he'd ever known.

Yes, Rabat. But not with any intention of reassuring the sultan of France's good intention. No, Telford had insisted, that particular horse already bolted.

Toto had regarded him suspiciously, her husband already gone off to yet another war.

'But still going back to Sidi Mohammed?' she'd said.

'Unfinished business.'

He had refused to explain any further.

Now, as the sultan's Cadillac dropped him at the Imperial College, across from the palace, Jack was greeted with formal deference by an officer of the Black Guard, in scarlet uniform, flowing white cape and blue cap. The soldier escorted him from the Moorish exterior, through the arabesque courtyards and gateways, to the incongruously European library building – which had, on his first visit, and again now – reminded him so much of his own red-brick Worcester Grammar School.

The familiar smell of libraries worldwide and, in the circular reading room, motes of dust floating in the archived stillness. The room was empty, except for the presence of Sidi Mohammed himself. He dismissed the officer, who bowed and left in a flurry of white silken billows.

'You remember?' said the sultan and set a hand upon the lectern at his side.

'How could I forget, Highness?'

Jack gazed again at the hand-painted oriental designs of the lectern's reading slope and, upon it, a thin leather-bound volume. Beneath the volume, the engraved brass plaque. He was no more capable of reading the Arabic script now than when he'd first seen it. But the translated words were burnished into his brain.

The edition of Life *magazine, with captions from the pen of journalist Mister John Telford, Englishman, for whom the free peoples of Morocco shall always hold a place in their hearts.*

Jack bit back on his nostalgia, his sense of pride. It hadn't been about the magazine, of course, but the mission he'd undertaken on the sultan's behalf to help thwart Franco's ambitions in North Africa.

'Your stay with General Massu and his wife – not too unpleasant, I trust.'

'There's a saying, is there not? About house guests and fresh fish – both starting to stink after three days.'

'And you were there two weeks.'

'Exactly, Highness.'

Telford doubted he'd ever see Massu or Toto again. It had become even more difficult in the second week, after the general had flown out with his troops and Jack had been left only with Toto – who had done her best to keep entirely out of his way.

'Effectively under house arrest,' he said, and looked Sidi Mohammed in the eye. The fellow was still handsome. Still the same immaculately white hooded robe. Still the same five o'clock shadow, the stubble now with a hint of misty grey. But Jack found the sultan gazing back at him.

'I see you are still adrift in the world, Mr Telford,' said the sultan.

'It seems so,' said Jack. 'And you, Highness, still a thorn in the side of the French.'

'As you now know.' He set his hand on the lectern once more. 'But I wanted to show you.'

Jack remembered the sultan's offer from all those years earlier. It wasn't just the lectern and its brass plaque remaining in place, but the promise as well.

'Morocco shall always provide a refuge for you. Whenever your soul is weary, you may return. Always a place for you here.'

But this wasn't the time for yet more nostalgia. There was business to be done. Telford nodded in acknowledgement.

'You understand, sir,' he said, 'that the general was convinced his agents had known I'd be on the plane with Ben Bella.'

'And so they did. My own agents simply needed to point them in the right direction.'

'I hated deceiving them. At least, at first…'

He had, indeed. All that pretence at not knowing Massu and Toto had been married.

'No, Mr Telford. You hated the idea of deceiving the comrades-in-arms you knew a dozen years ago. This General Massu and his lady wife are not the same people.'

Jack knew it. But could not avoid sensing Danielle's reproach.

'In any case,' the sultan went on, 'you got the story.'

He raised his hand in a way that was infinitely sublime, poetic, the most polite invitation Jack had ever received.

'It will embarrass the French, as well,' he said, obediently following the sultan back out of the library building.

'It's what General Massu wants, is it not? They get de Gaulle back. But I wonder if they realise – from what we hear, Madame Massu's ex-husband will be high in de Gaulle's government. Their Fifth Republic. Do you think the general knows – that he might not have quite the position of power he has come to imagine?'

'Interesting times.'

'My contacts tell me that, whatever the outcome in Egypt, General Massu will find himself back in Algiers – trying, and failing, to put down the battle for Algeria's independence. Another fight he cannot win. A poisoned chalice.'

Jack almost felt sorry for Massu. The sultan had halted in one of the courtyards. It had been twilight when Telford had arrived at the college but it was now fully dark, the sky all Indian ink, the sickle moon's blade of light reflecting on a scudding cloud, Jupiter blazing bright among the background of stars.

'He was right about Hungary, though,' he said.

The end of Hungary's short-lived revolution. Its new leader, Imry Nagy, had announced he would leave the Warsaw Pact – resulting in Soviet tanks immediately surrounding Budapest and crushing the Hungarian army. Thousands dead and, three days ago, Nagy's last dramatic broadcast before they came for him. Nobody – but nobody – was under any illusion that Nagy would ever be seen again.

'They believed the West would save them,' said the sultan, 'while, all the time...'

'While, all the time, the eyes of the world were on Suez.'

Only a week. British and French paratroopers landing at Port Said. An act of insanity to Jack's mind. Then, Britain had begun to broadcast – not through the BBC but through some bogus Cyprus-based radio station – bulletins designed to break the will of Nasser and the Egyptian people. It had dismally failed to do so. Yesterday, Eden announced a ceasefire. A week, and British troops had advanced a mere twenty miles from Port Said. Jack had been "released" – and Toto hadn't even said goodbye. But a subaltern had delivered Massu's instructions, arranged for Telford to wire his story to London. The response had been immediate. The D-Notice, precisely as he'd expected. But followed soon afterwards by a further message. One word: *Congratulations*!

'How delighted the Governors must have been,' said the sultan, 'to know they are now at liberty to save the free world yet again, this time in this Cold War you are fighting. Will they report the casualties?'

'At the BBC we rarely desire the distortion of information. So yes, the British, the French, the Israelis – two hundred killed? I picked that up on the news. But the suppression of the inconvenient? That's another matter entirely. So not a single mention of the three thousand Egyptians dead – most of them innocent civilians.'

'But you still have your job?'

'So it seems.'

The congratulations, Jack knew, would not have been forthcoming if Eden hadn't rowed back on his threat to the Corporation's funding. Somebody had negotiated a deal, a compromise. Of course, it would do Eden no good in the long run.

'Then, we shall be pleased to welcome you back yet again, Mr Telford. Next year, I shall take the throne.'

A couple of the sultan's similarly white-robed advisers – ministers perhaps – hurried across the courtyard and exchanged some urgency with their lord and master. Jack smiled to himself. King Mohammed the Fifth, he thought – it seems I have friends in high places.

'You think, Highness, that whatever the path which led us here, we may just have been spared World War Three?'

The sultan, now with his advisers in tow, resumed their journey towards the outside world.

'*Allahu Kabir*, Mr Telford. Hungary, the sacrificial lamb which distracts the Soviets going to war with the West over Algerian independence, over Suez. A Suez crisis, indeed.'

Jack took a final glance at the night sky.

'Crisis?' he said. 'Seems like such an inadequate word for such a tangled web. Almost Armageddon.'

'Ah, yes,' said the sultan. 'Armageddon. *Al-Malhamat Al-Kubra*. But not quite yet, it seems.'

No, thought Jack. Not quite. But he was thinking about the headline he'd attached to his copy.

Eden's Three-Way Lies to the British People.

It wouldn't be published, of course. Not in Britain anyway. But in France? Indeed, perhaps, in France. And he thought of another headline, a snappier headline.

Prime Minister's Suez Triangle.

Yes, he decided, that's the one.

Five

The Hamburg Incident

Friday 18th November 1960

'Hamburg?' said Jack.

'You can get there – soon?' Sydney Elliott crackled down the phone to him. Not the best connection.

'But rock 'n' roll – not my thing. And can't they spell?'

'Think about it,' said Elliott. 'Play on words, Jack. *Beat* – get it?'

Jack "got it" just fine, but he wasn't about to admit he'd actually thought it quite clever. Yet, Berlin to Hamburg to record some bunch of leather-clad scruffs everybody would have forgotten about by this time next year. Was this what life was going to be like now – working for commercial television?

'How long will it be, though?' he said. 'Before ITV starts showing productions of *Riddle of the Sands* in which Davies is seen pouring his breakfast from a prominently displayed Kellogg's Cornflakes packet? Or we see Captain bloody Birdseye sailing past in the background? Or Carruthers takes a whole scene to splash Old Spice aftershave on his face?'

'You're thinking of commercials in the States, Jack. And for a man who hates it all so much, you have a real ken for TV adverts.'

Elliott had never truly lost his slight Scots accent and Jack was now on a roll of his own.

'What about White Fang,' he said, 'with a Gibbs SR poster on the side of Grey Beaver's sled?'

Elliott laughed, both of them on the same page now.

'An ITV version of Dixon,' said Elliott, 'with Jack Warner spending all his off-duty hours fixing Formica to every damned thing in the Dock Green nick.'

'Seriously,' said Jack, 'why the hell would anybody be interested in this Hamburg bunch?'

'Grundy's idea. He wants to run a piece on how rock and roll is affecting the younger generation. You know the format.'

Searchlight, thought Jack. Reporting on Britain's social problems. Ten thirty at night, every second Monday – a small slice of serious viewing after a whole evening of Huckleberry Hound, Lloyd Bridges, *Double Your Money*, Arthur Haynes and *Wagon Train*.

'But why this bunch?' he said.

'Grundy again – and our Australian friend, too, as it happens.'

Our Australian friend, Jack laughed to himself. Poor Elliott – can't even bear to say his name. Yet *Searchlight* was Tim Hewat's brainchild. He was desperate, really desperate, to provide ITV with a "voice of working people" alternative to *Panorama* – which Hewat dismissed as the patronising voice of *The Times* and the establishment. A bit harsh, Jack thought, but he could see where the man was coming from.

'Somebody's told them these boys are going to make it big.'

'That's about the size of it. Can you do it – get to Hamburg and interview them? Get there tomorrow?'

Saturday 19th November 1960

By the time Jack climbed down onto the platform at the Hauptbahnhof Hamburg, he wished he'd decided to fly. Only the strangled state of his bank account had caused him to take the train.

But how could a hundred-and-sixty-mile journey take so damned long? It had left the station on Alexanderplatz with Teutonic precision, but then there had been the many delays.

It had to be taken into account, naturally, that Berlin – West Berlin, anyhow – remained an island surrounded on all sides by the Soviet-controlled territory of the Deutsche Demokratische Republik, the German Democratic Republic – East Germany.

The train therefore needed to travel westwards from Alexanderplatz until it reached the border crossing between Spandau – where Hess, Speer and a couple of the other Nazi scum remained in prison – and Albrechtshof. The halt there had been a lengthy one, with the East German frontier guards scrutinising everybody and everything on board. They had been especially officious in their inspection of Telford's own satchel contents.

Then, the innumerable stops across the western portion of East Germany – Wittenberge, Ludwigslust and the rest – until they reached yet another border crossing, this time between Schwanheide and Büchen. More searches and more document checks before they finally reached West German territory at last and completed the journey.

'They didn't find anything?' said Fox as they took a table in the station's cafeteria. Like Telford, Fox was now in his early fifties, his hair thinning, but the remaining strands still slicked down with brilliantine. He'd put on weight as well, a distinct paunch – and no longer in uniform. The David Niven moustache remained, however; though, his once debonair features rather spoiled by the thick spectacles upon which Fox had become dependent.

'Thankfully, no,' said Jack.

He lifted the trilby from his head and waved it enticingly towards his companion. He had no idea what the fellow's rank might presently be, but still military intelligence, or some branch of Britain's complex net of security services. Fox insisted on simply talking about "the firm" as though he was merely an employee of some backstreet engineering outfit.

'Please, try to be just a little circumspect, Telford.'

Fox glanced around to see if they were observed, then waved for the waitress, while Jack fiddled inside the hat's lining, produced a carefully folded sheet of almost transparent paper.

'Is that all there is?' said Fox. 'The firm rather expected...'

'A dossier?' Telford handed him the paper. 'You think I could have brought out a dossier? Anyway, this was all he had.'

They ordered coffee and strudel.

'What do you know about him, exactly?' said Fox.

Jack had once handed over a woman to the Soviet Zone's grenzpolizei border police, the Grepo – now the Stasi. He'd thought it was fitting and summary justice. Fräulein Vogel. In his dreams, he sometimes still heard her screams as they'd dragged her away. '*Why?*' she'd yelled. '*Why?*' Later, Jack had been contacted by the *Grepo* lieutenant involved in the whole thing, *Hauptmann* Hofert. For a long time, Telford had been convinced that Hofert was keen to enlist him as a spy, but the lieutenant had never pursued that avenue and, indeed, he'd occasionally fed Jack some snippets of information which Fox had found valuable – though, the incident in Vienna ten years earlier hadn't been one of them.

'As much as you,' said Telford. 'He seems to come and go pretty much unhindered. Always insists on playing me at chess, even though he knows I'm useless at it. We share a couple of glasses of *schnapps*, and away he goes.'

'And this time, he brought you this. But what did he say?'

'He simply said that this time there's a price. "*Tell your friend this time there's a price.*" That was it.'

The waitress was back, and wiped down their table.

'*Ihr Kaffee wird in Kürze hier sein, meine Herren,*' she smiled at them. Your coffee will be here shortly, gentlemen. Fox winked at her, muttered their thanks.

'You know what this is?' he said when she'd returned behind the servery.

'I glanced. An invoice for barbed wire. I was expecting nuclear secrets.'

'He gave you this – when? Last night, you said?'

A family came to sit at the table next to them. They looked as though they belonged to a different and earlier age, the father with beard and bow tie, the mother and two boys attired in a way that would have graced the previous century. Jack lowered his voice – unlikely they'd understand him, but still…

'I'd spoken to Elliott yesterday, then went to buy my tickets. Hofert turned up late in the evening.'

Fox followed Jack's lead and whispered as well.

'He knew, then – about the tickets.'

'I assume so.'

'And Elliott – you trust him?'

Jack laughed.

'I've known him more than twenty years. It was Elliott who first sent me to Spain.'

The waitress again, with a tray.

'Red?' Fox murmured.

Jack looked up at the waitress, searching for any sign she might be paying attention to them, but she was simply busy with the cups and plates.

'Moderately,' he said. 'You know he went to the *Mirror*? Masterminded their campaign that helped get Attlee elected.'

'And now working on documentaries with ITV. Isn't that a bit suspect?'

'We all have to earn our crust. And, at least,' Telford smiled, 'ITV brought us some good socialist morality tales with *Robin Hood*. But barbed wire?'

'Did you read how *much* barbed wire this is? It chimes with other things we've heard.'

'Such as?'

Fox speared a piece of strudel with his bladed pastry fork.

'You know I'm not at liberty to tell you. But, strictly between us, we've heard whispers the Soviets plan to erect a fence – to separate West Berlin completely from the East. A physical barrier between the two. Almost entirely stop the movement of folk and goods from one to the other.'

Jack whistled.

'That's big.'

'Bigger than you might think. I just had a call from Berlin. They fished Hofert's body out of the Spree this morning.'

Sunday 20ᵗʰ November 1960

'It's even worse than we thought, Telford.'

To Jack, it looked like Fox must have worked all night. The red eyes and the dark circles beneath. Animated to the point of hyperactivity. Coffee or drugs? One or the other. But he'd arranged a breakfast table for them at the elegant Restaurant Ehmke, somewhere between Ost-West-Straße and Katharinen-Kirche.

'Worse than German breakfast?' said Jack. 'I never quite got my head around it. All these years. But, stupidly, I suppose I'm going to miss it.'

He didn't need Fox to tell him. If the *Stasi* had killed Hofert, and they'd had any suspicion about the link between them, any hint that Telford knew about this Berlin wall of barbed wire, then his own life wasn't worth a tinker's damn, either. Game, set and match. Besides, the news of Hofert's death had upset him more than he could have imagined.

'The *Stasi*'s been breathing down your neck for years, old boy. But now they think they've got you. Seem to think you must have been Hofert's handler.'

Telford smiled and gazed around the ancient dark oak interior. It was quite a contrast to the bright three-storey street façade. They'd already worked their way through a basket of poppy seed rolls and butter, with a plate of Bergkäse cheese and liverwurst. Now, there was still more bread, this time with golden German forest honey.

'Not safe to go back?'

'Not even safe here, old man. We need to get you out – and fast.'

The waitress brought a steaming, steel pot of coffee and filled their cups.

'I need time to get my job done,' said Jack. 'Supposed to be interviewing this bunch of Liverpool lads for Grundy. God knows why, but...'

'Well, two birds with one stone, Telford. It just so happens that one of them's in a spot of bother. Some evil bastard's informed the authorities that he's under-age. Being deported – tomorrow.'

'Some evil bastard with a David Niven moustache?'

Fox ignored him.

'He'll need a representative of Her Majesty's Government to accompany him,' he said. 'Make sure he goes, at least. Diplomatic immunity, naturally.'

'There's all my stuff. Back in Berlin...'

'Not a problem. I'll arrange something.'

'And the lad...'

Fox consulted his notebook.

'Harrison,' he said. 'George Harrison.'

Monday 21st November 1960

Jack saw spooks all the way to the frontier station at Bad Bentheim. Another seemingly endless train journey: south and west to Bremen and Osnabrück before reaching the border. Once across, and feeling more secure upon Dutch soil, he relaxed for the first time.

He'd taken Fox's advice, simply observed the scruffy Scouse kid following his deportation instructions. Jack was disappointed, somehow expecting the boy to be a bit more – well, rebellious. But he'd turned up, meek as a lamb, at the Hauptbahnhof Hamburg in a scruffy old van, driven by a spotty juvenile boy and accompanied by a slender pixie, a girl with straw-coloured, mop-top hair.

And didn't these kids know anything about travelling light? My god, Jack had thought, everything but the kitchen sink! A suitcase, naturally. Though it was so battered that Jack doubted it could survive the journey. As well as the suitcase, an unmanageable black box – an amplifier, Telford would discover. In the lad's other hand, his guitar, in its own solid black shell. But this wasn't all, for the spotty companion had struggled with two cardboard boxes towards the station, while the pixie girl carried a couple of large brown paper bags, seemingly stuffed with clothes.

Jack had followed the encumbered procession to the ticket hall, then the buffet and finally onto the platform, before the tearful farewells and the inevitable struggle to get everything onto the train – at least, into a carriage corridor, since all the compartments had been crowded with squaddies or other travellers. Besides, with all that baggage, the lad would never have been able to stow it anywhere near the few available seats.

Easy enough for Jack, however, to squeeze himself into an empty space. He was, after all, accustomed to the vagaries and discomforts of military travel. The surrounding soldiers had also helped give him some sense of security in the midst of his paranoia about the *Stasi*. He'd shared his smokes, played a few hands of Seven-card Brag, and swapped some of the questionable jokes and lurid yarns he'd learned during the war and beyond.

They'd used the top of Jack's own attaché case for a card table – the case containing just enough for the couple of nights he'd expected to be away from Berlin. Fox had promised to clear his flat for him – and, hopefully, before the *Stasi* ransacked the place. Not much there for them to find, though. His record collection, his latest journals. Otherwise, he'd been in the habit of sending his few valuables to his sister, Mary, still in Worcester. Mary, now widowed. He'd not even found time to visit during his brief return to London sixteen years earlier. They spoke on the phone from time to time, but that was all. And now – where would he go, once he was back in England? A stranger in a strange land. Something in him wished he could stay exactly here, in this companionable cigarette haze.

But the lad's experience, out in the corridor, had been significantly less sociable. He'd been jostled repeatedly by soldiers trying to move along the narrow passageway, or enjoy some space to drink their beers. He'd been cursed for a bloody nuisance and worse. Though it had all come to a head twenty sluggish minutes after they crossed the border and were pulling into the station at Oldenzaal. They were due to halt there for a while, and Jack guessed there'd be a telegraph office, in which case he'd wire Elliott.

HAMBURG STORY COMING HOME STOP SEE YOU SOON STOP

Something like that. But, when he opened the compartment door, the Scouse kid was busy apologising to a sergeant, whose features reminded Jack of Ernest Borgnine – admittedly, a thinner version of "Fatso" Judson, but with the same slightly maniacal grin.

'Sorry, pretty boy?' said the sergeant – a Taffy, with the broad accent of the Valleys. 'Sorry, is it? Made me spill my beer, you 'ave.'

He gestured with the bottle's neck towards the damp stain spreading down the front of his battledress blouse. His shoulder flash identified him as a member of the Queen's Royal Irish Hussars. Tanks? Jack supposed so. And the sergeant was right, of course. The Harrison boy was, indeed, "pretty" in many ways. Something almost girlish about the translucent skin, the prominent cheekbones, the dark Spanish eyes. Only the thick brows and unkempt tumble of hair helped mark him for the handsome young fellow that he was.

'Give the lad a break, Sarge,' said Jack, then leaned in close to the fellow's ear. 'Just lost his mother,' he whispered. 'Heading back to Blighty for the funeral.'

The sergeant took a step back, perhaps in remorse or, perhaps, in response to the train coming to a halt in the station.

'Sorry to hear that, boyo,' he said, then turned to Jack, nodding towards the eye-patch. 'Copped that one in the war, did you?'

'Before,' Jack replied. 'But, listen, I need to get off and send a telegram.' He tapped a knuckle against the sergeant's bottle. 'Why not let me buy you another one? Bound to be a buffet here.' He turned to the lad. 'What about you?'

The lad smiled and looked down at the chaos around his feet and along the corridor.

'All my gear,' he said.

'What?' Jack laughed. 'Seriously think anybody's going to steal it?' He turned and opened the compartment door again. 'Hey, boys – somebody keep an eye on this lad's kit?'

There was a chorus of skitty comments, but the kid was persuaded to leave everything but his guitar behind, and the three of them stepped onto the platform.

'Before?' said the sergeant as they headed for the buffet. Another flurry of snow and an icy wind.

'Spain,' Jack replied, with a shiver, and the sergeant whistled.

'We 'ad two lads go from the pit. Never came back, like. Lucky, you was. Missed the big show, though?'

'Not really,' said Jack. 'Correspondent. Telford.' He stretched out his hand. 'Jack Telford. Where were you?'

'North Africa,' the sergeant smiled, and shook the proffered hand. 'An' Italy, like.'

The Scouse kid spoke for the first time. He was holding open the door to the buffet for his elders and betters.

'Arnhem?' he said.

'An' what would a lad like you know about Arnhem?' said the sergeant. They took a table by the window.

'Blew me away, mate. Stopped there. On our way here. In the van. Lost, like. But all the white crosses. Those boys who parachuted out. An' just got shot to bits. Memorial an' stuff. But nothin' about whose fault it was.'

Jack ordered beer for them both, then went to sort out the telegram. He left them arguing about Churchill. And Montgomery. And failed military strategies. The lad could, he was pleased to see, hold his own in an argument.

Tuesday 22nd November 1960

'Thought he was goin' to plant me,' said Harrison, leaning on the day ferry's rail. 'Yesterday. On the train. What did you say to him?'

The MS *Koningin Emma* offered an early morning salute from her horn as she edged away from the quayside. Strangely, Telford had recognised her, for she'd been one of the Allied vessels which had landed American troops in Oran, back in '42. Operation Torch.

'Told him you'd just lost your job,' Jack lied. 'That's the truth, isn't it? Otherwise, why would you be going back on your own, without the rest of the band?'

He offered one of his cigarettes and cast a baleful glance back at the ferry terminal, the enormous Haven station building beyond. The customs hall had been chaotic – luggage on trolleys everywhere, waiting to be checked and labelled at one of the two dozen desks. And the army transit camp alongside, where Sergeant Mervyn Davies would have spent the night before boarding the troop ship, still there in the harbour, almost alongside British Rail's SS *Amsterdam*, the night service ferry, waiting for this evening's crossing back to Harwich. It seemed strange, saying goodbye to the Continent this way.

'We were supposed to be goin' to Berlin after Chrimbo,' said the lad. 'Sixty marks a night in Berlin. Been practisin' my *gut Germen*, an' everythin'. Then they find out I'm not old enough to be workin' here.'

Jack experienced a moment of guilt alongside a twinge of premature home-sickness for Berlin.

'Will they keep your place open? Or is that the end of it?'

'Not sure I'll ever see them again. We were just about to start at the Top Ten.' He gave Jack a wistful smile. 'Great sound system at the Top Ten,' he said. 'An' then I get kicked out of town. They'll find another guitar, though. Do well, they will. Then off yer pop to Berlin. Always land on their feet, they do – John and Paul. An' Mrs Best's little lad, of course. But they have deaded me.'

He had this slightly annoying way of slipping into the voice of Bluebottle, from the Goon Show.

'Could be worse, George. If there was still National Service, you could be heading off to Aden with the sergeant.'

The ferry slipped smoothly along the fairway, running parallel with the breakwater. But the wind blew hard and Jack could see whitecaps on the open, grey waters beyond. They were steaming towards a rough crossing.

'Called up, like Elvis,' the lad laughed. 'Might 'ave made me famous.'

'That what you want?'

They passed the breakwater's lighthouse and immediately pitched in the swell. Jack had seen it coming, grabbed the rail and rode the moment. But it caught George unawares. He almost lost his footing.

'Bloody hell,' he said, staggering backwards. 'Bad enough on the way 'ere.' He steadied himself. 'An' famous? John and Paul just see me as their fave guitarist. But I want to be more than that. I *will* be more than that.'

'That's the spirit,' Jack laughed.

'You're a newspaperman, Jack. Think we'd get a headline outta this? *"Gear Guitarist Gets Jerry Jackboot"*. Eh?'

'Nice line. You should be writing songs.'

'Already have. Lads won't use them, though.

'Well, I'm not sure about the headline, but you could certainly help me. I've got some daft assignment. Write about this so-called "teenage revolution". Fancy giving me a few thoughts?'

But the thoughts would have to wait because, by that time, George was bringing up his fried egg and beans over the side. Jack wasn't entirely surprised. While he, himself, had spent a comparatively comfortable night at the Hoek's Hotel America, the lad's ticket had entitled him to the questionable privilege of "sleeping" – though he'd not actually slept a wink, apparently – on one of the docked ferry's

102

reclining seats, followed by a greasy spoon breakfast in the vessel's cafeteria.

Now, Telford helped him with his best *mal de mer* advice, led him to the topmost deck and sat him down on the floor, pretty much amidships, with his back against the white steel wall of the upper lounge. There, Jack took off his overcoat.

'First rule,' he said. 'Sit here like this, on the deck. And keep warm.' He wrapped the coat around the lad, like a blanket. 'Stay put,' he murmured, and found himself ruffling the boy's hair.

He went below, and watched the coastline disappear, a hazy smudge along the horizon. What next? Not only a stranger in a strange land, but also this strange end to a strange year. So many full-stops to so many of the lines in his life.

Jack had seen the news about Jacques Massu finally being dismissed from his command in Algeria by de Gaulle. And all those places he'd known so well in French Equatorial Africa, all the way from Brazzaville north to Chad, each now given their independence.

Then, perhaps, the last of the main Nazi leaders hunted down – Eichmann captured by Mossad in Buenos Aires, and awaiting trial for his worthless life in Jerusalem.

'There,' he whispered to the wind, whispered to Danielle. 'Let that be an end to them, my love. I wish I could have killed every last bloody one of them for you, but at least…'

It made him think of Massu again – or, more precisely, of *Madame* Massu, Suzanne – Toto – who'd been Dani's officer in the ambulance unit. Yes, he decided, best to remember them all the way they'd been, back then. Even the photo he'd carried, Danielle in her fatigues, was so faded and creased that her image had become entirely unrecognisable.

'And now,' he said, 'I have to start all over again.' He blew a kiss, south and east, to where he imagined Haslach and Danielle's final resting place must be.

Behind him, a bunch of English plum-in-the-mouth passengers were bemoaning the loss of empire, and snarling about Macmillan. It was his "Wind of Change" speech, Jack guessed, which had overwound them so tightly.

'Independence?' one of them sneered. 'Bloody Africans? Don't make me laugh. They'll all be starving in six months. Screaming for us to come back and save them.'

'Oh hell,' said Jack, turning to stare at them. 'Is this what I'm going back to?'

In fact, he was thinking about Macmillan, too. He'd met him, of course. In Morocco, with Josephine Baker. It had all been a bit embarrassing. The fellow had known Valerie Carter-Holt's father. He'd even introduced them. Yes, that had been a difficult day.

'Were you speaking to us, old boy?' said one of the Englishmen.

Telford was tempted to thump him. He remembered the day he'd landed a roundhouse punch against Hemingway's equally smug features – outside Paris, the day of the Liberation. But he simply brushed past this particular fool and headed to the saloon where they'd left the lad's boxes and bags, as well as Jack's own case, in the care of a pleasant family travelling back to Croydon.

He apologised for being away so long and settled down to read his book. Leon Uris. *Exodus*. The film version was due to be released. Paul Newman as Ari. Jack weighed the hefty tome in his hand and wondered how much Otto Preminger would have hacked out of the plot. Uris's account of the birth of Israel was certainly dramatic. But Jack found some of its descriptions offensive – descriptions of Palestinians in particular, and Arabs and Muslims in general. Besides, he didn't think it was even especially well written. But he was determined to get to the end, regardless.

Hard to concentrate, however, as the saloon passengers – individually, or by twos and threes – responded to the pitch and toss of the vessel by rushing to the toilets, or the outside rails. And, all through those hours, the *throb, throb, throb* of the engine room, the stink of oil, and the ever-present odour of vomit.

Miraculously, at the precise point when he was almost alone, the lad reappeared in the saloon's doorway, looking fresh as a daisy. A big grin, and he handed back Jack's coat.

'Hello, Eccles,' he beamed. Bluebottle's Goons voice again. 'Where did they all went, then? Did them all fallen in the water?'

'Feeling better, George?'

'Starvin' to be honest.'

Jack treated them to ham sandwiches and mugs of tea.

'An' what were you sayin'? Teenage revolution?'

'Sure,' said Telford. 'What about you? All those *Daily Mail* readers making you out to be juvenile delinquents. Reckon there's really a generation gap?'

'Too right! It was *their* generation landed us with the war, eh? All that suckin' up to Mister Hitler.'

'Bit of an irony, though. Lots of decent folk just wanted to avoid another one.'

Jack tried to chew his way through a piece of ham.

'Sure. An' they got it wrong. Time they moved over and give us young 'uns a chance. Too many old codgers runnin' the country.'

'What would *you* have done about Hitler, George?'

Harrison slurped at his tea.

'Dunno. But different. Been in Germany a while, now. Back home, everybody still thinks they're the enemy. Look at that Taffy sergeant – still got our army over there. An' all the Germans we've met? Some good mates. They're just – like us. Maybe, if we'd all done things different, Hitler wouldn't have had a sniff.'

It wasn't a million miles away from Jack's own view.

'You must have been born in the middle of it,' he said.

'Born in '43, that's me.'

'So, your dad came home?'

'Every night, like. Corpie bus conductor. Seems ye didn't get called up if you was a conductor.'

Jack couldn't remember whether bus conductor had been on the list of reserved occupations – not that it mattered much.

'What about your old fella, Jack – what did he do?'

'My dad? Shot himself.'

George recoiled in horror, but Jack pressed on.

'I was about seven. But the thought of going back to the trenches – being mutilated like so many of his mates had been… Just too much for him. Imagine? How scared you must be to top yourself, like that? To leave your wife and your kid behind?'

'Sorry for your loss, man.' The boy's features were stricken. 'But war, eh? Hell… You know, they reckon that we killed forty thousand people when we bombed Hamburg. Forty thousand. Just that one city. Somebody told me that's how many were killed right through the whole of the Blitz back home. Total, everywhere.'

'Sounds about right.'

'But now,' said George. 'The Bomb an' everythin'. They call *us* delinquents, Jack. But it's the world that's crazy. Teenagers? We're just tryin' to live a bit, while we can.'

Jack stirred his tea. It was thick and brown, much of it slopped onto the table every time the ferry slapped down from yet another swell. And now they were entirely alone, the very last of the saloon's passengers succumbed to the seasickness.

'A class thing, as well, you think?' he said.

'Class system's dead. They just don't know it, yet. Might take a while, like.' The lad switched to a broad imitation of a Lancashire accent. 'But 'ow would a lad like me 'ave earned this much brass before t'war?' Back to his own Scouse lilt. 'Almost got enough to buy my next guitar.'

Jack wasn't sure the British class system was anywhere near to extinction, but he laughed, all the same.

'And this new one will be...?'

A look of sheer rapture illuminated the lad's face.

'Gotta be a Gretsch, Jack. Eh?'

It meant nothing to Telford.

'Of course,' he said. 'What else?'

But he gradually moved the conversation back to the subject at hand. Labour shortages which had brought folk from all parts of the Empire – what was left of it. Harrison was excited by this mix of cultures, fashions and music they'd brought with them. Pop culture from the States, too, of course. Eddie Cochrane. Carl Perkins. Chuck Berry. All that colour, the way it had slashed aside the post-war gloom and infected this whole generation with its fire. The way it had almost managed to eclipse even the shadow of the Bomb.

By the time they were due to finally dock in Harwich, Telford had enough for not one assignment, but two. For now, for Elliott, Grundy and *Searchlight*, a pithy piece about rock 'n' roll and the teenage revolution. For another time, the Soviet plot to permanently partition Berlin.

'Will you get back to Liverpool tonight?' Jack asked him and glanced at his watch, then helped him with his belongings.

'Maybe, the late train.'

The sea had settled as they entered the mouth of the estuary, Felixstowe's Landguard Point to their right and Harwich itself to the left. In the early evening darkness, the red and green lights of navigation buoys flashed frenzied patterns through the beginnings of a bone-chilling fog.

'Anything I can do to help? I owe you, now – for helping me with the assignment. A few quid to help with the train?'

'I don't take handouts. And unless you know some way to get me back to Berlin with the lads...'

Sadly, no, Jack didn't know how to work that magic. So, he shook hands with the lad, wished him well, and picked up his own suitcase, before making his way to the passenger gangway.

No, he thought, I can't make that happen. But, then, there was Fox. Good at fixing things, that was Fox. Telford might not be able to get George to Berlin, but maybe it could be arranged for the band to also be deported back to Liverpool. Sure, he smiled to himself. Fox fits them up with some minor misdemeanour – just enough to get them kicked out of Germany, too. No guarantee they'd pick up the Harrison lad again, of course.

'But who knows?' he said to himself, as he set foot on English soil again after all those years. 'Don't suppose I'll ever find out, anyhow.'

By the time he reached the train station, he couldn't even remember what the bloody band was called. Maybe Elliott would remind him. But, one way or the other, a five-minute wonder, that was sure.

Six

The Mozambique Motorsport

Thursday 20th July 1967

Jack could hear Fred Astaire singing in his head.

> *'There may be trouble ahead,*
> *But while there's moonlight...'*

He'd been in Portugal long enough to recognise a secret policeman when he saw one. Salazar's International and State Defence Police. The PIDE. Jack had learned to pronounce the word *peed*, as a Portuguese would whisper it, whenever she or he dared. In fact, the PIDE agents were so obvious, he wondered why they didn't simply wear badges to that effect. Originally trained by the Gestapo, they'd never quite lost the stamp.

This one made a pretence of looking around the Lisbon airport lounge for an empty seat, before taking his cigarettes from inside the leather jacket and finally choosing the bench close to Telford.

Jack ignored him and unfolded the map.

Lisbon airport had changed remarkably little – apart from the Boeing jets which now came and went with bewildering regularity. Back in '43 it had been all Douglas DC-3s. The legendary, prop-driven Dakotas.

Telford saw again, as though it were yesterday, that image of Leslie Howard, racing onto the runway here, to catch the flight which would carry him to oblivion. Somewhere near Cedeira, on Spain's northwest coast.

I must visit, he decided, when Franco's dead. It was a hypocrisy, of course, this stubborn refusal to return to Spain while the Franco remained in power. For here he was, settled now in Portugal, ruled by a murderous dictatorship for even longer than Spain had been. But the opportunity had presented itself, and he had enjoyed Lisbon, even though his wartime visit had been brief.

'Travelling to Mozambique, *senhor*?'

'*Meu Deus*,' Telford replied. Good gracious. 'You have a quick eye.'

The title cover was barely visible. The latest copy of the Mozambique Automobile and Touring Club Map. The *Automóvel e Touring Clube de Moçambique*. Jack had no doubt he'd been followed when he bought it.

The agent lit a cigarette.

'And you, my friend,' he said, 'have good Portuguese.'

'I try.' *Eu tento.*

He'd been here four years already. And Jack's Spanish – as well as his grounding in Esperanto – had helped considerably.

'And yes, Mozambique. But I guess you already know this.'

'Not the safest place to be, *senhor*.'

Indeed not. The latest of Portugal's colonial independence wars. First, Angola. Then, Portuguese Guinea. And now, for the past three years, Mozambique. FRELIMO freedom fighters – or terrorist insurgents, depending on your viewpoint – already controlling a fifth of Mozambique's territory. Still, where *was* safe, these days? And danger seemed to wrap him like a shroud.

'Thankfully,' said Jack, 'I'm not there for the war.'

'The Grand Prix, perhaps?'

Telford was honestly surprised. Did they *really* know that much about his plans? Or simply an educated guess? The map, maybe.

'I'm happy to be there,' Jack admitted.

'Professional interest, perhaps?'

'You think *World in Action* would send me all the way to Lourenço Marques to cover Formula One?'

'What is this *World in Action*?'

Jack smiled. He supposed, in a way, this was exactly what his producer had done. This link, between the Grand Prix and sanction busting in Rhodesia. But it was a golden opportunity, as well. He'd used three seemingly interminable years back in England learning how to drive – and he'd ended up with something of a passion for cars. For racing cars, with all their thrills and spills. Who'd have thought?

'I'm guessing you already know,' he said. 'I'm a journalist.'

The agent grunted, and cocked his ear towards the nearest loudspeaker.

'You like?'

It was the other difference – the music. No rock n' roll in '43. So, he'd been wrong about that bloody band, after all. It now seemed impossible to escape them. And this one?

Good Day Sunshine.

It hardly suited Jack's mood.

The Harrison lad was very much part of the line-up, and Fox had delivered exactly as Telford had hoped he might. In private, Fox had even been known to claim credit for making the band what it was today. A bit of a stretch, naturally.

'I'm a journalist, not a music critic.'

'And an academic,' spat the agent, as though it were a leprous affliction.

'I deliver a few lectures in journalism at your fine university. Does that make me an academic?'

'But do you teach them, *senhor*, what a dangerous occupation journalism can be?'

Saturday 22nd July 1967

At the PIDE headquarters, in the heart of Lourenço Marques, Telford faced yet another interrogation. How many times had this happened to him? The customary sense of unease. His fingers went, almost involuntarily, to his eye-patch. The familiar ache returned.

He'd only been at the hotel for an hour when they came for him, brought him here. His first impressions, from the outside, had been that this must once have been a rather grand house. It filled the corner of a dusty road junction, broad and balustraded stone steps leading up from street level, at the corner itself, to a veranda filled with tiled mural panels – those elegant and traditional blue and white *azulejo* tiles which adorned so many fine buildings back in Lisbon, Porto and just about every other town in Portugal.

Inside, however, the place smelled like a butcher's shop, paint peeling from the walls. The spectral presence of pain.

'It says here that you wrote for this one?'

Lieutenant Machado pointed a bone-thin finger at his dossier, and Jack turned his head to read the entry. *Machado*, he thought. Spanish and Portuguese word for a hatchet. Yes, that was fitting. The fellow must have soaked himself in eau de cologne, but instead of masking the abattoir stench, it simply added to the building's sickly putrefaction and the stink of sweat wafting from the stained armpits of Machado's buttercream military shirt. The sleeves were rolled to the elbow, revealing spider monkey forearms.

'Indeed, that was me,' said Jack.

World in Action's 1964 production. *The Truth About Spain: an exposé of life under Franco.*

'This?'

Overhead, a ceiling fan rattled around but did little to disturb the heat. Somebody had told him this was the coolest month, the end of the dry season and, indeed, there was rain pattering at the window. It did nothing for his discomfort. And the rattan blades of the fan seemed to be playing a tune.

Do, Re, Mi, Sol, Fa…

'There may be trouble…'

'Yes,' said Jack. 'I wrote some of the script for that, too. Have you seen it?'

The lieutenant greeted the question with a look of pure contempt. It had been the following year. *The Middle East: growing tensions between Arabs and Israelis.* But Jack's most recent contribution to the programme didn't seem to be in the dossier. Last month, and the Special, *After the War*? Telford's analysis of the latest bloodbath between Israel and the Arab coalition.

'But now here to report on the Grand Prix, *senhor*? Please, be serious.'

The lieutenant fingered the truncheon, which lay on the desk next to his peaked cap. Jack understood the gesture perfectly and raised his hands in surrender, as a large fly settled on his interrogator's shoulder.

'Fair enough,' said Telford. *É justo*. 'My producers are also interested in the sanctions. Though, there *is* a link to the Grand Prix.'

'You will be aware, of course, that there is no evidence of any Portuguese involvement in breaking your sanctions. We are your country's oldest ally, are we not?'

Telford hoped he'd been sufficiently careful at his hotel for, among his paperwork, were clippings from last month's copy of *Anti-Apartheid News*. They were hidden inside the dust cover of his latest read, Capote's *In Cold Blood*. The true crime novel had just introduced Jack to the real-life Clutter family and, knowing the fate that awaited them, he'd lain awake half the night, wishing to hell that he could warn them.

'Are we not?' Machado repeated.

Telford looked him squarely in the eye, remembering the *Anti-Apartheid News'* compelling coverage about both the conflict here in Mozambique and also the sanctions – but, overall, about the unholy alliance between South Africa, Portugal and Rhodesia. It was less than two years since Rhodesia's Cabinet and their Prime Minister, Ian Smith, had issued that Unilateral Declaration of Independence from Great Britain, and incurred the wrath of both the British government and the United Nations. Sanctions imposed in an effort to bring them into line.

'Our oldest ally, indeed,' Jack smiled. 'And no, not Portuguese involvement. But South Africa? Now, South Africa's a different issue. All the same, I *am* here mainly for the Grand Prix.'

Lieutenant Machado stared at him. His emaciated features were hard to read. A poker face in more ways than one. Yet the dark, sunken eyes flickered, calculating. Was *Senhor* Telford dissembling? Well, of course, he was. It was a matter of record that the Royal Navy had successfully turned away oil tankers wishing to berth at Beira with cargoes destined for Rhodesia, through the pipeline. Now, the oil was simply being transported to Rhodesia directly from South Africa. And it was Jack's job to help confirm the evidence.

'So, who will you cheer for, *senhor*? At the Grand Prix?'

A trick question. Traditionally, all the competitors here would be from the South African Formula One championships – effectively, they'd all be Rhodesian or from South Africa itself. All one shade of apartheid or another.

'Oh, the winner,' Jack smiled. 'I'll definitely cheer for the winner. Just a shame you have no Portuguese drivers in the race.'

'Portugal – the poor man of Europe. Isn't that what you journalists like to call us? How could we afford to compete, *senhor*?'

'With all the wealth of Mozambique at your fingertips?' said Jack.

'The cost of bringing civilisation to the colonies, naturally.'

Oh, naturally, Jack thought. Only three per cent literacy and, beyond the large towns, according to *Anti-Apartheid News*, the vast majority still living in medieval levels of poverty. And here he was, in a capital city that didn't even have a decent airport.

'Civilisation and spiritual enlightenment, yes?'

Telford tried to keep the sarcasm from his voice, but he knew he'd failed miserably.

'You think,' snapped the lieutenant, 'that these FRELIMO terrorists are some indication that our efforts have failed? How typical of your decadent British liberalism. So totally at odds with the insurgents' landmines. With their cowardly attacks on innocents.'

'I've heard the arguments before, Lieutenant. In Algeria and just about everywhere else the oppressed have to fight for their freedom.'

Machado slapped the desk.

'Freedom?' he laughed. 'For these children? Give them freedom and they will destroy themselves in weeks. But very well, *Senhor* Telford.' He slid Jack's documents back to him. 'I have nothing further for you. Not for the moment, anyhow. So, enjoy the Grand Prix. Though, have a care. The world can be dangerous.'

Yet another warning. This was becoming monotonous.

Sunday morning, 23rd July 1967

There was something so entirely satisfying about being able to slam down a telephone.

Telford sat for a few moments in the booth, hoping to settle down and allow his anger to ebb; though, conscious of the queue out in the waiting area beyond the desks and operators.

'Gutless,' he said to himself. 'Totally bloody gutless.'

It was, he had to admit, at odds with the programme's reputation. Regularly threatened with legal action. Threatened, as well, by government and regulators alike. To be fair, *World in Action* usually went where angels – or, at least, the BBC – feared to tread. But not this time, it seemed. And it wasn't the sanctions. Nor the conflict here in Mozambique. Nor even the Grand Prix. No, it was Vietnam.

Jack made his way to the counter, took the bill and began counting through his wad of crumpled one-hundred *escudo* banknotes. *Banco de Moçambique*. But, all the while, Wallington's slightly slurred voice came back to him.

'I tell you, Jack. This time, they mean it. A D-notice.'

So, they'd be gagged.

'Whatever happened to publish and be damned?' Jack had demanded. 'We were happy enough to praise Wilson when we thought he'd kept us out of bloody Vietnam. But now...'

He'd paid a brief visit back to London in March, and taken part in the Grosvenor Square protests. Knocked about by mounted policemen. The long truncheons of the law. Arrested. Narrowly avoided being sent down. No stranger to torture and interrogation in foreign parts, he'd just never expected to be threatened with imprisonment in Britain.

'Now?' Wallington had said. 'We back off. The evidence isn't strong enough.'

'Then we do what we always do – play it in a way that points viewers towards the truth without risking a libel case.'

The truth? Telford admired Wilson. But the Prime Minister's public stance against going to war fell a long way short of openly condemning the Americans for their excesses in Vietnam. Understandable, maybe, that we'd not want to alienate them, given how much we owed them. But not even for their use of chemical weapons? Agent Orange? And the protestors in Grosvenor Square had been just as angry with Wilson as they were with Lyndon Johnson. But if they'd known about this...

'Jack, there's the D-notice.' Wallington had been exasperated, spoken to Jack as though he were a simpleton.

'We've got the statements,' Jack had protested. 'British servicemen willing to swear they've been training Vietnamese troops in counter-insurgency. By us. In Malaya, for god's sake. Wilson's claim that we've no military involvement's just a lie.'

Jack strolled back out into the heat.

The blare of a lorry's horn, as he jumped back, just in time, to avoid being killed.

'Bloody hell,' he shouted after the speeding truck. 'Bloody maniac!'

The sixties hadn't been easy and he'd not settled comfortably in Blighty after Berlin. He'd spent some time with sister Mary in Worcester, of course. Her husband, Charlie, had died a couple of years earlier, and she'd been left to run Weaver's bakery and confectionery shop on Friar Street, on her own. The five kids all grown and either married or working. The youngest, Harry, had got through university and was now working as a cub reporter for the *Worcester Evening News*. Ambitions to be as famous as his Uncle Jack, apparently. Idiot!

Jack had found a flat in London easily enough. But then there'd been the Cuba business. The threat that the whole world would be blown to hell. The shadow of the mushroom cloud. It was a cloud which seemed to have hung over him ever since. And, not long afterwards, Kennedy. Suddenly, Britain not only felt uncomfortable, but unsafe, as well.

Lisbon had been too good an opportunity to miss. And it had brought him here, as well. Not a bad place to fetch up, he thought. He stood in the shade of the Telegraph Office colonnade and lit a cigarette to settle his nerves, gazing down the dirt road and beyond the red pantiles to the Indian Ocean.

It was Wallington's warning that stayed with him.

'Anyway, Jack,' he'd said, 'there's been a development on the sanctions issue. Les and I are heading out to the Northern Cape ourselves. Hot tip. Trains carrying asbestos destined for Rhodesia. Heading your way. We'll film the shipments leaving Koegas and send you all the details. The official destination will be Beira, but we'll need you to be there and confirm it's then been routed directly across the border.'

'You're going on a spying trip to South Africa?' Jack had tried not to laugh. 'With Woodhead? Could be dangerous, Jeremy.'

'It's a dangerous job, Jack.'

Now, where had Telford heard that before?

'But safe enough your end,' Wallington went on. 'Just enjoy the Grand Prix and we'll let you know when we land.'

Safe enough? Jack hoped so.

Sunday afternoon, 23rd July 1967

The red Brabham Repco with the yellow trim roared past. If Love kept this lead, Jack could see him carrying away the Governor General's Cup. It would be Love's third win of the year and he was already a contender for the Championship. It had been a good move, swapping his old Cooper Climax for the former works car he'd apparently bought from Jack Brabham himself. Or so his companion informed him.

'One day,' she said, 'I will drive on this circuit.'

A young black woman? Telford wondered. How long will that take? He pulled down the brim of his Panama, so he could see better along the straight, a dozen cars spaced out, or fighting individual duels as they jostled for position, racing for the curve below the spectators' vantage point.

'I thought you wanted to be an artist, Reinata,' he said.

She laughed, and moved closer to him.

'I am an artist already.'

Reinata slipped a journal from her bag and quickly passed it to him, careful to mask the title; though, Jack saw it, plain enough. *Mozambique Revolution*. Issue Number 29, June-July 1967.

'Interesting piece in there,' she murmured. 'About the death of Chief Luthuli. But the photographs – they are all mine.'

Telford grabbed the journal as though it were white-hot, and slipped it inside his jacket. He looked around at the crowd surrounding them on the hilltop embankment, fully expecting a PIDE agent to arrest them both at any moment. But no, just a bunch of excited, young Portuguese lads. An occasional African face; though, not many. Down the slope, at the edge of the crowd, a Volkswagen Beetle belonging to the Public Security Police and sporting double loudspeakers on its roof. But that was about the only sign of authority.

'Official government guide,' Jack said, as quietly as he was able above the screaming engines, accelerating out of the bend. 'But distributing FRELIMO's newspaper. Are you trying to trap me, my dear?'

He loved the aroma which surrounded her, some heady musk-like scent that was new to him. And yes, she was attractive. Tall and big-boned, as his mother might have said. Her hair was a confection of tight braids spiralling down in a series of chains to her neck – chains mirrored in the green foliate patterns embroidered into the yellow cotton of her ankle-length tribal dress. Hell, here he was, almost sixty. But not too old – or so he considered – to be blind to the beauty of a person like Reinata Nyusi. A Catholic Makonde from the north, she'd boasted.

'It works well for me,' she told him. 'Access to the government offices here in Lourenço Marques. I gather information. I sell party membership cards.'

'Maybe, just a bit too much to trust me with, don't you think?'

'I was *told* to trust you, *senhor.*'

Jack laughed.

'Tingle,' he said, and she followed his gaze down onto the track, where Rhodesian driver Sam Tingle slid his racing green LDS Mark 3 through the curve. 'Second place?'

Reinata shielded her eyes from the sun and peered towards the finish line way down the straight, opposite the pit lane, where the scoreboard and celebrity stand were topped by a large Pirelli advertisement.

'Yes, second. Lap time…'

'Never mind,' Telford snapped. The other problem with his age. Failing sight in his remaining eye. 'Just who, precisely, told you to trust me?'

'The comrades, of course,' she told him, as though it were the most obvious thing in the world.

'Comrades here?'

'From Lisboa. Your reputation goes before you, *camarada* Telford.'

It was true that he'd established some good contacts already with the Party in Lisbon, but he was somewhat unnerved to find himself so readily on their list of trustees.

'Reputations have been known to kill,' he said.

'In the Wild West, maybe. Certainly, in Lisbon. They say you interviewed the boss of PIDE – about the girl!'

She could barely contain her amusement. But there was a hint of admiration, too.

Well, it was true enough. He'd made an early name for himself by securing a meeting with the PIDE's director, Fernando da Silva Pais and then hit this far-right fascist with a question about his daughter, Annie, who'd shamed daddy by running off to Cuba to serve Fidel Casto's government.

'It didn't exactly put me in their good books, Reinata.'

All about them, the boys had begun to chant.

'*Botha! Botha! Botha!*'

A blue and white car was jockeying for position with a green and yellow Lotus 21, a fierce contest between the two South Africans, Luki Botha in his Brabham BT11-Climax, and Jackie Pretorius in the Lotus.

'The lads like him,' Jack shouted.

'Luki the Legend. Privateer. No big company to back him. One man against the world.'

'That's what makes the sanctions busting work, too, isn't it? Rhodesia thumbing its nose, not only at Britain, but at the whole of the United Nations. And everybody at this end loves them for it.'

'They say there is a British man – I could not discover his name – who has approached the US Consul here. It seems he's been working in South Africa, helping to organise shipments for Rhodesia through the port of Beira. But now he's got himself in trouble with the South African police and was arrested for something else. Skipped bail and escaped to Mozambique. He has a dossier. He wants to use it to barter his way out of the country.'

Christ! Jack thought. Not another dossier.

'Interesting,' said Jack. 'I'll see what I can find out. But Beira seems to be yesterday's news. I'm chasing down trains carrying asbestos and oil, coming here to Lourenço Marques, and then…'

He'd seen enough of Beira, anyway – because the runway at Lourenço Marques wasn't long enough to accommodate the 707s of Transportes Aéreos Portugueses. So, a two-hour stifling wait at Beira before a further two hours for the flight from Beira to here.

'The train line runs to Malvérnia,' Reinata reminded him. 'Just two hundred miles, north and west, to the border. Then, straight on to Salisbury.'

Telford felt more beads of sweat trickling from the back of his hair and down his neck. He reached for his handkerchief.

'Doesn't it bother you?' he said. 'The line between resistance and collaboration?'

At the control tower, the loudspeaker crackled. Jack's Portuguese was good – but not good enough to cope with the whistling feedback of the announcement. But here came John Love, completing another lap. He'd started the race in pole position, and he'd kept the advantage. Sections of the spectators cheered him enthusiastically.

'It's a blurred line,' she told him, at last, 'and we want our independence. From Portugal. But from everybody else, as well. We all do what we must.'

'The Portuguese have been here a long time. Hard to shift.'

'Four centuries. But not in the north. My homeland, *Senhor* Telford. In the north, they only arrived seventy years ago. When you Europeans were trying to grab anything you could in Africa. We, the Makonde, have been protesting ever since. Peaceful protest. Until Mueda.'

1960, Jack knew. And the police had opened fire on a peaceful demonstration. Familiar story. Six hundred dead? The accounts varied wildly. But a massacre, whatever the death count.

'You think this will be their Vietnam?' Telford suggested.

Sam Tingle's green LDS took the bend, now a good twenty seconds or more behind Love.

'There are parallels, are there not? Here, too, they hold the coastline. But the interior, the *mato*? The highlands? Those belong to FRELIMO now. To our people.'

'You said, "freedom from everybody else". Who's on the list, Reinata?'

'We appreciate all the help from the Soviets, from China – and from our friends in Cuba. It made me smile, the story about your interview with da Silva Pais. Because the daughter made sure we were firmly on Fidel's map. Yet, Mozambique will not win liberty from one power, only to become a puppet for another. Not even Cuba.'

'Fair enough,' said Jack. 'But, one of these days, I must visit. Cuba, I mean.'

'The footsteps of Hemingway,' she laughed.

'You like Hemingway?'

She smiled as Jackie Pretorius hurtled past again, now plainly in third place.

'Who does not love Papa Hemingway?' Reinata asked him.

Well, thought Jack...

He still stung from his memories of Vienna, all those years back. But he'd followed Hemingway's subsequent story, just like the rest of the world. *The Old Man and the Sea*. The devastating plane crashes – not one, but two of them – in Africa during '54. His time in Cuba, which he'd finally left in 1960; though, remaining on good terms, they said, with Fidel. And then the suicide, at Ketchum, Idaho. Telford had written to Mary, of course, offering condolences – though she'd never really accepted her husband's death as suicide. Finally, there'd been the altar boy story. He saw it now, just as he'd first read the account. But he quickly dismissed the image. Too gruesome for such a fine afternoon.

'What are you thinking, *senhor*?'

'About Hemingway – and death.'

Not just Hemingway's, either, for Papa's demise had coincided almost exactly with the death of Jack's old friend, Sidi Mohammed – more properly, since Morocco's independence, King Mohammed the Fifth of Morocco.

Telford found himself sinking into a brooding despondency, reminders of his own mortality and, almost immediately, he experienced something which hadn't afflicted him since – when? Spain?

A vision of his father, in his First World War uniform, down at the edge of the track, his hand half-raised in Jack's direction.

'*Senhor* Telford, are you unwell?'

He turned to look at her, and heard the crowd yelling, once again.

'*Botha! Botha! Botha!*'

Here came the blue and white Brabham again, weaving in a terracotta haze of dust, through the pack, in the driver's wild efforts to catch Pretorius.

Telford glanced down the hill again. He shook his head to clear the vision. But his father's ghost remained. Jack grabbed Reinata's arm.

'We have to get away from here,' he yelled.

'What?'

Luki Botha had swung wide. It looked like he was going to use the bend's run-off area to give himself extra space. Yet, his supporters were themselves spilling down onto that same stretch of tarmac, desperate for a closer view of their hero.

'Now!' Jack shouted. 'For Christ's sake, now!'

She tried to shake free of his grip, but he could see what would happen next. See it as though it had already transpired. His father's warning? Maybe. Though, he didn't know which way to run. And he didn't care.

The first screams came to them with the simultaneous screech of tyres. A dull thud shook the ground beneath Telford's running feet, as he dragged Reinata behind him. Like a bomb going off. He saw cars snaking this way and that, across the track. Minor collisions. Pieces of bodywork thrown skywards.

He caught a glimpse of Botha's Brabham lifting above the heads of spectators. He watched those same spectators flinging themselves to the ground. The Brabham sailed through the air and came down through the crowd. It hit the slope with a sickening shriek of grinding metal. Luki Botha in his white overalls was tossed clear like a rag doll.

'Down!' Telford bellowed, as the vehicle's bonnet scythed toward them, slicing through two boys as it came. He fell on top of Reinata, pressed both their faces into the dirt. Yet, now, the musk-like scent threatened to smother him.

Something whistled overhead, and there was a siren. He risked a glance and saw the Volkswagen Beetle trying to force its way through panic-stricken spectators – and then onto the track.

'What the hell is he doing?' Telford murmured.

The fool was driving straight into the path of the oncoming cars. Reinata lifted her own head.

'Trying to reach the control tower? Stop the race? But are you hurt, *senhor*?'

She wriggled from beneath him.

'I'm sorry, Reinata. Just trying…'

'To protect me,' she said, scrambling to her feet. 'That English thing? To apologise for no good reason.'

Around them, all was carnage. A line of bodies strewn up the hillside. Some moving. Some not. A young woman sobbed, kneeling, covered entirely in engine oil. The engine itself had separated from the car and now pinned one of the lads face-down to the ground, where he cried for his mother beneath its murderous weight. Jack could not imagine the injuries it must have inflicted. He was astonished the boy was even still alive – though, he knew it would not be for much longer.

Reinata muttered a few words in what he assumed must be her own Makonde tongue, but she crossed herself as well, the meaning of her words clear enough.

'What was it?' she said.

He shrugged his shoulders, pretended he had no idea what she meant.

'Whatever it was that warned you,' she insisted. 'The old soldier?'

Telford froze.

'You saw him?'

'I live with the spirits of my family,' she said. 'You should not shun them. Or pretend they are not there.'

She stroked the dirt-smeared sleeve of his jacket – some gentle gesture of sympathy. But then she was gone from his side, making her way towards the nearest of the walking wounded.

Over the next fifteen or twenty minutes, perhaps longer, they did whatever was practical to help. Reinata, it transpired, had good first-aid skills and Jack had his own experience of battlefield injuries.

And this *was* a battlefield. Between them, they operated a basic triage system. Simple words of comfort, help on its way, that kind of thing, for those too badly hurt, beyond their abilities. For others, strips torn from the hem of Reinata's robe, or from Jack's shirt tails, to bandage cuts and abrasions. Anything to keep the flies away. For the flies were gathering. Great buzzing swarms of the vile creatures. Everywhere, the stink of fuel.

Further down the hill, Luki Botha. Somehow, he had survived. Unscathed? Hard to tell. Yet, he was there, helping others.

The police had arrived by now. The police and their dogs, trying to restore some order among the spectators. A cordon established so that the Red Cross, also on the scene, could get on with their work. The cordon serving, besides, to allow passage to those searching for victims of the crash.

The race had stopped, at least. Cars abandoned, haphazardly, around the distant pits. A babble of crackling announcements from the control tower.

'Not such a fool as I thought,' said Jack, as they helped two of the Red Cross workers strap the oil-covered woman to a makeshift stretcher. 'Whoever that was, in the Beetle,' he explained.

There were body bags, too. Corpses carried from the field, accompanied by grieving, inconsolable relatives or friends. Five of them teenagers? Six? A small boy, no more than a child. And two adults, a man and a woman. Just one of the dead remained where he'd fallen.

Another teenager, his face terribly mutilated. But African. A lone African among all those white casualties. Untended. Nobody searching for him. Telford wondered whether his family even knew he was here.

'We will make sure to post notices,' said Reinata, reading his mind. 'But...'

She didn't need to say it. There wouldn't even be a photograph to go on a poster.

'Is that it?' he said. 'The link. The sanction busting, the Grand Prix.' He pointed to the boy. 'That poor bastard?'

'The forgotten ones? Of course.' Her arm swept around in a ninety-degree arc. 'I pity the dead, *senhor*. All of them. But this?

Motor racing? White privilege. Privilege of the rich. Nothing here for my people. Nothing in Rhodesia for my people. Nothing in South Africa.'

'It will change,' he said. 'It has to change.'

'It will change when writers like you begin to tell the story of how *our* lives are shaped, or torn apart, by these things. The lives of ordinary Africans. Tell *that* in your programme. And when change happens, when there is darkness before the final dawn, remember how Europe enslaved an entire continent to feed their greed.'

'You know there will be hell to pay?'

'Yes, we know. But then will come the glory of a free Africa. All of it. Free, once more.'

Jack could almost see it. How the birth pangs and the early years of this new Africa would be more painful than the years of enslavement. But then? He hoped she was right. How many decades, though? How many lifetimes?

'Well, bring it on!' said Telford, while the words of the song played in his head yet again.

'Let's face the music and dance.'

Seven

The Lisbon Labyrinth

Thursday 18th April 1974

His tongue betrayed him. Partly the accent, that rare blend of English, Spanish, Portuguese and German, sliding like a silk glove pulled over each of his words, regardless of whichever among those four languages he chose to speak. And, partly, simple fear of the pain they might inflict upon him.

Jack Telford had been tortured in the past. In Spain, more than thirty-five years earlier. In '38. It had cost him his left eye, and much more besides. His interrogator now, as then, was a lieutenant. On this occasion, the fellow had introduced himself as *Tenente* Estéves. Slim and slight. A neat, civilian suit, naturally, but a lieutenant – a lieutenant firmly in the pay of a secret police force deployed by the regime that had ruled Portugal with an iron fist over the past four decades.

'We know you're a spy, *Senhor* Telford, but who for?'

The hammering on his door had come, as these things always did, just before dawn, and the agents had bundled him into their vehicle, driven him here to their notorious headquarters on the Rua António Maria Cardoso, in the heart of the Chiado District. Ironically, Jack could observe the place easily, just across from his new apartment – almost the first thing he saw each day when he threw open the shutters.

'If you have evidence that I'm a spy,' he said, 'it seems logical that you'd also know who I'm spying for.'

He tapped his finger on the impressively large file bearing his name upon a white label, and which lay accusingly on the table between them. It wasn't the first time they'd interrogated him, and he supposed it wouldn't be the last. Yet, so far, these had always been *entradas* as the locals called them. Routine. All the same, they were dangerous, these fellows. The regime may have changed the name, tried to soften the image, but nobody was fooled by their new DGS designation. Still the same old PIDE – Jack pronounced the word *peed*, in the Portuguese style. International and State Defence Police. Originally Gestapo-trained but their methods refined, more recently, by the CIA. Dangerous, but generally not very bright. And certainly no sense of humour. Still, Jack did his best. It would have been the caretaker, the *porteira*, of course, at his new place, who would have reported him. A well-known snitch, a *bufo*, for these secret policemen.

'You attended a dinner party last night. A meeting of dissidents – Ferreiro and others.'

'*Senhor* Ferreiro is a respected pillar of our community. I assumed I was safe from dissidence in his company.'

'And Commodore Lawrence?'

'What about him?'

'He was there too.'

'Can you imagine Allan Lawrence missing a good dinner party? Particularly his own.'

Lawrence provided a certain quality to Jack's circle of acquaintances – a younger Alec Guinness quality. Never without a collar and tie; neat linen suit; always unflustered; always cool – literally, for he knew every inch of shade, at each hour of the day, on the correct side of Lisbon's streets, all along the route from his home to his many favourite bars and eating places.

'Yet, he won't be attending any more, will he, *senhor*?'

Jack's acquaintances, who had been so scientifically tortured by these creatures, had once told him that you knew when a PIDE interview was no longer simply an *entrada* – because of the chill, which accompanies more serious interrogations. And he felt the temperature drop now, ice down his spine.

'Why would that be?' he said, flatly.

There was an alligator smile.

'Come,' said Estéves.

His chair scraped on the tiles and he stood, collected his paperwork from the table. Jack got to his feet, as well, followed him out into the corridor, his brain racing.

He'd left Lawrence around midnight, promising to meet him again for lunch today. Always a pleasure to lunch with Allan. Until recently, anyhow. He'd been complaining of headaches and fatigue for a while, a tendency to anger more easily. The stress of his work, he claimed. But, overall, urbane, ex-Merchant Navy, didactic. Thoughtful. He enjoyed nothing better than reciting large sections of Lorca, learned by heart. Jack had a particular affinity for Lorca. It had made them firm friends for the past four or five years. And friends, true friends, were a rare commodity for Jack Telford. So, what was all this about? Why did Jack feel this palpable sense of doom? As if there could possibly be any other answer.

In the basement of the PIDE building – the basement, which Jack had heard described all too often – there were white ceramic corridors and rooms that no sane individual would ever choose to visit in person. One of those rooms, he now discovered, was a mortuary. And there, on a slab, lay the body of his friend, the eyes partially open, the whites exposed.

Jack felt the floor turn to gelatinous mush, the wall tumble somewhat out of focus, his nostrils fill with the odours of disinfectant, and his own voice echo back to him as though he were talking in the public swimming pool.

'How?' he said, when he was able. 'And what was he doing here?'

'We needed to ask him a few questions, *senhor*. Routine. You understand? We were troubled by the company he's been keeping.'

'Spies?' said Jack. 'Like me?' The world steadied, though the nausea remained.

'Isn't that what you do? Spying?'

Lisbon, somebody had once told him, was the world capital of espionage. An inheritance from the Second World War, its neutrality making it a magnet for Allied and Axis intelligence operatives, for American and British exiles or traitors, and for all manner of double agents. He'd been here back then, of course. That terrible business with Leslie Howard. And it sometimes seemed that they were still there – the agents.

'I prefer to call it investigative journalism.'

'We think, *Senhor* Telford, that you could not sustain your opulent standard of living on a simple journalist's salary.'

Opulent? he thought. Where the hell does he get that idea? Yet, the other part was true enough. If he had to survive on the payments he received from the *World in Action* commissions, he'd have starved long ago. Fortunately, his journalism lectures at the University were a more lucrative source of income. But, for now, he sought signs of injury on the corpse; though, Allan looked as dapper as ever. Too clean to have been beaten. Too peaceful for electric wiring to the genitals. And he'd not been here long enough for their favourite procedure – the enforced standing.

'I manage to scrape a living somehow,' Jack told him. 'But these questions you needed to ask Lawrence so badly – they must have been deadly. I just don't understand how you managed to do it so cleanly.'

'This?' said the lieutenant. 'You're mistaken, *senhor*. This man's death is something of a mystery. Our doctors tell us he has been poisoned. That's something of an embarrassment for us.'

It wasn't unusual for folk to die in the cells of the PIDE – either here on the Rua António Maria Cardoso, or in their Caxias prison, off towards the coast – but it was unique for them to bother denying responsibility.

Now, why should this be so different? Jack wondered. And poison? Lawrence poisoned?

'Why do you need me?' he said, his thought processes blurred, confused.

'Not interested, *senhor*? You surprise me. What better justice than to have the murdered man's closest friend uncover the crime of passion that killed him. And a respected investigative journalist, as well. Perfect. For our own part, we are sadly and excessively overwhelmed with work to undertake the investigation ourselves.'

'You said a crime of passion. What makes you think so?'

'Because it cannot be anything else, *Senhor* Telford. You understand? Not political. It would not be acceptable if you concocted some political hypothesis.'

'Why should I come up with any hypothesis at all?' said Jack.

'That's a difficult question. Your friend's connections mean that we cannot simply allow the crime to go unpunished, unresolved. Yet, our own internal policies prevent us from doing so. You seemed the obvious choice to help us resolve the problem.'

'Obvious, because…?'

The policemen waved the file under Jack's nose.

'Our friends in the Guardia Civil, and among Spain's own intelligence service, shared some information with us. It was a while ago, when you first arrived in Lisbon.'

'An open file of their own? Intriguing.'

'About a mysterious death in San Sebastián. Many years ago now, but the case is still live. A crime of passion, as it happens.'

'I've no idea what you're talking about,' said Telford; though, he saw it again as if it were yesterday – his hands around Carter-Holt's neck as he held her down beneath the waves.

'How easy it would be, *Senhor* Telford, for us to make a link between the killer in one such crime, in San Sebastián, and the perpetrator of another, now, in Lisbon.'

'And my motive for killing my best friend, as a crime of passion? This is pure nonsense.'

'Not according to this statement.' He opened the file. 'A signed affidavit. From your lover, Lola Santos.'

'Lola? The singer?' Jack almost laughed. She was only half his age, one of Allan's own regular girlfriends. A dangerous liaison, since she was also married to one of the Communist Party's clandestine activists, Adriano Santos. But he doubted the PIDE knew this. Or did they?

'She says that you and Lawrence were both rivals. For her affections. She says you swore you would kill him if you could not have her to yourself.'

Now he did laugh.

'Please,' he said. 'This is too much. On that basis, would it not have made more sense for me to murder her husband? And when did you get this statement, Lieutenant? That's quick work, even for the PIDE.'

Tenente Estéves seemed shaken for the first time. As though he'd not thought of those obvious complications.

'Well, there it is. As I said, the Commodore was an important man. Essential that we should act quickly. We have a motive. We have a suspect. A suspect with a past record. Murder. You could rot in prison. Or you could find us a more acceptable alternative. What do you say, *Senhor* Telford?'

'If you put it so politely,' said Jack. 'I'm happy to ask around. See what I can find out.'

'I don't think you understand the urgency, *senhor*. We need that alternative suspect. Some proof. And we need it within the next seven days. Your friend was a British citizen, after all. Yet, he has died here, within our jurisdiction. The Ambassador is an understanding fellow, but he cannot simply ignore this. As I said, the connections.'

'So, you've made him a promise?'

'Seven days. And then I must hand over any evidence we've discovered. Is that plain?'

'I'm no detective. I can't promise to find this damned suspect. I'm not even sure I believe a word you've said. And, just to add insult to injury, I don't know anything about the circumstances. Poisoned – how? Did anybody bring him food? Was anybody with him when he died? Do I get to see the crime scene – if that's what it is?'

'There's little to tell. Our men picked him up at the Brasileira. Just after one. I asked him some questions. For maybe an hour. Then I left him for a while, in one of the cells. There was a guard outside. Nobody else. When I went back for him, he was dead. Just your friend. And his book.'

'What book'

'Perhaps, if we return to the interview room?'

Jack followed him back upstairs, churning all this over in his head. His friend dead on a slab in the PIDE headquarters. In a locked cell with nobody else present. Carter Dickson couldn't have written it better. Seven days in which to solve the conundrum, or the "evidence" – this nonsense about Lola Santos – handed over to the British authorities, and Jack himself served up on a plate.

But would they take Lola's alleged statement seriously? The Ambassador. Jack wished he had a fiver for every time he'd had to sit through one of those windbag speeches praising the Portuguese regime, while here, on the Rua António Maria Cardoso, one or other of Jack's colleagues or associates was suffering the torments of the PIDE's most skilled torturers. The regime's torturers – Salazar's regime until that old bastard had died, and Caetano had succeeded him as leader of the *Estado Novo*. All politics, of course. Petty bloody politics. So yes, the Ambassador would take it seriously. Allan's somewhat privileged position with the British Council would see to that.

'So, which is it?' he said, when they reached the ground floor corridor. 'This business of not being able to investigate for yourselves. Internal policies? Or overwhelmed with too much work?'

The latter, Jack concluded. They've been running around like rats for days now. Something in the air. I can almost taste it.

'Splitting hairs, *Senhor* Telford.' Back at the table, the lieutenant opened a drawer, took out a copy of Richmal Compton's *Just William*.

'He had this with him when you picked him up?' said Jack. He turned the copy in his hands. Then he opened the book to study the copyright page with its edition dates. George Newnes. First published, May 1925. On the title page, a pencilled dedication. Simple. *To Allan. From happy students.*

'Apparently,' said Estéves. 'At least, he clearly had it when he died.'

Allan Lawrence had strong views about Crompton – a great admirer of his style, claimed he was the most revolutionary writer in the English language. He was almost as fond of quoting from *Just William* as he was from Lorca. A distinct taste for the subversive, even subversion in a children's book.

'He had nothing else? Only the book?'

'Just these.' The lieutenant took a bunch of keys from the drawer. House keys. And the ignition key for Allan's great passion, his racing green MGB Roadster – though, Jack had noticed that he'd not driven it much recently. Still, here was the black leather key fob. 'You need them?'

'Perhaps,' said Jack, and dropped them, jangling, into his jacket pocket. 'And the poison. You said he was poisoned. But did your doctors tell you how? Or with what?'

'The doctors say cyanide. Glass fragment, some blood, inside the mouth. The pinkness of the skin. You see?'

Yes, Jack could see. But, again, he was taken back to his past. It seemed that, today, it was all catching up with him. The cyanide capsule he had left with Chrétien de la Marielle.

'No smell of bitter almonds?'

'They say it is something of a myth, *senhor*. Or, at least, that only certain people have the ability to detect its presence.'

'I still think I'd like to see the cell,' said Jack.

'And so you shall, *senhor* – if you fail to bring me what I need. You'll be able to study the cell at your leisure. Well, perhaps not entirely at leisure.'

'If I do this, it will be for my friend. You understand that, don't you?'

'However you wish to interpret this, *Senhor* Telford. A matter for you entirely.'

'And when will the body be released? Somebody will need to make arrangements for the funeral.'

'All in good time, *senhor*. Meanwhile, if you'd prefer to remain here, I could just hand over our evidence, sooner rather than later.' Jack touched a finger to the patch that covered his scar, his missing left eye. 'Painful memories?' Estéves smiled. 'And I appreciate the word games you like to play each time you visit us here. Sometimes, I sit at home, or in the bar, in the evenings. I amuse myself, remembering them. So, perhaps, you might enjoy this little game too.'

He saw the lieutenant reach beneath the table. A buzzer, loud and harsh. Jack turned, hardly saw the two thugs who hurled themselves through the door, wrestled him to the ground and handcuffed him while, at the same instant, dragging a sackcloth hood over his head.

He guessed they had been driving for thirty minutes. Thirty minutes of darkness, rolling around in the back of a van. Thirty minutes of complete silence, apart from the engine's noise and occasional squeal of tyres as they took a bend too tightly.

Jack had protested, though not for long, and with no response. Then he had fallen into a pit of pure terror. He had no idea what this was all about, but there was a real chance that he would die. He'd almost wet himself and, by the end, was shaking uncontrollably.

Telford was no stranger to physical pain and death. In fact, in many ways, they had frequently been close companions. But he had never lost his fear of either – never quite reached a concordat with them, as many others among his war-zone acquaintances had done. And, apart from the terror, there was his grief.

Allan Lawrence was gone. All this mystery around the circumstances. A real charmer, despite his recently acquired quickness to anger. Good friend. Great times together, playing tennis, out at the Club – though, at half Jack's age, Lawrence had worked hard at throwing the occasional game without the least sign of having done so. His death opened up that pit in Jack's stomach, into which the terror poured like a mud slide. Like losing a son. But the pit itself was aching loneliness.

They hauled him from the van and pulled the hood from his head, just outside a cemetery wall. Where? He had no idea. Driving for thirty minutes but, for all he knew, that could have been in circles.

'You understand the choices we now have, *senhor*?' said *Tenente* Estéves. 'How easy to make one's problems simply disappear.' Then he smiled again. 'But you see? We have a sense of humour after all.' He snapped his fingers, and one of his henchmen unfastened the cuffs.

Jack rubbed at his wrists.

'You went to all this trouble simply to make a point?' he said.

'For emphasis,' said Estéves, and he went to climb back into the van's cab. 'Remember, *Senhor* Telford. Seven days.' He reached beneath the seat, then skimmed something towards him. Jack caught it. A clumsy catch, the pages falling open. The copy of *Just William*.

Jack followed the van's dust cloud along the dirt track towards some houses, found himself in São Julião do Tojal. He knew the place, vaguely, but he had no contacts here. Not yet eight o'clock, a couple of bars already with breakfast customers. But Jack had no money. It wasn't normal to pick up your wallet and spare coins when the PIDE came to call so early. He hadn't even brought his cigarettes; though, he had no qualms about asking for one, in the Portuguese custom, from a man sitting at a café table. Then, he persuaded a taxi driver to take him, on trust, back to the apartment, paid the *taxista*, went straight for the cognac and another smoke – and he didn't stop trembling until both were consumed.

Where to start? he wondered. Whether to start at all. Or, maybe, go straight to the Embassy – though this didn't seem like much of an option. In any case, his curiosity was piqued. And he was deeply angry at Allan's death. No, his murder, he reminded himself. A waste. A stupid, bloody waste.

He changed, then took the keys Estéves had given him, took the book as well, and made his way to Allan's apartment. An elevator descent from the Bairro Alto, down Queimada, around the skirts of the Baixa, then up into the northern sections of the Alfama, to the Rua da Senhora do Monte, just along from the *Miradouro*. The keys gave him easy access; though, he couldn't help noticing the damaged woodwork around the lock. But was it recent? He couldn't tell.

And what was he looking for? He had no idea. There was the strangest sensation that Lawrence would, at any moment, come sauntering out from the kitchen with a couple of glasses in his hand. Jack almost thought it had come to pass, in fact, startled himself as he turned the corner into Allan's living room, caught his reflection in the full-length mirror. Yet, there was simply his own image – the hair turned prematurely grey, so many years earlier; the eye-patch; the surplus weight that he'd been carrying since his mid-forties; and that stupid affectation that he no longer noticed, the massaging of a guilt-ridden right hand by the more innocent left – more innocent, but with the tip of its little finger missing, a souvenir from Vienna.

Beyond the looking-glass, yesterday's papers were strewn across the floor. *Diário de Notícias*; *O Século*; *Portugal Socialista*; and a recent copy of *The Economist*. The headlines were consistent. Another Soviet nuclear test. ABBA still basking in the glow of their Eurovision victory. Franco's official visit to South Africa. Jim Callaghan attacked for promoting arms deals with Chile's new military *junta*. And that picture of Patty Hearst in the act of robbing a San Francisco bank.

The bookcases offered nothing but a reminder of Allan's eclectic tastes. Dickens to *Das Kapital*. Alongside, on a traditional dresser, there were framed photographs. A faded black and white of Allan's mother and father on their wedding day. They'd have to be told, of course. Where were they? Brighton, Jack recalled. And there was a wife. French? Yes, French. Monique. But they were estranged, separated, maybe divorced. Next, a professional portrait photo of Allan himself – his graduation from Southampton's School of Navigation. A slightly older Allan, drinking with some of his chums from the British Seamen's Institute, here in Lisbon – it looked like the Hot Club. And Allan with a group of his students – a bunch of Portuguese officer cadets. Where? Outside the Academia Militar, maybe.

Jack wandered around the remaining rooms, checked in all the obvious places but found nothing out of the ordinary – except, perhaps, the number of painkiller bottles on the bedside table, in the medicine cabinet, and alongside the cooker. The headaches must have been bothering him a lot. But then he remembered the dedication in the book, went back to it again. *To Allan. From happy students.* Not the best phraseology, he noted. His Military Academy English students. And was the book even a recent gift? It was a First Edition, and could have been presented to him at any time. He picked it up again, went to the last sentence, the closing words of the final story, *Jumble.* Then he turned to the beginning. Of course, he thought, it always helps to start at the beginning.

And Jack recalled that Estéves had told him about Allan being picked up at the Bar A Brasileira, after the previous night's dinner party. So, he walked there, asked their favourite waiter, Tomás, whether he'd served *Senhor* Lawrence, and whether he'd been reading, or had a book in his possession.

'*O Poeta?*' said Tomás. The Poet – that was the nickname by which they'd all known Allan, for many years. A lifelong admirer of Fernando Pessoa, and an avid poet himself. 'No, *senhor*. No book. No reading. Just a pretty girl. And, you know, the Lorca. *Por el agua de Granada, sólo reman los suspiros…*' It was a great impersonation, and Tomás smiled, then stopped, looked around. 'But then the spooks came for him. How is he, my friend?'

'I'm afraid he's dead, Tomás,' Jack replied. But he was still thinking about the bloody book.

Friday 19ᵗʰ April 1974

He'd lain awake most of the night and felt as though he'd only just drifted into sleep when more hammering on his door made him start from the sheets as though they were alive with scorpions. Yet, it wasn't the PIDE this time, merely that damned supercilious caretaker with a letter. It was written on the embossed and watermarked notepaper of the British Embassy, on São Francisco de Borja. Jack knew many of the Embassy officials very well, but he didn't recognise the neat handwriting and passed over the formalities, turning straight to the signature.

'My God,' he said, out loud. 'Good God in heaven.'

It was signed: *Ruby Waters (Miss)*.

He was carried straight back, the intervening years crashing away, to that awful day, on the dockside at Alicante, at the end of March '39. There had been a letter shortly after that, too, when he'd arrived in Oran. Her apology for abandoning him, a suggestion that they might "keep in touch" – as though there'd been nothing more between them. He'd ignored it, angry and hurt and alone. Then, one final letter, after the war. She had tracked him to Berlin, asked whether he'd like to meet. He had drafted a dozen replies, each more pathetic than the last, and all of them ultimately destined for the waste basket. Since then, nothing.

Dear Mister Telford

I hope this letter finds you well, and I am writing simply to let you know that I arrived in Lisbon recently to take up a posting here as, you might say, Queen Bee. I requested this posting – it is likely to be my last for the Service, I think – in part, at least, because I knew that you were in the city, also. I apologise if that seems rather forward but I offer the explanation in hope that you might consider a renewal of our acquaintance. I have followed your career with great interest over the years and, in the beginning, wrote a couple of times in the hope of making contact somewhat earlier. I have to assume that the correspondence did not reach you or, perhaps, that I had angered you so intolerably by my refusal to leave Alicante, you simply wanted nothing to do with me.

She finished by suggesting that, if he might be interested in sharing a coffee, he could leave a message for her at the Embassy. But, if not, she would understand perfectly.

Well, he thought, that's bloody decent of her. Then he put his sleep-starved head in his hands. Oh, hell. Isn't this all complicated enough already?

The training arena at the Santarém barracks, sixty-five kilometres northeast of Lisbon, was ripe with the scents of horse sweat, dung and saddle leather. In the centre, three swarthy troopers in shirtsleeves were struggling to control a wild chestnut filly with its left foreleg lashed up by webbing tackle to hobble its frantic efforts to escape. At the same time, an officer – Captain Marcelo, with his tunic and cap cast aside – deployed a sponge attached to a ten-foot pole, seemingly for the purpose of accustoming the beast to being touched and handled. Yet, the filly refused all attempts to pacify her and, after ten minutes, the captain lost patience, tossed aside the pole and, collecting his jacket and hat, gave orders for the troopers to take their charge back to the stables. On the farther side of the ring, six officer cadets were finally able to ride onto the outer track and begin some warm-up exercises at the trot.

'Mister Telford,' said Captain Marcelo, a speaker of perfect English. 'A pleasure to meet you. But I'm sorry about this.' He held up filthy fingers, then wiped them on his jodhpurs before shaking Jack's hand.

'No problem,' Jack smiled. 'And I'm sorry to bother you when you're so busy. I went to the Academy, and they suggested I should speak with you.'

The subaltern at the Academia Militar, in the old Palácio de Bemposta, had been helpful, also an admirer of Commodore Lawrence. It had been one of Allan's understated achievements – that, in addition to his tenure at the Seamen's Institute, the British Council, following a request from the Portuguese military, had appointed him as Lecturer of English to the Academia's Officer Cadets.

'But you seemed to have your hands full,' said Jack.

'In theory, young horses are easier to break in,' Marcelo told him. 'But that one – sometimes, they're just too spirited for ceremonials.'

'Then what? You cashier them?'

'Lord, no,' the Captain laughed. 'In those cases, we change tack and train them for eventing.'

'And the more successful graduates enjoy the rest of their lives doing parades?'

'A few. Depends on their temperament. But most of this intake will end up in Angola. With the Reconnaissance Group.'

Jack had seen the television images, apart from his first-hand experiences. Portugal's savage war against the Angolan liberation movements had been raging for thirteen years, with her armoured units proving ever less effective against the various guerrilla factions. So, the army had turned the Reconnaissance Group back into traditionally mounted cavalry, the Angolan Dragoons – a strategy that seemed to be partially working, though not enough to turn the conflict's tide entirely.

In any case, Portugal's colonial wars were deeply unpopular at home, with most of Jack's associates in Lisbon quietly rooting for the rebels, rather than the army. Meanwhile, more and more young men were coming home in body bags. Young men like these officer cadets, already taking their mounts over the arena's jumps, flights of steps and other obstacles.

'Impressive,' said Jack, as one of the cadets repeatedly swung from his horse's back, then leapt into the saddle again in a continuous series of fluid movements.

'Yes, Mister Telford. But you've not come all this way simply to observe our little performance.'

'That's true, Captain. I'm here in relation to Commodore Lawrence. You knew him quite well, I understand?'

'Knew?' said Marcelo, but Jack sensed that he'd picked up the past tense just a little too quickly, almost as though it was a prepared response.

'I'm afraid he's dead.'

'Sorry to hear that. He was a good man.'

No sign of emotion though, thought Jack.

'He obviously thought a lot of you, too,' he said. 'I understand you appeared as his guest speaker on occasion – his courses at the Academia. Do you mind if I ask you why?'

'Of course not. And it's quite simple. Your country is Portugal's oldest ally. Our units frequently receive visits from Britain's military advisers. Or from the United States. The cadets sometimes lose sight of the reason they need to study English so assiduously. And for the pilots, of course, it's essential. The Commodore asked me, a few times, to give some live examples of the ways in which practical application of the language has been crucial.'

Jack showed him the copy of *Just William*, opened at the page with the handwritten message.

'And this,' he said. 'I don't suppose it might be your writing?'

'As a matter of fact, yes, it is. However did you know?'

It sounded like sarcasm, though Jack had no idea why that might be.

'At the Academia, they told me that you and the Commodore were close. It seemed reasonable to ask.'

'Well,' said the captain, 'I'm pleased to say that my English has improved since those days.'

'It was a while ago, then?'

'Six years, I think. Yes, six.'

'It must have meant a lot to him. He had it with him when he died.'

'It was an important part of our curriculum.' The captain smiled. 'The pilots were only really interested in aviation English. And all the other workbooks and language tapes were supplied by the Americans. But for many of us – well, we enjoyed the Commodore's reading list. And *Just William*? An essay on challenging the established orders, he used to say.'

'That's pretty subversive – for a military academy, isn't it?'

'A modern satire? A book for school children? How could anybody object to that?'

'And this reading list,' said Jack, 'I suppose, your other books might have shared that trait – knowing the Commodore, I mean.'

'The others? Dickens, of course. *Hard Times. Animal Farm*. And we all enjoyed *To Kill a Mockingbird*.'

Jack took back the copy of *Just William*.

'And you've no idea how this one came to be with him when he died?'

'As I say, Mister Telford, it was a favourite of his. Otherwise, I'm afraid I can't help very much.'

Jack thanked him anyway, and Captain Marcelo walked with him to the barracks gate, past an old Daimler Dingo scout vehicle and a more modern Panhard armoured car.

'I hadn't expected the horses,' said Jack. 'Thought you'd all be charging around on these things up here.'

'Oh, in the modern Portuguese army, the cavalry gets to charge around on all manner of beasts.'

They shook hands, and Marcelo wished him good luck, began to walk away. Jack watched him for a moment, then called after him.

'Captain,' he said, and Marcelo turned. 'You wished me good luck. That was nice of you. Though good luck with what, precisely? And it's a strange thing, but you never asked me how or where the Commodore died.'

He could have waited for an answer, but he suspected it wouldn't take him very far. So, he fished in his jacket pocket, took out Allan's car keys, and sauntered out into bright sunshine, where he folded away the waterproof cover from the waiting MGB's windscreen and cockpit. He'd thought long and hard, back at Allan's Alfama apartment, about whether he should borrow the car. But it had been too much of a temptation, making the return journey to Santarém so much easier. And, as he drove down the approach road, through the open barrier, it amused him that the sentry snapped to attention when he saw the union jack fluttering from the car's radio antenna on the racing green front wing.

It was a pleasure to drive, naturally. Great fun. Almost enough to obliterate Telford's many preoccupations. But he faced a busy afternoon and evening. First, a telephone call to Allan's elderly parents in Brighton. He'd already conjured up an anodyne account that he hoped they'd swallow, but he would have to be sensitive on the matter of his possessions – the car, for example – as well as whether and when Allan's body might be flown home.

Then there'd have to be a visit to the Procurator General's office, to find out, diplomatically, how long the PIDE's investigation – his own, of course – might delay release of the corpse.

140

Third, a reputable funeral agent to be advised and put on stand-by for whatever eventuality might arise.

Fourth, a reply to Ruby Waters. He thought it likely that he would politely decline her proposal for a meeting. His priority, obviously, was to find some way of challenging Lola Santos – that bizarre statement she'd given to the PIDE lieutenant. But, meanwhile, there was his interview with Captain Marcelo to digest. Jack sensed that he was being deceived by more than just the PIDE, that the captain had been fully expecting his visit. And he was certain, beyond doubt, that this copy of *Just William* held more significance than Marcelo was admitting.

'You must tell me what happened to the boys,' said Ruby.

He'd arranged the meeting, after all, despite his doubts. And despite his less than successful afternoon. The Restaurante A Severa. An uncomfortable first few minutes; though, now marginally more relaxed.

'Fidel and Sergio?' Jack replied, and sipped at his Casal Garcia. 'I lost touch, I'm afraid.' It made his old bones ache, just thinking about it.

'I love your accent, Jack. You've become truly Trans-European, haven't you? But such a shame. About the boys. I was in Paris when the city was liberated. In '44. Long story. And I cried like a baby when Leclerc's Armoured Division came bursting into the Town Hall square. And who should be at their head? All those Spaniards from the Republic's army who'd joined the Free French. To carry on the fight against fascism. And there they were, at the beginning of the end. Tanks painted with all those names we knew so well. *Durruti* and *Teruel*. I thought they might have been there too – Sergio and Fidel – but I didn't see them. I asked; though, nobody knew them. They weren't there.'

No, thought Jack, but I was. Yet, why on Earth might she have even thought to look for Jack Telford there, with Leclerc's troops? Why, indeed?

'As I say, I lost track of them,' he lied. 'Lots of men got away. To Argentina and other places.'

She looked at him quizzically.

'Argentina, Jack?' She almost laughed. 'Sergio Sifre and Fidel Constantino?'

'Well, as I say… Anyway, here we are. You've been to Lisbon before, I take it?'

I would have recognised her anywhere, he realised. The same pixie face; the centre parting to her wavy hair; though, now peppered with grey; and more wrinkles, naturally, but those simply accentuating the laughter lines around her eyes.

'Once or twice,' she said. 'Though, it would be lovely to have a proper local show me around.'

'I've got some good Portuguese friends. I'm sure one of them would oblige.' But the words somehow made him choke, so that the end of the sentence was almost lost in a sob.

'Why, whatever's the matter, Jack?'

'Nothing,' he said. 'Nothing at all. It's just – well, a friend of mine, a very good friend, as it happens, he was murdered. Only yesterday.'

Was this why he'd agreed to meet her? Looking for pity? Shoulder to cry on? For somebody to talk with, when he had so few others with whom to share his grief? He could, after all, have paid this visit to the Fado house alone. But no. Portugal's most famous folk music held only limited attraction for him and, anyway, he'd decided he might need an accomplice. Or a witness. Something. And Ruby Waters was available.

'Murdered here, in Lisbon? What, a robbery?'

Then he saw a flicker of something cross her face. Did she doubt him? Or did she also consider that he might be implicated? She knew his story, of course. That list of the dead in Spain. I just thank my lucky stars, he thought, that she knows nothing of the others since then. He decided to change the subject.

'It's under investigation,' he told her. 'But how's your Portuguese? It might help me decide who'd be best – to act as your guide.'

'Mister Telford,' she said, with more than a hint of exasperation, 'I would be mortally offended if you chose not to even show me the sights.'

*

Dinner passed pleasantly enough. Reminiscences. Brief and diplomatic updates on their missing thirty-five years. Questions about how his career had begun – after university, but before *The Observer* and the *Mirror*. A couple of years as a cub reporter for the *Rhos Herald* in the depths of North Wales – a couple of years he'd been happy to forget for so many reasons. Depressing, Jack decided, the speed with which you can encapsulate almost half your life. But, at ten, while they were sharing an *arroz doce*, the lights went down.

'You have to go a long way to find a better Fado house than the Severa,' said Jack, as a guitarist and the first singer took up their spotlit positions to polite applause.

'Is she good?'

'Oh, yes.' He smiled. 'She's very good. Her name's Lola Santos. I'll introduce you. Later.'

Jack's reaction to Fado was always the same: the first few songs made the hair stand on the nape of his neck; the fourth, fifth and sixth left him somewhat bored, so that he began to fidget, look around at the couples gazing with desire into each other's eyes; and, after the sixth, nothing but a sense of gloom and suicidal tendency. In addition, among Jack's more radical friends, Fado was now somewhat disparaged – not quite the thing for proponents of liberal ideology.

'It's so romantic,' said Ruby. 'Hard to follow, though. Do you know what the words say, Jack?'

'Yes,' he said, cheerfully. 'She's singing about the true meaning of marriage and about how a man who does not regularly beat his wife is really not a man at all. That's Fado for you, I'm afraid, Ruby.'

Jack had tipped the waiter well for the privilege of access to the dressing room and now he hauled Ruby up the back stairs, along the dark landing, said goodnight to the guitarist as he passed, nodded greetings to the next act – Carlos Zel, another rapidly rising star among the *fadistas* – and pushed into the smoke-filled closet where Lola was still changing while, at the same time, trying to gulp down a glass of white wine.

'In a hurry, Lola, *querida*?' said Jack.

She jumped, dropped the glass, and it shattered on the floor.

'Jack!' She pronounced it like the French, *Jacques*. 'I thought it was you. At the table. You shouldn't be here.'

'Well, we enjoyed your performance so much. Let me introduce an old friend of mine. This is *Senhora* Ruby Waters. Ruby, this is Lola Santos. As you see, she's a famous Fado singer. And a liar.'

'Liar?' Ruby repeated, also in Portuguese. Then in English: 'Jack, doesn't that mean...?'

'Leave, please,' said Lola. 'Please, Jack.'

'Yes, a liar.' He spoke slowly, for Ruby's benefit. And for effect. 'I just told Ruby about my friend, Allan, being murdered.' Lola bit her lip, turned away. 'Ah, you see? News travels fast in Lisbon. But he was Lola's friend too, wasn't he, Lola? More than just a friend. Much more. Bad Lola. Because Lola's also married. To another friend of mine.'

'That's enough, Jack.' Lola Santos was racked by tears. 'Get out,' she spat. 'Now.'

'No, Lola, it's not enough. Because, Ruby, for some reason, Lola has given a statement to the secret police, claiming that she and I were also much more than just friends. And, worse, that I'd threatened to kill Allan.'

'Jack,' said Ruby, 'I've no idea why you brought me here. But I'm leaving. Right now.'

She was angry, and Jack knew she had every right. He'd not quite thought this through.

'They came to my house, Jack,' Lola confessed. 'A PIDE lieutenant.'

'Estéves?' Jack saw that Lola had caught Ruby's attention, that Ruby had stopped edging back out of the room.

'Yes, I think so,' said Lola. 'It was the middle of the night. He made us wake the children. He was playing with them, laughing with them, even though they wouldn't stop crying. And, at the same time, he was telling me about Allan. Poor Allan, Jack. Dead. I still can't believe it.' Tears began to stream down her face. 'Then he talked about Allan and me. Photos, he said. Photos they would share with Adriano. Then promises that they would cut me. In many places. The babies too. If I didn't write that stupid statement. And Adriano's already been interrogated by the PIDE, Jack.'

'Jack,' Ruby whispered, in English again, 'I'm not sure I'm following all this. Is she saying...?'

'Later,' Jack snapped at her, then turned back to Lola. 'He has? That's strange. I was with Adriano the night they took Allan. At the dinner party. He never mentioned it.' It was odd. Normally, those who'd been interrogated and lived to tell the tale would make sure they did exactly that – tell the tale. Unless...

'Why would that be, Lola?'

She shrugged.

'I don't know, but...' It was less than convincing. And then her face froze as she looked over Jack's shoulder. He turned. So did Ruby. The short and stocky figure of Adriano Santos stood in the doorway.

'What are you saying, comrade?' Adriano demanded. It was a good attempt at indignation, yet it sounded to Jack more like guilt.

'You never mentioned that the PIDE had picked you up, Adriano,' said Jack. 'I was asking Lola about it. Because of Lawrence. You heard?'

'I heard. Hard to believe. *O Poeta* – dead.'

Jack saw the look that passed between Adriano and Lola.

Shit, he thought. He already knows. About them.

'Jack,' said Ruby Waters, and touched his arm, 'perhaps, you'd walk me home now.'

'What did you tell them, Adriano?' said Jack.

'You accuse me, Telford?' He blustered into the room, chest out, his face flushed.

Jack had learned that it was always better to retaliate while a potential attack was still developing, while would-be assailants were still simply working themselves up to a frenzy. Yes, he could spend time trying to defuse the situation but this had, all too often, been to his eventual disadvantage.

At sixty-six, he should have known better. He knew that. Yet, his fist jabbed Adriano hard on the tip of the man's nose. He felt the pain and impact stab through his knuckles and wrist. He heard the grind and give of gristle. He saw the blood, the tears squeezed through clenched eyelids. He tasted iron on his tongue as, somehow, he managed to bite his own lip. And he smelled Adriano's aftershave and sweat. Lola's husband fell back, through the doorway, grabbed for the frame to stop himself crashing into the hallway but, by then, Jack had taken him by the lapels, spun him around, ready to smack him again. But Jack couldn't quite deliver the blow, for Lola was hanging on his right arm.

'Mr Telford!' Ruby yelled. 'For goodness sake.'

'I told them nothing,' cried Adriano, and aimed a kick at Jack's crotch. He missed, and Jack swung Lola around so that she slammed into her husband, sent them both sprawling back against a dressing table, scent bottles scattered, talcum powder clouding around them. Outside, somebody was shouting. He heard Ruby call his name again, too. But, by then, he had reached over, slapped Adriano hard. Once. Then again with a back-hander.

'Stop,' said Adriano. 'I had no choice. They threatened to kill the children.'

'I won't ask again, Adriano,' Jack bawled at him. 'What did you tell them? And quick. Otherwise, I take all this to Ferreiro and the Party.'

By and large, Jack had great respect for the Party members he'd met in Lisbon. Oh, there was the usual rash of well-paid intellectuals or professionals with their Mercedes and Porsches. The Orwell thing again. Some more equal than others. But, overall, they were good folk. Sincere. Dedicated to driving out corruption and repression. And, as one of the Party's leading activists in Portugal, Gaspar Ferreiro held great chunks of it together – at huge personal risk.

'No, Telford,' Adriano pleaded with him. 'That will be the end of me.'

He meant politically. Jack knew that. There were no *chekas* here. This wasn't Madrid in the civil war.

'Then, tell me,' said Jack.

'It was just a few names,' said Adriano. 'Unimportant names.' He paused, looked to see whether Jack was satisfied. But Jack had fixed him with his single eye, waited until he'd got the rest of it. 'And the dossier,' Adriano finally conceded. 'I told them about the dossier.'

Saturday 20th April 1974

Yet another night with little sleep. Yet another dossier. A night in which he replayed all those damned conversations in that futile, moronic manner of the insomniac – working through the things he might have asked or said if only he'd been sharp enough to think of them at the time.

Allan's mother and father: the stupid story he'd spun about the death being sudden and as yet unexplained. But Mister Lawrence Senior had been far from satisfied, insisted that he would 'phone the British Embassy himself. Meanwhile, yes, they wanted the body flown home. They would notify the estranged wife, Monique. They would take the next available flight to Lisbon, then make the arrangements themselves. And, no, none of Allan's possessions should be touched. They appreciated his concern, understood that he may have been Allan's friend, but...

At least, thought Jack, that saved me any bother at the Procurator General's office. In the same vein, he'd decided against advising a funeral agent – though, he'd found a couple of likely candidates in case Mr and Mrs Lawrence should need his recommendation on that score. Of course, that would all be somewhat academic if he couldn't find an alternative solution and the PIDE went ahead with the so-called evidence provided by Lola, about Jack being their main person of interest.

So far as Captain Marcelo was concerned, Jack imagined himself probing an obvious font of possibilities. If the captain had signed the book six years before, was that the same year he had graduated from the Academia Militar? Who were his fellow students in that class? Then a conversation about the reading list.

'Yes,' he should have said. 'I understand that *Just William* can be seen as a simple children's book. But *Animal Farm*? And Harper Lee. *Mockingbird* is, after all, a very overt attack on racial inequality, isn't it? That would hardly sit well with the Estado Novo's position on imperialism in Portuguese Africa, for example.

Oh, they might deny it, claim that their imperialism was based on fair treatment for all, but the realities of last year's Wiriyamu Massacre spoke of something entirely different. And *Hard Times* – how did Shaw describe it? *"A passionate revolt against the whole industrial order of the modern world."* Of course, there's the author's fairly silly portrayal of trade unions. 'Though, is that enough, Captain,' he should have said, 'for the regime to see it as anything but radical literature?'

But he hadn't said any of those things, and every time he went over the ground, Jack heard Marcelo in his mind, inventing ever more imaginative responses. Yet, none of them really satisfied Jack's curiosity. How had Lawrence got away, for so long, with the dissemination of liberal propaganda, here in one of Europe's most repressive dictatorships? Right at the heart of that regime, in fact. Come to that, *why* had Lawrence risked so much on this account? There were signs of hope for a new Europe, naturally; signs that the enlarged European Community would signal the death-knell for the regimes of Franco's fascist Spain, of the Military Junta's Greece and, by definition, of Caetano's *Estado Novo,* here in Portugal. But it all seemed a long way off, a pipe dream.

Nocturnal meanderings are never so neat in practice, of course. All this was threaded through with snatches of his confrontation with Lola and Adriano Santos.

The dossier. What dossier? Adriano only knew that he'd overheard a conversation between Lawrence and Gaspar Ferreiro, the word *dossier* mentioned. Yet, they had both clammed up when Adriano entered the room and, when he'd asked Gaspar later, the man he'd considered his closest comrade had denied any knowledge of the thing, claimed that Adriano must have misheard, dismissed him like an idiot.

So, Adriano wasn't trusted, then. And under questioning and threat from Lieutenant Estéves, what harm in mentioning it? Yet, even though he felt betrayed by Gaspar, Adriano hadn't been stupid enough to mention Ferreiro by name. Simply said it was some fellow he didn't recognise. They'd hit him a few times – but nothing that would show. Pressed him for another name. But he'd stuck to his guns. Betraying Ferreiro would be like betraying the entire Party, after all. And the dossier? Well, if it didn't exist, it didn't matter.

Jack's hands still hurt from the encounter, and he couldn't quite get the smell of Adriano's aftershave from his nostrils. *Old Spice.* Which brought him to the final weft in the baleful tapestry – Ruby's furious comments when they'd eventually left the Severa. Did he not recall how much she deplored violence? Could he truly not have gained the information he seemed to need so badly without resorting to beating that poor man almost to a pulp? It was a gross exaggeration, but Jack was indeed somewhat ashamed – more about the fact that he'd let her witness the assault rather than its actual execution. And there, of course, she had left matters.

'How dare you involve me in all this, Mister Telford,' she'd said. 'What a fool I was to think…'

Jack heard her words for the twentieth time but, on this occasion, there was something different. A background noise. Something out of kilter. He might not even have noticed an hour earlier, while there were still all those night-time sounds of the city, those that did not subside in Lisbon until three-thirty in the morning. Yet, now – soft, splintering sound, followed by a silence too profound to be natural and, at the end, something scraping. Something inside his apartment. An intruder.

It made his skin crawl, his bladder tighten, his armpits ooze with acrid perspiration. He seriously considered the option of slipping from the bed and hiding underneath, and he cursed himself for possessing no weapon. Jack kept a small box of tools for everyday repairs, but that lay in a hall cupboard and, by the time he'd found it, rummaged for a hammer or something equally lethal, he could be dead himself.

He thought he heard a footstep, finally swung his feet onto the bedroom tiles, tiptoed to the open door. His lightweight cotton pyjamas were unlikely to provide much protection, either, but he also couldn't risk dragging something more substantial from the wardrobe. Slowly, he peered into the hallway, which also served as dining area and library. At the far end was his living room, his study, and there he could see a dim light moving in the darkness.

In the short time he'd been here, there was never a problem with theft. It was a third-floor apartment and the street door was well protected. So, this was an audacious raid. No casual burglary. But there was plenty in the study he'd rather not lose or see damaged. In the drawers, which he could now hear being carefully opened, searched, closed again. Something specific being sought. And, because it had been so recently in his head, he thought once more about the dossier. Coincidence? Telford didn't believe in coincidence.

'*Você é muito cedo*,' he called. You're too early. '*O dossier.* I've not found it yet.'

Silence.

Jack readied himself for an attack. But the silence simply continued and, after several minutes, he looked down the corridor again. No light. He crept along the familiar hall, pausing often to listen. Still nothing. He arrived at the living room door, reached around the corner until he found the light switch. He was dazzled for a second but when his eye adjusted to the brightness, there was no trace of his burglar. No more than one desk drawer left slightly open, and the wooden shutter, with its broken catch, swinging on its hinges.

Since he had come to Lisbon, Jack couldn't recall anybody telling him that they'd visited the PIDE building of their own accord. There wasn't even a reception desk, for goodness sake, and when he had pressed a bell for several minutes, it was a confused agent who came to see what all the fuss was about.

Lieutenant Estéves seemed equally surprised to see him.

'I thought I should let you know,' said Jack. 'There was an intruder in my apartment. Last night.'

'I'm sorry, *Senhor* Telford, but – I don't understand why you've come to me with this.'

'I thought I'd better chat with Lola Santos, *Tenente*. I was curious about this affair that she and I seem to have enjoyed.'

'She claimed she'd made the statement under duress, I suppose?'

Oh, thought Jack, it would be so easy to say yes. To say I had a new statement from her. And then where would you be, Lola, my dear?

'No, not at all,' Jack smiled. 'And you can imagine how badly I felt that the whole thing had slipped my mind so easily.'

'I'm glad you both understand the realities of life. But this intruder?'

'Simply this,' said Jack. 'That Lola told me somebody may also have mentioned a certain dossier to you. And it struck me that you might be more interested in me leading you to this dossier than to the Commodore's killer.'

Estéves shrugged.

'Dossier?' he said. 'I'm afraid you're talking in riddles. Are you sure you heard correctly? And if you'd only just been told about this thing – whatever it may be – why would anybody imagine that you'd already possess it? Besides, I understand that it was especially noisy in the Severa last night.'

'Well,' said Jack, 'there we are. It occurred to me that anybody who'd been following my movements yesterday might just have suspected that I could, perhaps, have found this dossier even before I spoke with Lola. Wrong, of course, as I explained to my intruder. It seemed to satisfy him. And I shall spare you the line about me not having mentioned the Severa, shall I? But, perhaps, you could at least thank your man for having left my place so tidy. Though I've still no idea how he managed to get away so efficiently.'

Jack had a sudden image of Spider-Man.

'I suggest, *Senhor* Telford,' said the lieutenant, 'that you simply get on with the task at hand. The clock is ticking, after all. Ah, but one last thing?'

'Tell me,' said Jack.

'This intruder – did you get his name?'

Jack had recently spent a pleasant evening at the Cinemateca watching a sub-titled Bernard Girard movie, *The Happiness Cage*. Not a brilliant film, as it turned out; though, it had introduced him to an actor he'd not seen before. American, of course. A fellow called Christopher Walken. And Jack had been instantly struck by the similarity between Walken and the man now facing him across the desk, Gaspar Ferreiro. Admittedly, Walken's shock of hair was mousey, while Ferreiro's thatch was pure black. But they shared the same build, the same piercing eyes, the same hint of prettiness about the face, which was at once appealing and disturbing.

Jack had met Gaspar many times. He wasn't as close to him, not by a long chalk, as Allan had been. But impressive, that was how Jack thought of him. An economics graduate, now in his mid-thirties. A man with two lives. Finance Director for Fabrigaz by day and, more privately, often in company of student leaders, metalworkers' union organisers, or the clandestine members of the Portuguese Council for Peace and Cooperation. Association with any of those could have guaranteed him a possibly lethal encounter with the PIDE. But it was Gaspar's involvement with the Portuguese Communist Party that put him most at risk.

Lawrence would never talk to Jack about this in any detail, but it was plain that here was one of the Party's cadres, holding things together while the *de facto* General Secretary, Álvaro Cunhal, remained in exile, now in Paris. It made the point, Jack supposed, for Cunhal had engineered a remarkable escape from Peniche, back in '61. It was almost the stuff of legend. But, by then, Cunhal had already spent twelve years in prison for his beliefs.

'I think we should go and get a coffee, Jack,' said Ferreiro, pronouncing the name much as Lola Santos always did; though, in Gaspar's case, with even greater exaggeration of that Portuguese sibilance that Jack loved so much. 'Better than trying to talk here.'

They took the stairs to the ground floor.

'You know, of course?' said Jack.

'I've heard the stories. Still can't believe it. He was a dear, dear man. But you should have come to me sooner.'

'It was a busy day, Gaspar. And I wasn't sure whether I should involve you. Not until last night, anyway.'

In the square outside, old men were playing chess in the sparse shade of jacarandas that were still awaiting their lavender blossoms while, across the street, the city's street cleaners were washing down the cobbles.

'What about this place again?' Jack pointed at the café where, a couple of weeks earlier, a group of them had gathered, Allan Lawrence included, to watch the Eurovision Song Contest final, broadcast live from the Brighton Dome.

'Are you still lusting over those Swedish girls, Jack?'

'No,' Jack laughed, as they placed their orders. 'Katie Boyle's more my type. Nearer my age too.' The Swedish band had won easily, he had to admit. But he doubted that anybody would hear of ABBA, ever again. Yet he'd thought so about The Beatles. Even so, all those sequins. Too much. 'Anyway, I was secretly rooting for Olivia Newton John.'

'Traitor,' said Gaspar. 'We all thought you'd put money on Paulo.' To be fair, on this point also, the Portuguese entry had done well. *E Depois do Adeus*. 'And if you didn't,' Ferreiro went on, touching the side of his nose and winking, like a conspirator, 'you should have done. You'll be hearing it again before too long.'

'Well, it's difficult to avoid the damned thing. I'm sick to death of it already.'

But he sensed that Gaspar intended something more profound.

'Or am I missing something?' said Jack.

Gaspar waved a hand at him, dismissed the subject.

'Just tell me – what happened to Allan?'

Jack told him the story, all of it, including his exposé of Adriano Santos and the information he'd leaked to Lieutenant Estéves. He finished only as their coffees arrived.

'I'm sorry, Gaspar,' he said, as he took his first sip at the *bica*. 'I'd rather not have broken this to you.'

'Adriano was always loose-lipped. We had quite a few people picked up yesterday. I'd guessed already it must have been Adriano. I suppose, I should be thankful that he didn't drop my name. But if they question him further…'

'And I'm sorry about Allan,' said Jack. 'I know you were close.'

'He was wonderful company, wasn't he?' Gaspar paused, looked away for a moment. 'And well connected. Did he ever tell you the stories about when Salazar died?'

Salazar had ruled Portugal as Prime Minister with a rod of iron since 1932. In '68, he'd fallen from a chair, suffered a cerebral haemorrhage, and been replaced by Marcelo Caetano. All the same, Salazar had lived on until his eventual death in 1970, with his closest advisors allowing him to think he was still in power.

'Allan had heard from some comrades in Madrid,' Gaspar continued. 'They were really pissed off that Salazar had popped his clogs while Franco looks like living on forever. They'd heard about the chair, though – and they'd sent a message to Allan, asking whether he could arrange for Spain to borrow the chair for a while.'

They both laughed.

'And then there was his other friend, that poor bloody German brain specialist from Porto. Huber. The regime flew him to Lisbon to see if he could help. How Allan came to know him, I've no idea. But he can't have been a bad fellow. Told Allan afterwards that it was something of a dilemma. What should he do? Everything he'd read about Salazar screamed at him to let the bastard die. But there was his Hippocratic Oath, his commitment to saving life. Even a life as worthless as that of António de Oliveira Salazar. And that's what we need now, of course. A decent physician who can tell us all about poisons. You're sure that Estéves said cyanide?'

'Yes, certain. They must have given it to him, mustn't they?'

'That doesn't make a lot of sense, either. He was exceptionally well connected. It made him a bit untouchable. Or so we thought. But then there's this deadline they set you. Seven days?'

'And Estéves reminded me this morning. The ticking clock.'

'You've got some balls, comrade. Strolling into the PIDE headquarters to complain. But I can see why Estéves might think that seven days is important. They'll still be following you, I guess.'

'I learnt a few tricks in Spain,' said Jack. 'One or two. And during the war. I think if anybody was tailing me, I would have given them the slip before I came here.'

'Oh, bloody Adriano,' Ferreiro sighed. 'What do you know about the dossier, Jack?'

'Nothing at all. Or even if it exists. Was Adriano telling the truth?'

'As it happens, some of it was meant for you?'

'The massacre?'

For Jack, the penny finally began to drop. Elliott had been in touch again – *World in Action* desperate to do a programme about Angola, about the Wiriyamu Massacre. But from the inside. And Allan had promised Jack that he knew exactly where to find such a source.

'Yes,' said Gaspar. 'The massacre.'

'That enough to get him killed?'

'It was only a small part of the dossier, Jack. The part he meant for you. But the rest – Well, the rest was something of an insurance policy. No, that's not right. More like a bequest.'

'From you? From the Party?'

'No, Jack. From Portugal. To the world.'

'I'm not sure I understand. But Allan had this dossier?'

'I gave it to him myself. You're certain you searched his apartment properly?'

'I'll do it again. His office at the Seamen's Institute, too.'

'You'll be wasting your time, Jack. If the PIDE have been in your apartment, they'll have gone through all the other obvious places. With a fine-tooth comb.' Then Gaspar gripped his arm tight. 'But if you do find it, my friend,' he said, his voice now ice-cold, 'you will make sure that it comes straight back to me, will you not?'

Jack shook his arm free.

'Even the parts meant for me?' he said. He intended sarcasm, but Ferreiro seemed to take the question seriously.

'Even those, Jack. Look, are you still planning to go ahead with this thing tomorrow night?'

Jack had arranged it a week ago. Just a few drinks and a bit of food at his apartment.

'I certainly haven't had time to cancel,' said Jack. 'Do you think anybody will still come? With all this going on?'

'It will serve as something of a wake for Allan, no?' said Gaspar. 'And, maybe, a chance to talk some more. So long as you don't invite the *Comandante*, this time.'

Sunday 21st April 1974

Comandante Fernando da Silva Pais was the PIDE's director-general, its head. And Jack had taken great delight in inviting the man to one of his social gatherings – much to the discomfort of Jack's other guests. He had once succeeded in interviewing Silva Pais and – smoothly, of course – asked after the man's family.

'All well, I hope, Commander?' he'd said.

It was a barbed question because, though it wasn't public knowledge, the man's daughter, Annie da Silva Pais, had run off with a Swiss diplomat to join the Cuban Revolution and, ever since, she'd been working as one of Fidel Castro's personal interpreters. Yet, Jack had done his research. He was close to things, that way. But no, *Comandante* Fernando da Silva Pais hadn't been on Jack's guest list for tonight – although, Miss Ruby Waters had most definitely received a belated invitation. Delivered to the Embassy by Jack, in person, that very morning. Sunday or no Sunday, he'd told the sentry, it was imperative that Miss Waters received the note as quickly as possible.

'And yes,' said Jack. 'I appreciate that it's only eight o'clock, but I was up early.'

It had been one of the most difficult things to write. An apology for the other night; though, without any sense of grovelling. And yes, of course, he recalled her aversion to unnecessary violence very well – admired her for it immensely. Condescending? Yes, he supposed so, but he could barely forgive himself for breaking her trust, and asked to be excused on the basis, first, that he had lived alone and selfishly for far too long and, second, that he was still reeling from the loss of such a close friend. Then an enticement. The offer of a cordial evening in the company of some very amiable *Lisboetas* and, at the same time, something that he wished to share with her – a memento of their time in Spain together. He doubted she would come, but it was worth a try.

From the Embassy, he dropped down to the river, at the old Alcántara deep-water wharves. He turned right, westwards, along the dock road, past the many warehouses, the smell of hemp and copra, tobacco and rum, determined to take his normal Sunday stroll out to Belém. It was his main form of exercise these days, helping to clear the smoker's cough from his early morning lungs. He often had trouble with his knees, though. They plagued him at times, particularly during those already unequal tennis matches with Allan Lawrence. The aches and pains of approaching old age, he assumed. But after a few minutes, he was under the rust-red girders of the Salazar Bridge, and his first uninterrupted view across the Tagus, with its steady procession of ocean-going vessels. Two kilometres to the other side? He supposed so. Views across to Almada, where the huge statue of Christ the King easily rivalled its counterpart in Rio.

Jack wished that he could have shown all this to Ruby Waters. But he couldn't see that happening now. His own fault, naturally, and he buried his self-criticism in a resumé of those anomalies still hovering from yesterday's discussion with Gaspar Ferreiro.

First, the nods and winks about that Eurovision entry. *"You'll be hearing it again, before too long."* Where, in God's name, had Gaspar been? You couldn't move in Lisbon without hearing the damned thing played in every other bar. *E Depois do Adeus*. But, maybe, that was nothing.

So, second: Gaspar's comment about understanding why Estéves might think a seven-day deadline important. Jack had no doubt, now, that this dossier was the thing Estéves truly wanted. It existed – but why? A bequest from Portugal to the world? That implied some sort of testament. In the event of what? It was only weeks, back in the middle of March, since an armoured column had rebelled against the government, driven towards Lisbon. Yet, they'd been halted by Caetano's Republican Guard, surrendered without a shot fired. The country had held its breath, because there'd been rumours of a military coup and revolution for months.

Two of the army's leading generals, Spínola and Costa Gomes, had already been sacked. Spínola had even published a book, demanding reform: *Portugal and the Future*. Surely, everybody had thought, after that thwarted rebellion, there'd be reprisals. Yet, nothing. Punishment for the troops directly concerned, naturally, but Caetano had simply mocked those involved, safe in the knowledge that his security forces had their finger on the pulse. "Is that the best they can do?" Caetano had seemed to say.

Now, however, there were new rumours. May Day coming up. Huge demonstrations planned. Maybe, more than just demonstrations. Still ten days away. And if this dossier held any details of the plans for whatever might be on the horizon, perhaps, that made sense of the deadline. If the PIDE had picked up on the potential for May Day as a flashpoint – and it was impossible that they had not – then they would, of course, be anxious to know the opposition's intentions in advance. Anxious, but probably not much more than that. Caetano's arrogance was astonishing. His secret policemen were almost casual about the way they would snatch and torture anybody they thought might be plotting against the regime, then simply toss them back onto the streets at a whim. It was this that allowed Gaspar and his comrades to continue their activities – clandestinely, but only just.

And the cruelties of Portugal's foreign policies were paraded before the world, only thinly disguised as a necessary defence against Communist insurgency.

So, here was the third, and last, of his anomalies: this business of the dossier holding some source materials for Jack on the Wiriyamu Massacre.

FRELIMO, the Mozambique Liberation Front, had been at war with Portugal for ten years in a bid for independence – after 400 years of Portuguese colonisation. Jack had been there, seven years earlier. He'd reported on the conflict several times, with information supplied by his contact, Reinata Nyusi. Offensive and counter-offensive. Reports of casualties were confused. But conservative estimates put civilian deaths at twenty thousand, and fatalities among Portuguese soldiers at, perhaps, three thousand. The official casualty figures were, of course, much lower.

And then, just before Christmas '72, word had started to filter through about a massacre of villagers, at Wiriyamu. A hundred men, women and children. A massacre committed by the Portuguese 6th Commandos. It had been an embarrassment – especially when Caetano's Foreign Minister had visited London the previous summer and been greeted with protests and demonstrations. But, in Jack's view, with so many doubts still hanging in the air, one that Caetano himself had been able to ride easily.

New revelations at this time, though? If they existed, they could just provide a last straw, perhaps. And, for Jack himself, this was manna from heaven, given the apparent *World in Action* interest in the story.

Yet, what did all this mean? If Ferreiro had helped Allan Lawrence to compile the dossier, and the dossier contained material specifically for Jack's use, Allan must have been intending to share those contents with him sooner rather than later. And, to Jack, that spelled one thing only – that the dossier could not be far away. But where? Allan had left no clues, could not have had too much concern about it being discovered accidentally.

Jack began to make a mental note of other places he should check – Allan's locker out at the tennis club, for example. And, so far as the dossier itself was concerned, it seemed that the PIDE had no real idea of its content, only knew about its existence when they'd pulled in Adriano Santos for routine questioning. They would already have known about Allan's affair with Lola, of course. And Santos had mentioned the dossier in connection with Lawrence, either through malice, because he knew about the affair, too – or simply to buy himself some credit with the PIDE. One way or the other, the PIDE had taken Allan for interrogation but, before they'd got too far, and it then being the middle of the night, they'd locked him in the cell where, according to Estéves, he'd been poisoned. If that was true, why had Allan been killed? Jack began to edge towards an uncomfortable conclusion.

It took him a full half-hour to walk from the Salazar Bridge to the Torre de Belém. He loved it there. No finer place, he always thought, than resting in the shade of the old tower's colonnades and watching the river's ebb and flow. And, unusually, today he was not alone. There was a woman. Fifty? Trouser suit. Expensive camera, taking snaps of the Monument to the Discoveries, some way back upriver. He watched the woman. Not Portuguese, he decided.

'Good morning.' He risked the greeting in English. She turned, briefly, but ignored him. '*Bom Dia*,' he tried again, and the woman turned once more.

'I'm sorry,' she said, with a Southern States drawl that could have come straight from *Gone With The Wind*. 'Did you say something?'

'Forgive me, but I was going to suggest that, if you wait another hour, the sun will be this side. It won't be in shadow then.'

'It was the shadows I wanted. Plenty of normal tourist angles already.' She adjusted the enormous zoom lens. 'And with the right filter – there.' A couple more adjustments and she stepped back, framed the monument in one of the colonnade's arches. 'Such a shame, don't you think, that we can't go to the top? The views must be swell.'

'Oh, I've been to the top,' Jack told her. It had been with Lawrence, of course. Allan could get in just about anywhere. 'They're talking about a public viewing platform. One day, maybe.'

'Literally friends in high places,' she said. Then, 'Something funny?'

Jack looked again at the prow-shaped concrete and rose-tinted stone, jutting out from the waterfront – impressive, even from this distance, a good twenty-minute walk back towards the city. It was typical of the Estado Novo. A highly romanticised tribute to

Portuguese colonisation, the base lined by its statues of Vasco de Gama, Magellan, Bartolomeu Dias and the rest, all crowding behind Henry the Navigator up at the front – in that prominent position, Portuguese folk would say quietly, just like Salazar, not through merit but because so many of those others with influence had pushed him to the fore.

'Not really,' said Jack. 'And the photos – for professional purposes?'

'I'm under contract to *Holiday* right now. You know it?'

'You might find this hard to believe, but I wrote for it once.'

'Say, that's some coincidence,' said the woman.

'I don't really believe in coincidence,' Jack told her. No, he thought, I don't, do I? He looked at the woman with fresh eyes. Superficially attractive, high cheekbones. But a harshness around her eyes. The sort of harshness he'd seen before. 'But I'm sorry,' he said, 'should I know you?'

'Well, I'm not Burri, nor Krainin. Not Capa. Not Doisneau.'

'Obviously not. All men. But you could be Eleanor Antin; Shirley Burman; Eva Rubinstein; Kay Lahusen.'

'Impressive,' she said. 'But Lahusen's a lesbian. You think I'm a lesbian – Mister...?'

'I told you,' said Jack, 'I don't believe in coincidence. Shall we stop this?'

'I'm sorry, but did I do something to make you so tetchy, sir?' She stretched out her free hand. 'My name's Mary Lou De Witt. Maybe we need to start over? Gracious me, I seem to have offended you somehow. I was just kidding, you know? About the lesbian thing.'

Jack bit his lip, finally offered his hand. Caution's one thing, he thought, but when the hell did I ever become so eaten up by cynicism.

'No, it's nothing,' he said. It's just – well, I normally have this place to myself. And I lost a close friend recently. I seem to be seeing spooks everywhere, as you might say. My apologies. And yes, start over. Good idea.'

He introduced himself and, a while later, they were sharing coffee and custard tarts, *pasteis de Belém*, among the blue-and-white tiles in the Antiga Confeitaria de Belém, along from the Jerónimos Monastery. Cakes had become one of Jack's passions – a way, he always joked, to bring some sweetness to his life. The *confeitaria* was a tourist trap, of course, but they managed to find a table, swapped pleasantries, backgrounds. She'd not been in Lisbon long, just this short-term assignment. Lisbon for the more discerning American visitor. Emphasis on culture. Perhaps, he could give her a few pointers. And, Lordy, what a heap of luck, meeting another stringer. Pure Texas.

'Now, I might not have a lick of sense for asking this,' she said, 'but you mind telling me what happened?'

She waved her fingers in the general direction of his eye-patch, and he told her the story. One of the stories, anyhow. The one about the swimming accident at San Sebastián. The rocks. His eye. All such a long time ago, though.

'And I really need to be going,' he finally apologised. 'But if you're not busy tonight, why don't you come over to mine? I've got some friends over for drinks. All very informal.'

'Bless you,' said Mary Lou, 'that's awfully nice. And I'd love to come along – if it's not going to cause too much of a ruckus, that is.'

No, not a bother, he told her, gave her the address, the time – and then remembered his invitation to Ruby Waters.

'So, Jack,' said Gaspar Ferreiro, 'here we've been waiting all this time to see you with a woman in your life, and tonight you turn up with two. Don't you British have a saying about that?'

Jack hadn't believed his apartment could hold this many people. Where the hell had they all come from? The air was already thick with a fog of cigarette and cigar smoke.

'That's buses, my friend. And I had no idea they'd both accept.'

It looked as though Ruby was interrogating Mary Lou De Witt intensely; though, they were out on the terrace, surrounded by some of Jack's other guests – as well as all those he couldn't recall having invited at all. A couple of army officers he didn't know from Adam. He needed to ask Ferreiro about them, but Gaspar only seemed interested in the women.

'Tell me again,' he said, 'how you came to meet them both.'

'Suspicious?' Jack laughed. 'No need, Gaspar. I've known Ruby Waters for thirty-five years. From Spain.'

'I'm sure, Jack. And you're certain it's no more than coincidence that she's come back into your life just now? This week.'

I don't believe in coincidence, Jack thought, yet again. But Ruby...

'Well – not coincidence. Not entirely. To be honest, she seems to have got the posting to Lisbon deliberately. You've made me feel rather foolish now, Gaspar. She wanted to renew our acquaintance. That so hard to believe?'

Gaspar pursed his lips.

'And the American woman?'

'You're going to tell me she's with the CIA,' Jack grimaced.

'The PIDE have been employing women for the past ten years. You know that, Jack. And they love to follow the CIA in most things. Why should this woman not be an agent, too? You just met her?'

Jack explained. Yes, another bloody coincidence. Ferreiro urged caution.

'But there are a few things I need to explain,' he said. 'And some people you should meet. I took the liberty of inviting them – I hope you don't mind.'

Jack did mind. He wasn't made of money, after all. He'd hired *Senhora* Fortunata Ventura from across the street to do the catering. She was busy now, scuttling between the kitchen and the large living area, making sure that the guests were fed but frequently catching Jack's eye, darting exasperated shards of anguish at him for his lack of planning. *Merda*, how did he expect her to feed them all?

And then there were the drinks. But those bottles of the Minho's finest Alvarinho, the Dão Nobre *reserva*, and the Alentejo *rosado*, were all disappearing fast, along with his private stock of Warre's white port. There was nothing more he could do for the moment, however, and Gaspar was leading him towards the army officers. But, before they could get there, Ruby Waters pushed through the guests to intercept them.

'Jack,' she said, 'might we have a word?' She looked terse, and Jack hoped she'd not come simply to make a scene. But he introduced her to Ferreiro, who instantly adopted a charm offensive towards her, begged leave to borrow Jack first. Just a few minutes, he promised. And, when she agreed, Jack detoured her courteously into an appropriate circle of conversation. Most of the men in the room had arrived wearing black armbands, and the talk, of course, was all about Allan Lawrence.

'I hope she won't find that too tedious,' said Gaspar. 'She didn't know the Commodore, I don't suppose? Anyway, here we are.' The two army officers. 'Perhaps, gentlemen – somewhere a little more quiet?'

They all shook hands, exchanged names, and Jack took them back past the kitchen to the hallway door and narrow stairs that led up to his private area on the roof. It had been advertised as a roof garden when he'd first rented the apartment; though, there wasn't enough room to swing a small cat. But the view was good.

'It occurred to us, Jack,' said Gaspar, when they'd each lit a smoke, 'that much of what's happened won't make sense unless we give you some additional background. Hipólito, perhaps you'd begin?'

'Before that, *Senhor* Telford,' said the cadaverous cavalry Lieutenant Gouveia, 'I have to say, I'm not entirely happy about this. Gaspar may have vouched for you, but...'

'For heaven's sake,' spat the other lieutenant, the more debonair Abel Romão, 'let's just get on with it. And then get out of here. You know the opposition party here in Portugal, *senhor*?'

'The MDP, yes, of course.'

'You might not be aware that the Democratic Movement also has an arm within the military,' said Romão.

Jack looked at Ferreiro.

'It's not truly much of a secret,' said Gaspar. 'The Armed Forces Movement has been around for a while. Caetano is aware of it. But, as usual, he's happy in the knowledge that the PIDE and his informers are keeping him abreast of developments. Now and again, he takes a head or two. Nothing more.'

'Spínola and Costa Gomes?' Jack asked.

'It wasn't the best moment for the General to publish his book,' said Lieutenant Gouveia.

'And this Armed Forces Movement,' said Jack, 'Spínola's its head, I'm guessing.'

If so, Jack feared it. Spínola had fought as a volunteer for Franco's fascists during the Spanish Civil War, and then served as an observer with Hitler's Wehrmacht at Leningrad.

'That's a bad guess, Jack.' Ferreiro smiled at him. 'Our movement here in Portugal cannot be organised that way. Democracy can only come to us through the will of the military, that's true. But only sitting alongside the will of the people. And the will of the economy. You understand? Change, when it comes, cannot be through a palace revolution.' He squeezed Jack's arm.

'Portugal's true friends in the army, *senhor*,' said Romão, 'understand – *must* understand – that we can only ever be caretakers towards democracy.'

'Caretakers. From what point will you become caretakers, Lieutenant? My God, when has there ever been a military coup that served the needs of the people?'

Ferreiro smiled at him.

'Who said anything about a coup, Jack? In any case, there are just as many officers in the army that we can't trust at all. But everything in good time. There's still the economy to discuss, you know? You'll understand better than any of us what happened in Spain, back in '31.'

'Capital fled the country along with the monarchy. How can you stop that happening here?'

'We have friends, Jack. In Cuba, France, Italy and Germany. Certain deals have been made...'

'The dossier,' said Jack. 'The bequest from Portugal. In case all your other plans go wrong.'

'That's just a part of it. But...'

Ferreiro didn't finish. The door burst open, and there was Ruby Waters.

'What a fabulous view,' she said. 'Oh, I'm so sorry. Have I interrupted something important?'

'Not at all,' said Gaspar, in English. 'We were, as you say, admiring the prospect.'

'The view,' Ruby tried to correct him.

'Perhaps,' Gaspar smiled.

'*Senhor* Telford,' said Lieutenant Gouveia, 'perhaps, we should conclude this another day. But, for now, please remember what we've said. Caretakers. Nothing more.'

The four men shook hands again and the officers began to take their leave, clicked heels, polite nods of the head for Miss Waters.

'There's just one thing,' said Jack. 'Curiosity. But when did you both graduate from the Academy?'

The lieutenants glanced at each other, but it was the taller, skeletal fellow, Gouveia, who answered.

'Six years ago, *senhor*,' he replied. 'The Class of '68. Why do you ask?'

Jack shrugged his shoulders.

'Just curious,' he said.

'And, you and I, Jack...' said Ferreiro. 'Later?'

'Please,' Ruby insisted. 'It was simply that Mister Telford enticed me here with the promise of some memento from our days in Spain. And I need to speak with you, too, Jack.'

'Of course,' Jack told her. 'We should go down again. The library...'

'Spain,' said Ferreiro, and flicked the remains of his cigarette out into the night sky. 'Terrible days. Jack's told me a little about his time there. But he's very secretive. And a memento? If it's not too private, I should love to see it.'

Back down the stairs, Gaspar in the lead, anxious for Ruby's safety on the high risers.

'And how did you find the conversation?' Ferreiro asked her. 'Not too dull, I hope?'

Ruby insisted that it had been fine, yet hung back, turning to touch Jack's leg.

'Caretakers?' she whispered, 'What was all that about? But, Jack, I have to speak with you.'

Yet, by then, they were in the noise-filled hall again, the open plan dining area and bookshelf-lined walls across from them, filling the space between Jack's bedroom and the galley kitchen.

'Just over here,' said Jack, leading them to the nearest shelves and swapping pleasantries with some of the guests huddled around his table. Among them was Mary Lou De Witt.

'Oh, Jack,' she beamed. 'There you are. You've been neglecting me and I'm mighty sore with you. What's that you've got?'

Jack had already taken the battered old sketchbook, with elaborate reverence, from between two large volumes of Luís de Camões. It was an exquisitely private thing. For the past thirty-five years it had been his carefully guarded companion whenever it was reasonably safe to have it with him and, if not, then secured under lock and key, often in the strangest of locations.

He had kept it, he now supposed, against the possibility of this very moment. To be shared with Ruby Waters. It troubled him a little that Ferreiro should be here, too, but not excessively. Whereas the presence of a virtually total stranger – attractive as Mary Lou might be – suddenly seemed insupportable. He saw the look of offended shock on De Witt's face, realised that he was clutching the sketch pad protectively to his chest. Tight to his chest.

'Jack,' he heard Ruby Waters saying to him. It was the most tender of reproaches. 'It's all right, Jack.' There was a tear on her cheek. 'I know what it is.'

But Mary Lou De Witt had snatched up her purse. She looked livid.

'Well, forgive me for intruding,' she snapped. 'I reckon I'll take a rain check on the rest of the evening. I appreciate the invitation, though. Sure, I do.'

Had anybody else noticed the sudden chill? Jack didn't think so. There'd been a couple of turned heads. Nothing much. He was aware of Gaspar offering to help Mary Lou find a taxi, and he recalled leading Ruby to a relatively quiet corner, where she carefully turned the stained and fragile pages, which had once belonged to their friend, Sergio Sifre. She laughed when she came to the images of a Chinese girl, the hand-scribbled lines of Lorca's poem. But then she closed the book.

'Jack,' she looked up at him. 'I've been trying to tell you all night. That woman. I've seen her before. She was at the Embassy, on Friday. With the American Ambassador.'

Monday 22nd April 1974

'I did as you asked, Jack,' said Ruby, as they climbed off the old Number Twenty-Eight tram. 'Though, it raised a few eyebrows. But nobody seemed to know much about her. She was simply introduced to the Ambassador pretty much as you said. A photographer. Here on a cultural mission. She'd been given permission to take a few shots, and then left. Oh, this is the stop for the castle. I remember this.'

'But today,' Jack assured her, 'we'll explore some bits of the Alfama that tourists never get to see.' He steered her over to the terrace, the Miradouro das Portas do Sol, in any case. For that remarkable view down over the terracotta-tiled rooftops to the wide Tagus.

'Looks like a good place to have coffee?' she suggested.

'We've only just started,' Jack laughed. 'Oh, don't tell me – you've turned into one of those old ladies who can't go ten yards without a coffee and toilet stop.'

'How dare you, Mister Telford. It was you, I recall, who was so badly out of breath when we caught the tram.'

'That's the cigarettes, I'm afraid. And you have to give me some leeway today, Ruby, for having been up half the night, finishing my piece. Deadline to meet.'

He'd been in the grubby little studio before dawn, recording, then making arrangements for the tapes to be shipped to London.

'Still not hit the Pulitzer, then?'

He was tempted to tell her how he'd turned one down, in '45, but this was neither the time nor the place.

'Not exactly. But let's go back to Mary Lou. Ferreiro made an interesting point. Women agents in the CIA. You ever come across one?'

The CIA had become something of a *bête noire* for Jack, as for most others on the Left. Their practice of helping to overthrow populist governments in exchange for improved American business interests had almost become old hat, a familiar pattern of replacing democratically elected leaders with ruthless pro-USA dictators. They'd done it in Iran in '53; Guatemala in '54; the Congo in '61; Indonesia in '65; Cambodia in '70; and, of course, in Chile, just the previous year. Poor Allende, thought Jack. Countless others, too.

And that business with Hungary in '56. All apart from their bizarre involvement in Cuba, in Laos, and in Vietnam.

'Well,' said Ruby, 'I probably shouldn't tell you this. But when I was in Athens, there was a woman there. You'd swear butter wouldn't melt in her mouth, Jack. But, my goodness, the stories. She'd served with the OSS during the war. She was with the Agency, I've no doubt of it. And not in a secretarial capacity, either.'

'So, what did you make of Mary Lou?'

'Too young for you, Jack. That's what I made of her. But, look. Do you mind if I get something off my chest? To be frank, I had no intention of attending your little drinks party.'

'Ruby, if this is about the other night...'

'It's partly that. Naturally it is. But your note, Jack – it touched me somehow. I've become far too rigid with age, I'm afraid. I don't suppose either of us is the same person we were, all those years ago. And then, when you showed me Sergio's sketches. You remember, Jack? That beach. Near Alicante.'

'I remember. A few brief moments of sunshine in all that filthy darkness.'

'So, why is that particular day the one I remember so vividly? Well, it doesn't really matter. The important thing is this. I'd like to draw a line, Jack. In the sand, so to speak. On that day. Let's start again, Mister Telford. May we? You'll need to tell me more about whatever it is you've become embroiled with this time. But, apart from that – well, as I say...'

Jack briefly recalled Gaspar Ferreiro's suspicion about what had brought Ruby back into his life at this precise moment, but he dismissed the thought. It wasn't this particular episode in his life he'd struggle to explain – it would be his story about Danielle. But that would have to keep for now.

'There's something I should tell you, though,' he said. 'About Sergio and the *Capitán*.'

'No, Jack.' She bristled, defences coming up. Like the old days. 'A line in the sand must be exactly that. It was sweet of you to keep Sergio's sketches, though. All these years. My goodness.'

There was a twinge of the old jealousy, a vivid recollection from another long-ago day. She had been teasing him, as she'd often done.

Her coquettish taunt that she may one day marry *Capitán* Fidel Constantino. '*Bear him many fine children*,' she had said. '*Settle down somewhere peaceful. A pretty little place. Dorset, perhaps. Cottage garden. Wildflowers everywhere*.'

'Come on,' said Jack, 'this way.'

He led her down the flight of sloping steps, the Rua Norberto de Araújo, into the maze of streets beyond. Up and down narrow thoroughfares, winding their way through waves of washing, woodsmoke and cooking smells, barking dogs, suspicious glances from the etched and ebony-eyed women, from their curious children, until they reached the Church of Santo Estêvão. Another *miradouro*. Another fine view of the river. They chatted about the architecture. All the normal things. And they stopped often to take water at the fountains, to complain about their aching limbs, the curse of encroaching old age. Then, in the Rua dos Remédios, they finally surrendered to the temptation of a small bar, with shaded tables outside, a cool breeze wafting up towards them. Cold beer.

'This is good.' Ruby sipped through the froth. 'But I need to be back at work this afternoon, Jack. And you look as though you could do with catching up on some sleep.'

Jack took his handkerchief, wiped the sweat from beneath the edge of his eye-patch.

'And you want to know about Allan Lawrence,' he said.

'I found out a great deal about Commodore Lawrence from your friends last night. But the dossier – and those young army officers. What is the mystery here, Mister Telford?'

'The two lieutenants I can now explain, I think. The Portuguese opposition, it seems, includes a substantial force within the military. Dangerous. They call themselves the Armed Forces Movement. But Caetano doesn't appear too worried by them. And my good friend, Allan Lawrence, seems to have played some part in politicising them. Yes, I know. But he's been teaching at the Academia Militar and apparently using every subversive text available.'

'*Animal Farm*?' she laughed.

'Good guess. And quite how much that's helped to influence those officer cadets themselves, I've no idea. But he must have had many friends in very high places to pull that off.'

'Did that get him killed? Is that what you think, Jack?'

'I don't believe so. But this dossier – that's a different matter. And, Ruby, I hate to ask you. I just need to know – how much of this might have to go back to the Embassy?'

He expected an eruption, yet it didn't materialise. Only a difficult silence.

'I rather respect the fact that you appreciate my dilemma, Jack,' she said at last. 'Duty came between us once before, and I should hate that to happen again.'

'But you can't ignore your responsibilities any more than I can.'

'Besides – and I never thought I'd hear myself saying this – there's my pension to consider. Well, I'm glad you find that funny, Mister Telford. Anyway, perhaps I might offer you a token. The office gossip. Caetano himself may not be too concerned about the Opposition's activities, but some of his diplomats certainly are. Rumours, Jack.'

'About May Day.'

'And those rumours are causing ripples at the Embassy too.'

'Panic about what happens to British business interests in Portugal if there's a change of regime,' said Jack. 'I can imagine.'

'Is that what we're talking about, Jack? Some attempt to overthrow the Estado Novo?'

Jack was suddenly on his guard, recollections of Ferreiro's words: *"Change, when it comes, cannot be through a palace revolution."* No? he wondered. Then, what sort of revolution, precisely?

'I've really no idea,' he said. 'But let's suppose you're right. Hypothetically. The threat to British business?'

'No,' she murmured. 'Not that at all. Something far more important. Look, this is serious intelligence. You can't use it. Off the record stuff. Simply a token, as I've said. Between you and me.'

He spread his hands.

'Fine,' he said.

'During the war, Jack, two things happened. First, Britain borrowed heavily from the Bank of Portugal. The debt was – still is – colossal. Second, because of Portugal's neutrality, the Nazis smuggled enormous quantities of gold here. You can imagine where that gold came from, can't you? And, at the end of the war, the Allies had a policy of recovering all Nazi gold and restoring it, wherever possible, to the countries and victims from whom it had been stolen.'

'I remember it vividly,' said Jack. 'I spent some time in Berlin, after the war, with the Monuments and Fine Arts folk. There were still hundreds of them all over Europe, putting some of that bullion and artwork back where it belonged.'

'But they never came to Portugal, Jack. We made sure that Portugal should be treated as an exception.'

'A blind eye turned to her gold reserves in exchange for a deal on Britain's debt?' he said. It made sense.

'It was a deal that both Salazar and Caetano have been happy with.'

'But if there should happen to be a change of government...'

'A new regime, leaning more towards handing over the Nazi gold, whatever's left of it, while insisting, at the same time, that Britain's debt should be paid in full – well, you can see where that might lead.'

He could, indeed. Britain already in the grip of economic crisis, three-day week, power cuts, this threat of petrol rationing, strikes galore.

'It could tip the balance, Jack,' she said.

'Gaspar – Ferreiro,' said Jack, 'he describes this dossier as a bequest, some sort of testament about Portugal's secrets. I'm guessing it may contain some of their plans, justifications for whatever they're plotting. And more – some idea that, if these plans don't work out, whatever's in the dossier might damage the Estado Novo just enough for the next attempt to be more successful. This thing you've just told me, that would damage them too, wouldn't it? Nazi gold. Like a buried treasure map.'

'But it would damage Britain just as much, Jack. And, perhaps, that's why they entrusted it to your friend. Have you thought of that? Such a dossier, revealed by a prominent British citizen – that would carry a lot of clout, wouldn't it?'

'And there was me,' said Jack, 'convinced that your being here in Lisbon really was just a coincidence, Ruby. Am I being played, again?'

She set down her glass, placed her hand gently on his arm.

'It's just this, my dear. That, if you manage to uncover this damned dossier, there may be worse options than letting the Embassy know about it. I'm sure we could sort something out. We're due for a Ministerial visit quite soon. Maybe, hand it to one of the MPs – somebody you'd trust. I'm just afraid, Jack. If it's already taken one life, I don't want it to take another.'

It had been a strange couple of hours. Ancient archways, tiled walls, the old Jewish quarter, interlaced with their exploration of more recent mysteries: cyanide poisoning, and its possible administration to Allan Lawrence in a locked cell; the certainty that the poison could only have been administered to him by the PIDE themselves; the incongruity of their denial; the potential significance of *Just William*; the obvious link between rumours of further unrest and the PIDE's need to find the dossier.

In this way, they came down towards the cathedral, the Sé de Lisboa, and heard the first sounds of a noisy demonstration. They followed the sheer limestone flank of the church, past orange trees, to the road junction just below the cathedral steps, where tourists were busily taking snaps of riotous students – flared trousers and beards; girls in bright Bohemian dresses and sandals; a young hippy with a loud hailer, bellowing Maoist slogans through howling electronic feedback; placards; chanting; a drum band; and whistles. Deafening.

'Bloody Maoists,' Jack shouted over the din.

'Students, Jack,' she laughed. 'You were young and impetuous once, weren't you?'

He would have commented but, by then, there were sirens from all directions. Behind them, in the Cruzes da Sé, black vans screeched to a halt, disgorged units of the regime's anti-riot shock police. A cordon was already forming, men with shields and batons, helmets and Alsatian dogs while, further back, a water canon came trundling up the road.

'We need to get out of here,' Jack yelled, and pulled Ruby towards the cathedral's entrance, where the tourists were still clicking their cameras, despite the efforts of some Republican Guardsmen – like science fiction star-troopers in their face masks – trying to push them back into the church itself.

The students weren't especially numerous – perhaps, two hundred in all – but, by the time Jack and Ruby reached the steps, the demonstrators were already hemmed in by police lines across each of the three streets that met here in the Y-junction. A couple of the young women tried to escape through the grey uniforms on the Largo da Sé but they were beaten savagely, Jack saw, not with the wooden batons themselves, but with the metal grips, gashing them bloody. Some of the lads ran forward, hurling stones and bottles while, on the small plateau outside the cathedral doors, some of the tourists began screaming, panic setting in as the scene turned ever more ugly.

'Inside?' Ruby cried, but Jack shook his head. They were now, themselves, in an impossible position.

The tourists were pressed up against the portico, penned by the paramilitary guardsmen, and being manhandled inside, out of harm's way, but also beyond bearing witness to the violence now unleashed on the protestors. Jack and Ruby were only metres from the cathedral's interior, but unable to penetrate the detachment of policemen separating them from sanctuary.

'Hey, let this woman through,' he said, but they ignored him and, not for the first time, Jack found himself wondering how these animals could possibly have anything in common with the Portuguese he had come to so admire. It was a familiar feeling from his time in Spain.

By now, the shock police were advancing on all fronts, shields raised, missiles bouncing against them, occasionally penetrating their ranks, finding a target. Yet, these were minor victories, for the police lines soon stopped, regrouped and, at their rear, Jack could see new weapons being deployed.

'My God,' said Ruby. 'Tear gas.'

The canisters, lobbed into the air, fell into the demonstration's centre, billowed smoke and created chaos. Within seconds, he could hear people coughing, yelling with the pain. Some of the students pulled bandanas or scarves up around their faces, while others were caught unawares, inhaling the irritant shards of noxious CS2.

'Hey,' Jack shouted again at one of the guardsmen.

They'd now succeeded in getting most of the tourists through the doors, but that didn't help Jack.

The fellow turned, pressed a gloved hand against Jack's chest and shoved him back, so that he stumbled down the first couple of steps. He scrambled to his knees, Ruby coming to help him, and he pulled the handkerchief from his pocket. 'Quick,' he said, 'tie this round your nose and mouth.'

Then the vapour reached him, curling tentacled wisps of the stuff. It felt like he'd taken a lung full of fire. The taste on his tongue was bitter, pungent. He gagged. He thought he was going to vomit. And then his eye began to feel like it was pierced by needles. The pain was excruciating. He was drowning, gasping for breath. Every breath burned more, suffocating him. He tried to rub his face, but felt Ruby grip his wrists.

'No, Jack,' she cried, coughing and choking, too, despite the makeshift mask. 'Don't rub it. Come on, we've got to get out of here.'

She was pulling at him and, through it all, he could hear the anguish of those suffering the full brunt of police brutality. The guardsmen on the plateau had left a couple of men to keep the tourists within, while the rest charged down the steps, almost trampling Jack and Ruby in the process, and adding their own individual violence to the carnage below.

Snot gushed from his nose and wouldn't stop. Through the blur of his vision, Jack saw that some of the students were escaping, staggering off down the streets, helping each other to get clear. And there, waiting for them, just beyond the smoke, were the PIDE agents. Unmistakable. They could have been extras from one of those '40s and '50s Gestapo movies, *Odette* or *13 Rue Madeleine*. They had spray cans of their own, marking the fugitives with indelible red paint – casually, as though raddling their flock after a sheep dip. They would round up the stragglers later. At their own leisure.

Jack was terrified, incapable, fighting in vain to remain calm, lungs still roasting, desperate for just one mouthful of clean air, while Ruby dragged him across the flagstones, her own breath coming in rasping spasms. Yet, she hauled him all the way back down into the Cruzes da Sé, in the direction of those parked riot police vehicles. More PIDE agents here and, among them, Lieutenant Estéves, weaving through the beatings and kickings like a sinuous ferret until, catching sight of Jack and Ruby, he strolled towards them.

'*Senhor* Telford,' said Estéves. 'Just fancy.' He turned, scrutinised Ruby. 'And this – a friend?'

'She's nothing to do with this,' Jack wheezed. 'She's…'

But, by then, Estéves had taken a can from his pocket and sprayed Ruby liberally across her shoulder and defensively raised arm.

At the Embassy, Jack was astonished by the nonchalant reception he received. He wasn't helped by the raging headache with which the CS2 had left him; though, some minor functionary understood Mister Telford's concern. He was certain that, in the circumstances, Miss Waters would be released very soon. A simple misunderstanding, surely. A case of being in the wrong place at the wrong time. No, the Ambassador himself was in Porto today but Mister Telford mustn't worry. The matter would be dealt with urgently. A communiqué to the State Defence Police. Yes, they had the details of Lieutenant Estéves and were certain this would help to expedite matters. Jack raged for a while until, eventually, he was politely escorted from the premises.

From there, he went directly to the PIDE headquarters. As before, he had to wait - pacing, anguished, his vision still gritty and painful – before Estéves granted him an audience.

'I want to see her,' he raged.

'Did you think I sprayed her for pleasure?' said the lieutenant.

Jack and Ruby had been at a fountain, dousing their heads in cold water, when the PIDE car had come skidding up the road, the agents knocking Jack aside as they'd bundled Ruby into the back seat.

'Why? Why take her, not me?'

'She's perfectly safe,' said Estéves. 'For now.'

Jack noticed a muscle twitching constantly along the lieutenant's jaw. He'd not seen that during their previous encounters and there was an unaccustomed tension about the man, some of his *sang-froid* dissipated.

'What the hell do you mean? She's a member of the British Embassy staff. You've no right to hold her.'

'I don't see any representative of our friends at the British Embassy here to argue your case, *Senhor* Telford. But I'm sure the Ambassador will remind my superiors of your friend's status in due course. We're incredibly busy at the moment, though, as you've seen.

It could be several days before we're able to work out exactly where the lady in question is being held.'

'She's not here?'

'Truly, I have no idea.' The lieutenant's response was impatient. 'That was an illegal assembly, after all, and there were many arrests.'

'Miss Waters had nothing to do with the demonstration, Lieutenant. You know damned well she didn't.'

'I know nothing of the sort. Not until we've interviewed her. And, by then, anything might have happened. You take my drift, *senhor*? It would be a tragedy if your Miss Waters should happen to suffer the same fate as poor Commodore Lawrence – simply because you failed to complete your investigations on time.'

'For pity's sake,' said Jack, 'if you don't respect her position at the Embassy, you might at least give some consideration to her age. She's almost sixty, man. She could be your mother.'

'My mother would have more sense than to get involved with some communist protest.'

'But that's not why you picked her up, is it? I've got your message about this so-called investigation, Lieutenant. Loud and clear. You'll gain nothing more by keeping her.'

'It really isn't a matter of what I might gain, my friend. More a question of what you may lose.'

'Some day, Estéves...' Jack began, but the lieutenant quickly opened the office door, held up a hand to silence him.

'Please, *Senhor* Telford,' he said, 'a hasty threat is long lamented.'

Jack blustered past him, stopped in the foyer to light a cigarette, steady his nerves, and his trembling hands. But, as he left the building, a couple of PIDE agents were entering and, involuntarily, Jack almost greeted one of them. He knew the man's face, though he couldn't quite place from where that might have been. His previous visits here? He thought not. The thugs who'd bundled him into the van? No, he'd remember those two Charlies for a long time. Somewhere else. And the fellow deliberately avoided any eye contact with him, simply shouldered Jack aside and disappeared down the corridor.

He knew he mustn't panic now, but Jack was riddled by guilt at Ruby's kidnapping. Because that's what it was. And while the tales of men tortured and abused in the PIDE cells were told aloud, and with passion, the fates of women prisoners were only ever whispered, quietly, in the darkest corners. He needed answers, and he could think of nobody else who might provide them than Gaspar Ferreiro. It was Gaspar who had helped compile this bloody dossier, after all.

Had Ruby been correct? Did it contain details of Nazi gold and British debt that just about everybody would want buried? Or did it have clues – more than clues, maybe – of whatever the regime's opposition might be planning? And did Ferreiro have some inkling about where Allan Lawrence might have hidden it? But Ferreiro was neither at his office nor at home. Nobody knew his whereabouts. He had gone to ground.

There was only one lead left to follow, and that was Allan's locker at the Lisbon Tennis Club. So, he went to pick up the MGB again, with only the merest twinge of guilt about using it, and drove out to Monsanto.

The staff at the club had heard the news but were reluctant to allow the Commodore's locker to be searched without some legal authorisation. Jack played the PIDE card again; though, it didn't help on this occasion, and he had to settle for a compromise by which the Club Secretary would open the locker, allow Jack to see but not touch the contents. It was a waste of time. The locker held nothing but a neatly laundered set of Allan's tennis whites, his tennis shoes, two favourite rackets hanging in their presses, and a thin rain jacket. Nothing else.

Jack drove back into town both dispirited by his lack of progress and plagued by visions of Ruby's incarceration. He thought seriously about 'phoning London. She'd mentioned a forthcoming ministerial visit, had she not? Perhaps, if he could find out who the minister might be – maybe, Sydney Elliott could help. *World in Action* had its own long arm, after all.

Yet, his thoughts annoyingly insisted on returning him, over and over, to that PIDE agent who'd refused to meet his gaze when he left their building. And he was just turning back into the Rua da Senhora do Monte when he worked it out.

*

Later, at the Restaurante A Severa, Jack was careful to stay in the shadows, so that Lola shouldn't see him in the audience. But, perhaps, it wouldn't have mattered. Her singing was awful tonight, the normal exaggerated drama of the Fado diminished by Lola's own raw emotions weeping through the performance. She ended only to a mere ripple of polite and somewhat embarrassed applause, while he tipped the waiter even more than usual, took special care to wait while the acts changed and the landing fell quiet.

He found her, dressed only in a white nylon slip, slumped over her dressing table, still crying.

'What's happened, Lola?' he said from the doorway.

She spun around.

'You,' she spat, through the tears and the running nose. It wasn't a pretty sight. 'Haven't you done enough damage? They came for him again this morning. For Adriano. I can't find out where they've taken him. It looks bad. And all your fault. Yours. You bastard.'

It was hysteria. He understood that.

'My fault because I've not managed to find this bloody dossier, I suppose? But why can't your friend in the PIDE help you find him?'

'What friend?' she said. But the tears had stopped, suddenly. And she'd turned away, could only look at him obliquely, through the mirror. 'I have no friend in the PIDE.'

Jack reached into his inside pocket, took out his cigarettes, his lighter, and a sheet of paper.

'Here,' he said, and held out the packet of *Gigantes*. She took one. He lit it for her. 'And wipe your nose, Lola. You look a state.' Then, while she grabbed a handful of tissues, cleaned herself up, he unfolded the paper. 'This friend.'

It wasn't a bad likeness, and it had only taken him a few minutes to sketch out the details. The lips were thin; the face and head almost impossibly square; the nostrils flared; the eyes small, close together, a slight turn in one of them; and the hair almost a mockery of Hitler's quiff. A man Jack had only seen once before their brief encounter at the PIDE building. That had been at the Severa too. With Allan, to watch Lola, naturally.

Jack had gone to the toilet and, when he'd returned, it had been this man, at the table, threatening Lawrence – or so it had seemed.

But he'd muttered some final drunken nonsense when Jack appeared, then staggered out again. Allan had brushed it aside. Just some drunken hustler, he'd said. Yet, the thing that had struck Jack was the fellow's similarity to a picture he'd recently seen of the real Butch Cassidy. Not a bit like Paul Newman. But square-jawed. Like in this drawing.

Lola barely glanced at it, simply looked up at him, the tears all gone.

'Can we go somewhere else, Jack?' she said.

Tuesday 23rd April 1974

Long past midnight, but the theatre bar at the Trinidade was only just getting lively. Plenty of corners, though, where you could shout at the top of your lungs and not be overheard. Still, it took long enough to get the story out of her, even then. But it had a ring of truth about it.

Lola had been an Alfama street urchin and, like many such girls, she'd been forced to make a living any way she could. Did Jack understand that? Yes, of course he did. And some of the men, she'd said, had been PIDE agents. Not that they talked about it. But everybody knew the PIDE. They'd pick up the girls on some pretence of an arrest, but then…

It was a risky business. All the usual dangers plus the added factor that these were supposed to be the Estado Novo's upholders of Catholic morality. It was more than the girls' lives were worth to even whisper about the PIDE. But there was this one among them. This man, the one that Jack had drawn. Oh, he had some very special needs. Needs that only Lola had been able to satisfy.

'You want to know, Jack?' she said. Jack's interest was certainly piqued but he declined her offer. No, he told her. He just wanted her to get on with the tale. What the hell had any of this to do with Lawrence?

The PIDE officer had sought her out quite regularly, maybe once each month. Even after she'd started to make a name for herself as a singer. Even after she'd married Adriano.

It was like a drug, she insisted. And this man hadn't minded her getting married. Quite the opposite. It was a righteous thing, he reckoned. For a good Catholic girl. God would bless her marriage. So their little business arrangement had continued. How could it not?

Only, then, she had met Lawrence. He'd seen her at one of the bars, singing. Long before she came to the Severa. She'd loved him from the start, spun him all the usual stuff about an unhappy marriage, and Allan had swallowed it – just as Jack knew he, too, at that age, would probably have done. Lola was an attractive woman, even with all the knocks that life had given her. So, they had fallen into a strange quadrangle for a year or more.

Lawrence never talked much about his political involvement in Lisbon, but she'd picked up snippets from Adriano about him, here and there. Until, one night, with Adriano away, she'd asked him openly about it. They'd made love on the rug in Allan's apartment, then held each other, listened to music on his record player. Dylan. Oh, how she worshipped Dylan. Early Dylan. *The Times, They Are a-Changin'*.

And so they were, Lawrence had assured her. But he had also made her realise how deeply he was involved. Far more than her husband. Then, the inevitable promise. *"If anything ever happens to me, if I'm taken…"* It was the book, of course, as Jack had known it would be. Instructions on where to find it. Insistence that he must have it.

'But why?' Jack pressed her. 'Why *Just William*?'

She had no idea, almost forgotten about it. Yet, it had come back into focus that night at the restaurant. The PIDE agent had seen them together and, worse the wear for wine, had approached Allan in a rage. A jealous rage? She couldn't say, and Lawrence hadn't even known that the man existed, but he'd figured that he was with the PIDE. Everybody knew the PIDE, didn't they?

'And this PIDE agent,' said Jack. 'He has a name?'

Vítor, she told him. He had only ever been Vítor. She'd never believed it was his real name. But a sergeant, she thought. And, that night, Allan had demanded to know what was going on. She'd invented a story, and he'd been gracious enough to pretend to accept that as well. Though, a few days later, he'd reminded her. About the book.

That was – well, months ago. Months in which she kept her grubby appointments with the PIDE agent. She'd had to remind him many times that, without her, his special predilections would never be satiated, and that seemed to keep him under control - until, those few short nights before, Vítor had arrived at her door.

He'd taken great delight in telling her that her precious bloody Commodore was in custody. She'd been terrified for Allan's safety, then remembered the book, and been convinced that it must be important. So, she'd used her hold on the agent, persuaded him to break into Allan's flat, find the book, take it to him in his cell. Jack recalled the damage he'd seen, around the lock at Allan's place. But then, Lola told him, just a couple of hours later, Estéves had come calling, broke the news that Allan was dead, demanded that she write the statement, incriminating Jack.

'And now Adriano, Jack,' she said. 'What more can they want?'

'My guess is they were satisfied with his story, Lola. To start with. About him not knowing the man who spoke with me about the dossier. But something's changed. I could sense it in Estéves. And this business of them taking Ruby. All of a sudden, they're under more pressure. They can feel something coming and it's making them jumpy. I hate to say this, but if they've had Adriano since yesterday morning, they'll know now. That it was Ferreiro. That's why he's gone to ground. He's no fool.'

'Why couldn't you just find the damned dossier for them?' she yelled. 'It can't be that important. It's the only way.'

'But I don't know where it is. And, even if I did, I wouldn't be handing it to Estéves, Lola. It seems like – I owe it to Allan. To get it back to Ferreiro.'

'But Adriano…'

'You must forgive me, my dear, if I say that your concern doesn't quite ring true after everything you've told me. Unhappy marriage? And the tricks you've turned for this Vítor. But I guess we can safely conclude that it was Vítor who fed Allan the poison, don't you think?'

It was a huge relief in one way. He'd been plagued by that uncomfortable conclusion since Sunday morning – that, somehow, it must have been the Party that had arranged it. To prevent Lawrence from talking.

'No, Jack. Don't say that,' she sobbed. 'That would be – as though I'd killed him myself. I loved him, Jack, whatever you may think of me.'

'There's no other possibility, Lola. You may have had enough hold to persuade this Vítor to take him the book, but presumably you didn't bother to make sure he kept Lawrence alive? No, I thought not.'

And, in desperation, making himself feel filthy, depraved, he had begged her. For Ruby Waters. Could Lola not see her way clear to one further liaison with the fellow? Persuade him to arrange Ruby's release?

'Well,' she said, without thinking, without even blinking, 'that would, of course, be so much easier if we had the dossier.'

It was almost three in the morning before Jack got home. And he still wasn't sure he had the full story. Certainly not about the book, anyway. What was so special? He fetched it, went through it page by page, scrutinised it for notes, special markings. He even held each of the pages up to the light, on the off-chance there might be something watermarked or invisibly embedded in the paper. Nothing. Just that dedication, written by Captain Marcelo on behalf of his graduation year. There was nothing else for it. He'd have to drive back out to Santarém, ask the captain all those questions he'd failed to think about until after their last meeting.

He didn't remember sleeping, though he must have done; finally got out of bed at eight, then started the rounds of everybody he'd invited to his little *soirée* on Sunday evening, as well as all those he could remember seeing at Allan's own dinner party on the night he'd been taken.

He'd started with those he knew were closest to Ferreiro, explained how urgently he needed to find him. They were sympathetic, naturally, shocked that the PIDE should have snatched Miss Waters. At her age. No offence, of course, but a damned disgrace. Intolerable. And yes, they would make some calls, use whatever limited influence they might possess. It was a similar story everywhere he went. Lots of welcome good intentions, but no tangible results.

By lunchtime, he was bone-tired, and still needed to make the drive out to Santarém – but not without a couple of strong coffees and then *camarões ao alho* with cobs of bread to soak up the chili-spiked hot olive oil. As it happened, his favourite bar for garlic prawns wasn't too far from Allan's apartment and the MGB's parking spot, but he'd only just ordered, his thoughts somewhere else, when he became aware that he had company.

'Well, Mister Telford.'

'Mrs De Witt,' he replied. 'I should have known.'

'You mind?' She pointed to the spare seat at his table.

'Might I order you some prawns? They're very good here.'

'I ain't never developed a taste for garlic, Mister Telford. Makes life mighty difficult for me over here, but I get by. Nice offer, though. And I'd happily share a wine with you.'

'Sorry, I've got a long drive ahead of me. But let me get you a glass.' He shouted to Hugo behind the bar, called for a *vinho verde*. 'And so, Mrs De Witt, what brings you here? More photographs?'

'I'm guessing that your Miss Waters told you she'd seen me at the Embassy. Am I right?'

'Miss Waters doesn't believe in coincidence, it seems, any more than I do.'

'And now she's missing. That's some edge you've got in your voice, Mister Telford. If you don't mind me saying so, you sound a tad like the drowning man too proud to take hold of a life ring.'

'I never appreciated that the CIA's involved with rescue work,' he snapped, ignoring the temptation to make some trite comment on how she'd known Ruby had been taken. And Hugo was at the table, pouring a generous helping of *Orlana*.

'This wine's good,' she smiled. 'But I wonder if you can possibly have any idea of the agency's place in the world.'

'I read the news. Bay of Pigs. Jakarta. 'Nam. Shall I go on?'

'Are you a communist, Mister Telford? Your files are a bit contradictory.'

'If I was a card-carrier, Mary Lou, your files would be very explicit indeed.'

'A fellow-traveller, then. Isn't that how you describe yourselves?'

'I think it's how the Party describes us, actually. I prefer the CIA terminology. Pinko. It has a nice ring. And what about Lawrence? Your files on the Commodore must be interesting.'

'I guess you'd say that. And your British Intelligence certainly thought so. They'd be drawn to him, wouldn't they? That gift for languages. The Cuban ruckus caught us all on the back foot. A guy like your Commodore, he'd have been mighty useful.'

He could have told her a story – about Allan and Cuba, but she wouldn't have appreciated the yarn.

'He was a natural linguist,' said Jack. 'A brilliant one, as you say.'

'Sure,' she said. 'Just a lover of languages. And you still think the PIDE poisoned him? On what evidence, Mister Telford? You're supposed to be an investigative journalist.'

'Until we get a pathologist's report from the Procurator General's office, or his parents arrange a post-mortem back home, we've no way of knowing any different. But, like I said, I've got a long drive ahead. It's wonderful bumping into you again like this, but I really don't have the damned dossier, if that's what you're after.'

'Well, I ain't sure where you may be going, Jack, but it might be worth planning ahead before you make the trip. Lots of places on lockdown just now, they tell me. And the dossier? I doubt there's much in there we don't already know.'

Jack laughed.

'I appreciate the advice,' he said. 'About the trip. How funny if it turned out you were really a travel photographer after all. But I'm guessing that, if the CIA knew so much about the dossier, you'd have shared that with the PIDE by now.'

'You reckon? Well, let me paint you a picture, Jack. And yes, I know you've been here a lot longer than me. It'll be familiar. But I'd like you to look at this picture with fresh eyes. American eyes. Can you do that? Because here's what we see. Go back fifteen years. Portugal's already a basket case. It survives by selling sardines and a few bottles of wine, right? Cheap textiles. But she's got some important African colonies. Good trade for us. Oil, you know? And we're happy with the regime here. There's no other game in town, so far as we're concerned. If there had been, we'd most likely have offered them a deal. Our help to get them into the driving seat, in exchange for a good climate. For American business interests.'

'And for US Containment Policy. Isn't that what you call it? Anywhere a progressive, liberal-leaning government pops up, you panic about the spread of Communism, blockade the place. Oh no, I forgot, you don't like blockade, do you? Sounds too much like an act of war. So, another euphemism. Quarantine. That was Kennedy's take on what you were doing to Cuba. Quarantine. Like those poor bloody Cubans were sick. The virus of socialism. So, build a wall around it, choke it at birth.'

'Gracious me, you're mixing us up with the East Germans and the Ruskies, Mister Telford. But let's stick with Portugal for now. See what happens next. So, Salazar takes his eye off the ball and ends up with liberation movements springing up all over his African colonies. He fouls up, and no matter what help he gets, it's clear he can't win these wars. No way. These wars eat up fifty per cent of Portugal's budget. Productivity drops to the worst in Western Europe. There's almost more Portuguese leaving the country than living in it. Labor unions may be illegal here, but they've got strikes coming out their ears. Our companies, Jack. Big multinationals like ITT, going down the tubes. And it gets no better with Caetano. But you know what? There's no obvious alternative. Normally, we can see somebody. Like talent scouts. That guy, we'd say, he looks good to go. It's a doozy, though. Because there's nobody. Nobody except the opposition.'

'There's always Spínola,' said Jack. 'He's your sort of man, isn't he? Fought for Franco. Friend of Hitler's Germany.'

'Lordy, Jack. Sometimes I think you just ain't got a lick of sense. It was Spínola who fouled up in Angola. Then again in Guinea-Bissau. And have you read this book of his? Heavens, I never saw such a load of phooey. So no, Jack, not Spínola. I want you to hear this, Mister Telford. That we're all working real hard here. Me, the American Ambassador. All of us. To persuade the Secretary of State that we need a different take on this one. Not to do too much by way of helping the Estado Novo out of the fix it's got itself into. So, it might just be important for you to chew on that some. Just in case you find that dossier. Just in case you might be tempted to trade it for Miss Waters. Just in case you ever have a need for that life ring, after all.'

Telford was driving too fast. He slowed, momentarily. Then lost himself again in Mrs De Witt's Texas drawl. She was right. He had absolutely no proof that Allan had been poisoned and, worse, he still had no viable story to tell the Commodore's parents when they arrived. There'd been a message for him. Their flight to Lisbon booked for Thursday. Two days away. But there was no way for Jack to either prove or disprove Estéves's version of events. Just that old logic. Why would the PIDE, of all people, bother denying it if they'd killed him themselves?

For the rest, what was he supposed to believe? That Kissinger and the State Department might, here in Portugal, come down on the side of the good guys for once? Preposterous. No, this was just another ploy. Give him a softer option for handing over the dossier. And, contrary to what De Witt had claimed, there must be powerful stuff inside.

There was only one flaw. That Jack had given up all hope of ever finding it. And he was now considering another plan. Why shouldn't he just compile a dossier of his own? He had the skills. And it wouldn't be the first time. He thought about Berlin. Those tapes he'd made for the World Service. If only they knew! So, when he got back to the apartment, he'd make a start.

But when he arrived at the barracks in Santarém, he was forced to consider Mary Lou's intelligence afresh. Worth 'phoning ahead, she'd told him. Places in lockdown. What was that, anyway? Some prison jargon, he thought. Yet, so it was, here. The approach barrier remained firmly closed to him and the road solidly blocked by an armoured car. The sentries were polite, however. Apologies, but Captain Marcelo wasn't available. Well, what about Lieutenants Gouveia or Romão? Just on the off-chance. The sentries seemed unsure but, no, they said – they thought not. He tried several other angles, but no success.

It was now much later than he'd intended. Bloody Mary Lou De Witt, Jack thought. He felt exhausted, drained, totally depressed. Visions of Ruby Waters, the PIDE cells – images that needed to be buried, and fast. So, he stopped at the first decent-looking bar on the road home, swallowed another *bica*. Mistake. By the time he came out again, it had started to rain, and he realised he had no idea about how to raise the soft top. Another half-hour in the drizzle while he worked it out. He was soaked. Cold. And it was now dark. It had been dark for the past hour and a half. Ten o'clock. Thirty-five miles still to go, give or take. Still tired, despite the coffee. He found himself mesmerized by the wipers; forced his eyes wide, rubbing them frequently. There was traffic; though, not much. Lights occasionally dazzling him. That awful sensation when his head would occasionally jerk forward and he'd know he had dozed. Just a split second. But dangerous.

He took the bend doing fifty. Perhaps, a bit more. He realised it was tighter than he'd thought, and jerked the brake just too sharply. Jack felt the MGB's rear end start to slide. He turned the wheel into the direction of the skid. Textbook. And, too late, he cursed himself for not using the seatbelt. But then he felt, rather than heard, something give, and the rear end snapped away from him, throwing the MGB into a spin.

He let the wheel run through his fingers and the car twisted fast, very fast, anticlockwise, to the left, completely out of control. It jerked a couple of times and then hit the embankment. He thought, stupidly, about Mr and Mrs Lawrence – about how he would explain the damage to them. But, by then, he had hit something. He couldn't see what it was in the dark, but it was enough to flip the vehicle. He had the sensation of time frozen, of complete, eerie silence as he became airborne. There was nothing. A vacuum, a blur, where his thoughts had once been. Upside down, though still in his seat, trying to throw himself sideways, across the handbrake, reaching for the passenger seat – anything to which he might cling.

And then it struck.

Wednesday 24th April 1974

He saw the windscreen shatter, the header rail collapse as it hit the road, the rubber seal whipping around his head, and the wipers torn clean from their wheel box nuts. The bonnet's stripped metal was screeching along the road surface, and the dashboard top ripped loose, sliding back to wedge his right hand between its underside and the steering wheel. Jack could feel his grip failing. His head hit the fabric of the soft top, the road surface beyond, then his left shoulder, twisting him around, dragging and bouncing him until, at last, the MGB ground to a halt. His left hand was free, clutching the seat frame, while the right was still trapped. Blood was oozing from it, lots of blood; though, he felt nothing. Not then. It was just his head. As though he'd been hit with a sledge-hammer. And it was warm, wet.

There was a smell, too. Petrol. He realised that the engine was still running. He had to get out. But with his hand trapped, he couldn't work out how. The car was on its roof, and his legs were still imprisoned in the tight and narrow footwell, his backside hanging somewhere between. One of his feet was caught under the accelerator pedal.

Bloody car! Hard enough to get out of the damned thing when it was parked at the roadside. But, he finally managed to drag the foot free; a contortionist's trick as he tried to kick the driver's door open. No good; though, at least, he could reach the ignition key. Thank Christ they'd had the sense to locate it, there, in the middle of the dash. He reached for the key – but the bastard thing wouldn't turn. Stuck fast. He tried, and tried again. Nothing. And, now, he was afraid. Very afraid.

In truth, he could barely see, there in the gloom, with only the dashboard lights for company. But, wriggling until he was almost on his back, he managed to slowly swing his knees, brace his feet above him, against the drive shaft tunnel and handbrake, then painfully pushed upwards, lifting the car no more than a millimetre or two – but enough to scrape his smashed hand free from under the steering wheel.

He cried out with the pain of it, but at least he was now able to edge his way towards the passenger door, aware that he was already soaked with the petrol oozing along the road surface and through the hood. He reached for the door handle, fingertips just curling around the chrome, levered it down. Nothing.

He stank of petrol now, and he knew it was only a matter of time before a spark from the engine or the electrics might blow the whole thing to hell. He edged forward, took a slightly better grip on the handle, pulled again. And the lever snapped. God-damned bloody idiot, he told himself, remembering that the car was upside down, and that the lever should have been pushed up, not pulled down.

He felt for the window winder, turned it and breathed a sigh of relief when the window slowly began to shift. Bit by bit, until it was fully open. It was the devil's own job to heave himself far enough across, reach out through the open window, and work the door release button from the outside. It did the trick though. The door gave, slowly at first, but then opened fully, and he slithered like a snake out onto the open road, where the headlights carved rainbow-studded beams into the darkness and the rain.

He staggered through the glare, around to the driver's side, just as a truck came around the bend behind him, its lights blazing through the downpour. He waved furiously, both arms flapping, and the lorry driver slammed on his own brakes, hammering on the horn, jolting to a halt with only metres to spare.

Jack's heart was pounding, his legs weak, yet he heaved the MGB's other door open, found the ignition key again and, this time, managed to switch off the engine, but left his own headlights beaming down the road. Then, he sank to his knees, pain burning through his hand, his arm, his shoulder, his head.

The truck driver stayed put for a while, fiddling about in his cab, looking out, peering down at the wreck through his own rain-splashed glass, occasionally poking his head through the side window to shout stupid questions about whether Jack was all right. But he was out of his vehicle now, shining some sort of hand torch, like a bicycle lamp, staring at Jack in disbelief. I must look a bloody mess, he realised.

'It's not as bad as it looks,' Jack shouted. 'But can we get this thing off the road, do you think?'

The driver wandered over, one hand thrust into the pocket of his bib and brace overalls.

'You need a hospital,' said the man.

'Yes, but are you able to tow it off the road?'

'I'll get a rope.' The driver nodded. He looked at Jack, sniffed, then studied the upturned rear axle with the lamp. 'Here's your problem,' said the man. 'Part of the differential. Come through the casing plate. Gear oil every-bloody-where. British engineering! *Merda.*'

Jack was in no position to disagree.

'Can we shift it?' he said.

'Sure,' said the driver. 'But what's this?'

He was peering inside the wheel arch, shining the torch down past the side of the tyre. There was something there, fastened tight to the arch itself with a sort of duct tape, and wired in place, too, top and bottom to the panel bolts. Jack knew, of course. He should have worked it out earlier. Where else would Lawrence have hidden something so valuable other than in his own most precious possession? But his head was swimming and he had to steady himself, cling to the bumper.

'You got a pair of pincers, by any chance?' said Jack.

The former Royal Hospital, now the Hospital São José, had been in the same location since 1492, the year that Columbus sailed off on his first famous voyage of discovery. And it felt, to Jack, as though he'd been waiting almost that long for some attention. He'd caught a glimpse of himself reflected in the admissions window. Gruesome. As if somebody had tipped a bucket of abattoir blood and guts over his head, and that he'd then dipped his hands and arms in a second pail of the same stuff.

Yet, the receptionist hadn't spared him even a glance. He'd been given a number, sent to a seat in a waiting room crowded, even now, long after midnight, and where, once again, nobody seemed to notice him. His head hurt. So did his hands, his shoulders, his neck, his back. Christ, he hurt everywhere. But the dizziness seemed to have passed. There was little chance of losing his place, so he carried the dossier – his handkerchief folded around its spine so he could handle it without getting the buff manilla too fouled up – to the washroom, where a spluttering tap allowed him to gingerly swill away some of the filth from his fingers.

Once more in his seat, he unfastened the string from the cardboard button, glanced inside, careful to keep the contents hidden from other prying eyes, and frequently checking out all corners of the waiting room in the paranoid belief that, even here, he might be observed.

At a cursory examination, it was much as he would have expected. A batch of signed and witnessed statements: victims of terrible torture at the hands of the PIDE; insider observers who'd been present when bodies had been dumped, or fished out of the river; forensic evidence demonstrating PIDE involvement; financial and economic assessments – Nazi gold and its sources, and the links to Britain's wartime debts to Portugal; a fascinating account about the assassination, back in '65, of the exiled "Fearless General" Humberto Delgado, near Badajoz, by a PIDE agent, named here as Casimiro Monteiro; another account, apparently by the same informant, of Monteiro's indiscriminate use of parcel bombs against FRELIMO guerrillas and civilians alike, but in supposedly friendly Tanzania; and page after page of signed declarations from army officers, attesting to the true numbers of Portuguese soldiers killed in Angola, Guinea-Bissau and Mozambique, as well as summary reports, putting the total fatalities among the military at over eight thousand – compared to the several hundred claimed by the regime – and the seriously maimed or injured at fifteen thousand. Civilian casualties? Fifty thousand in Mozambique alone, according to these seemingly reputable sources.

Lots of photos, too, of course. Body bags, and scenes of Portuguese atrocity. Affidavits relating to Wiriyamu. All of it invaluable for Jack's potential *World in Action* piece. And embarrassing to the Estado Novo, without a doubt. But worth all this grief? Worth Allan's death?

The crucial papers were, of course, buried somewhere towards the back. Lists. Names of officers active within the Armed Forces Movement. Some names that Jack knew. Majors Vitor Alves and Otelo Carvalho. Captains Vasco Lourenço and Casanova Ferreira. Communiqués from army units in each of the colonies. A widely developed network. One page even detailed the Movement's objectives and aspirations – their Last Will and Testament to the outside world. Many names that meant nothing to him. Another list, too. More army officers, but marked in red and many with the initials ANP in brackets. Active members of the Acção Nacional Popular, he assumed. Yet, Jack was far too weary and sore to absorb it all. Information overload. And, fascinating as all this might be, he could feel himself nodding off from time to time.

He dozed for a while. Some strange dream about Ruby Waters. And, when he woke, the familiar panic about her fate was back with a vengeance. Then, when he'd been in the waiting room for two hours, with little sign of the queue getting any smaller, he got up, went back to admissions, thanked the woman politely, and told her he thought, maybe, he'd come back another day. She smiled at him, nodded.

He eventually flagged down a taxi prepared to drive him right across the Barrio Alto to the British Hospital on Rua Saraiva de Carvalho. Little England – St. George's Anglican Church; the British Cemetery; and the Estrela Hall Theatre. Private hospital, naturally. Somewhat against the grain for Jack. But he knew he needed treatment. They admitted him with exaggerated politeness while, at the same time, checking that he possessed the means with which to pay for his treatment. A modicum of deference when he mentioned the BBC World Service, open admiration when they received details of his medical insurance, sheer delight when they were able to take his credit card as a hostage against any misfortune.

They tried to separate him from the dossier, of course. And they failed miserably, began to treat him as though he might be more than simply eccentric, like a child. Patronising. But bloody efficient.

They carefully examined and dressed his right hand. Miraculously, nothing broken. Not even his skull. An attractive nurse, with some Eastern Mediterranean accent, Israeli perhaps, cleaned his head wound, too. Jack had expected stitches, but she carefully explained that, instead, she was tying together strands of his hair, from each side of the wound, to close it. He felt each pull, painful, but not too bad. A spot of glue on each of the crossed strands. It would all grow out, in time, naturally, she assured him. And what a good thing he still had such a head of hair. At my age, he thought. Is that what she means? Grey but plentiful. Then, a young doctor checked whether he had lost consciousness or was suffering from memory loss, dizziness, nausea. Lights were shone into his eyes, and his skull was gently explored for swellings. Insistence that Jack must be x-rayed before they could even think of discharging him. And yes, they would call another taxi for him, to get him home.

He clung to the dossier through the x-ray process, and only went back to it while he waited for the results. This time, he turned straight to the final few pages and their clipped attachments. But they made no immediate sense. Some of it seemed to be encoded. A heading: 740501. The First of May? So it seemed. Then, this: *E Depois do Adeus* 23:00. That bloody Eurovision entry again. What the hell? Next, another musical entry: *Grándola, Vila Morena* 00:30. Finally, lists of numbers, lots of them, which could easily be latitude and longitude references. And times, perhaps. Like this: 38.7598 09.1723 03:15; 38.7199 09.2098 03:15; 38.6896 09.1771 03:15; 38.7756 09.1354 03:30; 38.7628 09.1039 03:45.

Jack was still pondering the significance – though, he now thought it was obvious when the Israeli nurse popped her head around the door.

'This way, Mister Telford,' she smiled. 'Doctor Huber is ready for you now.'

'You are a lucky fellow, Mister Telford.' The doctor's accent was almost stereotypical, war movie German, as he peered at the backlit screen, examined each of Jack's x-rays in turn. Left side, right side, top view. 'And would you not care to set down your documents? You might be more comfortable.'

'I think I'll hold on to them, if you don't mind. No offence, Doctor, but they were a bit hard to come by. A stroke of luck, really. So, I suppose you're right.'

Huber went back to the first x-ray, studied the image of the vertebrae closely, then came over to probe behind Jack's ears with unnaturally cold fingertips.

'You may experience some pain and stiffness here for a while. There is a little damage to the tendons and ligaments, but nothing major. I understand there was no actual collision?'

'No, I suppose not. In the sense that I didn't actually smack into anything. Just my head. On the road. And the poor bloody car's finished, of course.'

'Well, I can't give you anything for the car, Mister Telford, but I am happy to discharge you so long as you promise to go home and rest. I can also give you some painkillers. You may need them.'

'Did you prescribe them for Commodore Lawrence, Doctor?'

It was an unfortunate thing that Huber looked so much like Heinrich Himmler. Mid-forties. Wire-rimmed spectacles. Franco-style moustache. But it rather set Jack against him, now that he recalled where he'd heard of him before. And now that he remembered all those pills in Allan's apartment, when he'd first searched it.

'We have met?' said the doctor. 'I do not recall. And Commodore Lawrence was a patient of mine, yes. But what has this to do with your own case?'

Good question, thought Jack. Given that I don't believe in coincidence. Do I?

'Directly? Nothing. At least, I don't think so. But we have mutual friends, it seems. Both in Allan Lawrence and in Gaspar Ferreiro. Close friends. Yet, you don't seem too surprised or shocked at Allan's death.'

'My private emotions are truly none of your concern, Mister Telford. And, professionally, I was only informed yesterday. There seems to be some confusion about the cause of death; though, he was in the custody of the PIDE, I understand. Now, may I write you a prescription or not?'

'Gaspar told me a story about you recently,' said Jack. 'That you were one of the doctors flown here to examine Salazar. That it gave you something of a dilemma.'

'An amusing anecdote, but no dilemma. The Prime Minister had survived a cerebral haemorrhage. But he was in no immediate danger of dying and it was, therefore, my duty to prolong his life to the end of its allotted span. That is my calling. To prolong life wherever that may be possible.'

'But you were in Porto then, I think. I didn't realise you'd moved to Lisbon.'

'A year ago. Just after the time – well, never mind. I am sure there must be other patients waiting for my attention. I shall assume that you do not need the prescription, Mister Telford.'

'Just after the time – what, Doctor? The time Allan Lawrence began to suffer with the headaches. Is that what you meant?'

'I was going to say, just after my father died. Allan was my patient. Confidentiality. You understand that, do you not?'

'I understand that he's dead, Doctor. And I also understand there's something you're not telling me. Allan put the headaches down to stress at work, whatever that means. Was it something else?'

Huber stood, folded his arms across the front of his white laboratory coat, clicked his teeth together continuously while he collected his thoughts.

'He talked about you,' he said, at last, his tone softer now. 'During his consultations with me. Sometimes, when we met outside. He had great respect for you, Mister Telford. And yes, there were the headaches, of course. But the fatigue, also. Some evidence of mood swing. Nausea. Classic symptoms. In the end, I had to instruct him not to drive.' Jack felt himself flush. 'Ah,' said Huber, 'I see. You were driving the Commodore's pride and joy, I suppose? Well, he would have preferred that to seeing it sit and rot.'

'Classic symptoms?' said Jack. 'Of what?'

'You may have been his friend, but there is still patient confidentiality to consider. Whatever his cause of death, I am sure there will be a post mortem.'

'If you'll forgive me for saying so, Doctor, I think anybody else might have assumed that it was something to do with the PIDE. Do you have reason to believe it may have been something else?'

Huber turned his back, shuffled the papers on his desk.

'Why would that be, Mister Telford? And I have no idea. All these questions. Well, I suppose, it does not matter now.' Huber shook his head, turned to face Telford once more. 'But regardless of how our friend actually died, he also had a brain tumour. A particularly malignant one.'

Five in the morning, and he was just getting back to his own apartment. He remembered, just too late, not to slam the door of the taxi so that, when he let himself into the old building, there was the caretaker, the *porteira* informant, peering from around the dingy door of his downstairs lodge. Jack tried to hide the dossier but he didn't imagine the *bufo* would be so well-briefed by the PIDE that he would pay it much heed. But it reminded him that he would need somewhere to hide the thing while he decided what to do next, and while he tried to get cleaned up. To sleep. There was nowhere obvious, but he finally settled on sealing the folder and its contents inside a plastic bag, then carrying it up the narrow stairs to that tiny terrace, which passed for his roof garden.

In truth, it was no more than a modest balcony, projecting from one face of the L-shaped architectural features at each of the building's upper corners, almost set into the roof itself. Both to left and right, white balustrades extended some way – to the next projection on one side, and to the actual corner on the other. These were the balustrades enclosing true terraces for the expensive penthouse apartments. Jack knew that the flat on the northern side, 4D, was empty, and by carefully climbing over his railing, hanging on with one hand, hanging precariously over the street below, he could reach over and slide the dossier, in its waterproof covering, between the first two balusters of the vacant apartment's terrace. He'd just have to hope that nobody would be coming to view the place over the next few hours but, with that done, he went back down, dumped his clothes in the kitchen, and ran a bath.

Now what? he thought, as he soaked in the tub, his cuts and bruises stinging.

He recalled, again, the times that he'd seen Allan over the past year. And yes, there'd been the headaches, an occasional lapse in his usual debonair composure. But brain tumour? The poor bugger. Terminal, perhaps? Huber hadn't said so. Only that it was serious, malignant.

So, Jack felt duty-bound to remember his friend afresh, pushing aside the frequent temptations to mull over the dossier and its contents, remembering the man, wondering how much else there had been in Allan's life that Jack himself had not known. That image of him with Lola Santos. Bob Dylan on the record player. *The Times, They Are a-Changin'.* And so they were, he'd assured her. What had she said? *"But he also made me realise how deeply he was involved. More than my husband. Far more."* How deeply might that have been? Then the strange promise he had compelled her to make. *"If anything ever happens to me, if I'm taken..."* The book. What was so important about an old copy of *Just William*?

Yet, there was something else too. That if the PIDE sergeant, this Vítor, had administered the cyanide to Allan, how had he accomplished that? How easy was it to get hold of cyanide, anyway? These days, at least. He had a brief flashback to Nuremberg, all those years before – though he quickly reburied the memory, and returned to his current conundrum. Jack had only viewed the body briefly, but he felt certain that, had there been any sort of struggle between killer and victim, there would surely have been some sign, some evidence.

An hour later, wrapped in his dressing gown and eating bread with apricot jam in his kitchen, he considered more immediate matters. Recovering the car, for example. There was a garage, just down the road, with a tow truck. He'd walk down there in a while, ask them to sort things out for him. Then, Allan's mother and father. They were due to arrive just the next day. Should he 'phone them, find out whether they already knew about Allan's medical condition? Forewarn them? Tell them about the car, even? Later. Later.

For now, there was only one thing. One big thing. Ruby. And the dossier. How to play this? There was the obvious option: simply head back to Estéves and report his findings so far; about this Vítor; and hand over the dossier. Except that Estéves had never actually admitted that it was the dossier he was after. *"Dossier?"* he'd said. *"I'm afraid you're talking in riddles."* Besides, was he likely to simply accept that it was one of his own men, after all, who'd poisoned Lawrence? A crime of passion, yes. It seemed that Estéves had his wish in that regard; though, it would hardly be the type of passion for which he'd hoped.

Finally, there were the dossier's contents to consider. Handing them over would be a betrayal of all the friends he'd made here. A betrayal of his own beliefs. A betrayal of Allan Lawrence himself if he was, as Lola had said, so very deeply involved. A betrayal, he was convinced, of an opportunity to overthrow the whole of the Estado Novo's stinking regime. But through a military coup? That couldn't be right. Where did military coups ever happen, without the CIA being up to their necks in them, replacing one regime with the USA's own puppet dictators? Could Gaspar, the Party, the whole of the Portugal's opposition movement, truly be chancing their arm on a military takeover?

*

It was Jack's fourth visit to the PIDE headquarters in less than a week. A record, surely, he thought, as he waited for an audience with Director-General Fernando da Silva Pais. He'd been here for an hour already and it was getting late. He wondered, idly, whether the Director kept normal office hours. What did you do, for goodness sake, after a day spent managing a workforce of psychotic torturers and thugs? Go home and have dinner with the wife? Chat over a glass of wine about the rigours of the daily drudge? Feet up, slippers on, watch the TV?

Well, perhaps, he said to himself when he was finally admitted, surprised to find himself alone with the man in the Director's relatively simple office. Florid. Amiable. Army uniform.

'*Comandante*, you may remember that we met a couple of times before. A drinks reception at my apartment. And you were kind enough to allow me to interview you.'

'I know who you are, *Senhor* Telford. Lieutenant Estéves keeps me fully briefed on the case. I bitterly regret that the Commodore should have died while in our custody, and it's no secret that I am not particularly enamoured of the way in which the investigation is being progressed. But there are certain pressures upon us at the moment. You've found our mystery killer, I hope? Completed your task?'

'For the sake of Commodore Lawrence, sir, I shan't insult your intelligence by beating about the bush.'

'That's a shame. It is precisely the game that I thought you enjoyed. Keep your friends close, your enemies closer. I think that's your philosophy. But it's a game that works both ways, is it not? Your little party entertained me as much as my presence must have amused your associates. Useful. It helped me to identify potential assets. Like yourself, *senhor*.'

'I did wonder. It all seemed a bit too easy for Lieutenant Estéves to put me in such a compromised position. To find the Commodore's killer, or take the blame for it myself. But it soon became clear that the hunt might actually be for something else. There was no logic to putting me in the frame for his murder, except that I was close to him. Available. And that, because we were close, I was, perhaps, the person most likely to easily succeed in finding that thing. A certain dossier?'

The Director's feigned surprise was unconvincing.

'A dossier? With relevance to the case in question? How interesting. And you now possess such a dossier?'

'I could have it here for you within five minutes. But, first, you have to show me that Miss Waters is alive and well.'

'*Senhor* Telford,' said da Silva Pais, 'within five minutes, one of my men could persuade you to tell me this mysterious dossier's whereabouts without my Directorate having to barter for it.'

'Then, please proceed, *Comandante*. I'm not a particularly brave individual; though, age has lent me a certain *sang-froid* about the perils of life. But this really is the final throw of my dice so far as Miss Waters is concerned.' And so it was. Jack had been back to the British Embassy twice during the day, certain that, at last, the authorities must have taken action on Ruby's behalf. But nothing. More obfuscation. Everything possible being done through diplomatic channels. Simply a matter of allowing those channels to be followed. 'Miss Waters, you see,' Jack pressed on, 'is the nearest thing I have to a family, I now realise.'

'And why have you not undertaken this negotiation with Lieutenant Estéves, *senhor*?'

'Perhaps, you should read the dossier first, sir. In private.'

'The killer?'

Do you really care? I wonder, thought Jack, but he took a moment before he replied.

'I only know this, *Comandante*. That Lieutenant Estéves believed there was some mystery. Commodore Lawrence locked in a cell, albeit temporarily. Between interviews. Nobody in, nobody out. Classic. Ellery Queen could not have done better. But now I know that wasn't quite the case. One of your agents paid him a visit. I've no idea what his real name might be, but he calls himself Vítor. A sergeant, I think. Whether he killed Lawrence, that I can't say. But he was certainly the last person to see him alive.'

'I should have guessed,' said Jack, as the guard let him into the cell, 'that you'd manage to find a five-star room even in this bloody place.'

He'd rehearsed the line, but then his emotions almost choked off the last few words. And she had flung herself at him, wrapped her arms about his waist, buried her head, the cushioning waves of her hair, into his chest. 'Steady,' he chided, wincing as she pressed against his aching ribs and back. 'I'm too old for this. Brittle bones, you know.'

In truth, he was right. He'd not been taken to the infamous basement but to a wing on the ground floor. This cell was light, reasonably furnished.

'Jack,' she said, holding him now at arms' length, 'please tell me you haven't done something foolish to get in here.'

'Not a lot of choice. Our own Embassy, Ruby. Your employer, for God's sake. And they've done nothing.'

'And you look like hell. As though you've been in the wars.'

He explained. The crash. The discovery. The dossier's content. The trade he'd done with the *Comandante*.

'He's insisted, of course. A chance to examine the dossier in detail. See whether it provides enough information to declare Allan's case closed. Sheer nonsense, naturally. But I'm required to come back tomorrow. Noon. Can you possibly bear to be here until then?'

'But you've no guarantee, Jack, that they'll keep their end of the deal. Why should they? Once they've got the dossier. And what's in the damned thing, anyway? What was so important?'

'It was like Gaspar said. The Last Will and Testament to the outside world from a failed revolution. Or, rather, one that was never going to happen. Naturally, as any good reporter would have done, the best bits I've kept for myself. All the stuff about Wiriyamu. But the rest, Ruby, they can have. It would have been a military coup, my dear. Can you imagine the carnage? And how the Opposition could have been taken in by the idea is just astonishing.'

She let go of his arms. Her face was set, near to tears again.

'Jack, don't do this. Not for me.'

'I'm sorry, my dear, but I've no option.'

He left her, and the guard locked the cell once more. But, outside, on the Rua António Maria Cardoso, he'd gone no more than a block before a car pulled up alongside. A black Mercedes 280S. The back door was flung open.

'Get in, Mister Telford.' It was Mary Lou De Witt.

'Thanks,' said Jack, 'but I prefer to walk. And have you been waiting all this time? I'm really sorry if I've kept you. All for nothing too, I'm afraid.'

'You found it,' she said. 'The dossier?'

'I'm afraid I've no idea what you're talking about. But, if you'll excuse me, I've got a deadline to meet.'

'Jack, don't be a fool. You can't trust these people. Whatever you're planning, it won't work.'

'Too late, I'm afraid. Now...'

'Jack!'

He slammed the car door, crossed quickly and cut down the steps of the Travessa dos Teatro where, he knew, he could lose himself and stand the least chance of being followed. Within two hours, he'd retrieved the dossier and delivered it back to the *Comandante*'s office.

After that, there was nothing to do but wait until tomorrow. Noon. Ruby Waters. And maybe some explanations. But, meanwhile, there was the Bar A Brasileira. There were bottles of wine. There were toasts with Tomás the waiter to the memory of Jack's best friend, Tomás's best customer, Allan Lawrence. There was music that carried him late into the night. And the music, inevitably, included that bloody Eurovision entry. *E Depois do Adeus.* Paulo de Carvalho.

'Tomás,' he just about managed to say, 'what programme's that?'

'Emisores Asociados, *senhor*,' the waiter told him.

Jack peered at his watch, could barely make out the fingers. Ten fifty-five. He laughed.

'Not eleven, then,' he said. 'Not eleven.' And he drowsily began to imagine all manner of things that might have been.

Thursday 25th April 1974, Afternoon

The 'phone was ringing, and though he tried to put his head, his pounding head, under the pillow, the damned thing wouldn't stop. He stumbled out of bed, glanced at the clock. Eleven-thirty. Hell, he was supposed to be back at the PIDE building in half an hour. Was that what the call was for? About his meeting with the *Comandante*? Good news? Bad? He staggered through the hall and dining area, past the kitchen, grabbed the 'phone.

'*Estou*,' Jack shouted. Hello – yes?

'Jack, is that you?' Sydney Elliott's modestly Scots accent on the other end. From London.

'Sydney. What…?'

'Trust you to be in the middle of another revolution. And on your birthday, too.' My birthday? thought Jack. He was confused, pulled himself together. Yes, my birthday. Trust bloody Elliott. Probably got it written on his calendar.

'Thanks,' he said. 'I'd forgotten. But did you say…?'

'How's it going? The Revolution, I mean. Not the birthday. I didn't really think I'd catch you in. Just 'phoned on the off-chance.'

'Revolution? I don't think so. Hang on – I'm just looking out of the window now. It's quiet enough. No, I thought not. No gunfire. Nothing. Somebody's pulling your leg.'

'Don't be bloody stupid, Jack. It's been on the news all morning. Where the hell are you, exactly?'

He slammed the 'phone down, washed and dressed within minutes, didn't bother to shave. From the camphorwood chest in his library, he grabbed the tape recorder in its black leather carrying case, stopped just long enough to check that he had a spare cassette and extra batteries. Ah, the wonders of modern technology and Japanese ingenuity. The Panasonic RQ-421S. He slung the strap across his shoulder and chest, went down the stairs at a reckless speed for a man of his age, and found the caretaker-snitch sitting on the building's front steps, nursing a shiner. Somebody had thumped the little bastard. My God, thought Jack, Elliott must be right.

There was an excited crowd at the tram stop, and they were headed, every one of them, for the Largo do Carmo. It was all going on, they said. There, in the square. Who? he asked. Which side? Nobody seemed to know. Not in detail. But the general consensus was that Caetano was done for.

The small square itself was one of Jack's favourite places in Lisbon. A cut above the bustle of the Chiado district – literally, for it stood near the top of the Santa Justa elevator, on the edge of the Barrio Alto. Normally peaceful, decent bars and cafés, shaded by jacaranda trees, an ornate fountain in the centre. Yet, today, it stood almost empty while, huddled in the side streets at each of its corners, there were packed crowds, noisy but pensive.

'What's going on?' said Jack, to nobody in particular. 'Is it right? Caetano's in the Carmo?' The National Guard barracks was in the top right-hand corner. He'd heard the rumour on the tram, over and over again, that Caetano and other prominent ministers had taken refuge there. And, if so, what did this all mean? In his wildest dreams, he'd never imagined this was possible. The dossier – how had that all played out? Was any of this even vaguely connected to his actions yesterday? Impossible. Crazy.

'Like rats in a trap,' a young woman yelled. One of the Flower Children, Bohemian dress, sheepskin jacket. And the trap now seemed to be closing, one way or the other. A column of armoured cars trundling into the square, a broad and raucous procession following behind, almost surrounding them. Among the newcomers, a face Jack recognised. A local journalist, Abel Guerra, whom he'd met a few times. Short, neat man, with a beard.

'Abel,' Jack shouted. 'Thought I'd missed all the fun. You been here since it started?'

'Somebody was hammering on my door at six,' said Abel. 'I was sure it must be the PIDE. Nearly shit myself. But just my brother. Told me the military had taken over the city. No idea for which side, though. So I got myself off to the Terreiro do Paço. And there they were, in the square. I bumped into one of our photographers, and he knew the captain in charge, Maia. This is his column. That's him.' He pointed at the soldier, combat fatigues and bush cap, holding a loud hailer, standing on the front of his armoured car. Jack thought he looked like Humphrey Bogart. 'He seemed okay,' Abel told him. 'So I went and asked him. Whose side are you on? I said. And he recognised me. Knew about all the trouble I'd had with the censorship and the PIDE. "Well," he said, "let me put it this way – we're doing this so, in future, you'll be able to write and say whatever the hell you like." The bugger almost made me cry, Jack. And you know what? For the first time in my life, I honestly felt like I belonged in my own bloody country.'

Jack couldn't help himself. He threw his arms around the man, hugged him tight. But he was torn. He should be at the PIDE headquarters. For Ruby. What the hell would be going on there, right now? Yet, there was work to do here, as well. The crowds were being kept back by a cordon of soldiers, and the armoured cars had advanced to the northern end of the square, guns trained on the Carmo barracks. But Jack was thinking about the dossier again.

'They played it, didn't they?' he said. 'They played Zeca. At one in the morning?'

Protest singer Zeca Afonso's revolutionary marching song had already become an anthem.

'*Grândola*. Yes. How the hell did you know? I didn't hear it myself but the presenter on Rádio Renascença apparently read out the first line just after midnight, a signal for something to kick off. Everybody who heard it said it was so obviously a message. But can you believe it? Catholic radio station, also. Now, the whole place has gone mad with it. You should have seen the crowds earlier, Jack. Marching down here. The flags. Everybody singing the words.'

'Then, let me guess. They took the Lisbon barracks, the radio and TV studios, the airport – a whole pile of other military objectives. All around three o'clock, right?'

'For somebody who thought he'd missed everything, you're well enough informed, Jack. God bless the BBC, eh? And yes, they made the announcement at four-twenty. Representatives of the MFA. On Rádio Clube Português.'

'That all makes sense. My God, Abel, they did it. And last night. They brought it all forward. Oh, bloody hell. Any more broadcasts since then?'

'One every hour, more or less. Telling everybody to stay calm, stay at home – that sort of stuff. Not that anybody's taking any notice. And what do you mean, brought it forward? Who did?'

Jack ignored the question.

'No opposition?' he said.

'Some, yes. But remarkably little. Apparently some units turned out with orders to attack the MFA troops, to fire on them. Only none of them have done that. Most just surrendered. There was a frigate, also – anchored in the river. Rumours that she was going to fire on the crowds. But nothing. Not a shot. I was on the Arsenal, an hour ago, I guess. And there was this army big-wig. A colonel or something. Trying to get one of his officers to fire on some MFA soldiers who'd blockaded the street. But this officer, he's not having any of it. So the colonel thumps him. Three times. Then he storms off. Never seen anything like it.'

'Civilian casualties?'

'None. Not one.'

Can that be right? thought Jack. And have I got this all so badly wrong? A military coup with no deaths? Christ, this could restore my faith in human nature. Well…

'Listen,' he said, 'I'm going to try to 'phone London.'

There were two telephone boxes, just the other side of the jacarandas, in front of the fountain.

'Are you mad?' said Abel. 'What if there's shooting?'

'It would have happened before now, my friend,' Jack laughed. 'I'll be fine.' And he strolled over to the first box, only to find that the handset had been ripped out. The second looked more hopeful but, when he got there, some bloody Englishman was chatting with his wife about what time he'd be home for dinner. Bizarre. But Jack used the following few minutes getting his recording machine ready. He'd try to phone the BBC direct and make the broadcast down the wire, but he'd record it, too, if possible. Yet he was thwarted again, emptied his pockets of coins so he could make the call, got through to the main switchboard at Bush House and asked for the Portuguese service extension. All lines engaged. Apologies.

'Look,' he said, 'this is important. You must get a message through to them. Tell them it's Telford. That they should 'phone me back on this number. At – let's see – three-fifteen, say? You got that?' He gave them the number and then, outside, he began to record.

"Here in Lisbon's normally tranquil Carmo Square, the people of Portugal are making history. For, today, they will try to overthrow the right-wing regime that's kept them enslaved for the past forty-one years.

"At every corner of the square, in a slight haze of diesel exhaust fumes, I can see hundreds of men and women, even children, handing out food, cigarettes, bottles of milk, to the soldiers who, with their armoured cars, have come to help free them from repression.

"But, in the streets behind the crowds, behind those troops, commanded by Captain Maia, are others – members of Prime Minister Marcelo

Caetano's National Guard, men still loyal to the regime, men under orders to strangle this revolution at birth.

"Caetano himself is currently at bay, there in the Carmo barracks. Nobody knows what else awaits us behind those walls. Will he remain at bay, or will he unleash the National Guardsmen on the people's army?

"And that sound you can hear – there, now – comes from the rotors of a helicopter gunship. On whose side, we do not know. Everybody here holds their breath. The world holds its breath, as well. Yet, as the helicopter passes overhead, disappears into the distance, the crowds, the soldiers, too, relax. This revolution, it seems, is still far from over."

On the Rua António Maria Cardoso, there was a very different crowd. A crowd swarming like an angry hive. Ten minutes' walk away, yet another world.

The street was narrow, a canyon with towering walls on each side: people clustering around the top of the Travessa do Teatro steps; around the line of Volkswagen Beetles and Squarebacks, Citroën 2CVs, Cabrios and Panier vans parked along the narrow pavement to the left; around the yellow tramcar that was now trapped outside the old municipal theatre; and around the military jeep, parked fifty yards from the PIDE building itself. Only a jeep, and a thin line of soldiers, some sailors, too, taking shelter in the lee of the high garden wall and gateway, which ran from the jeep to the front of the three-storey headquarters.

This contingent of the Armed Forces Movement – unlike those down at the Carmo barracks – seemed wholly inadequate. For, as Jack knew only too well, the PIDE interior was like a fortress and, today, it was well garrisoned. He could see the front windows from here, the long balcony, as well as, over the top of the garden wall, some of the side windows. There were agents at all of them. Some in blue uniforms, some in military combats, some in civvies. But they were all heavily armed.

Jack was breathless, frantic. And his cuts and bruises seemed even more painful. How the hell was he going to get inside? There didn't seem to have been any shooting. Not so far. But how long could that continue? He could have cut the atmosphere there with a knife. It was ominous.

'Telford.' It was Mary Lou De Witt. 'You've got some nerve, mister, showing your face. And how, in the name of all that's holy, did you get here? The National Guard's got all the streets sealed off.'

'You'd be amazed how persuasive a set of BBC credentials can be,' he smiled, though he could see that she wasn't amused.

'Do you know what you've done?'

'I gave them the dossier,' he said. 'What choice did I have?'

'Choice? What choice d'you think you gave your friends? A well planned operation for May Day has to be brought forward at the drop of a hat. If we'd not been able to tip them off...'

'The CIA's claiming some credit for this? America's suddenly become the champion of progress? And, for your information, they had no need to bring anything forward.'

'For pity's sake, Jack, you gave them the dossier. You gave them the date, all the details.'

'Don't be so bloody stupid, Mrs De Witt. I changed the date. To the First of June. Just an extra insurance policy. A few other things too.'

'Wait. Are you telling me...? There were arrests. During the night. But mostly officers supposed to be loyal regime supporters. A real ruckus. Did you know about this?'

Jack smiled, pleased with himself, for once.

'There were two lists,' he said. 'One with leading officers of the MFA, the other with those who are paid-up members of Acção Nacional. I just re-typed the lists. Mixed them up a bit.'

'Some folks might think that's mighty smart, Mister Telford. But I ain't one of them. Just how, exactly, do you think the Director-General of the PIDE is likely to cut up, now he knows you've tricked him? What price the life of Miss Waters after that?'

'He's in there?' Jack knew she was right – that he'd probably done more to endanger Ruby than protect her. 'Christ, is he?'

'So far as we know,' said De Witt, 'he's holed up with Caetano down in the Carmo. But we can't be sure.'

Jack thought about all the time he'd spent doctoring the dossier.

'You could have got her out?' he said. 'Was that the lifeline?'

'I reckon. You could have brought the dossier to us, Jack. Or, better, just left it hidden some place. But hell, that's spilled milk. And you know what? For me, America's always been – what did you call it? Champion of progress. Heck, I like that. Sure do. But progress? That kinda depends on where you stand. Eye of the beholder. One person's progress, another's prison. Ain't that right? I'm a God-fearing person, Mister Telford, but sometimes my country moves in mysterious ways, too. And did you ever meet anybody who didn't believe they were one of the good guys – regardless of which side they'd picked?'

'I appreciate the homespun homilies, Mrs De Witt. Truly, I do. But, right now, I need to work out how to get inside that damned building.'

'Looks to me like nothing much is going to happen here a-whiles. Why don't we head back down to the Carmo, see if we can get ourselves some help? That's if you think those BBC credentials can carry two, Jack.'

He didn't feel the need to tell her that the credentials were now somewhat out of date.

'I don't think I can leave here right now,' said Jack, but De Witt gripped his arm.

'Come on. You'll do no good here. And you may just be missing that Pulitzer Prize-winner your files tell me you've always hankered for.'

The files were obviously incomplete; though, she was right. This portion of the game was stalemated. For now.

'Fine,' he said. 'But it's safer this way.' Down the Teatro steps again. 'And maybe I could ask you something.'

She laughed.

'Yeah, sure. So long as it ain't an invitation to dinner. I don't mix business with pleasure, Mister Telford. Not normally, anyhow. Not that I couldn't be tempted, mind.'

'To be honest, I wanted to ask you about poison. Poison pills, to be precise.'

'That's a less than flattering response, Mister Telford,' she said, as they crossed Picadeiro, talked their way through a National Guard cordon, and headed down the next set of steps to skirt the side of the National Theatre. 'This about the way your friend died?'

'I remember when Gary Powers went down – the U2 incident. There was a lot of talk about him being equipped with a suicide pill. Is that a state secret? I was never sure. Are they easy to get?'

'I guess, if this is off-the-record, I don't mind telling you I've come across them from time to time. Saxitonin. It's a very potent neuro-toxin.'

'What about cyanide?'

'What about it? Saxitonin's far more effective. To get hold of potassium cyanide, these days, isn't so easy. You telling me that's what killed him? I don't want to seem callous, Mister Telford, but gracious me, an old-fashioned L-pill? Lordy, I figure you'd have to find a Nazi German army surplus store to get your hands on one of those.'

The call came through at three-fifteen sharp, and at least there was no time difference between London and Lisbon.

'Yes, Telford here,' he said. And they put him through to the Portuguese desk, to the news editor there – Santana, himself Portuguese – who chatted with him while the technicians completed all the sound-checks and readied themselves to both record him down the wire, but also to transmit the broadcast live. 'And I suggest you get a move on,' said Jack. 'Things are happening.'

They finally gave him the green light – verbally, of course – and Jack switched on his own recorder, told the story yet again. Carmo Square. Forty years of repression under the regimes of António Salazar and then, more recently, Marcelo Caetano. Regimes that had brought misery to millions, both in Portugal itself and in their African colonies. But, last night, all that had begun to change. Portugal's Eurovision Song Contest entry, *E Depois do Adeus*, just before midnight to put the Armed Forces Movement, the MFA, on alert. Then, an hour later, the protest song, *Grândola, Vila Morena*, given as the signal for these army captains – men sworn to free Portugal from its fascist dictators – to move into action. And they had done so. He listed their objectives, the ease with which they'd been captured. Then a piece about the background here in the square.

"*But now,*" he said, "*at three-thirty on this fateful afternoon, there is renewed tension in this normally peaceful place. The soldiers of the Revolution and the soldiers who've been sent to stop them – a powder keg,*" *which any spark could ignite. But the waiting crowds have grown anxious, silent. Because, in the Carmo barracks, just across from where I stand, the regime's leadership and its National Guard supporters remain as defiant as ever. While I watch, the commander here, Captain Salgueiro Maia, climbs once more onto the front of his armoured car."*

Jack paused, held up the handset, caught a few of Maia's words for atmosphere, as the captain shouted through his megaphone. He wondered, for a moment, whether Maia had also been one of Allan's students at the Academia Militar – another student of *Just William*.

"He calls on the National Guardsmen inside the barracks to surrender. He gives them an ultimatum. Surrender now and there will be no repercussions, he says. But, if there is no surrender, he will not hesitate to blow up the gates, to take them by force. As he speaks, I can see the crowd edging back a little, uncertainty replacing some of the earlier euphoria. We all wait. Captain Salgueiro Maia looks at his watch. He hasn't given a time limit for their response, but the sudden silence in the square is full of foreboding. Maia jumps down from the armoured car, shouts some instruction to the vehicle's commander. Maia looks at his watch again. Three-thirty. Oh, my goodness..."

The *bark-bark-bark* of the heavy machine gun echoed between the buildings in the square, a pause, then a second burst. It was deafening, there in the confined space. The quick stink of cordite, pigeons rising in panic from the jacaranda trees, a few screams from the crowd, as the bullets kicked dust, splinters of plaster and brick, from the white walls of the barracks, a row of craters gouged above the entrance archways and empty, striped sentry boxes. Jack suddenly felt very exposed.

"As you've just heard, Captain Maia has opened fire on the National Guard headquarters itself. Warning shots. But, so far, at least, no response from those inside. No. Wait. A sergeant has just called Captain Maia to the radio post on the edge of the square. He's taking a call. I can see him nodding, speaking into the handset, giving it back to the radio operator. Now he's lifting the megaphone again, addressing the crowd. He tells them that General Spínola – something of a hero for many Portuguese, and an outspoken critic of the regime's colonial policies – has been in telephone negotiations with Prime Minister Caetano. Those negotiations had broken down, he says, but have now resumed again. He reassures them, makes

a speech about Portugal's future and, suddenly, all the optimism of this revolution – this Captains' Revolution – returns."

'Mister Telford.' The news editor broke in, and there was something in his accent-laden English that reminded Jack of Allan Lawrence. 'Great work. But that sounds like a very good place to cut the broadcast. We're working on it now. Will you come back to us if there are more developments. And give my love to Lisbon. I was born just two streets away from the Carmo. Wish I was there.'

'It's quite something,' said Jack. 'But I'm not planning to go anywhere. This story will carry on running for days yet, I guess. Months.'

'Ah,' said Santana. 'No need to worry about that, really. We'll be sending out a team. This evening. Helpful if you could brief them when they arrive.'

'Will I be leading?'

'Well, no. Not exactly. New girl on the block. Understand? Young blood. Susan Rhodes. You'll like her.'

Yeah, thought Jack. Sure, I will.

Thursday 25th April 1974, Evening

Mary Lou De Witt found him an hour later. By then, he'd had plenty of time to fume over Santana's news. But what could he expect? Nobody wanted the old hands any more. No respect for experience. For age. Well, bollocks to the BBC. He'd talk to Sydney Elliott.

Meanwhile, it seemed that negotiations had broken down and the MFA forces, supplemented by a tank, which had roared and squealed into position in front of the Carmo barracks, while Captain Salgueiro Maia began a lengthy countdown, a five-minute warning, after which, he had promised the crowd, the building would be demolished. He had begged the crowd to pull back or, better, to go home. But nobody seemed to have any inclination to leave.

'It won't happen,' De Witt told him. 'We just had word. A message on its way from Spínola to Caetano. Everything arranged. Caetano's going to respond. A bit of face-saving. He'll only surrender to a General Officer – that will be Spínola, naturally. Needs assurances that government won't fall to the mob. Given a respectable break, to build up the drama, Spínola will show up in person, escort Caetano off to somewhere safe.'

'So,' said Jack, 'it will be Spínola, after all. Power to the generals again. Your CIA buddies must be really pleased. All this, so we can swap Spínola for Caetano. Brilliant. Meet the new boss. Same as the old boss.' The 'Sixties bands weren't entirely his thing, but he had a certain admiration for Pete Townsend and *The Who*. Natural rebels.

'It's never over 'til the fat lady sings, Jack. But we've got other things to worry about right now.'

'I'll let you worry about them, Mrs De Witt. I'm heading off to find somebody who can get Ruby out of that place.'

'That's what I meant. In a very short while, that nice Captain Maia is going to announce that the PIDE – the DGS as they now are – is being abolished. Forthwith, Jack. You know what that means?'

'They'll know they're on their own. You think they'll make a last stand?'

'What the hell have they got to lose? Caetano and the Boss Hogs may get away with what they've done – but not the PIDE. The crowd will want blood – and the PIDE know it.'

'You've got a team ready?' he said. 'How do these things work? And what price am I going to pay for the lifeline?'

'If what you tell me is true, Jack – about the dossier – I guess we're already in your debt, ain't we? But no team. You've been watching too many movies. Just you and me, Mister Telford. And a friend on the inside to let us through the back door. Seven-thirty. On the nose.'

'Do I, at least, get a gun?'

'You know how to use one?'

'It's been a while,' said Jack. 'But I'll get the hang of it again quickly enough.'

'Like I said, Jack. Too many movies. I was kinda hoping we could do this quietly.'

It was a long wait, and passions were still running high outside the front of the PIDE headquarters. Huge numbers but, like the Carmo square, everybody pressed back against the walls, crammed down side streets and alleys. Somebody said there'd been shots, but nobody hurt. But who had fired them, that all seemed a bit vague, and De Witt went off to speak with the MFA officers. Jack, meanwhile, talked to people in the crowd, scribbled notes, used his recorder a few times. Yet, at seven-fifteen, Mary Lou was back at his side.

'You sure we don't need guns?' he said, as she steered him to the municipal theatre, where a woman was waiting for them, promised to look after Jack's Panasonic, led them through a maze of passages, up stairs and down, until they came at last to an emergency exit, opening onto an alley that ran along the back of the block. They followed it.

'Here,' said De Witt. The PIDE building's rear was a far cry from the elegant façade, out on Rua António Maria Cardoso. Dingy, gloom-laden, cast-iron fire escapes and piping, crumbling masonry and a loading bay that might have belonged to any backstreet sweat shop.

Jack could only imagine the gruesome bundles, which must have been shipped through the rusting doors over the years but, at half-past the hour, prompt, they heard a bolt pulled, the lock turned. De Witt dragged a document from her suit pocket, something that looked official.

'And no guns, just this. Keep a cool head, Mister Telford. Act like we belong here. Okay?'

He followed her through the door into a storage area. Nobody there. Whoever her insider contact might be, they had made themselves scarce.

'But now we're here,' she said, 'it's up to you. Lead on, Jack.'

'If we can get to the main entrance, I'll be able to find her,' said Jack. 'This way?'

He headed straight along the corridor in front of them, down the centre of the north wing, Jack calculated. It was busy with armed agents, cigarette smoke, sweat-stinking tension, acrid. Each of the agents eyed them with suspicion as they passed, yet nobody took the trouble to stop them. At the end of the corridor, swing doors gave access to a stairwell and, along to the left, Jack could see the vestibule and the custody desk area.

'This right?' said De Witt.

'Interrogation rooms are down there.' Jack pointed. 'Then, around the corner. They were holding her further round, that way. And I take it you've worked out how to get her released?'

'Just keep going, Mister Telford. We'll be fine.'

He wasn't reassured, yet he set off along the patterned tiles anyway, excused himself as they edged through the PIDE men. De Witt attracted some angry demands, though her brandished document helped open the way, the agents really too busy arguing, shouting, clustering around the barricaded front doors, to properly study the contents. But the second half of the passage was empty. Perhaps it was going to be easier than he'd thought. If, of course, Ruby was still in the same cell.

'Almost there,' he said, as they turned the final corner – and walked straight into Lieutenant Estéves. Ruby Waters was being pushed along behind him, dishevelled, distraught, her arms pinioned by that same Butch Cassidy lookalike – the sergeant, Vítor.

Estéves, at least, was armed. Self-loading rifle. He levelled it.

'How the hell…?' he said. But his surprise was short-lived. 'Telford. What excellent timing. The best. We were just about to process your reward for the dossier you left with us. Then have it dropped off for you. Gift-wrapped.' He gestured with his weapon towards their captive.

'Ruby,' said Jack, 'what have they done?'

Her eyes were wide with fear. Terror. Grief. He'd never seen her in such a state, her legs so weak they could barely keep her upright. Were those bruises on her face? Had these bastards knocked her about? Yet, she didn't answer him. It almost seemed that she couldn't even see him.

'If you've hurt her…'

'But this is perfect,' the lieutenant laughed. 'Now you can be here to watch. To receive your reward in person. What do you think, Sergeant?'

Vítor laughed too, but it was cold, sickening.

'Lieutenant, you'll want to read this,' Mary Lou De Witt told him in surprisingly good Portuguese. 'A diplomatic request from the US Embassy, endorsed by our State Department, that Miss Waters should be given over into our care, and an offer of asylum for any representative of the State Defence Police who ensures her safe conduct there.'

Estéves snatched the letter from her.

'How did you get in here?' he said, at last, when he'd finished reading.

'The back door was open,' said Jack. 'Careless. Now, Lieutenant, what the hell's been going on? Ruby, speak to me.'

'You just wandered in?' said Estéves. 'You two? Alone?'

'Just us,' said Mary Lou. 'But we've not got much time. The offer...'

She never had the chance to tell him.

Estéves swung the rifle's butt upwards, the flat of it smashing against De Witt's cheek bones. It sounded like shells crushed underfoot. Her head snapped to the right, spittle spraying from between her teeth, and her knees buckled.

Ruby screamed, and Vítor wrapped his arm around her throat, at the same time pulling an automatic from the holster at his waist. He aimed the pistol at Jack, who froze. The lieutenant was pointing the rifle at him, too, for a moment, until he was satisfied that Jack would cause no trouble. Then he smiled again.

'Bastard Americans,' he said. 'And bastard English. Who gives a shit?'

He lifted the rifle again, brought the butt crashing down once more on Mary Lou De Witt's already lifeless head. And Jack simply reacted. No plan. No thought for consequence. Just a reflex, a spasm of his muscles, launching him forward. Yet, only far enough to stop him dead as his solar plexus collided with the jabbing muzzle of the gun. It doubled him over, sank him to the floor, groping for breath.'

'You are too old for heroics, *Senhor* Telford,' said Estéves.

The basement cell was only a few doors from the mortuary where Jack had viewed the corpse of Allan Lawrence, perhaps, the very one in which the Commodore had died.

'You planning the same for us?' Jack groaned. They'd virtually dragged him down the stairs, re-opened the head wound from the car crash. He'd felt those carefully knotted twists of hair, the gash itself, coming apart, the blood flowing afresh. It was trickling down his neck, even now. 'The cyanide?'

'Did you bring some with you, *senhor*?' said Estéves. Then he feigned shock. 'Oh no, this is too rich. You never worked it out, did you? Shall we tell him, Sergeant? About your stupidity?'

'Jack,' Ruby murmured. It was the first time she'd spoken. 'Get me out of this place. Please...' Her teeth were chattering. Severe shock. She was in a bad way.

'Let her go,' Jack told Estéves. 'You don't need her now. You've got me. Isn't that what you wanted?'

'But this is more interesting, don't you think? And it seems we have time to kill, while we wait for reinforcements. Then we'll teach those Commie pigs outside a lesson or two. So, how to amuse ourselves? Sergeant Vítor had some very original ideas so far as your woman's concerned.'

Jack was sick to his stomach. Lola Santos had never gone into detail, but Jack's imagination conjured some awful visions. He fought hard to blank them.

'You wouldn't dare,' he spat. 'You bloody animals.'

'Oh,' Estéves grinned, and he pressed the rifle's muzzle hard against Jack's skull, 'he already dared, my friend. It was something to behold. And animals? Yes, that's pretty much how I saw it. Strangely moving though, to see him do that with an old bitch like this.'

A voice in Jack's head began to scream, and it wouldn't stop. Beside him, Ruby Waters was being violently sick on the floor.

'Of course,' the lieutenant went on, 'he didn't really deserve any sort of reward. Not after your friend the Commodore. Though, of course, you don't know, do you?'

Jack wasn't even sure he cared any more. He just wanted the clock to turn itself back, or for him to wake from this nightmare.

'Well,' said Estéves, 'I shall tell you anyway. That our Sergeant Vítor was so besotted with his whore Fado singer, he brought Lawrence the book. You remember the book? He only admitted this later, naturally. And, hidden in the spine of the book – there was nowhere else it could have been – a glass ampoule of potassium cyanide. The inside of his mouth was cut from where he'd bitten it. Killed himself, Telford, before we could get what we wanted from him. What do you think about that? Suicide is a mortal sin, such a selfish thing, don't you think?'

It was a knife, and it cut open Jack's heart. An old wound. Almost as old as Jack himself. Yet, a wound that he thought had healed thirty-five years earlier. On the dockside at Alicante. Here it was though, back to haunt him again, and now all wrapped around this black pit of hell into which he and Ruby Waters had fallen.

'It's an option you should consider yourself,' Jack spat at him. 'Right now. Because, I can promise you, that's going to be the only painless way for you to finish this.'

He was filled with more cold fury than he had ever known, yet his brain yelled at him that his words could be nothing but empty threats. Time, though, he thought. Buy time. Time. Time for what? He had no idea, but he longed for a moment to put his arm around Ruby, to hold her just once, just one last moment. To put right the horrors he seemed to have brought down upon them.

'Time to kill?' muttered Estéves. 'Is that really what I said? It's going to give me great pleasure to watch you die, *Senhor* Telford. But not nearly so much as drinking your pain when you see how we finish your woman.' He turned to Vítor. 'Get on with it,' he said. 'And take all the time you want.'

It was a moment. Only a moment. Estéves glancing away, the rifle's muzzle straying slightly to one side.

A movement in the doorway.

Crack, crack, crack.

Three shots that roared around the room, two of them carrying away the side of Vítor's head, spraying blood and brains across the wall, across Ruby's own face. Her scream. Jack's grab for the lieutenant's gun, his dive forward that knocked Estéves to the floor, both of them locked together, rolling over and over. A distorted vision of Mary Lou De Witt falling into the room. Ruby Waters crawling towards Vítor's body, like some demented inmate of Bedlam. Jack was forced onto his back, Estéves above him, pressing the cold steel of the rifle into his windpipe, crushing it. Those eyes. Like a maniac.

Crack. The lieutenant's lower jaw disappeared in bone, and teeth and blood, flung him away, onto his side, the gun skittering across the floor.

Estéves got to his knees, tried to crawl after it, tongue lolling from the mess where his chin had been. And Jack followed; though, all he wanted to do was stop, to sleep – but not to die.

Christ, how he ached.

Yet, he hurled himself on the lieutenant, screaming, and threw his left arm around the man's gore-soaked throat. Jack slammed his right hand against the other fist, pressed with every ounce of strength he still possessed.

Estéves stank of hair oil, cheap aftershave, and he made a frightful gurgling noise, thrashed from side to side to break loose, clawing at Jack's arm. Then, he tried for his face, but only succeeded in ripping away the eye-patch.

Jack shifted his grip. He was still bellowing, some war cry litany of every profanity he'd ever heard, telling himself, time and time again, that this creature deserved to die, that he was less than human, that killing Estéves was not like killing himself. Not like that, a voice inside him sobbed. Not like that.

But he had to focus. Keep pressing, though he knew that his right hand was too weak to keep this up for much longer. It had never been the same since Spain. Some psychological debility. Estéves was still reaching for him, could only find his hand, but had dug his nails deep into the flesh at the base of Jack's thumb, tearing at it, an agony of ripping that only served to fuel Jack's rage, fire his failing strength.

Estéves began to crawl forward again, reaching for the rifle, his knees trying to find purchase on the slippery floor. But he was going nowhere. Jack's weight was impossible for him to shake off. And Jack had never yet stopped screaming, forcing himself to look at the ceiling, to ignore the sweat now trickling through the lieutenant's hair at the back of his Brylcreemed head.

It was taking too long. How long, normally? He couldn't remember. Four minutes? Five? But every time Jack's grip loosened, Estéves would grab a breath – a terrible bubbling sound. How long had it been already? And how long could Jack keep this up?

It was not just weakness of muscle, of course. He could feel himself sinking. Almost into lethargy. Split personality. One part of himself playing through the evils that this bastard had committed. Those nightmare visions of whatever they'd done to Ruby again. But the other part – that one was riddled with doubts. Did Estéves have family? Kids? Jack looked away from the ceiling now, desperate for help. Yet, all he saw was Ruby, pummelling at Vítor's body. And he saw De Witt too, slumped, unconscious, in the corner. He was on his own with this.

The lieutenant still struggled, still scratched, still crashed about, trying to shake himself free. Then, Jack sensed that moment when it all became a little less desperate, the fight not yet gone from him but, perhaps, beginning to ebb at last.

Jack yelled even louder then, shouting anything that went through his head, anything that would sap Estéves's morale, his energy, his will to carry on the struggle. Yet, it was far from over. It became easier, yes. But Jack forced himself to think of the lessons he'd learned. A long time back. About cutting off the blood to the brain. About how long that took. About how, if you eased the choke hold too soon, the blood would go coursing through again, the target live to fight another round. So, he kept the grip, that animal scent of imminent victory bringing him new vitality, fresh strength.

'Jack.' It was Ruby, standing at his side. Some of the madness seemed to have cleared from her eyes, and her hand rested on his heaving shoulder. 'Leave it, Jack.'

Time had stopped at some point. His arm was still around the lieutenant's throat, and he couldn't feel it any more. It was completely numb. But he was simply supporting a dead weight.

Painfully, he unlocked the choke hold, allowed Estéves to slump forward. Above them, distant but clear, he could hear more shooting. Intermittent fire. Jack hadn't paid it great heed earlier. But he realised that, in the moments after Vítor was killed, the shots had been echoed. Upstairs. And there they had not stopped. There'd been continuous firing for how long? It couldn't have been more than five minutes, not really, yet it felt like hours. Had De Witt triggered some other gun battle? Had the Revolution gone wrong? Had those reinforcements – those for which Estéves had so hoped – finally arrived? They would find out soon enough, Jack supposed.

Still kneeling, he took hold of Ruby's shoulders.

'My sweet woman,' he said, 'what have I done to you?'

'Don't, Jack,' she sobbed. 'Please. Not now. Just get me out of here.'

He could barely move, but he managed to crawl over to Mary Lou De Witt. She was groaning, softly, and must have been in awful pain. He prised the automatic from her fingers.

'I thought you said no guns,' he whispered; though, she couldn't answer. He got her to her feet, all the same, and they hauled each other up the stairs. It was chaos. PIDE agents running in and out of rooms, some wounded, the corridor filled with gun smoke, deafening sounds of battle.

So, they went unnoticed, three more blood-smeared, walking wounded. Yet, they dragged and supported each other, stumbling straight to the back of the building, along the rear corridor, out into the alleyway.

Jack hammered on the theatre's stage door until the same woman opened for them, gasped when she saw them, hand going to her mouth. But she must, by then, have become accustomed to the bloodshed. For, in the theatre foyer, it was another abattoir. Medics, caring for dozens of wounded people, people from the crowd and, in the corner, several dead, covered by blankets. Outside, the bullets were still flying.

Friday 26th April 1974

In the early hours of the morning, Jack hobbled gingerly around the corridors of the English hospital. They'd stitched his head properly this time, and the back of his right hand, too, where Estéves had gouged out a significant amount of flesh. Otherwise, the nursing team had told him, he was in remarkably good shape. Once again, they omitted to say, "For your age." But he knew that's what they meant. Yet, "in good shape" was the last thing he felt. Every step was murder.

However sore he might be, though, it was insignificant compared to the treatment both Ruby Waters and Mary Lou De Witt were receiving. The CIA agent had been rushed straight into theatre. She was still there. Severely fractured skull, with all the associated complications, and her cheek bones smashed in three places. Ruby, on the other hand, was heavily sedated. Two teams of doctors had examined her but, on the basis that Jack was, factually, no more than a friend, they refused to divulge their prognosis. He must be patient, they'd told him. In her own good time, perhaps, she would be able to tell them more. For the time being, she seemed in no immediate physical danger – needed rest and quiet.

So, Jack, in hospital dressing gown, retrieved cigarettes and lighter from his discarded clothes and, left with his own tormented imagination, he took himself out through the main entrance, lit one of the *Gigantes*.

Lisbon was sleeping, it seemed. At last. The latest news told how General Spínola had indeed arrived at the Carmo, and gone inside with Captain Salgueiro Maia to accept Caetano's surrender. Caetano had then been spirited away in an armoured personnel carrier. Yet, still a final moment of tension. The National Guards, almost refusing to believe the surrender, had become edgy, a real threat.

But a young girl had appeared from nowhere. A young girl with a single red carnation. She'd carried it from her mother's side, and walked purposefully to where the National Guardsmen had their weapons at the ready. Slowly, that tiny angel of peace had lifted the flower, slid the stem into a rifle barrel. The National Guardsmen seemed confused, but then the crowd had begun to applaud, to cheer. More people came forward, more red blossoms bursting from the muzzles of guns, large and small.

And just my bloody luck, thought Jack, that I wasn't there to record it.

Victory, all the same. And the crowds, they said, had gone wild. Fireworks. The Carnation Revolution. A crazy street party, marred only by the news from the PIDE headquarters. There, a gun battle had ensued. Nobody knew how it had started, but shots had been heard. And the PIDE had opened fire on the crowd. Four dead. Maybe, five. Almost fifty wounded, some seriously.

Jack had seen them, in the foyer of that other theatre, yesterday evening. Casualties among the PIDE agents? Unknown. Yet, the building had finally been taken. Jack had no way of knowing whether Adriano Santos had escaped or not. He didn't really care.

By eight, he had taken a taxi to his apartment, washed and changed, retrieved some papers and other stuff that he'd hidden away. It took a while, for the streets were full once more, the revellers having rested and now resumed their celebrations in earnest. Red carnations everywhere – not a gun barrel without one.

He made the return journey on a crowded tram, full of jubilant, singing passengers. *Grândola, Vila Morena*, naturally. Then he walked to the small car park reserved for the hospital's doctors. Huber turned up a few minutes later, driving a battered old Mercedes. Very old.

'The job doesn't pay well, Doctor?' said Jack.

'Mister Telford. I drive this through nostalgia, to tell you the truth. A family heirloom, you might say.'

'Inherited from your father?'

'As it happens, yes. But you must excuse me. I have an appointment. What about you, though?' It seemed like an afterthought. 'Have you been receiving treatment again?'

'We were caught up in the fighting at the PIDE headquarters, I'm afraid. I suspect your appointment might be a consultation with a friend of mine, Mrs De Witt.'

'You're acquainted? Good gracious. A small world.'

'Smaller than you might think, Doctor Huber. You told me once about your calling. You remember? To prolong life wherever that may be possible.'

'That is correct. But, as I told you, I cannot discuss...'

'Perhaps, you might explain to me how your ethics stack up against supplying Allan Lawrence with a potassium cyanide capsule.'

'Whoever told you that, Mister Telford, I can assure you... Though, you have said it yourself. My calling is to prolong life wherever that may be possible. You were the Commodore's friend, also. You would not have wanted to see him die in agony? Intolerable agony. Sometimes, a shorter life lived in laughter is better than one languishing in pain and lamentation.'

Yes, Jack had learned that lesson from his father. But was this an admission? Jack took it to be so; though, the doctor's features betrayed nothing.

'I have no proof, of course,' said Jack. 'You needn't worry. But I found these papers recently.'

From his best tweed jacket, he produced some of the documents he'd kept from the dossier and, this morning, brought from his apartment.

'I was intrigued,' he said. 'The reports written for the Communist Party about the Nazi gold held by the Bank of Portugal. All these dates and times. The names. Most of the reports signed by Herr Walter Huber. Not you, obviously.'

'Obviously,' said the doctor. 'My father.'

'He must have had very intimate knowledge of the transactions.'

'A highly respected economist, Mister Telford.'

'Was that before or after the war?'

'After, naturally.'

'And during?' said Jack. 'I suppose, I wouldn't find any record of a German economist called Huber until – when? 1946? In Porto. He must have left you some interesting souvenirs. Of his previous life.'

'He told you that?' Gaspar Ferreiro had come out of hiding overnight, picked up snippets of their story, tracked Jack down to the hospital without much difficulty. He looked exhausted, grateful even, for the horribly weak coffee served up in the hospital's waiting lounge.

'I didn't press him,' Jack murmured. 'There seemed no point. It felt like I've caused enough pain this past twenty-four hours.'

'But he'd given Allan the capsule. You're sure?'

'The tumour was inoperable. Simply a matter of time. I'm guessing that Huber found the pill among his father's things, after he died.'

'It's built into our Portuguese sense of humour,' said Gaspar, 'that, here, anybody German must somehow be related to a Nazi war criminal. One of those given refuge by Salazar. I just never dreamed… About Huber's family, their background.'

'That's Huber's business. But it's hard to explain why else Huber himself would possess a suicide capsule. It was De Witt who made me think of it. Some throwaway comment about where you might find one. In a Nazi army surplus store, something like that. Seems, she was right. Huber gave it to Allan against the day when the pain might become intolerable, the end inevitable. Past the point where prolonging life was even relevant any more.'

'And the good Commodore,' Jack pressed on, 'stashed it down the spine of his *Just William*. Well, why not? His favourite book. Easy for somebody like Lola to remember. A final fond memory of all that time he'd spent teaching subversion at the Academia Militar through Richmal Crompton's fables. All or any of those things. I've no idea. By the way, I take it that Captain Maia was one of his students too?'

'Salgueiro? Yes, naturally,' said Gaspar. 'And the PIDE too stupid to know that English literature could be helping stir up a revolution. But the Commodore's plan – it all turned on Lola Santos doing as he'd wished. She's hardly reliable, Jack.'

'But she loved him, I think. Genuinely. He made her promise to get the book to him, wherever he might be, because he assumed that, when the time came, he'd likely not be at home.'

'But he couldn't have guessed, could he? About the PIDE?'

'He was no fool, Gaspar. He knew damned well how dangerous that bloody dossier must have been.'

'It was important, Jack. Like I told you, if this had all gone wrong – and, thanks to you, it very nearly did.'

'Then, maybe, you should have been more honest. You knew I was looking for it. And you knew why. By the time I found it, you'd...'

'If you want the truth, Jack, I knew the Commodore was much smarter than you. I was certain that, wherever he'd hidden it, you wouldn't find it. It was meant to stay hidden, remember? Only to see the light of day in the event that this revolution failed. To undermine the regime in the eyes of the world. In readiness for the next one. If you'd been a better driver, Jack...'

Smarter than me? thought Jack, without any rancour. Yes, Allan was always that. At first, I thought of him as my young protégé. But, later, I came to realise it was somewhat the other way around.

'If I'd been a better driver, then I'd not have found it. And then, what? They had Ruby, for God's sake.'

'And you seriously think they'd have harmed her? Then? When they still felt safe, untouchable. Whatever they did to hurt her, Jack, they did for simple, petty revenge. But only when they knew they had nothing to lose. Because you'd cheated them – made them look fools even in their own eyes. Revenge, Jack. You caused them to seek revenge.'

It was the very thought that had plagued Jack, though he still kicked against it.

'Not that simple,' he said. 'The night Allan was taken, they knew cyanide killed him, Gaspar. They already knew there was a dossier. One of your own Party cadres had told them, remember? Adriano. And, some time later, that bastard Vítor owned up to taking him the book. They must have known. How could they not? He was either poisoned, or killed himself. Either way, the PIDE must have worked out that he'd died to protect the dossier – that it was a damned sight more important than they'd reckoned. After that, it was only a matter of time before they found it, or discovered what it contained. And then where would you have been, Gaspar?'

'Jack, I like you. A great deal. And I understand that nobody ever enjoys accepting the blame for their own mistakes. Always easier to shift the blame to somebody else, isn't it? But here – well, it leaves you in a difficult position. Staying in Portugal, I mean.'

'They may have uncovered the plan before you could launch. A dozen different ways. Without my help. And if they'd wrecked your – what are you calling it, by the way? Revolution or military coup?'

'Oh, it's a revolution, my friend. And they could never have discovered its blueprint without your help, I'm afraid. That's what I mean – about the difficulty of your position here. You're not likely to be very popular among the new leadership. But our workers have forty years of scores to settle. They'll take control of the factories and the land. For a while, at least. And the price? We've had to agree that Spínola will take charge. For now. Until elections can be arranged. A cast iron guarantee. Free elections. You see, Jack?'

Jack reached for the side pocket of his jacket, took out the copy of *Just William*.

'I think Allan Lawrence would approve' he said. 'And I thought you might like it. A souvenir.'

Gaspar accepted the book, ran his fingers appreciatively over the cover.

'And a reminder, perhaps? About not letting authority get too big for its boots? Well, there'll be no more dictatorships here, Jack. But at least Cunhal's coming back. And Soares. Can you see the dream? The possibilities here for Portugal to be at the heart of a European federation. A federation of socialist, progressive states. Set a spark that will drive Franco out of Spain, at last. That will take Greece out of the Colonels' control. That will unite us with the GDR. With comrades in Italy and France.'

'Britain, too?' said Jack.

'Jack,' Gaspar laughed, 'the Left in Britain would never, in a million years, be able to agree on anything at all.'

Susan Rhodes seemed impossibly young to be here, in charge of an entire BBC crew, and to cover the complexities of revolution. But at least she had brought back his Panasonic.

'There was a young woman at the Municipal Theatre,' she said. 'Very keen that we should get this to you.'

'Good. On the money the Beeb pays me for my stuff,' Jack replied, 'I certainly couldn't have afforded to replace it.' He checked that the tapes were intact, safe.

'Have you got anything good on there?'

'Sadly, nothing at all,' he lied.

'That's a shame. But Santana said you'd be able to help us. Set up some interviews. A few of the key figures, naturally. But I'd really like to get into the guts of this thing. The real story. From the ordinary person's point of view.'

'That's very egalitarian of you, Susan. But I don't think I can help very much.'

'You resent me being in charge of the team, Jack? Instead of you?'

'A little,' he said. 'But it's more pragmatic than that. You see, Susan, I've finally decided it's time to go home. Jump before I get pushed, I suppose. And, besides, yesterday taught me something. You may find many sorts of people here in Lisbon. Foolhardy? Yes, some. Indomitable? Thousands of them. But ordinary? I wouldn't have a clue where to look, my dear.'

Mary Lou De Witt was drowsy, but she could speak. Just. Through teeth kept almost, but not quite, clenched shut by her wired jaws, and the bandaging that encased almost her entire head.

'You'll be eating through a straw for quite a while, they tell me,' said Jack.

'Purée of beefsteak, I hope,' she told him, like a ventriloquist. 'How is she, Jack?'

'Not good. I don't know what they did to her. It's driving me crazy.'

'Then, why not let it go? Strong lady. If she needs you to know, she will say.'

'Maybe,' said Jack. 'That's probably good advice. And I owe you. For saving us. Though, God alone knows how you managed to shoot so straight, given the state you were in.'

'Truth, Jack? Couldn't see a damned thing. Figured it didn't matter much. Couldn't have made it any worse.'

'I'm glad I didn't know that at the time. We'd have managed somehow, though, I guess.'

'I call that bold talk for a one-eyed fat man, Jack Telford.'

Jack laughed, surprised himself by being able to do so. But he liked the comparison with Rooster Cogburn.

'A bit of a paunch, I'll give you that,' he said. And nothing we couldn't sort out, he told himself, with less cake. Or if Allan was still here for the tennis. Then he shut down that train of thought as far as he could.

'And where did you learn that choke hold?' said De Witt. 'War?'

'Yes, the war. An American, as it happens. An American training the Spanish Republican contingent in the French Foreign Legion. Crazy world, eh? Maybe, a story for another day. But, you see? Some of my best friends have been Americans. Just so long as they're not weaving plots through the CIA, Mrs De Witt. I still don't get it, you know? What you're doing here.'

'Mustn't make me laugh, Jack,' she mumbled. 'All cock-a-hoop here. Nice revolution. Peaceful. More or less. We called it right. Just my job. But next? Normal ruckus. Reds will want a second Cuba.' She paused, wearied by the effort. 'Rest will all split,' she pressed on. 'Maoists. Trotskyists. Shit, that's hard to say with your jaw wired. Anarchists. Never agree. Never do. You seen that. Spain. But we'll have Spínola. A while. Then elections. And only one game in town for us. Socialist Party. Pity. But can't be choosers. Agency can't back them. Not officially. Kissinger won't let us. Undermine the rest, though – the Reds. Make sure they can't win.'

'And then you'll help give them all the trappings of Western democracy. New conservative parties. Social democrats working alongside communists and others on the Left, but only so long as it suits you. Only so long as it takes you to convince the people of Portugal that what they really need – investors, entrepreneurs, international bankers and the rest – will simply sit on their hands so long as communists remain part of the government. The people will ditch them then. That's what you're banking on. And the Left will split, of course. Like it always does. End of revolution.'

'Left never needs help to split, Jack. Lots of chaos on the way, of course. Strikes. But we'll have done our job. Saved Gulf Oil. Great news for the world. Don't you think, Jack?'

Jack could have wept. Ruby's eyes were still haunted by whatever she'd experienced, as though it had tipped her into permanent madness. But he'd accept De Witt's advice. If Ruby could endure it, he would have to learn to do the same.

'The road to hell,' he said. 'Paved with good intentions. Gaspar Ferreiro made it clear that's how they'll see it. The dossier. That I should have just left things alone.'

'What will you do?' she said, almost a whisper.

'Speak with Elliott again. See if there's any work for me. *World in Action* again, maybe. I don't know. Yesterday, in the Carmo Square – before all this – I met a man I knew. Abel Guerra. Another journalist. He said that it was the first day he'd ever felt like he really belonged here, in his own country. But me? This is the first time I've ever felt like a foreigner, an outsider. Irony, no?'

There was a nurse in the doorway.

'Excuse me, Miss Waters,' she said. 'But you have another visitor. From the Embassy. If you'd rather they came back later...?'

'No,' said Ruby. 'It'll be fine.'

'Oh, this should be good,' Jack raged, as the nurse disappeared. 'Now the bastards turn up. Well, I'll have a few words...'

'Jack, please. I could not cope with any more. Could I just hear what they have to say?'

228

So, Jack sat and seethed, while an absurdly young Third Secretary – recently graduated, of course – purred apologies for the delay in the diplomatic negotiations to free her from captivity. Agreement had been reached late on Wednesday evening, he claimed, for her release yesterday morning. But then – well, she was obviously aware that it had hardly been a normal day. The little bastard even had the temerity to laugh about it. Intolerable, of course, that she had been kept in such poor conditions. Did she wish to make a formal complaint? Understandable that she should be distressed.

'Distressed?' Jack yelled. 'Distressed? Why, you jumped-up little squirt. Have you any idea what she's been through?'

In truth, Jack had no real idea either.

'It's a difficult situation, Mister…?'

'Telford,' said Ruby. 'This is Jack Telford. BBC World Service. Sometimes, anyway. And you must forgive him. We've both been through a lot in the past twenty-four hours.'

'Mister Telford?' The Third Secretary smirked. 'Oh, jolly good. My lucky day. I was supposed to track you down later. You've been rather mentioned in dispatches, I'm afraid. You were a friend of Allan Lawrence, of course. The Ambassador has been speaking with the Commodore's parents. They're booked out on the first flight, as soon as the airport's open again. The Procurator General has completed his inquest, it seems. A post mortem. And confirmation from Lawrence's own consultant, Herr Huber.'

'Cause of death?' said Jack.

'Oh, brain tumour. Didn't you know?'

'Was there a reason the Embassy didn't investigate the death? Independently?'

'Was there a reason we should have done so?'

Jack shook his head.

'I suppose not. But why was I mentioned?'

'The car, of course. It seems they intend to press charges. You were driving without the owner's authority – the deceased, of course. No insurance cover and – well, we can find no record of you having a driving licence, Mister Telford. But, perhaps, we should discuss that later. For now, I have some private information for Miss Waters. Would you mind?'

Jack looked to Ruby for a lead.

'Why don't you get a smoke, Jack?'

And he did just that, cursing his luck that, on top of everything else, he'd now face a court case about the bloody car. After fifteen minutes, he watched the Third Secretary leave, returned to Ruby's room.

'They've offered you promotion, I suppose,' he said. 'Or a plum posting to Paris? To keep you quiet.'

'They've offered me a retirement package,' she said, quietly.

'Will you take it?'

'That depends, Jack. It's a very generous package.'

'Depends on what?'

'You remember I told you once? Failed miserably to make you jealous? That I was thinking about marrying Fidel Constantino? Settling down somewhere peaceful?'

'Of course I remember. There were going to be lots of fine children as part of the deal, weren't there? And a pretty little place in Dorset, with a cottage garden. Nice idea. Though foolish, as we both now know. You still thinking about the settling down thing? Not the kids, of course, but...'

'Only if I had somebody to share it with, Jack. And no, not much chance so far as the kids are concerned. Not now. But for the rest? Nothing foolish about Dorset and the cottage, is there? I think we can manage comfortably, even after sorting out that little problem of the court case. What do you say, my dear?'

It was late in the evening, and Ruby was sleeping again, more peaceful now. They had reached an amicable agreement: Jack would never press her on what had happened at the PIDE headquarters; and neither of them would ever broach the subject of *Capitán* Fidel Constantino again. Agreement. It sounded so clinical. And, with time to think about it, Jack was simply afraid. He had made a commitment to somebody. After all these years of living alone. It seemed ludicrous. Yet, he could taste the potential sweetness of it. Like *pasteis de Belém*. And Dorset...

'I'm sure she will be fine, Jack,' said Gaspar Ferreiro. 'Once she's back in England, this will all seem like a bad dream.'

'Not all of it, Gaspar. Not by a long chalk. Ruby Waters is resilient. She'll need to be if she's going to put up with my little foibles. And the past few days have been like negotiating a maze. A labyrinth. A moral labyrinth, apart from anything else. And the PIDE – well, we've reached a position on that. But the rest? Do you think we'd have missed a single moment? The revolution? It'll be quite something for us. Something to take into exile.'

Ferreiro smiled.

'I shall like to think of you that way, Jack. In exile. But you will marry her?'

'Oh, yes.'

Jack was warmed, sweetened, simply by the thought, despite his trepidations. And somewhat resenting the thirty-five wasted years. Yet he recalled the words that Fidel Constantino had spoken to him. *"Has she saved you yet, English?"* And Jack prayed that she could, after all that time, still be his salvation, his redemption.

'Then, you must invite me. To the wedding. I should like to see England. But, for now, I need you to hand over any of the documents you've kept. Or notes you took. And your word that all the contents remain confidential.'

'The new bosses will keep the Nazi gold, then?'

'It will cause problems. But we can't survive without it, they tell me. And if we returned it – well, we'd have to call in Britain's debts. That would never do, eh?'

'What about the Wiriyamu stuff?'

'That, you can keep, Jack. The world still needs to be reminded about what Salazar and Caetano have truly been. The grief they've inflicted on Angola and Mozambique puts their policies into sharp relief. So, tell the story, Jack. Push it down the world's throat. About the massacre. About all this.'

'You know, Gaspar, that you can't trust the Americans. The CIA – they'll do everything they can to smash your dream. Your European federation of socialist states. They'll poison it, the way the Spanish Republic was poisoned in the run-up to '36. Don't let that happen here, Gaspar. Not civil war.'

'In Spain, Jack, the country allowed itself to be divided by propaganda, by slogans. Day-in and day-out, for five years. Until the propaganda and the slogans became more real than truth itself. And, when that happens, there can be no common ground. Only lethal division. Compromise will be the price we'll have to pay. But our bottom line will be consensus, I hope. Consensus is the only true democracy, isn't it? Without consensus, there's simply chaos. At least the colonies will get their independence. That's all guaranteed. But you should be proud, too. Of the part our good Commodore played in all this. The part he played in helping set us free.'

And I am proud, thought Jack. If I'd ever had a son, I would have wanted that son to be Allan Lawrence. He envied them, those parents of his friend, coming to collect his poor, mortal remains, to take them home.

'You're very philosophical about all this, Gaspar. The revolution only a day old and you've already accepted that it will fail. I don't understand. How do you keep your faith – as a socialist?'

'Because I know which way the wheel of social progress turns.'

Jack remembered being told almost precisely the same thing, in Spain, in 1939.

'Slowly,' said Gaspar. 'That's how. But always forwards. Whatever happens here, it will be far from failure. All infinitely better than what we've had. Just so much less than it might have been. No matter how harsh the winter, Jack, come spring the carnations always bloom anew.'

Eight

The London Luncheon Club

Friday 31ˢᵗ August 1979

'Is this how it's always done?' said Jack. He found himself surprisingly bedazzled by the opulence of the Garrick Club's dining room.

'A foible of mine,' his host smiled, the voice as familiar as a comfortable old slipper. 'It's the way we've always done it. And I am truly sorry about the short notice.'

They had a table by a window. If he turned his head, Telford could see down into Garrick Street itself, and across into Floral Street, both of them busy at this time of the afternoon. But, in here, the world was strangely isolated from the bustle and noise outside. Time stood still. The crimson walls, covered from end to end with the painted portraits of its patrons, and the other *dramatis personae* who had graced the place with their presence for a century and a half.

'It's a pleasure to be here,' Jack replied, for want of anything more profound.

'And a pleasant journey, I hope. Dorset, isn't it?'

Jack had chosen the onion soup from the *entrées*, not sure if he could cope with the mussels, the snails, or the scallops. He wiped his lips with the linen serviette.

'Just on the edge of Lyme. Pretty little place. With a cottage garden.'

Yes, they'd found one, just as he'd promised Ruby. He remembered how amused she'd been when they'd received the call from the assistant at Broadcasting House.

'They must have the wrong Jack Telford, surely,' she'd laughed.

It had happened before, after all. Six years ago? Seven? A famous interview when the Beeb thought they'd landed a major coup for the programme by inviting thriller writer Alistair MacLean onto the show – only to find they'd got the wrong Alistair MacLean.

'And Mrs Telford? She's well, I trust?'

'Ruby,' Jack told him. 'Like the rest of us, feeling her age, Mr…'

He still wasn't entirely sure how he was supposed to address his host. In truth? He was somewhat in awe of the man, the legend.

'Please, you must call me Roy. Though, it's customary, when we record the programme, not to call me anything at all.' The smile was entirely disarming. 'Something, I'm afraid, that Tallulah Bankhead, for one, could not quite grasp. It was Roy this, and Roy that. And then that memorable moment when I asked if she'd be able to survive on the island. "Why, Roy," she said…' He had Bankhead's drawl off to perfection. '"Why, Roy, I can't even get my key in a door, darlin'."' Priceless.'

'I'll try to remember.' The waiter removed his empty soup plate. 'But I wish I'd known about the Bankhead story when Ruby was giving me hell for coming here.'

'Oh, dear. The Garrick's reputation for being men-only, I suppose.'

'It doesn't quite chime with your foible, though. Does it? For bringing all your castaways here. Women included, I assume.'

Roy's voice dropped to a warm whisper.

'It's the thing about the Garrick. The club itself has rules. They don't specifically preclude women. There simply are no women members. But guests for lunch? Not a problem.'

'I rather think that, for my wife, that would simply make matters worse. And will you be asking me the same thing you asked Tallulah – about being able to survive?'

'I shall certainly be avoiding anything relating to the Women's Liberation Movement, Jack. Though, perhaps, we should get to the questions later. And the music, naturally. But, first, a word about the process?' He looked up as a second waiter, elderly, with a distinctly Spanish accent, brought their main courses.

Elderly? What was Jack thinking? The man must be at least a decade younger than Telford himself.

234

'Yes,' said Roy, 'the *coquelet* is mine.'

'The process,' Jack repeated, and lifted the napkin to clear space for his own salmon. 'All recorded beforehand? Next Friday?'

'Correct. We record the interview itself in the studio. Then, the technical boys work their magic.'

Telford could almost hear it, the seagulls' cries above the soporific strains of *By The Sleepy Lagoon*.

'We record the music during the interview, as well?'

'Gracious, no! Dear me, that would be a disaster. No, that's the technical boys again.' Roy picked up his wine glass and Jack sensed some embarrassment on the part of his host, as though the admonishment had been a little too harsh. '*À votre santé*, by the way.' Jack raised his own glass. 'But yes, all that fading-in, fading-out, timing the length of the piece. Leave all of that to the experts, don't you think?'

Jack had never thought about it. He'd been a regular listener since they'd settled at the cottage. But he'd always imagined that it happened exactly as he heard it. The questions, then Roy carefully playing part of the chosen record on a turntable. He felt like a fool. He was, himself, in the industry, after all. He knew how these things worked. But the programme had somehow retained a significant slice of magic for him – for Ruby, too. And now it felt like the magic had been taken from him.

'So, the questions?' he said, still savouring the flavour of butter-baked asparagus.

'You know, Jack, that I have a reputation for not actually asking questions. Most of our castaways accuse me of simply making statements. Which is precisely where we'll begin. A introduction. "My castaway this week is international journalist and broadcaster, Jack Telford." You see? And then I'll remind everybody that you were chosen as Foreign Reporter of the Year at this summer's British Press Awards.'

'I don't think I deserved it.'

Jack picked at the salmon, dipped a piece in the *meunière* sauce. In truth, he was desperate for a smoke.

'Well, we can't have any self-deprecation on the programme. And it seemed perfectly appropriate to me. An award in memory of a murdered journalist, and you breaking the case – the story?'

'There were three *Sunday Times* reporters who probably did more than me. I just knew Cairo. From the war. And I knew enough about the CIA to make the link between David and the Agency. We're going to talk about this – in the interview?'

Roy almost choked on his chicken.

'Good grief, no! We move straight to me telling the listeners about you being born and brought up in Worcester. One of my famous statements of undisputed fact: "Jack, music mattered very much to you." And then, you say…?'

'Oh, I say something about how there was always music in the house when I was growing up. Just after the Great War, of course. My father had died. And I imagine that music was my mother's way of holding on to his memory. There was an old wind-up phonograph – a Victor, I think – and Mother would have me crank the handle while she listened to my dead father's favourites. These were records like *Alexander's Ragtime Band*. Lots of Irving Berlin, now I come to think about it. But music's been one of my passions ever since.'

'Perfect. Just perfect.' Roy sipped at his wine. 'And the dreaded moment when I ask whether we could have your first record.'

Jack picked up his own glass, but he simply swirled the Chardonnay around the bowl. It was bloody good stuff, a Corton-Charlemagne *Grand Cru*.

'It's not easy, is it? If I'm going to survive for a long time, then it needs to be music to lift the spirits, stuff you can bear to hear over and over again. That's not necessarily the same as our "favourites." But, if survival is only likely to be short-lived, the music needs to be poignant. Full of unashamed nostalgia.'

Roy looked bored. How many times had he heard this argument?

'You may just be over-thinking this, Jack. What did you choose, in the end?'

'Oh, a good marching song to start, I think. *It's a Long Way to Tipperary*, please.'

'Good choice. I don't think we've had that one before. There's an old John McCormack recording. 1914, I think. Which will lead

236

me nicely to my next trigger point – about your father dying on the Western Front.'

'No,' said Jack, 'I'm afraid…'

He had no chance to finish. A tall, exceptionally good-looking fellow had clamped his hand on Roy's shoulder. Telford looked up at a face he knew, but to which he was struggling to attach a name.

'Roy, dear fellow,' the newcomer boomed, the voice as familiar as the face. Rich, all the sweetness of Victoria plums. 'What's this? Another castaway? And you've still not included me on your list?'

'You're on the list, Donald, as I've told you many times before. But yes, this is Telford. Jack Telford. I'm afraid he's bumped you down the ladder again.'

Donald? Jack searched his memory in vain. He recalled a couple of likely films. *The Cruel Sea. Above Us the Waves.* Archetypal naval officer parts. Donald…?

There was some further good-natured banter before the fellow sauntered off to find his own table.

'Lovely man, our Donald,' Roy whispered. 'But he's not even on the list yet. Now, you were saying…?'

Jack had to admit that he rather shared Ruby's viewpoint. Why was he on the programme, rather than Donald what's-his-name? And what *was* his name? Dammit, he still couldn't remember, and he certainly had no intention of demonstrating the faulty memory of his advancing years by asking Roy to remind him. At seventy-one, it was a deadly curse. But Ruby would know.

'Jack?'

'Apologies,' said Telford. 'Miles away. But no, I'm afraid not. My father died in the second year of the war. Hardly a glorious death. Caught a chill, somewhere in Flanders. Complications set in. They sent him back to the Red Cross Hospital at St Albans. He died there. Actually, he killed himself. Couldn't face the prospect of going back to that senseless butcher's yard. And his fear of the trenches was so strong, he chose suicide over the slim chance that he might come home intact to his family.'

'You're happy to talk about that.'

'It was a long time ago.'

'Then, maybe, think about your second record. I'll mention that you won a scholarship to Manchester University. Owens College?'

'You have no notes,' said Jack.

'All up here.' Roy tapped his forehead. It rather rubbed salt in the wound.

'Owens College, indeed,' Jack sighed. 'Strong links to the Mechanics' Institute. Lots of Left-wing politics. And I ended up editing the college magazine. President of the Esperanto Movement, too. And our signature tune? *When the Red, Red Robin Comes Bob-Bob-Bobbin' Along.*'

He omitted to mention that it was also a favourite of his gran's; though, too many painful memories there.

'The Al Jolson version, of course? Now, Jack, you graduated with a First Class Degree in History, and then went to London University where you studied for a Diploma of Journalism.'

'It was the only one available in Britain at the time.'

The waiter was back, cleared their plates and asked if they'd care to see the desserts menu.

'Not if you have the *tarte au citron*, Ramón. If so, we shall each sample its glory. But,' Roy turned his attention to Jack once more, 'that diploma took you into Fleet Street.'

'Not at first. A couple of years learning the ropes in North Wales.' Recollections of his gran, again, which needed to be quickly put back in their box. 'Later, I started with *The Observer*, and then went on to work for the *Mirror*. But I resigned from the *Mirror* when their anti-appeasement stance veered towards re-armament and a war-mongering editorial line.'

He was about to expand, though both of them were distracted by a modest commotion over at the dining room's entrance. Modest, yes, but enough to slice through the otherwise genteel and hushed conversations at the tables. A loud cockney accent demanding to know why the fellow's usual table wasn't available, and the monkey-suited maître d's attempts to placate the newcomer and his guest.

'Sid Yobbo,' Jack groaned, stealing the phrase that *Private Eye* had already coined for Jameson.

'He's not so bad when you get to know him,' Roy grinned. 'Hardly on the same political plane as you, though, Jack.'

'I might have fallen out with the *Mirror* over appeasement, but the paper's heart, otherwise, was generally in the right place. Yet, there stands the man who dragged it into the gutter. Topless girls. In the *Daily Mirror*!'

'You'll be no great fan of the *Star*, then.'

Last year, a further step in Jameson's career. Editor-in-chief of the *Daily Star*.

'I thought we'd reached rock-bottom with *The Sun*,' Jack murmured, as the argument with the head waiter seemed to have reached some compromise. 'But – look out, he's coming this way.'

Jameson, crossing the dining room and, escorted by the maître d', had seen them. He grinned, his gleaming teeth just too large for the mouth in which they were housed.

'Blimey! Jack Telford.'

He swung away from his escort.

'Give us a minute, will yer? I need a word with this geezer. An' Roy, my old mucker. Don't tell me you've got Telford on your bloody desert island?'

Ramón was at the table again, set down the plates of lemon tart and a small jug of *crème anglaise*.

'Indeed, I have, Derek. Just getting ready for the interview. Over a quiet lunch. Or so I'd hoped.'

The barbed hint, delivered with such courteous cultivation, seemed to miss its mark entirely.

'Well, at least you won't be missed Jackie boy, eh?'

Jameson stroked his Picasso-esque silk kipper tie as he spoke, and turned to his blond, wide-eyed companion.

'See, darlin'?' he said. 'Best thing to do with commies. Send them all to a bloody desert island.'

Jack wondered how many people thought of him that way. There was the saying, *"show me who you walk with and I'll tell you what you are"*. On that basis, maybe, it was fair. He'd had some good friends who were members of the Party. But it was just another label, in the end. And labels were lazy, dangerous. Left? Right? The world wasn't that simple.

'Yeah,' Jameson laughed. 'Good idea, Roy. Can I give you a list of others 'e could take with 'im? Hahaha. Just jokin', Jackie boy. Just jokin'.'

Perhaps the maître d' imagined there'd be a fight, for he tried to interpose himself between Jameson and Roy's table.

'Your table is ready, *monsieur*. If…'

Jameson edged the poor man aside.

'Know what the bloody fools have done, Roy? Given my table away to some poofter, that's what.' He glared back down the dining room to the corner window, then glanced down at Jack's dessert. 'An' I wouldn't eat that, Jackie boy. Last time I tried the bloody lemon tart, I had the squits for a week.'

'It can be a tough life, sometimes, Derek,' said Telford, 'for us working class lads.'

'Come on, Del,' said the woman – the recent third wife, as Jack recalled from the coverage of the wedding. 'I'm famished.' They'd both plainly had a few drinks too many. The curse of the industry, of course, for she was a decent journalist in her own right, too.

'Well,' said Jameson, 'there's workin' class, an' there's workin' class, Jack.'

But he seemed to lose interest in the conversation just then, and turned again to the maître d'.

'Right you are, mate,' he beamed at the poor man. 'Lead on, Macbeth. An' let me know, Roy,' Jameson shouted back. 'As soon as you get rid of all those commies, I'm happy to be on the programme.'

Jack saw Roy physically shrink, as Jameson and his wife were led away to the farther end of the banqueting table which ran down the centre of the dining room, collections of guests scattered along its length.

'I'm truly sorry, Jack,' he said.

'Not a problem. East End boy made bad, eh?' He'd seen that somewhere else, as well. 'I just hope he's not right about the lemon tart.'

'Well, you were very diplomatic, Jack. You see? Appeasement. Wasn't that what we were talking about – before we were so rudely interrupted? You resigned from the *Mirror*. So, a committed pacifist by then. And your pacifism took you to Spain.'

Jack set down his spoon, wiped his lips with the napkin again.

'No. That was my new editor, Sydney Elliott. I'd just gone to work for *Reynolds News*. Remember it?'

'The best Sunday paper ever.'

'Until they killed it,' said Telford. New title, the *Sunday Citizen*. Tabloid format. But its last edition had hit the streets in '67, while he'd been in Mozambique. 'Elliott had been doing a lot to raise money for the people of Spain. Civil war still raging, still in the balance. And then he saw this bizarre brochure in a local Thomas Cook window. He'd brought it into the office. Organised tours of Franco's battlefields. So, he sent me on one of them to cover the story.'

'Astonishing. And your time in Spain, Jack – how do you describe it?'

'Like *For Whom the Bell Tolls* meets *The Thirty-Nine Steps*, I suppose.'

Roy smiled.

'We might use that, in the interview. And your third piece of music?'

'It has to be something Spanish, doesn't it? And nothing reminds me of my time in Spain more than *¡Ay, Carmela!*'

'I have a horrible feeling the Gramophone Library might struggle with that one, but we'll do our best.'

'I can help, if not,' said Jack. 'One of my own. 1937 recording by Voces Asturianas.'

Ramón had returned and overheard the conversation. He carried away the dessert plates, smiling, quietly humming the song's refrain. Jack wondered whether the waiters here, like all the waiters in Madrid during the civil war, were anarchists, as well.

'But it was thought you'd died in Spain, Jack. There was an accident.'

'Yes. An accident. Swimming accident.'

'And the accident to your eye?'

'That's another story entirely.' He spooned up the last of the *crème anglaise*. 'But you like the new patch? A parting gift from friends and comrades in Lisbon. Finest Alcanena leather, soft as silk. Plenty of stretch in the headband, as well. Fits like a glove.'

'The stitching is remarkable. But beyond repair – the eye?'

'Some Harley Street quack offered me cosmetic surgery. A glass eye, you know? But, at my age? And Ruby loves me just the way I am, it seems.'

Indeed, she did. Whatever had happened to her in Lisbon remained unspoken. The horrors into which he'd plunged her seemingly forgiven, if not forgotten. She'd married him, when all was said and done. Yet, there were times when her eyes became shrouded and grim. On those occasions, he knew enough to leave well alone, until she forced herself back into the present.

'I saw,' Roy was saying, 'that you'd spent a few months with a group of Republican guerrilla fighters, carrying on the fight against Franco's forces even when the war itself had basically been lost.'

'I owed them something. We had scores to settle. A spell in Madrid, while the Republic fell apart around us. Then east to Alicante for the final tragedy of the war.'

Ramón was back, to take their orders for coffee.

'And forgive me, *señor*. But did you say Alicante? I am from Alicante. My family, also.'

Jack glanced up past the immaculate white jacket, the black tie, to the Spaniard's trim but grey-tinged Van Dyck beard and moustache.

'I have fond memories of the city, Ramón.'

The waiter stood for a moment, as though he wanted to ask something. But, finally, he simply promised to bring their coffees, and left them.

'Have you been back to Spain?' said Roy. 'Since Franco died?'

'Not yet. Though, I'm planning to. As soon as I can pluck up the courage to tell Ruby.'

The truth was that Spain, and Alicante in particular, held memories for them that were both fond – and not so fond.

'Anyway, I ended up in Oran and was still there when France fell to the Germans. So, I joined the Free French. De Gaulle's people found out that I was a correspondent and I became part of his press corps. Specific responsibility for liaison with the BBC. I was mainly attached to Leclerc's Division.'

'Was that difficult?'

'The toughest times of my life. But at least the Corporation must have appreciated me, even if de Gaulle did not.'

And there was that other loss. Danielle.

'So, Jack, record number four?'

'This was the hardest one. To start with, I thought, what else but Piaf, singing *La Marseillaise*? And then, I wondered about *Le Chant des Partisans*. But, in the end, it has to be Josephine Baker.'

'You knew her, of course. During the war.'

'She was a good friend.'

There'd been his final visit with her, when the fighting was over. May '45. Her beautiful Gothic mansion on the Seine. Her plain grey blouse, the striped slacks, the sunglasses. *La Baker*, in all her glory. The lake. Almost Givenchy. The lily pads. The reflections of yellow and green. He should have gone to her funeral, four years ago, now. A state funeral, for goodness sake. Everything she deserved. Twenty thousand mourners. Her tomb at Père Lachaise. But he'd not been able to summon the courage. Too many memories. The same when Toto Torrès – Suzanne Massu – had been laid to rest, with far less ceremony, even more recently.

'And the song?'

'*J'ai deux amours.*'

I have, indeed, had two loves, he recalled.

'Another story, Jack?'

'Not the one you're imagining, Roy.'

'A story you can share?'

'No,' said Jack, more abruptly than he'd intended. In his mind, he saw Danielle again, just as he'd last seen her, driving away in the old Dodge ambulance.

'Fair enough, Jack. But, cast away on your desert island, would you try to escape?'

Telford imagined the waving green palm fronds, the crashing of breakers on the sand.

'Definitely. I seem to have spent my whole life escaping from something or other. I joined the Corporation at the end of '44, renewed some old acquaintances but London brought back too many old memories. So, I had myself posted to Europe again.'

'You covered the Berlin Blockade and the Air-Lift in '48.'

'And the death of Stalin in '53. The Suez Crisis in '56.'

'Record number five, please, Jack.'

'Something from the 'Fifties, then. Fats Domino and *Blueberry Hill*.'

Actually, Jack had really wanted the Gene Autry version from *The Singing Cowboy*, but he'd once written a piece about the song's place in the campaign for civil rights – about how this sleepy ballad, and Domino's performance of it, had suddenly both made rock 'n' roll acceptable and ended the American TV ban on black rock artists appearing on national television. Another quiet revolution.

'Fats Domino and *Blueberry Hill*. You're breaking new ground with some of these, you know, Jack? For some reason, most of our castaways seem to feel obliged to only request classical favourites. Now, you spoke about Sydney Elliott earlier. But you were both reunited in the 'Sixties.'

'We hadn't spoken for thirty years. And I can't blame him. I gave him some sleepless nights when I disappeared in Spain, I think. But out of the blue he called me. He'd gone over to the other side by then – *Granada Television* – working on *World in Action*. He needed a researcher, and I joined him. I've been with the team ever since. Except for some freelance work, back with the Beeb.'

'**And** your sixth choice of music, please.'

'Did your researcher tell you I once met George Harrison?'

'Not that I recall. That's something of an oversight – for both of us. I like to do my own research, for the most part. This would be…?'

'In nineteen sixty itself. Hamburg. So, in the hope that we get decent weather on this desert island, what about *Here Comes the Sun*?'

'And you found the sun yourself, Jack. A move to Portugal.'

Ramón brought the coffees, Telford's espresso and Roy's *café au lait*.

'May we smoke?' said Jack.

'Of course, *señor*.'

The waiter lifted an ashtray from the neighbouring empty table and Jack lit a Capstan.

'It didn't quite work out as I'd planned. Portugal, I mean. Looking forward to a quiet retirement. But, then, two things happened. My very good friend, Allan Lawrence, died there. And, almost the same day, the Portuguese Revolution began. The Carnation Revolution, you remember?'

'I heard your very moving broadcast from Lisbon on the morning of the Revolution, Jack. You deserved a Pulitzer for that one alone.'

Telford wondered whether he should mention the Pulitzer Prize for Correspondence he'd actually won in '45 – and been tempted to accept, until he'd realised that all those who'd helped him earn the damned thing were either dead or gone. Or betrayed. Accepting the Pulitzer would have been like betraying them, as well. In the end, he'd politely declined; though, he knew that would all sound a bit egotistical.

'But now that you've retired,' said Roy, 'do you have any plans?'

'I'll be writing my memoirs, of course. It seems the proper thing to do. The Right-wing in power again. Time to remind people how easy it is for fascism to spread.'

'And will we finally find out what really happened to you in Spain?'

'Perhaps. We'll have to see, won't we?'

'Record number seven, then?'

'Given the election result, I can't think of anything more appropriate than Jake Thackray and *The Bull*.'

Ruby had dragged him off to see Jake perform at the Lyme Regis Folk Club and he'd been impressed. It was only days after Thatcher's victory back in May, and this one had brought the house down.

> *The bull is the biggest of all.*
> *He is the boss, he is, because he's big and we are small.*
> *But the bigger the bull, the bigger the balls.*
> *The bigger the bull, the bigger and quicker and thicker the bullshite falls.*

'That one might be a little contentious, Jack. Let me get back to you. But, then, we'll come to the part where I say you'll be given a copy of *The Complete Works of Shakespeare* to take with you. And you can also take either the Bible or another appropriate philosophical work.'

'I never quite worked out how everybody finds a copy of the Bible there. Did the Gideons get there before us? But yes, I'll swap the Bible for something else, if I may. Jacob Bronowski's *The Ascent of Man*, I think.'

'Of course. And one other book?'

'My constant companion during that trip to Spain in '38 was Tolkien's *The Hobbit*. It hadn't been published long but I lost that copy while I was there. I'd like to read it again, I think.'

Roy signalled to Ramón, that universal gesture requesting the bill.

'And one luxury?'

'A typewriter, please. Lots of paper too, if I may?'

'I'm sure that can be arranged. Now, your final choice of music?'

'Oh, Ruby's been civilising me. Introduced me to opera. So, at least you get one piece of classical stuff. My favourite. From *La Bohème*. *O Soave Fanciulla*.'

'Jack, you've been wonderful company and I'm looking forward to the interview. Shall we adjourn to the Irving for a G&T?'

They rose from the table and headed towards the door. Roy collected his bill from the maître d' – it was plainly going on his account – and turned as Jameson yelled some raucous farewell. But it was Ramón who intercepted Telford.

'*Señor*, you don't remember me. But I served with *La Nueve*. I remember you, *señor*. From Pocklington.'

'I'm sorry,' said Jack. 'There were so many…'

'You do not need to apologise, *caballero*. I was wounded at Écouché, and sent back to England. I've been here ever since. But I wondered, *señor*, whether you knew about Granell?'

Telford heard the words, and knew it could not be good news. He'd written to his old friend, now and again, to the restaurant on the rue du Bouloi, but they'd not been in touch with each other now for – what? Fifteen years? Probably more. He turned to his host, apologised, promised he'd only be a minute.

'No, Ramón, I don't know about Granell. Is he…?'

The waiter nodded.

'Yes. In Valencia.'

Jack had no idea he'd even returned to Spain.

'After Franco died?'

A shake of Ramón's head.

'No, *señor*. Before.'

246

Now, that was surprising news. Even in his latter years, Franco hadn't been above inflicting punishment on those who'd fought against him. And Amado Granell...

'He died there?' said Jack. 'In Valencia?'

'No, *señor*. He was killed there.'

The maître d' prevented any further discussion, smiling deferentially at Telford but making it clear that Ramón must return to his duties. Jack tried to make sense of all this, his brain suffering an overload of confusion. He apologised to Roy as he rejoined him.

'It's not a problem, Jack. But everything OK? You seem a little distressed.'

'No, it's nothing,' Jack lied.

'Anyway,' said Roy, leading the way to the Irving Room bar, 'there was one more thing, my thanks for stepping in at the last minute.'

'Stepping in?'

'Oh, my goodness. When they 'phoned you – they were supposed to say...'

'Say?'

'Jack, we were scheduled to have Norman Mailer. But he had to cancel at the last minute. We've rearranged him for December.'

'And I suppose,' said Jack, 'that I was the only available option.'

Ruby's jibe, he realised, that they must have the wrong Jack Telford, hadn't been quite so far short of the mark, after all.

Nine

The Valencia Conclusion

Saturday 21ˢᵗ February 1981

'So, you bought the shop from this man – when, *señor?*'

The shop owner was probably forty. Intelligent eyes, full of fire. Jack held up the photo again, while Ruby wandered among the washing machines and refrigerators, the kettles and toasters.

'Ten years ago? Yes, it must have been. I was recently married, and looking for work – or even a small business. Anything to give us some extra income while I wrote.'

'An author?' Ruby shouted from behind an electric cooker.

'A science teacher, *señora.* But the pay wasn't good and I wasn't sure I'd find a publisher. So, this…' He waved his arm around the store. 'This helped to keep us afloat.'

'A book?' said Jack.

'Yes, a book. *The Secret Life of Copernicus.* It was a success. And I owe it all to your friend.' He tapped the photograph. 'A good man. Very guarded, though. Gave nothing away. Even the paperwork, all conducted through a third party, a woman from Orihuela. So, I never had his name. But generous. I could not have afforded to buy the place otherwise.'

It had been quite a process, so many favours that Jack had called in, simply to track Granell's probable journey from Paris back to Spain. First to Santander, then to Barcelona, before Valencia and, finally, here to the shop on Alicante's Avenida del Poeta Zorrilla.

'And you still have no idea,' said Jack, 'who this man might have been?'

248

The shopkeeper replied with one of those Spanish faces, the jutting lower lip and the eyes dancing from side to side, while his hands fluttered like butterflies. No, he had no idea.

'Then, I shall tell you an interesting story, *señor*,' Jack smiled at him.

He kept it reasonably brief. How Amado Granell Mesado had been born in Burriana, north of Valencia. How he had married an Orihuela girl and run a shop there, too – bicycles and motorbikes. Afterwards, the civil war, and Granell had fought for the Republic to the very end. A spell in Vichy French internment camps in Algeria until de Gaulle's Free French army was formed and Granell, along with hundreds of other former-Republican soldiers, joined Leclerc's 2nd Armoured Division.

'A motorised infantry regiment,' said Jack, 'with an entire company of Spanish troops. The Ninth Company, to be exact. *La Nueve.*'

The shopkeeper looked astonished.

'Is this true, *señor*? We carried on the fight – against Hitler? Against Mussolini?' He almost choked on the words, a tear running down his cheek. 'Without them, Italian troops, German bombers – without the other *fachas* – Franco could never have beaten us.'

'No, he couldn't.' Jack put a hand on the man's shoulder. 'And yes, you carried on the fight, right to the end.'

Telford saw Ruby's reaction, too. She was toying with a pretty coffee percolator, blue and white ceramic. She offered him a sad smile.

'And not just *La Nueve*,' said Jack. 'Whole units of Spanish troops fought all through the Italian campaign. And in the French resistance. Thousands of them.'

'How could we know? How? Too dangerous, even to mention the war, while Franco was alive. And not much better now. This Amnesty Law – so we all forget the atrocities, the war crimes, regardless of who committed them, or for how long. That's what it is – a law of forgetfulness.'

Jack had wondered about this, so very often. Did Spanish kids never question why, in school, Spanish history stopped in 1929 and didn't start again until 1950?

'Franco certainly wouldn't have been happy,' he said, 'about anybody knowing Granell's story. You see, *señor*, here's the thing almost nobody else knows, either. That when Paris was liberated from the Nazis, in August '44, the first Allied troops to fight their way into the city weren't Americans or British. Not even French. They were Granell's men. Spanish Republicans. *La Nueve*.'

Now, the man wept in earnest, uncontrollably. And Ruby wept, as well.

'When you find this man's resting place,' murmured the shopkeeper, 'you will say a prayer for him.'

Sunday morning, 22nd February 1981

'Hard to recognise the place,' said Ruby.

'It's more than forty years,' Jack laughed. 'What did you expect?'

'Somehow, I thought...'

'That they'd still be here? Sergio and Fidel?'

Jack felt the familiar pang of guilt. The two friends had shot each other on the quayside at Alicante rather than be taken by Franco, but Ruby had always refused to let him speak of the tragedy. He carried it alone.

She shook her head.

'No, but...'

The beach itself was still the same – more or less. The beach house *casitas* remained. But the fishing boats, which had once been pulled up on the shore, were now gone, apparently moved to a fishermen's quay beyond a new breakwater, away beyond the pinewoods. The old Hotel Moñino was now a fairly swanky beachside restaurant, closed for the winter. Two other hotels had sprung up, the Miramar and the Hotel Las Dunas.

The sea remained, too, of course. Gentle, lapping at the sand. Inviting. He was still a keen swimmer. A sea swimmer, for as much of the year as possible, as his gran had instilled in him. But here? As ice-cold, he imagined, as when they'd been here with the boys. He shivered in his overcoat, pulled the collar up around his ears.

'That's not changed, though.' He gazed north, where the bay was enclosed by the long ridge of the Cabo de Santa Pola, and he remembered how they had watched the tiny black specks of Italian aircraft circling above, a bombing raid against Alicante, on the farther side of the headland.

'Let's find somewhere to eat,' said Ruby. 'It's made me sad, coming back.'

They climbed back into the cramped SEAT they'd hired the night before at the airport – hired in Ruby's name, naturally, since Jack still had no licence. They found a bar, up on the town's Calle Mayor, where they ate fresh sardines and *gambas al ajillo*.

Later, they took the Alicante road, drove back through the city until, thirty-five miles further, they came to the tourist sprawl of Benidorm.

'Christ,' said Jack, 'I thought Franco had made a mess of Guernica – but poor bloody Benidorm.'

'And now, Mr Telford? Where next on this Magical Mystery Tour?'

'Next stop, Sueca. An hour and a half. Two, maybe.'

It took two, climbing up and over the scrub-covered mountain range, which could have graced episodes of *The Cisco Kid* or any of the recent spaghetti Westerns. Then down onto the open plain, the orange and lemon plantations, the dull, flat, rice-growing wetlands, towards Valencia. They arrived just after noon. The cemetery wasn't hard to find, and neither was Granell's tomb.

Typical rows of crypts, five and six storeys high, and each *nicho* sealed with its own square slab bearing the name of the deceased, many bearing flowers, or Catholic crucifixes, rosary beads and other personal religious symbols.

In Granell's case, there was a grey marble tablet, at shoulder height, dust-covered and seemingly neglected. Jack cleaned it with his handkerchief until it gleamed once more, revealing a beautifully engraved upright silver palm branch alongside Amado's name – the palm branch embellished with the letters S. L.d.H.

'They erected it in his honour, when his own people had forgotten him.'

'Legion of Honour,' said Ruby.

'The Society. It's how I tracked him down.'

251

But Ruby knew this already. She'd helped him when he'd contacted them. The Society, in turn, had put them in touch with the French consulate in Valencia – from which he'd discovered more details of Granell's death.

'And the accident, Jack? Do we know exactly where…?'

'Accident?' He polished the marble one more time.

'You know what I mean,' she snapped. 'Don't be so bloody pedantic. And can we get out of this wind? I'm freezing.'

Jack straightened up and winced. Aches and pains. Stiff from the drive. Yet, at almost seventy-three, at least a reminder he was still alive. It was when the aches and pains stopped that you had to worry. And if it wasn't for the cough…

That bloody tune ran through his head. *Deutschland, Deutschland über alles.* The public services advertisement, he remembered, and the words of which Tony Hancock had so memorably set to the tune of the German national anthem.

Coughs and sneezes spread diseases,
Trap your germs in a handkerchief.

'Just feels wrong,' he said. 'Leaving him here. Lost count of the times he saved my bacon. But sure, let's hit the road.'

He wrapped his arm about her for the warmth, led her back towards the car.

'It all seems a bit strange. Did I ever tell you about being in Vienna for the premiere there of *The Third Man*?'

He opened the car door, helped her into the passenger seat since, despite not having a licence, he'd insisted on driving after they'd stopped for those prawns in garlic oil.

'And now,' Ruby laughed, 'you see yourself as Joseph Cotten? Going back to find out what happened to Harry Lime.'

Sunday afternoon, 22ⁿᵈ February 1981

They arrived in Valencia in time for the lunch appointment. They'd checked in at the hotel, and then walked for just five minutes to reach the Casa Montaña.

'So good of you to meet us on a Sunday,' Jack said to their host, as they sat at the Montaña's bar, picking at the *torreznos* and sipping beer.

'It's good, *monsieur*, for us to have somebody with whom to lunch at a civilised hour. These Spaniards!'

Madame Baudouin pursed her lips in mock disgust. She was prim, *petite*, and had made it plain she was merely the honorary consul, now – though, she seemed to have a prodigious store of archives at her disposal.

'In any case,' she went on, 'the least we could do for a holder of the *Croix de Guerre*, is it not? Something of a legend – the man who saved de Gaulle's life?'

Ruby looked at him, her mouth hanging open, her eyes wide.

'Long story,' Jack told her. In truth, however, he hardly remembered the details. He had the photographs, somewhere in his papers, along with the medal itself. But he had reached that point in his life when he was no longer certain whether he recalled the events themselves, or merely the images in the photos.

'But I really appreciated the information you sent,' he said to the honorary consul.

'Sadly, there wasn't much to tell.'

She set down her beer glass and offered him a cigarette. Gitanes. Jack politely declined. Strong French tobacco was just a bit too much, these days. But he quickly provided a light, wondering whether she'd be interested in the lighter's history – the gold lighter once belonging to von Choltitz, the German commander of Paris. Yet, the moment was passed, and *madame* Baudouin was in full flow.

'He'd been driving here from Alicante. Some problem with his French army pension and we needed paperwork from him. But he never made it.'

'Sueca,' said Ruby.

'Sueca,' repeated the honorary consul. 'Only one witness. A truck on the wrong side of the road. Granell swerved to avoid it, and…'

'The truck didn't stop?'

'No, *monsieur*.' She helped herself to another piece of the *torreznos* and crunched through the belly pork's crispy coating. 'And the witness couldn't remember any markings.'

'The witness still around?' Ruby asked.

'It was nine years ago, *madame* Telford.'

'Suspicious?' said Jack. 'The truck having no markings?'

'Who can say? We know Franco had issued an order for his arrest. But that was just after the civil war. And then, in '64, there was the celebration. Twenty-five years of peace.'

'Peace?' Jack laughed. He lit one of his own smokes, then turned his head for the inevitable coughing fit which followed. 'For all Franco's victims? How many, by then? Thousands? Tens of thousands? Bloody butcher.'

'*Eh, bien*, there was some notion of amnesty. Probably how Granell managed to come back.'

'False passports, maybe?' said Ruby, before draining her own glass.

'My point, *madame*, is that he'd been in Alicante at least a few years. And, so far as we can tell, he kept himself to himself. They probably didn't even know he was here.'

'And if they did know,' said Jack, 'they would have had plenty of chances to pick him up without this thing with the truck.'

'Unless,' said Ruby, 'it took until '72 before they found out? And, maybe, then needed a quick solution to their problem?'

Sunday night, 22nd February 1981

The hotel bed was comfortable enough, but there was little chance of sleeping. Impossible even to read. But Telford didn't mind. Ruby was huddled beside him, in the darkness, her head nestled into his shoulder. The winceyette pyjamas were hardly alluring but they provided a more comfortable form of intimacy.

'Festival?' she whispered, as another set of explosions shook the windows. They were a troubling reminder of too many battles.

He set down his book.

'Probably somebody's birthday. For the real thing, we'd need to be here next month. *Las Fallas*. Non-stop fireworks, twenty-four hours a day.'

She stroked the side of his face, ran a finger carefully over the scar of his left eye socket. It still seemed a wonder to him that she did not find it repulsive. But, then, it still seemed a wonder that she was with him at all. At the cottage, every morning was a miracle. There, they had separate beds – partly from the habit of them each having spent so many years living alone, with their own selfish routines. And, partly, a legacy of whatever had happened to her in Lisbon.

Few annoying habits, though. Neither of them. Yes, there was the issue of which way to replace the toilet rolls – Ruby insisting on the paper hanging down at the front, and Jack, more pessimistic, worried about the thing unrolling accidentally, reversing them so the paper hung down at the back. His pessimism was, he supposed another foible. Ruby was distinctly a glass half-full person, while Jack one of those who insisted on looking both ways in a one-way street. But these were minor irritations. So, he would awake each day at first light and immediately thrill anew to the sound of her gentle snores.

'Think I'll give *Las Fallas* miss, Jack Telford. I need to be back in my garden.'

'Just a couple more days,' he said. 'We'll meet up with Aurora.'

Aurora, Granell's first wife, and the mystery woman – the Orihuela woman – who'd negotiated the sale of the shop in Alicante, and now living in Valencia.

'But I think it's just going to be a dead end,' he said. 'Sorry, no pun intended.' He could positively feel the reproachful look on Ruby's face, but chose to shrug it off. 'But no chance, now, anyway, of finding out what happened, is there?'

'I still don't understand. Did he do something so awful in the civil war that they'd still want to kill him for it?'

He felt the warmth of her whispered breath against his shoulder.

'Not just his part in the civil war. Though – well, he'd been a major in the Republican army. Very senior.'

'Franco would have given him a death sentence?'

More fireworks, tiny shards of red and yellow light dancing through the gaps in the half-closed *persiana* window blind. He thought about Sergio and Fidel – their certainty that their own parts in the war would seal their fates. Their roles – and their relationship. Franco's Catholic fanatical crusaders would have made them pay with their lives for this particular sin, alone.

'Probably, he would. But then, serving with Leclerc – the Republic still at war with Franco's friends…'

'Unforgivable.'

She poked a finger through an opening in his own pyjama top and tickled his chest. He hugged her still closer, wondering whether the shared bed might lead to something else. They were, he decided, yet again, a companionable couple. Despite Lisbon, they had their moments of passion. But those, too, were comfortably companionable.

'The worst thing, though?' he said, now needing to get the discussion out of the way. 'After all that was over, Granell was a big player in the secret negotiations between the Republican Left and the Spanish royal family. They were still in exile. Portugal.'

'Democracy with the compromise of a constitutional monarchy? It's what happened four years ago.'

Constitutional monarchy, thought Jack. Now, there's an interesting oxymoron, if ever I heard one. It had never really made sense to him, neither at home, nor abroad. Heads of state determined by nothing other than hereditary privilege? Not a system to be trusted.

'Franco was dead, though,' he said. 'But, back then? Late-40s? It was anathema to Franco. The final nail in Granell's coffin. Literally, maybe.'

Ruby stretched her neck and gently kissed his cheek. Further firecrackers in the street below, like the rattle of a machine gun, and the smell of gunpowder reaching them, even though the window itself was shut.

'And here we are. Back in Spain, after all this time. We've seen the world, you and I. But Spain, Jack. Are you glad?'

He turned, and brushed the curls from her forehead – the curls she had finally allowed to turn grey.

'Yes,' he said. 'Glad.'

It was not entirely true. He loved the country, but so many bad memories here, as well. So much menace.

Monday 23rd February 1981

They were due to meet people from Granell's trade union but, as they left to find breakfast – coffee and grilled croissants at a bar, Jack hoped – they were stopped by the receptionist and handed a message. Apologies, but the meeting would have to take place, instead, during the evening. Something urgent had come up. And there was an odd ending to the note.

Take care, and stay safe.

'Strange!' said Jack.

But that left them with the whole day to kill. Their arrangement to meet with Granell's ex-wife, Aurora, wasn't until the following lunchtime.

So, it was off to the Plaça de la Reina, to the cathedral, and to the plethora of churches – at Ruby's insistence – all located within a few minutes' walk of the square. So many churches!

Ruby took photographs in each of them, keeping a record of the location in a small notebook, and going through reel after reel of Agfa film. Jack had something of a phobia about cameras – they reminded him too much of Valerie Carter-Holt – and he amused himself by compiling a list of collective nouns for Catholic churches. A host. A mass. A blessing. It was endless. It caused him to giggle from time to time, so that he was eventually asked to leave the Church of San Juan del Hospital. Outside, he tried to remember all the other saints for whom the churches were named: Santa Catalina; San Martín; and Santo Tomás, among several others.

Another list of collective nouns began to form and, to Ruby's annoyance, he insisted on sharing these with her as they walked to the Museum of Fine Arts.

'Jack,' she said, 'I sometimes wonder whether I've married a schoolboy. An ageing schoolboy.'

He sulked through most of the galleries – the Gothic and Renaissance stuff, the Goyas – but he came to life again with the exhibition of work by Sorolla.

'I've never seen anything like them,' he laughed, intoxicated by the sun-drenched beach scenes, the pure joy of them, the light on sea and sand. The children swimming. The blinding blues and whites, the burning yellows and orange.

'You know what the Spanish call his style?' said Ruby.

He shook his head, filled with the wonder of them.

'*Luminismo*,' she told him.

'Good word.'

He was staring at the painting simply called *Boys on the Beach*. It reminded him of his own childhood, and those excursions to the lido at Grimley-on-Severn. What had his gran taught him?

'Swimming,' she would say, as she showed him the finer points of advancing from doggy paddle to something resembling front crawl, 'is the best form of exercise for both body and mind. Swimming in the sea is better than swimming in a pool. Swimming in a pool is better than no swimming at all.'

And this: 'There are only two sorts of people in the world, John – those who swim and those who learn to drown.'

She had taught him much more, of course – and especially during those precious weeks back in '34 when he'd been so wet behind the ears. But, best not to think of that, now. Indeed, he *never* thought about it. He'd not, really, ever accepted her loss.

'Yes,' he said, wishing he could be one of those boys in Sorolla's painting. '*Luminismo*.'

Later, they ate lunch at a fish restaurant near the port, before retreating to the hotel for a much-needed *siesta*. This was nothing to do with being in Spain, however. It was almost a daily ritual, wherever they happened to be. Simply a feature of their advancing years.

But, at six that evening, they braved the gathering darkness and a short-lived but icy shower of rain to reach the car and drive to the headquarters of the Comisiones Obreras union confederation for the Valencia Region. *CC.OO. del P.V.*, as the sign in huge red letters declared across the front of the building. The place reminded Jack of the Madrid's Gaylord Hotel, back when, during the siege, it had been home to the Russians dispatched there to help the Republic. Soviet austerity in the architecture.

It was *madame* Baudouin's suggestion that the meeting had been arranged.

'Yes,' she'd said. 'Yet another black mark against him, so far as Franco was concerned.'

For Granell, of course, it would have been unthinkable not to be in a union and, on his return to Spain, he'd inevitably become involved in those clandestine "workers' commissions" – an almost literally unholy alliance between the Spanish Communist Party and various Catholic labour organisations – established in opposition to the Francoist yellow unions and even the Socialist-affiliated General Workers' Union, UGT.

'You think they'll know anything here, Jack? Just because he was a member?'

They climbed the steps to the front doors. Unusually, there was nobody else on the street. Not a soul. Complete silence.

'An important member. Who knows? They have a lot of influence. This past six years, they've grown from almost nothing to be the biggest union in the country. Confederation, really. Made up of lots of separate unions.'

'Like the TUC?'

'Yes, like the TUC. But different. More – well, revolutionary, maybe.'

'*Sindicatos*,' she said, as though it were self-evident. The Spanish word for trade unions; though, here, the roots of the word ran so much deeper. Syndicates.

'Sums it up in one, my love.'

Syndicalists. Like those in Britain in the early days of the century. Workers' organisations, believing in direct action to improve workers' conditions, rather than relying on government to do it. So, he'd expected a hive of activity. Yet, the foyer was empty, eerily silent, nobody at the reception desk.

'Hello!' Jack shouted.

No response.

They waited for five minutes, Telford pacing up and down the tiled floor.

'Perhaps, they're all in a meeting,' Ruby suggested.

'Perhaps.'

He tried the double doors at one side of the reception area. Locked. But, on the other side, they opened onto a wood-panelled, dimly lit corridor with offices on either side. From the farther end, the muffled sound of voices.

'Well, nothing ventured…' said Jack, and strode off in that direction, with Ruby following behind.

'It could be private, Jack. Are you sure…?'

There was a modest conference hall, a small lecture theatre, adorned with union posters and long banners bearing slogans and the *CC.OO.* logo. Near the rostrum, a group of twelve or fifteen men and women, gathered about a radio set upon a table. In the Spanish manner, every member of the group was speaking at the same time, so it was impossible for Jack to hear their words, or the radio itself. But the babble of voices conveyed its own impressions. Anger – and fear. Consternation – and caution.

'Excuse us,' Jack called out, and every one of them spun about, surprised. Perhaps, a little afraid, he thought. 'I'm Telford. We had an appointment.'

A quick huddle of conversation, and one of the men came forward.

'*Señor* Telford.' The fellow was Jack's age or thereabouts, with corduroy trousers and a thick cardigan over a collarless shirt. 'Have you not heard?'

'Heard?'

The babble began again, and Jack tried to make sense of what he was hearing.

'A military coup, Jack?' said Ruby. 'Is that what they're saying?'

'We thought it was a joke,' said the man. 'Marcelino...' He turned to point at one of his companions. 'Marcelino brought us the news. We didn't believe him. But when we turned on the radio...'

A single radio station had been broadcasting live from Madrid, covering an early evening meeting of the Spanish Parliament, the *Cortes*. Nothing very dramatic, simply a formality vote to confirm the election of the new President, Leopoldo Calvo-Sotelo. Suddenly, listeners could hear shouting, and the reporter covering the event telling the world that scores of Guardia Civil agents had invaded the chamber. He'd identified their leader, a Lieutenant Colonel Tejero, who could then be heard ordering everybody to stop, to get on the ground. Angry voices, a lot of yelling, and shots fired.

'And now?' said Jack.

'And now, the broadcast from Madrid cut. But here...'

The man did his best to silence his comrades, and though it was less than successful, Telford could at least make sense of it.

'This is all we can get now,' said the younger man, identified as Marcelino. 'Every station.'

Military music, interrupted by a recorded statement in the name of General Jaime Milans del Bosch.

"I must inform you that a state of emergency now exists within the Valencia region. Martial law has been declared and a curfew will be in place from ten o'clock this evening, Tuesday, twenty-third of February. The curfew will remain in force until further notice and those found breaking its conditions will be severely punished."

A warning, too, that any strike or lock-out, any abandoning of work for other unauthorised reasons, would be considered as sedition and the culprits treated accordingly. Everybody knew what that meant.

'The other regions?' said Jack.

'We don't know. And I'm sorry, *Señor* Telford, if you've had a wasted journey. But I suggest you return to your hotel. Safer there.'

'This can't be right,' said Ruby. 'Not again, surely.'

But Jack wasn't so certain. Spain's path along the road returning to democracy had been full of potholes – sometimes yawning sinkholes. Francoist elements in the army openly showing their displeasure that socialists and communists were now back in public office. Another general, Alfonso Armada, publicly espousing the removal of President Suárez from power and replacing him with a military leader. Telford had followed all this with interest, including the dismissal of yet another general, the previous year, for plotting against the government.

'The message, this morning,' Jack said to them. 'About putting the meeting back to this evening. Did you know?'

There'd been those words at the end: *Take care and stay safe.*

'Sense of something in the air,' said Marcelino. 'And you have a certain reputation, *señor*. Did you not smell it, too?'

Jack decided that his nose for danger had not been quite so acute since Ruby entered his life again, though he wasn't about to admit as much.

'Too much stink from last night's fireworks, I guess. And my wife's right – the government's bound to deal with this. But I think it

261

was good advice, about heading back to the hotel. If there's nothing we can do here…?'

Nothing. There were farewells. More warnings to be careful.

But as Jack and Ruby were letting themselves out of the building, there was an old, too familiar sound, which sent chills down his spine. The squeal of link pins as they rolled around the length of tank tracks, and the accompanying raw grind of the tank's engine. Not one tank, in fact, but two of the monsters, rumbling along the street.

'Christ,' said Jack. 'It's real. Maybe, better to stay here? I don't fancy running into a roadblock or something. Soldiers stoked up and ready for a fight?'

'But not safe here, either, Jack.'

She was probably correct. How long before they decided to round up the union leaders? It was all too predictable. It was always the same. Here in '36. In Jakarta. Chile. Athens. South Africa. Now Spain's turn, again.

'Although, maybe strength in numbers?' she said, as more women and men arrived outside the building, running up the steps. Heavy coats against the evening cold. Blowing on chilled fingers. Animated, concerned chatter. Raised fist salutes.

Jack and Ruby followed them back into the hall, into a barricade of noise. Outsiders, they were on the receiving end of suspicious glances; though, nothing staunched the flow of shared news.

'The bastards have put two thousand troops on the streets.'

'Occupied the *Ayuntamiento* and the court buildings.'

'Tanks – dozens of the bloody things.'

From beyond the walls, they could hear the muffled cackle of stentorian announcements.

'They're everywhere,' somebody shouted. 'Loudspeaker trucks.'

And then, there was the speculation. The rumours. But that same younger man from earlier, Marcelino, slammed his hand on the table, again and again, until some semblance of order was restored.

'Comrades,' he cried. 'It's bad enough as it is. No point guessing what might happen next.'

'And we've got a job to do,' said his older companion, the fellow with the cardigan, as still more people arrived. 'This curfew – we'll have members coming out of work at ten. They'll walk straight into all this shit.'

'We need to get around as many of our workplaces as possible,' said Marcelino. 'The hospitals. Factories with shift changes. Try to make sure everybody finishes early, wherever they can.'

Telford remembered Madrid during the siege – the warnings for folk trying to retain some normality, still going to the cinema or the theatre. Warnings to leave before the curtain fell, because Franco's artillery always aimed at the streets outside such venues at finishing time, hoping to target departing audiences. Get out early, but not so easy at work.

'What about the membership records?' said one of the newcomers. He was deeply tanned, perhaps thirty, with a sparse beard and dancing, intelligent eyes. Vaguely familiar eyes.

'Good point, Joan,' said Marcelino. He pronounced the man's name in the way of the Catalans and Valencianos. Jo-anne. 'You know somewhere we can hide them?'

'I do, but I'll need a car.'

'We have a car,' said Jack, before Ruby could stop him. 'And happy to help.'

'*Señor* Telford,' said Marcelino, 'this isn't your fight.'

Yet, somehow, these things were always Telford's fight and, ten minutes later, they were edging through the city streets, Joan in the passenger seat, navigating, with Ruby squashed in the back, along with all those green cardboard bankers boxes, filled with files, stacked to the roof, and all the SEAT's small boot filled, as well.

'How far?' she said.

'Seven kilometres,' Joan replied. 'Give or take. But we won't get there without a few detours. Watch out for checkpoints.'

Jack fought against the temptation of speeding, for the roads were generally quiet. Army convoys, here and there, buses still running, but not much more. And it was stupid, of course, driving without a licence and the likelihood of being stopped.

'But we're headed where, exactly?' he said.

'Sant Pau,' Joan told him. 'San José – the Jesuit College.'

Telford almost lost control of the car.

'The...?'

'I was a novice there. Two years. Took my vows and became a Jesuit brother. Then sent to Central America. Well, I volunteered to go.'

On one of the wider palm-lined avenues, a loudspeaker truck passed them, travelling in the opposite direction and playing loud martial music, its headlights creating tiny rainbows through the drizzle.

'Wanted to see the world?' said Ruby.

'Something like that. The Society had a network of schools and I, too, it turned out, had skills as a carpenter. They thought I might be useful.'

'But you're not a priest,' said Jack. 'Not now?'

Joan shook his head.

'No, not now.'

'I sense a story,' said Ruby. 'What happened?'

'Nicaragua happened,' Joan told her, as he gazed out of the window at rectangular turrets of the Generalitat Palace, which Jack and Ruby had visited earlier.

Earlier? To Jack, it felt like weeks ago.

'The revolution?' he said.

'The revolution, *señor.*'

There was something about this young man which reminded Jack of those among whom he'd shared so many dangers in Normandy. But something which reminded him, too...

'A liberation theologist with a gun?' he said.

'I wasn't the only one. And there wasn't much choice.'

Jack had followed the events in Central America closely over recent years. Honduras, Guatemala and El Salvador. Popular guerrilla movements fighting cruel civil wars against CIA-backed despots. But, most of all, he'd been intrigued by Nicaragua's successful revolution, just two years earlier, which had overthrown the brutal regime of dictator Anastasio Somoza.

'Caught up in the fighting?' said Ruby, hastily turning to stop the pile of boxes falling on her as they turned a corner just a bit too sharply.

'Not caught up,' Joan replied. 'I chose sides. Simple as that.'

'The world revolution?' Jack suggested. He'd heard this sort of speech before. In truth, he'd heard himself making them.

'There may only be one world revolution, comrade. But it's made up of lots of smaller revolutions. Each a bit different, but each with the same purpose – to make the world a better place. And, in those revolutions, we can each only do whatever we are able, small or large. From each according to their ability, to each according to his or her needs.'

'A Jesuit Marxist revolutionary,' said Ruby. 'That's quite a mix.'

'The core principles of Christianity, of Marxism, of Islam – they're not so very different. It's men who corrupt those principles, is it not? Fanatics. And it's those men we must depose.'

'Back long?' Jack asked him.

'A year. And now it looks like we all need to choose sides one more time.'

They were given cheese, *jamón* and wine when they safely delivered the union's membership records into the Jesuits' safekeeping. There was some better news, as well. Apparently, the local air force base commander had refused to comply with the rebels' demands and, instead, threatened to scramble his fighter jets against them.

By nine, they were back at the union headquarters; though, by now, there was a machine gun post on the corner, the weapon itself trained on the building from a hastily constructed parapet of sandbags. Yet, it was unmanned, a couple of soldiers idly smoking nearby.

'Let's see if there's anything else we can do,' said Jack, starting to climb out of the car. But Joan grabbed his arm, told him they'd done enough.

'And there's the curfew,' he said. 'No disrespect, but I don't think you'd want to spend the entire night here. Seriously, my friend, you should both go back to your hotel. Get some sleep. We'll see what the morning brings.'

'He's right, Jack,' said Ruby. 'Tomorrow's another day.'

Joan shook their hands, wished them a goodnight, and headed for the steps.

Telford started the engine again and pulled his door shut. Then, he thrust it open once more.

'Wait!' he called out. 'We don't know your name. Joan...?'

'Sifre,' the younger man shouted back. 'Joan Sifre.' And, with a wave of his hand, he was gone.

They both sat in silence.

'Is that – just coincidence?' said Ruby, at last.

Jack slammed the door, and pulled away. He didn't believe in coincidence.

'I guess it's a common enough name, my love.'

'But...'

'Yes, I know.'

It had only been yesterday, after all. On that beach beyond Santa Pola, talking about their old friend. In his suitcase, at the hotel, Jack had brought the copy of Sergio Sifre's sketchbook, but he'd left it there, in his luggage. He'd intended, of course, that they'd sit on the sand and turn its pages together, as they sometimes did, back at the cottage. Those beautiful illustrations Sergio had drawn to accompany Lorca's poetry. *La señorita del abanico*. And the intimate likenesses of Fidel, pencilled with a lover's hand.

But it had been too cold for sitting on the sand. And those moments always somehow turned sour, Ruby still refusing to ask the question, and Jack honouring her wishes, though anguished by the pain of keeping the secret to himself. He'd resisted the desire, in Alicante itself, to visit the port, to stand once more on the quayside where he'd cradled poor Sergio's head in his bloodied hands, where he'd seen Fidel's body floating in the water.

'*Hombre*,' the Republican soldier had told him, all those decades past, shrugging as though what had happened to them was obvious, 'they shot each other.'

Jack had seen that the man was holding Sergio's sketchbook, and had snatched it from his hands, taken it with him aboard the *Stanbrook* – carried it with him all these years.

'Perhaps, tomorrow...' said Ruby.

'Maybe,' he said, and he rubbed at the eye-patch though only to mask his true intention of wiping away the tears.

Thirty minutes later, they were back at the hotel, in time to hear a radio broadcast by the President of the Catalan government, calling for peace and assuring listeners that the Spanish king, Juan Carlos, had everything under control.

'Whatever the hell that means,' said Jack. They were both exhausted, but he was never going to be reassured by a royal promise. 'And a military coup – but the king's got everything under control? How?'

It was a distraction, at least, from the Sergio saga. They'd not been able to leave it alone.

'Yes, tomorrow,' Ruby had said. 'We find Joan again, and just ask him – whether he had relatives who fought in the civil war. Uncle, perhaps. Something like that.'

Jack had offered her the same non-committal assurance. Maybe. Maybe, tomorrow. But, for now, there was this crowd of guests in the hotel restaurant, trapped here by the curfew. Everybody shouting at once. Everybody shouting louder than the radio – now returned to playing martial music. Everybody with an opinion – and several of the Spaniards, women and men alike, stridently supporting the coup, just as they'd supported Franco, just as they supported him even now, even in death. Telford expected blows to be exchanged at any moment.

'Perhaps, best to go up to our room, after all,' he said, when it was all beginning to get entirely out of hand. 'I'm scared I'll end up thumping one of those fascist bastards.'

Tuesday 24th February 1981

He slept, but not for long, Ruby shaking him awake. She was still dressed.

'Jack,' she said. 'Jack! There's something going on. The noise from downstairs. It suddenly went quiet. But they've started up again. Only, it's different, now. I think I can hear the television.'

Telford listened. She was right. It was the thing about Spain. This modern Spain. You couldn't go anywhere – local bar or the finest restaurant – without an old black and white TV blaring in the corner. Until last night, at least, when the televisions had all lapsed into lifelessness. Somehow, the sound was distinctive. He thought about getting dressed himself, but a television broadcast? Not to be missed.

Jack slipped a dressing gown over his pyjamas, and they took the stairs down to the basement, where the same crowd – maybe with a few additions, Jack thought, were gathered in front of the screen. It sat on a table in the corner, alongside the glass-domed bar on which the *pintxos* were normally displayed.

In Britain, there would have been a reverential silence, had the queen deigned to appear on television, at one in the morning, in full regalia, to make a statement to the nation. But here? The same abrasive arguments as earlier – though, perhaps, marginally more muted. Yet, there he was, King Juan Carlos, monochrome, but in person. Full army general's uniform, medals galore, and filmed in some royal palace, against the backdrop of a tapestry full of heraldic symbolism. He'd obviously been speaking for some time but, once Jack had attuned his ear to the Spanish, concentrated on the speech itself, he heard most of the final words.

'*...will not tolerate... the actions or behaviour of anyone... through use of force... to interrupt... the Constitution... approved by vote in referendum.*'

There was an appeal for serenity. For public confidence.

'Is that it?' said Ruby. 'All over?'

'That depends. On how much authority he carries. On the military governors in all the other regions. We'll know better in the morning, I suppose.'

They slept very little but, over breakfast in the morning, the TV channels kept churning out the same bulletins. Endlessly repeated highlights from the king's broadcast. Snatches of the country's two main union leaders, one Socialist, one Communist, appealing for calm. Grainy coverage from outside the Congress building in Madrid, showing the deputies emerging, one by one, from their overnight ordeal as hostages. There were raised fist salutes and cries of *¡Viva la Libertad!* Long live Freedom! Singing crowds cheering their release.

'And Tejero?' Jack asked the guests at their neighbouring table.

But the lieutenant colonel who'd led the coup was apparently still inside, still in the Chamber of Deputies.

'They just reported,' said the elderly woman at the table, 'that he was shown an early edition of *El Pais*, listing all the army commanders supporting the king. Every region – except here. Knew his goose was cooked. Started releasing the hostages. Hopefully, he'll do the decent thing…'

She put two fingers of her gnarled right hand against her temple. '*Pfff,*' she said.

'And here?' Ruby asked her. 'In Valencia?'

'They arrested Milans del Bosch two hours ago,' said the woman's husband. 'Though, it looks like some of his men are still holding out – looking for some sort of amnesty, maybe.'

'And they not only arrested the general,' laughed the wife. 'They arrested his tank, too. Seems like they're going to put it on display somewhere – make an example of it.'

Yes, thought Jack, that would be Spain!

'I just hope they make them pay,' he said, later, as they headed back to the union building.

There were still armoured vehicles and checkpoints here and there. But these soldiers had obviously been ordered to smile as they did their duty. No helmets. Flags fluttering from every available antenna.

'You sound so bitter, Jack. You don't need to take everything so personally.'

Do I not? Telford thought. Fascists. Danielle. Mauthausen's gas chambers and ovens.

'What other way is there?' he said. 'And look at this lot. You think it's not personal for them, too?'

Impossible to park anywhere near the confederation's headquarters. Crowds filled the street. Placards and flags, white lettering on blood-red banners.

'They must have been up all night making those,' Ruby laughed, as one of the flags was thrust into her hand.

It wasn't yet eight o'clock and already so many thousands that there was less chance of finding Joan Sifre than peas in a *paella*.

'Where are we headed?' Jack asked a group of young women, all leather and studs, piercings, chains and tattered tartan trews, multicoloured Mohican haircuts.

'The Generalitat, comrade!' they shouted, as though it might be the Bastille. Perfect unison. Fists raised skywards.

'Civil government building,' Jack told Ruby, who was busy waving her flag in the midst of the girls. They made a strange contrast, the elderly Mrs Telford and these exuberant punks. But they stayed together when the demonstration finally formed and began to snake its way, generally west and northwards, though with many twists and turns, across the Ciutat Vella, the old historic heart of the city, and around the cathedral.

'Making a point, don't you reckon?' he said; though, he now rather wished he'd stayed at the hotel. It was a clear morning, but cold. And the exertion had brought on the bloody cough, again. So, he was pleased when they finally reached the Plaça de Manises and the Gothic, fortress-like bulk of the Generalitat Palace, flanked at either end by menacing square towers. The square itself wasn't particularly grand but it was packed to capacity by the time they got there, and so, too, were the surrounding streets.

'Why here?' Ruby asked him.

'Us, or them?' Jack nodded his head towards the punks. But he went on to explain that this was the administrative base for the Valencia Regional Council. 'Next year,' he said, 'they become an autonomous region. Even more devolved powers. And all this...' He waved his hand around the square, echoing now to shouts of *Huelga General! Huelga General!* 'They seem convinced the Council must have known about the plans for the coup. So, the threat of a general strike.'

They spent an hour pushing their way through the demonstrators.

'Reminds me of Lisbon,' she shouted, at one point.

He turned to see what she meant, afraid she was remembering whatever they'd done to her. But, then, he recalled that other demonstration, outside Lisbon's cathedral, the riot police and the tear gas.

'Not quite the same,' he said.

The cordon of Guardia Civil officers guarding the building's front entrance, at the base of this nearest tower, seemed pretty relaxed. But, less so, the groups of armed civilians scattered among them, and waving old rifles, even a few shotguns, in the general direction of the protestors.

'And those?' she said. 'Didn't have time to get their uniforms on?'

He laughed.

'Somatén,' he told her. 'Militiamen. A Catalan thing, originally. From the Middle Ages, I think. Disbanded a couple of times, but then became a national outfit under Franco in '45. Officially disbanded again a couple of years back but, here and there, they still exist. Fascists, licensed to carry guns.'

'Listen,' he said, overcome with negativity, 'there's no sign of Joan. Shall we give this up and go for coffee?'

She handed her flag to another of the demonstrators.

'Good idea.' She linked his arm, rubbed his back as the coughing caught him yet again. She'd told him often enough that he needed to see a doctor but, for now, she simply gave him that familiar look of admonishment. 'But I was thinking about what he'd said – Joan, I mean. About liberation theology. Isn't that just a contradiction?'

'You think so? I realised a long time ago that there's a simple difference between liberal thinkers – even if they happen to be Jesuit priests – and the most reactionary conservatives.'

'Far left, or far right?'

For a moment, he considered making a joke of it since, in truth, he'd rather lost his sense of direction. But then he spotted a sign for the cathedral, and the moment was lost.

'Both,' he said, as he led her through the scrum along the narrow street on the Generalitat's southern façade.

'And the difference?'

They'd emerged alongside a neat public garden, filled with still-naked trees. Beyond, the enormity of the Plaça de la Virgen. They already knew this square from yesterday's jaunt around the tourist spots. Here, the Turia fountain, the pink stone elegance and dome of the basilica and, in the farthest corner, the cathedral's Apostles' Gate doorway, and the curved wall of archways, Colosseum-like, which seemed to join them

'The difference,' he murmured, and edged them towards the nearest bar. 'I guess... Well, liberal thinkers – and I put us both in that boat, my dear... Liberal thinkers spend most of our time trying to rationalise what makes the reactionaries tick. The theories just keep getting more and more complex.'

At the entrance to the bar, Ruby changed her mind.

'Coffee later?' she said. 'I'd rather see the cathedral. I think I can hear those reactionaries of yours laughing at us.'

She patted his arm. It was the gentlest of censures, but he still ignored it.

'Exactly,' he said. 'We might not like them, detest them, even. But we always believe they can somehow be redeemed. See the light.'

'And the more we try to rationalise their politics...'

'That's probably the point – it's not politics, at all.'

They stood back to admire the doorway, four pointed arches joined together in a single framework for the sculpted and weather-worn apostles, virgins and angels for which it was famous. Above the arches, a rose window. Behind them, the chanting and songs of the demonstrators still filled the morning. From inside, a choir.

'I read yesterday,' he said, 'that when the Moors were here, this was where their main mosque stood. This, the main entrance.'

'Beautiful, Jack. Can we go in?'

Telford tried the door and it opened easily. Inside, there was quite a contrast. Plain white walls in the Baroque style and hung with gilt-framed Renaissance paintings. Further into the cathedral's depths, the choristers practised their *Miserere mei, Deus*.

'Is that what happens?' she whispered. 'The more we rationalise, the louder they laugh?'

Because, fundamentally, Telford decided, they have nothing but their hatred for the rest of us. For no more complex reason than that we *are* liberal-minded.

'We might not like *them*,' he murmured, 'but they despise *us* to such an extent that only our total annihilation will satisfy them. They hate us so much, they don't care how much damage they do to themselves – just so long as we get wiped out in the process.'

It seemed to Jack that the choir echoed the pessimism in his soul. Three choirs, in truth: the first two singing alternating sections; the third, responding in plainsong.

Libera me de sanguinibus, Deus
Deliver me from blood, O God

'In the end, though, don't we always win?'

It wouldn't be 1984, Telford knew. Orwell had underestimated the date. But it was coming. The totalitarian superstate kept in place, this time, by overwhelming masses, concerned more with personality cults than political realism.

'In the end?' he said. 'Think about it. Reactionaries loathe the idea of collectives. Any sort of collective. To them, collectives stink of socialism. Yet, they hate us so much that, whenever they want to destroy us, they have to band together to accomplish their goals. Imagine how much that must fuel their fanaticism.'

There are none whose hate burns so fiercely as those who hate themselves.

'Yet, still we win.'

Miserere mei, Deus; secundum magnam misericordiam tuam.

'Because, so far, our collectives have ultimately been bigger than their own. But, one day, Ruby… One day, we'll still be trying to make sense of them, and the bastards will outnumber us. They'll still be laughing while they lobotomise each and every one of us.'

Tuesday afternoon, 24th February 1981

To his horror, Jack realised that Granell's first wife lived on the fourth floor of the apartment block – and the ancient lift doors were sealed with an ominous orange sign. Black lettering. *Fuera de Servicio*. Out of Order.

Fifteen painful minutes later, he'd reached the landing, bent double, gasping for breath, and one of the worst coughing fits he'd ever experienced.

'But not bad…' he wheezed, '…for a one-eyed…fat man.'

'Just a bit overweight, Jack,' said Ruby. She'd struggled somewhat coming up the stairs, as well; though, she'd managed better than Telford. Yet, he looked up into her face and saw worry etched into her beautiful wrinkles.

'Never fear, he said. 'As soon as we're back… the doctor… I'll make an appointment.'

'Good. Because you're certainly no Rooster Cogburn.'

She was right, but he'd enjoyed the comparison ever since the CIA woman Mary Lou De Witt, had taunted him that way, back in Lisbon.

Whatever became of her? Jack wondered.

The dark mahogany opened at the far end of the short corridor. A woman appeared in the doorway. Mid-fifties, he calculated. Cornflower blue and purple floral-patterned frock.

'Great heaven,' said Jack. *'De tal palo, tal astilla.'* The apple, indeed, did not fall far from the tree.

'Everybody says the same,' the woman smiled. It was Granell's smile. The features aquiline, too, like her father's, just as Jack had last seen him. Amado would have been about the same age, back then, as the daughter must be, now.

'Aurora,' he laughed, and rubbed at his chest to settle and soothe the last of his convulsions.

Within the apartment, the furniture was traditionally sombre. Heavy, dark as the door, every available inch of open wall space filled with religious prints and posters, images of the Virgin and several wooden crucifixes.

In a worn armchair, before an electric fire, sat the other Aurora, the mother. She was frail, wrapped and belted in a raspberry-pink candlewick housecoat. The whole place smelled of mothballs. Camphor and the unmistakeable odours of old age; though, she could not be so many years older than Jack, himself. Not yet eighty, he decided. She couldn't be. But hardly spared them a glance, focused instead on the television, its volume turned to maximum.

'Seen the latest?' she shouted at him without any welcoming ceremony.

Not so frail, after all, Jack realised. And he had to admit they'd not heard any more news for the past hour or so.

'Tejero,' said the old lady. 'Traitor just surrendered. Arrested! Should have been shot.'

It was amazing to Telford that the wretch had held out so long. Eighteen hours? More or less. While his accomplice, there in Valencia, General Milans del Bosch, had given up at five that morning, over seven hours ago, now.

'All over, then,' he said.

'It is never over, *señor*,' she snapped. 'Never.'

Well, that was true. Just look at this past twenty-four hours. Another bloody coup. And what was all this with the king? Perhaps, he'd spent too much time around conspiracies. But a military coup - only one in which the leaders of the insurrection left the king free to make a broadcast to the nation. His assurance that he had things under control. It had nagged at him ever since. Wouldn't this mean that Juan Carlos might come out of this as a hero, legitimising the monarchy at a time when so many still called for its abolition?

'*Mamá*,' said the younger Aurora, turning down the sound on the TV to a more bearable level, '*Señor* Telford knows this. He's been fighting the *fachas* all his life, I think.'

Jack was taken aback. Had he?

'That's kind of you to say, but...'

'My husband is very modest,' said Ruby. 'He does not accept compliments with any grace.'

'*Papi* spoke about you often enough. I always felt as though I knew you. From afar, perhaps. But my brother speaks English and sometimes we have seen something in a foreign newspaper that you have written. Amado has translated it for me.'

'I'm truly flattered,' Jack told her. 'And your brother – another Amado.' He smiled at her. 'I should have known. Will we meet him?'

'Amado,' said the old lady. 'My Amado.'

The son, or her husband? Telford wasn't sure.

'Not this time,' said the daughter. 'He's out of the city. But if you come back another time...' She stopped to tell her mother what was being said, raising her voice again. Then, she turned back to Jack and Ruby. 'But please, sit. There's coffee on the stove and Amado went to visit Lina. To fetch something you'd like to see, perhaps.'

Lina, the second love in Granell's life. Marcelina Gaubeca. Living in Valencia, as well, Jack knew. And when the coffee arrived, served with bite-sized sugar-coated pastries, Aurora went to the large sideboard and produced a small tray, covered with a red silk cloth. Like a magician, she lifted the cloth away with a flamboyant flourish.

Granell's medals. Of course. Several campaign medals and the *Croix de Guerre*. The ribbon, green and red.

'The same as yours, Jack,' murmured Ruby, in English.

'But I never got this one.' Jack pointed at the blood-red ribbon of the *Légion d'Honneur*. 'This one is very special. It's these, though...'

He picked up, in turn, Granell's dog tags, his old compass, and the whistle he'd been so fond of blowing, to issue orders, when they'd been in the thickest of the fighting.

'He saved my life,' he shouted to the old lady. 'Not once. A few times. I'd never have survived the war...'

Telford watched a tear trickle down her cheek, and choked back one of his own. Ruby hugged him.

'When did you see him last?' the younger Aurora asked.

'At Leclerc's funeral. '47. We wrote to each other for a while afterwards. He was always full of hope – for Spain. For you. For his family. Knew he'd come home, one day.'

'He survived all that,' said Ruby. 'The civil war. The world war. Exile in Paris. Only to be run off the road by some maniac.'

'When you wrote to me, *señor*,' said Aurora, 'you told me you wanted to find out what happened to him.'

Telford paused before replying, then addressed himself to the old lady, who was busily chewing on one of the pastries.

'It always seemed too much of a coincidence, *señora*. Franco was never one to forgive and forget. And when Amado came back...'

'Did you think, *Señor* Telford, that we would not have investigated *Papi*'s death ourselves?'

Jack felt the colour rise up his neck. He toyed with the eye-patch, a common enough affectation on the rare occasions when he could be embarrassed.

'No, Aurora,' he stuttered, 'I didn't intend...'

'We never managed to find the driver or the truck. There was only one witness and the descriptions were vague. But some of our people went to all the bars on the road north of Sueca. A long way north.'

Jack hadn't thought of that – though, by now, that particular trail would have been so cold, it would have been frozen solid.

'Anything?' said Ruby.

'Not much,' Aurora smiled, while her mother seemed to have fallen asleep. 'But in one of them, our vague descriptions rang a bell. There'd been this old fellow. One too many brandies with his breakfast. They'd warned him not to drive, but…'

'Accident, then?' Jack murmured.

Aurora snorted with derision.

'If you call being killed by a drunk driver an accident, I suppose so.'

'Shame,' said Jack, swallowing the dregs from his coffee cup. 'A waste.'

He felt himself being brought close to tears again. Old age, he decided. Sentimentality. Granell would have had sharp words for him.

'And a particular shame for Jack,' said Ruby, linking his arm. 'He rather saw himself as that fellow in *El Tercer Hombre*.' The Third Man.

Aurora laughed; though, this time more affably.

'He thought he would find *Papi* here alive – hiding in the sewers of Valencia?'

'Something like that,' Jack told her. 'I know – stupid!'

'No, *Señor* Telford. Not stupid, not really. And, in a way, I suppose you were right. Look what just happened. The *fachas* are always with us. But at least the principles my father fought for, they're strong enough to keep them at bay – for a while.'

For how long, though? It sounded like some sort of cliché, but he knew that, in this instant, she was right. And in this sense, Granell was, indeed, still there – in spirit, anyway. It eased his gloom a little.

'Imagine the time,' he said, adopting his best smile, 'when Spain decides to remember, rather than forget. To honour him the way the French have done.'

'We shall work on that,' Aurora replied. 'One day, *señor*. One day.'

Her mother stirred from her sleep, and started as she came awake. She stared at him, seeming confused by this stranger in her home.

'Time to rest,' she shouted at him. She repeated the word, even louder. *Descansar*. 'Rest!'

Telford thought about it as he struggled all the way back down those endless flights of stairs. Almost as hard as climbing up the bloody things. She's right, though, he decided. This path on which I set out after the war. He remembered Strasbourg. He saw again the face of Chrétien de la Marielle. Revenge.

Fighting fascists all his life? He didn't think so. But Aurora was right. There were plenty of others to carry on that particular work. Others inspired by the example of giants like Granell.

One of the last performances he'd seen in Berlin had been Brecht's *Die Mutter*, and there were those lines for the Pelagea Wlassowa title character. Her song, *In Praise of the Fighters*.

> *Those who are weak don't fight.*
> *Those who are stronger might fight for an hour.*
> *Those who are stronger still might fight for many years.*
> *The strongest fight their whole life.*
> *They are the indispensable ones.*

Yes, Jack, he urged himself. Maybe, time to simply set down the burden.

He rested when they reached the ground floor, just in time to see the engineer remove the Out of Service sign from the lift doors.

'There,' the fellow beamed at them. 'All fixed, now.'

Ten

The Dorset Obituary

Monday 25th April 1983

'Odysseus had it easy,' Telford murmured to himself as he eased his way down the concrete steps to the austere promenade, and the beach. 'Only adrift for ten years after his war. But me? It took me forty!'

Forty years before he could finally come home – apart from that brief spell after Berlin. And all those journeys; the places he'd seen; the treacheries he'd known; the friends and the enemies; the secrets he'd discovered; the dangers he'd come through. Unscathed? Hardly. Though, just look at what he'd found at the end. Had it been worthwhile? Had he made a difference somewhere along the road? Somewhere in those forty long years? He hoped so.

But the journey this past six months – the cancer!

The stupid thing? He'd been expecting it. And there'd been that fateful day with the consultant. All dicky bow and Brylcreem.

'I'm guessing you know what I'm going to tell you, Mr Telford.'

'Cancer,' Jack had replied. 'Lungs?'

'Gracious, no. The problem with your lungs is emphysema. Bad enough, but if you give up those damned cigarettes, and with the help of a bronchodilator, we could keep you going for a good while yet. The cancer, however…'

'Then…?'

'Testicular, I'm afraid. Did you not suspect…?'

He had not. It had felt very much like one of those "good news, bad news" jokes. A young man's cancer, the consultant had told him.

'Aching scrotum?'

'Yes, sometimes, but not always.'

'Ache in your back and losing weight?'

'Symptoms of old age, surely.'

'Cough? Sore chest?'

'That's why I came, in the first place.'

All very treatable, though, he'd been assured. Possibly, an operation. And the inevitable jest.

'Don't worry, it's why God gave you two!'

Radiation therapy. Chemotherapy, too. All to be decided when they had a clearer picture.

'And the prognosis?' Jack had demanded to know. 'How long?'

'Give up the Capstans. Cut out the drinking. Take the treatment. Excellent chance of surviving. Maybe, five more years? Statistically speaking, of course.'

'Statistically,' said Jack. 'Yes, of course.'

He'd picked up the inhaler, and it helped – a little. And he'd made all the appointments for his further tests. But give up the smokes? Fat chance!

The drink, he minded less. But he'd work on that, after today. It was his birthday, for pity's sake, and Ruby was taking him to the Bell Cliff later. A glass or two of their best red wouldn't go amiss.

He walked eastwards, a hundred yards, with the cliff face rising to his left – Back Beach, his favourite – and laid down his towel. Then, he lifted it again, to clear some of the stones beneath and, as had happened so many times, he turned over a decent-sized ammonite in his fist.

The tide was a fair way out, but already on the turn. Another four hours, he calculated, before High Water. A perfect incoming tide. He was still a strong enough swimmer, but these days he wouldn't risk the ebbing currents. No, today it would be the cold that would challenge him. That, and the climb back up those damned steps to the car park.

From behind him, he heard the voices of his neighbour's children, Tim and Tilly.

'There's Mr Telford,' Tilly screamed, and raced towards him. 'He's going to swim! He's going to swim!'

For some reason, it had become a favourite entertainment – watching him shiver as he took the plunge. His mind went back to those Sorolla paintings in Valencia. *Boys on the Beach.* He just wished to god there was a modicum of Mediterranean heatwave here. But he couldn't fault the quality of the light. It was a beautiful day. *Luminismo*, indeed.

'You look like the *Six Million Dollar Man*,' Tim laughed. It was the tracksuit, of course. Darkest purple, heavy velour. Several decades too young for him. But Ruby had insisted. Good for the warmth, she'd said. Though, to Jack, it reminded him of East End gangsters and Black Power salutes.

Tim's mother cuffed the boy playfully around the ear.

'How are you, Jack?' she said, while the dad shook his hand.

'Fair to middling,' Telford replied. 'Can't complain. And no bugger... oh, sorry!'

He swung around to see whether the kids had heard him, but they were already out of earshot, once more. He smiled.

'And nobody,' he went on, conspiratorially, 'takes any bloody notice when you do. Isn't that what they say?'

He and Ruby had decided to keep Jack's prognosis to themselves. For now, certainly. Nothing to tell, really.

'And what d'you reckon, Telford?' said the father. 'Will Thatcher call the election?'

'Soon,' said Jack. 'She's bound to do it soon, while she's still riding high on the Falklands thing. Give it a couple of months and the propaganda will have worn off – everybody will start remembering what a mess we're in.'

He'd picked up his pen again – well, his typewriter, in truth – during those three months of the previous year. The *Belgrano*. There'd been Reagan, too, of course. And Lebanon.

'Oh, and memoirs,' said the mother. 'Ruby says you're writing your memoirs.'

'Ah, that's a bit of an exaggeration, my dear. Just some notes, really. No intention of publishing, or anything like that. But my sister Mary's children – one of them's turned out to be a journalist, too. Tried to persuade him to look for a proper job, but...'

There was so much he'd omitted. Emotional things. Things too close to home. Things too painful for a simple committal to paper. Danielle, of course. But a few things, as well, of which he was somewhat embarrassed – and about which he'd never spoken to anybody. Those earliest stupid mistakes, for example. His first entanglements, before he'd joined the *Observer*. He shook his head, to dispel the memories, to put them back in their box.

'I think you're not being entirely honest, Mr Telford,' she laughed. 'Ruby tells me your nephew – Tom, isn't it? Anyway, Ruby tells me Tom thinks you're quite the hero.'

'That's Ruby for you,' said Jack. 'But, maybe, Tom will see some value in the notes.'

He excused himself, of course, wanting to get changed and take the plunge. But he watched as the family continued its walk towards the children's favourite rock pools. Nice kids, he thought, and then laughed. All of them! For the mum and dad seemed like mere youngsters to him, as well.

He struggled out of the jogging trousers, slipped off the eye-patch and tossed it down onto the rest of his clothes, then pulled on his bathing cap. He looked back towards Lyme itself, the length of the beach. The rocks, the corrugated ripples of damp sand out towards the water and, closer to him, the neat lines of brown-fronded seaweed like tram tracks across the shingle. All that crushed seashell. It made him smile, remembering the local folk festival they'd attended just two weeks earlier. He'd not been dealing very well with the prognosis, but one of the performers had been a brilliant wordsmith and comedian. Birmingham-born, but now living in Beer, the fellow had told the audience how this very stretch of beach had inspired him to write his shortest poem. And when he'd finished writing, he'd decided to set it to music.

'You'll probably know the tune,' he'd said. 'So, feel free to join in.'

Then, he'd begun to sing. The familiar, simple notes of the Christmas song. And the crowd had howled with laughter.

'*Shingle, shells. Shingle, shells. Shingle, all the way.*'

Jack had found himself laughing, as well. Almost couldn't stop.

Yet, the smile vanished from his lips, as the water triggered goosebumps up his shins, and shivers up his spine.

'Christ!' he shouted.

He pressed on, a small wave soaking his thighs, making him jump, and the next, as he came down, reaching his groin. He winced.

'There, you bastard. Serves you right.'

He'd found himself talking to the offending testicle on more than one occasion, and wondered whether there might be any scientific or medical research to confirm his increasingly stubborn belief that immersion of one's balls in ice-cold sea water would just provide the magic cure he so hoped might exist.

Five years? No more? Bollocks to that! But, however many were left, what would he do with them?

The water hit his midriff. Now or never. As always, he launched himself into the sea on his side. He struck out, with leg kicks, like a frog, swimming on its back. Long, sweeping strokes , faster and faster, until his blood finally adjusted to the water's forty-nine degrees. As always, when he swam, he could almost hear his gran whispering encouragement in his ear – though it still pained him, after all this time, the suddenness with which she'd been taken from him.

He rolled over onto his belly and closed down the memory. Front crawl. He'd do his usual. Half a mile only. Eastwards, along the line of The Spittles. Then, trot back along the beach. He'd be almost dry by the time he got to his towel.

But, after ten minutes, he stopped to tread water, watched as an oil tanker came into view, out on the horizon. The sky was blue, a few white clouds. All things considered, it had been very beautiful, thought Jack. His life. Most of it, anyhow. The dark phantoms of Normandy, of Nuremberg, and much more, seemed finally to have been laid to rest. But now it also seemed to have been so brief.

He closed his eyes and fell into a waking dream. Spain. A beach. The sea. Then, with another ten minutes to go, he allowed the water to close over his head and savoured the dancing patterns of light just below the surface. The peace.

Wednesday 27ᵗʰ April 1983

Elliott discarded another attempt at writing the obituary. An awful sense of *déjà vu*. Yet, this was no piece of prescience. This would, indeed, be the second time he'd been called upon to fulfil this duty. The last time? October '38.

He'd never expected he'd have to do it again. Telford was younger than him, for pity's sake. Six years younger.

But the ironies. Then, the apparent swimming accident at San Sebastián. Now, this.

His neighbours had seen it all. Jack emerging from the water and picking up his towel. They'd seen the moment of absolute panic on his face. Fleeting. Momentary. Then, he had fallen.

It had, at least, been quick.

Otherwise, Elliott could have believed that, somehow, this might be yet another hoax. He still expected that Jack might appear at his own funeral, or in another six months, with that annoying grin on his face.

Yes, bloody Telford. He could be an annoying devil when he chose. But Elliott already missed him.

And he knew that, this time, it really was the end.

The End

But if you enjoyed this story and want to know more about my other novels – or better still – to sign up for the monthly Inner Circle newsletter, just visit the website: https://www.davidebsworth.com/
Also, if you're able, please feel free to write a short review, maybe, on Amazon or Goodreads, etc.
And remember, if you've any questions, I always love hearing from readers. My e-mail: davemccall@davidebsworth.org

Notes and Acknowledgements

After we published *A Betrayal of Heroes*, readers began to ask awkward questions about how Jack Telford's life went after his exploits at the end of the Second World War. In the beginning, I impatiently pointed them in the direction of the novella I'd already written, *The Lisbon Labyrinth*, set in Portugal during 1974.

But that sparked still more questions. How did he end up in Lisbon, of all places? The novella didn't tell us much about the intervening years. A clue, here and there, but nothing more.

Still, a while earlier, I'd scribbled a piece for a book blogger, who'd asked me to imagine one of my characters appearing on *Desert Island Discs*, and I'd dutifully obliged. Jack's fictional interview with Roy Plomley in September 1979. So, I had the music, the tracks of Telford's life story. And, from these fragments, these long short stories – or short novellas – began to take shape.

In truth, I wrote them more for my own enjoyment than anything else; though, I hope that readers who've enjoyed *The Assassin's Mark*, *Until The Curtain Falls* and *A Betrayal of Heroes* might find some pleasure in them, as well.

I was inspired to write *The Nuremberg Effect* after reading David Nasaw's wonderful book, *The Last Million: Europe's Displaced Persons from World War to Cold War*. While Britain undoubtedly suffered badly from the Blitz and from the Second World War as a whole, the after-effects for large parts of Europe were horrendously worse. Total devastation of towns and cities across northern France, Belgium, Holland, Poland, western Russia – and yes, of course, Germany. As many people killed in that single night's bombing raid on Dresden as had died in Britain collectively throughout the entire Blitz. And then, there was the starvation, the disease, the total economic collapse. And the refugees. Millions upon millions of refugees. The logistical nightmare of trying to relocate them. My final understanding about how the rest of Europe sees the EU so differently from many folk here in Britain.

The Berlin Protocol sprang from two sources. The first was the accounts I kept reading about the large numbers of Germans who, long after the war, still thought that Hitler had been a wonderful fellow and, at the time of pulling this anthology together, I have been living through the Trump era. I couldn't help seeing the parallels. But the second was Kevin Prenger's *War Zone Zoo*, and that tragic story about how, by 1945, less than one hundred of Berlin Zoo's original 3,500 animals had survived.

So far as *The Vienna Premiere* is concerned, I have to be honest and say that Ernest Hemingway wasn't actually at that first showing of *The Third Man* in its dubbed German version. But the background to the premiere is accurate enough, and the premiere did coincide, more or less, with the destruction of the real-life and notorious Benno Blum gang, pretty much in the way I've described. But the story of the movie itself is intriguing and has all those controversies – about the "cuckoo clock" speech, and about whether Graham Greene had himself been inspired to write the original story, and the character of Harry Lime, because of his own personal involvement with that other "third man", Kim Philby.

Factually, however, in 1950, the Café Papageno was in the Soviet Sector of Vienna.

The Suez Triangle sprang from my fascination with a couple of frequently recounted conspiracy theories. First (though this one is far more than simple theory), that Britain and France colluded in the Israeli invasion of Egypt in 1956 by issuing an ultimatum they knew the Egyptians would have to ignore, and thus give them an excuse to also invade – on the pretext of protecting the Suez canal but, in reality, to regain control of the canal itself. Second, the theory that, to keep Egypt's ally, Soviet Russia, engaged elsewhere, the CIA had instigated the anti-communist Hungarian Uprising to take place at the same time, and knowing it was doomed to failure from the outset. That, and the simultaneous capture of Algerian independence leader, Ahmed Ben Bella, which also served to distract the world's press from what was really happening in Egypt.

Thanks to a particular episode of the TV series, *The Crown* (Season Two, Episode One), lots of readers will now be far more familiar with this story. But I'd also introduced the real-life characters of Jacques Massu and his lover (and later, wife), Suzanne 'Toto' Torrès in *A Betrayal of Heroes*. And here they were, again, in this much later and very different piece of history.

How did it end? Ahmed Ben Bella remained in prison, after the hijacking of his plane, until 5th July 1962, the day that Algeria was officially declared to be independent. He became the country's first President, between 1963 and 1965, but he later went on to fulfil a range of political posts until his death in 2012.

I needed Jack to have a reason for getting out of Germany in 1960 and I couldn't think of any better companion for him on the journey than George Harrison. So, apologies to George's widow, Olivia, and son, Dhani, if I've got any of the details wrong but I relied on countless sources to try to catch the flavour of this important episode in the saga of The Beatles.

For the *Mozambique Motorsport* yarn, again, I wanted to bring together various threads. These included: the reason for Jack being in Portugal, in the first place; the now largely forgotten story of Portugal's dictatorship years, and especially its brutal colonial wars of the '60s and '70s; the whole story of the Rhodesian Sanctions; and, finally, some reflection on the hidden part played by Britain in the Vietnam War. I hope it works!

The Lisbon Labyrinth is a work of fiction, but one based on factual accounts of the Portuguese Revolution of 1974. It's also laced with anecdotes borrowed, as usual, from family and friends; though. the characters themselves are not intended to represent real people, with the exception of Abel Guerra, who is based on the journalist Adelino Gomes. Fernando Eduardo da Silva Pais, on the other hand, was factually the Director-General of the PIDE secret police, until it was disbanded on 25th April 1974. He died in 1981.

So far as I know, there was never an intention to launch the revolution on any date other than 25th April – so I hope those who were directly involved will forgive the "poetic licence" I've taken in that regard. Apart from all the documentary resources upon which I relied for the background, I owe an enormous and posthumous debt to my cousin, Brian McCall, from whom I largely stole the story. Brian was there, in person, and may well have been the real-life professor at Lisbon University who used a range of subversive English-language texts while teaching the army officers who would later go on to play such an important part in the Carnation Revolution.

I wrote *The London Luncheon Club* as an afterthought, but arising from the blog post I mentioned earlier. It's a fairly accurate reflection of the way in which the late-lamented Roy Plomley actually prepared for the programmes.

Simply for information, and in case anybody was wondering, the BBC's *Desert Island Discs* did, indeed, feature Norman Mailer in December 1979. Donald Sinden was the show's castaway in August 1983. And Derek Jameson, only in July 1994.

For the Valencia story, I owe a great deal to my real-life friend and comrade, Joan Sifre. Joan was there at the time of the 1981 coup and he kindly provided the first-hand anecdotes on which the story was based. He went on to become the General Secretary for the Comisiones Obreras union confederation for the Valencia region. I hope he might not mind me using his name for the character in this particular yarn – especially as it was too tempting not to make the link with my Sergio Sifre character in *Until The Curtain Falls*. There are more details of Amado Granell's family and how he was finally commemorated on my website.

The Dorset Obituary, I think, needs little explanation. Though, I should admit to having borrowed the poem about the beach after it was performed at the 2025 Wrexham Carnival of Words – our literary festival with a difference – by poet, singer and natural comedian, Rob Barratt. But it was actually written by brilliant poet and performer, Merv Grist, who then kindly let me use the lines. So, my huge thanks to Merv – and to Rob, as well.

Sydney Elliott, who appears in just about all the Jack Telford novels, died in 1987, at the age of 85.

But for those already asking whether this is, indeed, the final Jack Telford story, I have to say that there's already another in the pipeline. The keen-eyed will have spotted that, now and again, there are vague references to how Jack got into journalism in the first place. During his lunch with Roy Plomley, for example, when questions were asked about how his career had begun – after university, but before *The Observer* and the *Mirror*. A couple of years, we're told, as a cub reporter for the *Rhos Herald* in the depths of North Wales. So, yes, one more outing for Jack. A prequel, really, set in 1934 during his time with the *Herald*. It's working title? *Evil In The Steel*. Watch this space!

My thanks, of course, as usual, to my editor, Nicky Galliers; to my cover designer, Cathy Helms; to my principal "beta reader", Ann McCall; and to the wonderful Helen Hart and her team at SilverWood Books for assisting with the technical publishing processes. In addition, a further friend, Holly Thorpe, was kind enough to help me with some difficult rewriting of the opening story. Finally, and most of all, my undying gratitude to all of you who read the story!

David Ebsworth, May 2025